Harmattan Rain

HARMATTAN RAIN

a novel by

AYESHA HARRUNA ATTAH

PER ANKH
the african publishing cooperative
Popenguine, SENEGAL, West Africa

Cover Art: Inse Armah, Popenguine
Author's Photo: Sidy Almamy Sow, Dakar
Typesetting and Design: PER ANKH
Print funding: Natalia Kanem

PER ANKH
B.P. 2 Popenguine
SENEGAL, West Africa

ISBN: 2-911928-12-1

Dedicated

to

my family

Acknowledgements

I would like to thank Trust Africa and Per ANKH for the fellow-ships awarded during the period in which this novel was written.

I acknowledge with gratitude the guidance Ayi Kwei Armah gave me during the nine-month period of writing. Without his mentorship, wisdom and humor, this book would not have come out so soon.

I am indebted to Natalia Kanem and Abdul-Rahman Harruna Attah for funding the publishing of *Harmattan Rain*.

Immense gratitude goes to my aunt, Phyllis Christian and to my editors, Nana Yaa Agyeman, Michelle Johnson-Murray, Natalia Kanem, Pearl Kyei and Akinloye Ogundipe for their attention to detail and invalu-able suggestions.

Finally, I thank my family and friends for their support during the book writing process.

Contents

PART ONE

One
Khaya Tree

March 1954

On the day after the first rainfall of the year, Lizzie-Achiaa stood under a neem tree in front of her father's compound, a convinced young woman.

She was convinced that there was more to life than working on Papa Yaw's unproductive farm, helping Mama Efua with chores and having inane conversations with Asantewa.

Times were hard in Adukrom No. 2. Owusua, her eldest sister had died the year before. Swollen shoot disease had infected plants. Her father's cocoa farm had been no exception, and of course, he was quick to use that in his defense of trying to marry her off. But she was convinced life would get better and she didn't have to marry someone she didn't love.

She stared at the neem leaves, resplendent after their wash. She was convinced that outside Adukrom No. 2, there were interesting people and she had proof—her tall enigma from the north, Bador Samed.

Before any friendship had developed with Bador, however, she'd regarded him just as everyone in the village had—with mistrust. He'd showed up early one Saturday morning and stayed on for two years as the medicine man's assistant. She welcomed his friendship when everyone in her house was mourning Owusua and wouldn't give her the time of day. Their conversations were the perfect escape from a house where death had left its stubborn mark. He would be sending for her any minute. She waited impatiently.

She looked back into her father's compound. The laterite huts capped with thatch roofs seemed in need of redoing, with cracks snaking

3

their way from foundation to roof. Her half-sisters ran around, pushing each other, lifting their dresses, laughing with the freedom only children have.

"Sister Lizzie," a boy's voice said. She turned around and saw Kojo dressed in a pair of torn brown shorts. "Good morning," he said. "Please Brother Bador wants to see you."

"Thank you," she said, glad she didn't have to keep waiting. She noticed that Kojo's small shoulders had risen with self-importance, obviously because of the message he was sent to deliver. As they walked away from Papa Yaw's, she bent over to pluck two globular pods from a shrub pushing out of their path. She handed one to Kojo and shook the other in her hand. "You don't have to come all the way with me," she said. To Kojo, this task was probably a big deal—having Bador Samed bid him on errands. His eyes widened, pleaded with Lizzie. "Give me the pleasure of finishing this task," they seemed to say, but Lizzie wasn't about to be swayed. She stared at him until he realized he wasn't needed anymore. She strode on, passing by the Aduhene's compound.

Lizards scuttled out of her way as she arrived at the Insu River. He wasn't there. She stared at the river, running on young and wild, rejuvenated by the rainfall from the day before. She sat down under the tall *khaya* tree, which had become their spot. She hit the pod against her shin, listening to its rattling. She fussed with the black cloth she was wearing.

"Do you know what that's for?" a voice asked, startling her.

"You scared me!" Lizzie said, turning around to see Bador Samed grinning. His head blocked off half of the sun, and all she saw were teeth.

"Sorry I'm late," he said. "Opanyin Nti caught me just as I was leaving and made me mix herbs for him."

"I just got here myself," she said. "What were you asking me about?"

"The pod you're holding," he said.

"This?" She shook it again. "It's *tutotuto*. A cheap children's toy," Lizzie said, smiling and raising her nose toward the sky.

"True," he said walking around her, "but did you know that the leaves of the plant are great for curing snake bites?"

"Really?" Lizzie asked. "I didn't know that. See, what would I do without you?" She laughed and hit her forehead with the pod.

"A lot, my dear," he said, sitting down across from her. "You're one smart woman. I'm just here to help you believe in that fact." His skin, the color of laterite, looked redder with the sun bouncing off it. His small eyes shone. They were gentle and ageless. Every time he looked at her, his eyes seemed to pierce her existence. He wore a black and white striped smock and white shorts.

"How do you know I'm smart?" she asked.

"Because like souls find each other. We're two smart souls." He looked at her and reached into his pocket, extracting a small white container and a thin piece of brown paper. He popped off the lid of the container, poured dried leaves onto the paper and rolled it.

"Can I smoke too?" she asked.

"No, you can't."

"Why not?"

"Because I don't want my wife smoking," he said.

"I'm not your wife," she said, "yet."

The river gargled on indifferently. Bador Samed closed his eyes.

"Is that what it is today?" he asked, opening his eyes. A smile spread across his face. "You're not my wife, eh?"

"It's not that. I just don't understand why you can do some things and I can't just because I'm a girl … a woman."

"I said I don't want 'my wife' smoking and nothing about women in general," Bador Samed said, still smiling.

"Wife, woman. You meant it as the same thing," Lizzie said. She turned round and shifted her gaze from the colossal roots of the *khaya* tree, up along its trunk to the point where its branches kissed the sky. When she looked back down, Bador Samed's face was an inch away from hers. She inhaled the strangely sweet smell of tobacco. He leaned forward slowly. His eyes narrowed. She looked at him, her heart beginning to sprint. This was the first time she'd been that close to any man. She closed her eyes.

"Relax," he said, planting his lips on hers. They tasted spicy and felt moist. All she heard was the Insu River splashing on in its infinite course. She opened her eyes. Bador Samed was back in his original position, smoking his tobacco. She thought him so beautiful. Of all the men in the village, he was the only one she'd ever been interested in. It was his foreignness, his eccentricity and that he wasn't staying in Adukrom No. 2 all his life.

"When you make it to Accra," she said, catching her breath, "you'll start learning the white man's medicine and save enough money for me to come join you."

"You keep saying that," Bador Samed said, stubbing out the tobacco stick on the wet grass. "You always talk about what I'll do, but what do you want to do with your life?"

She was taken aback by his question. She was lucky her father had sent her off to school—the only girl in the village to finish secondary school. Bador was right—with all her school knowledge, who did she want to be? She wanted to find answers to why people like her sister died, to leave Adukrom No. 2, to meet more people like Bador Samed. People who weren't afraid of limits.

"To be your wife," she said, grinning widely, knowing her response would irk him.

"Seriously, Mrs. Samed."

"All right," Lizzie said, smiling. "I want to look after people—sick people."

"That's more like it," Bador Samed said, getting excited, his eyes lighting up like a five-year-old who'd been offered sweets.

"I want a big family, but you can't have any other wives. As annoying as Papa Yaw is, I don't understand how Mama Efua shares him with two other women," Lizzie said, drawing a circle in the damp loamy soil with the pod.

"There'll be only one Mrs. Samed," he said, taking Lizzie's hands into his and holding them. His hands felt calloused and were stained a reddish-brown hue. I've never been so happy, Lizzie thought. I shouldn't be, especially not with Owusua gone. She stared at a seedling that was pushing out of the soil.

"Are you all right?" Bador Samed asked. She remained quiet. "You're thinking of your sister, right?" he asked. She nodded. "We all go to the ancestors eventually, Lizzie. Some people leave faster than others."

"She was so young. She didn't ask to be sick."

"Lizzie, some of us will die violently, some through epilepsy, some in sleep. But we'll both come up with remedies to make people live longer."

Lizzie smiled and said, "Let's go to Accra." Her chest rose. It was a rash decision, but one she'd convinced herself about on the spur of the moment. There was no turning back.

"Are you serious?"

"Yes," she said. "I have nothing to do here."

"What about your family? Will Papa Yaw let you go?"

"I'm not telling them. We'll elope!"

"I like your energy," Bador Samed said. "But we have to plan this properly. I need money. We need a place to stay in Accra. We need to work on all those details."

"I thought you were spontaneous," Lizzie said, stretching out her lower lip.

"I am, but with you coming along, I want things to fall in place perfectly."

"Let's leave in a week."

"Fine, a week it is, my dear. But first ... come back here tonight."

Lizzie knew why Bador Samed told her to come back. This would be their pact, their nonverbal way of sealing their deal. For her, it would also be an act of defying her father. Her way of making sure he couldn't marry her off to anyone else.

*

Three days passed and Lizzie hadn't seen or heard from Bador Samed. She thought it strange and began to cook up excuses for him. Maybe because he was planning their escape, he didn't want to be seen with her. He was smart, that Bador Samed! But, she wanted him to touch her again and make her feel like the only woman in the world and she wanted to plan their future, even if it was just in talk. She sat in front of the rectangular room she shared with three of her sisters. I have to find out if he's well, she thought. Springing up from the stool she'd been sitting on, she marched out of Papa Yaw's compound.

Kojo's older brother was sitting under the mango tree in front of his house, scrubbing his teeth. She quickened her steps so she wouldn't have to talk to him.

"Lizzie, darling," he whined. He was so sickly, even his voice carried no timbre.

"Kofi, I'm coming," she said, trying not to look into his eyes. She wasn't going to come back. She walked past the Aduhene's compound, past a string of similar huts and stopped in front of Opanyin Nti's hut, where she saw the medicine man stirring an earthenware pot of neem leaves.

"Good afternoon, Opanyin," she said.

"Lizzie, how are you?" he asked, looking up.

"Opanyin, I'm fine. Is Bador Samed in?" The medicine man's eyes watered. He shook his head. "Do you know where he is?"

"Lizzie," the medicine man said, looking her in the eye. "The last time I saw him was three nights ago." How strange, she thought. That was the day they'd made plans to run away, the night they'd sealed their deal. Had he left her all alone? She didn't think that was possible. He couldn't have just used her, could he?

"Has he gone to find some ingredient for you?" she asked, hoping that the old man was getting senile and had forgotten.

"No. You remember how he just appeared?"

"Yes."

"I think he just vanished from our lives in the same way. There are some things you should just let be, Lizzie," he said, bending over his pot, adding more neem leaves. He was obviously being mysterious. Maybe Bador Samed would come back for her. Maybe he'd gone in search of money. He must be preparing for their elopement.

"Thank you, Opanyin."

"You're welcome, my daughter," he said, stirring his brew.

She walked to the Insu River. As she sat under the *khaya* tree, she battled with opposing thoughts. One part of her was swelling with the surety that Bador Samed was simply getting things ready for their flight. The other was confused. He would have given her some clue that he was leaving to prepare things, but he'd said nothing.

As the Insu River ran its indifferent course, her eyes traveled along the trunk of the *khaya* tree. Where are you? she wondered. She would be so miserable if he never came back.

*

Lizzie stood in the entrance to her room, watching Agya Kwaku walk out of Papa Yaw's compound in a huff. She saw her father shuffle behind him, chewing stick in mouth, his head bent obsequiously low.

"Oh, Agya!" Papa Yaw said. "The girl didn't know what she was saying. Agya, wait small …"

She wanted to hear what her father was saying to her suitor, but his voice became smaller the farther away he walked from the compound. She patted her plaited hair, hoping she hadn't been rude to Agya Kwaku. The truth was that she was still reeling from Bador Samed's disappearance. No one had seen him. He hadn't written to her. Nothing! He was the only man she wanted to be with and now that he'd disappeared, she wasn't in the mood to be married to just anybody. Besides, now that she'd been tainted, would anyone want her?

She turned around, ready to pull back the tattered red and green curtain that covered the entrance to her room, when her shirt was tugged on from behind. "What's your problem …" she started. Papa Yaw whirled her around. She saw a thick neem branch in his hand.

"You useless, good for nothing," he spat out, hitting her shins with the branch. He reeked of stale palm wine.

"Papa Yaw, why?" Lizzie asked, a frown creasing her forehead. Papa Yaw was always abusive. She'd found it strange when he hadn't reacted to her refusal of two of the men he'd brought over. Both times, he'd served her a dish of silent treatment and hadn't resorted to violence. Now he was behaving just like she'd expected him to.

"Come here!" He walked to the middle of the compound.

"No," Lizzie said, lifting her right leg up the ledge into her room. Her father clutched her shirt, dragging her away from the door. Her foot landed on the rough ledge. "*Agyee!*" she screamed out in pain. He hit her shin in rapid strokes with the branch. Its leaves and yellow fruits were still intact. She tried to run into her room, but his grasp was too strong. He spun her around.

"You think of no one … but yourself," Papa Yaw yelled, spitting out bits of chewed stick. "You think I enjoy begging in front of all these men? Eh? First you rejected Mr. Sam. I didn't say anything. Then you did the same to Wofa Atta. Still I remained quiet." With his left hand, Papa Yaw adjusted his heavy, black and white *kente* cloth, which was nestled around his shoulders. He spat out his chewing stick. "Today, after being rude to Agya Kwaku, you think I'll let you go scot-free?"

Lizzie tried to break into a run, this time aiming for the compound's exit. As she lifted her legs off the ground, Papa Yaw yanked her shirt. She lost control of her legs and landed on the ground, grazing her buttocks. Her father struck her head with the branch. He swiped at her neck, slapped her back. Lizzie tried to get up, but her father kept hitting her. The lashes kept coming. She tried to block them, tried to second-guess where the branch would fall, but each time he moved on to another part of her body. She saw Papa Yaw look up and followed his gaze. Her brothers, sisters, mother and stepmothers were trickling out of their rooms. She crawled toward the exit.

"Papa Yaw is beating someone!" a shrill voice shouted, inviting all in the village to come over and witness the spectacle. This was one of the things Lizzie hated the most about the village. Everyone was in everyone's business. She picked herself up close to the exit, noticing that people lined the periphery of the compound and had completely enclosed her and Papa Yaw.

Papa Yaw came after her. As she tried to escape, the crowd wouldn't part. Obviously they wanted a good show at her expense. Her father pulled her plaits, dragging her back toward the center. He lashed her arms rapidly. She flailed her arms, trying to stop the contact of the rough branch on her flesh.

"Useless, selfish girl," Papa Yaw shouted. He let go of Lizzie's hair, and again, she tried to dash for the exit. He caught her shirt and unleashed a string of lashes on her arms.

"God, show your might!" Lizzie heard her mother cry out.

"You little witch," Papa Yaw went on. "Do you want us to all die from hunger? Eh?" He pointed in the direction of his cocoa farm. "If you married Agya Kwaku, he would give me seeds for free, I would plant them, then after the rains, I would yield a healthy harvest to feed all your greedy mouths. But you … you think only of yourself!"

Lizzie was quiet as tears flowed from her eyes. She wanted to stop them but she couldn't. She looked at her feet, blurred by her tears. The neem leaves were falling and landing on the ground. Lizzie heard her mother still crying out.

"'I am not interested … I am not interested!' You think it is for you to decide?" Papa Yaw asked her, rapidly striking her legs. She tried to dart toward her second stepmother's hut, where the thatch wall had fallen over. Her father was faster. He caught the cloth she wore around her waist, spun her around and struck the branch against her left shoulder. "Agya Kwaku is an honest man. He would have taken good care of you. But you …" She covered her shoulders with her hands. He hit her shins. "But you selfish …" She tried to buckle her knees. "… think of only …" Before his last stroke hit her, Lizzie grabbed and held on to the branch with her right hand.

She felt the flesh on her arms blistering. She stared at Papa Yaw, his yellow eyes bulging, capillaries dancing about on them.

"Leave it!" he spat out. Lizzie clutched the branch firmly.

The Aduhene came in through the crowd and touched Papa Yaw on the arm. "I beg you," he said. "Let the girl go."

Papa Yaw shook the chief off. Lizzie felt her tears drying on her face. She wasn't letting go of the branch. She saw Papa Yaw's eyes redden as he tried to extricate the branch from her grasp. His muscles were taut. His cloth slipped off his shoulders. As Papa Yaw tried to save the falling cloth, Lizzie heaved the branch with all the energy she could muster, pulling it out of his fingers.

"Go back to your houses. I beg you," the Aduhene pleaded with the gathered crowd. His voice was too soft. Nobody seemed to hear him.

"No more nonsense," Papa Yaw shouted. He cleared his throat loudly, spat on the ground and stomped off, red-eyed, to his room.

Mama Efua ran to Lizzie, who was still standing in the middle of the compound, branch in hand. The leaves had gathered at her feet and she was now sobbing uncontrollably.

Two
Seeking Refuge

April 1954

Lizzie and Asantewa dragged the foam mattress they'd taken out to air toward the entrance of their room.

"Wait," Lizzie said, walking into the room. She bent down to pick up a torn blue and orange cloth from the floor. She knelt on the cold concrete and started wiping the damp rectangle on which they would place the mattress. Spreading her arms in broad strokes, she tried to erase the dark patch imbued into the concrete. No matter how hard she pressed the cloth, the patch stayed permanent. She couldn't stay in Adukrom No. 2 any longer, living like this, she thought.

"Ah, Lizzie! When are you going to finish wiping?" Asantewa complained, struggling to fold the mustard-colored mattress through the door. "It won't get dry. It never gets dry." Lizzie looked up at Asantewa. The tattered red and green door curtain, with prints of birds in flight, veiled her little head. Her skinny arms dangled over the cratered foam.

"You're right," Lizzie said, getting up. They pulled in the mattress, letting it land carelessly over the dark patch. Lizzie then pushed the head of the mattress against the red wall. Green, orange and brown craters streaked the mattress surface—urine and blood stains from over the years.

Asantewa picked up a faded blue and white cloth from a heap of clothing atop a black metal trunk. She tossed the cloth at Lizzie, who caught it, opened it up and spread it over the cratered foam. As Lizzie tucked it under the mattress, Asantewa seemed ready to throw herself onto the bed when her knee hit the trunk.

"*Agyee!*" she cried out.

"Serves you right," Lizzie said. "Are you hurt?"

"No. But this trunk keeps hitting me," she said, laughing. She lowered herself slowly onto the mattress. "I think it wants to come to Suaadie Girls with me."

"Then what will those of us left here use for our clothes?"

"I don't know," Asantewa said, rubbing her bony knee.

"Papa Yaw will give you the same wooden box he gave me," Lizzie said, joining Asantewa on the bed. She picked up a green shirt and folded it absentmindedly. Everyone she cared about was leaving. First Owusua died. Then that Bador Samed just disappeared. Now Asantewa was going to school. Why couldn't she leave too? Adukrom No. 2 was stifling. "How I wish it was me going," she said.

"But you've already gone," Asantewa said. "Aren't you tired of school?"

"It's not even about school. It's about a world away from Adukrom No. 2." This girl probably has no idea what I'm talking about, Lizzie thought. "I'm sure you'll like Suaadie Girls," she said, standing up. She made for the only window in their room. She unlatched the wooden shutter and pushed it open. She saw her mother's hut on which a big crack in the sandy wall crept up to the thatch roof.

"Lizzie, you really like that brown blouse," Asantewa piped up.

"Because it suits me," Lizzie said, turning to look at Asantewa. "You're too skinny. You'll disappear in even this small blouse I'm wearing. I was going to suggest you take my uniforms, but they'll be too big on you."

"Mama Efua said we'll alter your uniforms. I'm not getting new ones."

"Oh, all right."

"I wish you were still at Suaadie," Asantewa went on. "It would have been nice if we were both in school at the same time."

"I know. But that's life, my dear," Lizzie said, drawn again to her mother's cracked wall. She sighed and walked back to the mattress.

"What are you going to do without me around to bully?"

"Look at you!" Lizzie said, laughing and sucking her teeth. "We have at least five more months together before you leave."

"Are you going to keep working with Papa Yaw?"

"Asantewa, good question." In Adukrom No. 2, that was all she could do, wasn't it?

"He should pay you …" Asantewa started.

"Lizzie! Lizzie-Achiaa!" Papa Yaw's thick voice boomed into the girls' room, slicing through their conversation. "Elizabeth Achiaa Appiah! Queen Elizabeth!"

"What does he want?" Lizzie whispered. She sat up, folding the clothes frenetically. She knew what he wanted. Why else would he be shouting her name for the whole of Adukrom No. 2 to hear? The lilt of his palm wine-laced voice made her touch her arms. She shuddered. The blisters had just begun to heal.

"Please follow me. Come, come," she heard Papa Yaw say to someone. "Lizzie!" he yelled, his voice inching closer. Lizzie was still rubbing her arm, staring at Asantewa.

"Number four in four months," Asantewa quipped, simpering. Enough is enough! Lizzie thought. "One for each month of the year."

Lizzie felt the scars from the last beating itch as the memory danced through her mind. The scars prickled, reminding her of what would happen again, because she was going to say no. She had to say no. She remembered the neem leaves falling at her feet. There was only one solution. Run. But where to? She could go back to Suaadie Girls. Wouldn't that be too easy? Oh God, she groaned, what am I going to do? She wasn't going to marry some old farmer. No!

"Lizzie, won't you answer Papa Yaw?"

"I'm coming," Lizzie said. She got up and made for the door. As she drew aside the door curtain she almost ran into Papa Yaw.

"Ah, Lizzie-Achiaa," he said, wrapping his blue and green cloth around his shoulder. "Why have you made me scream like a madman?"

"Sorry, Papa Yaw," Lizzie said, looking over his shoulder.

"My voice has even gone now, eh! What are you doing?" Papa Yaw rewrapped his cloth.

"I'm coming, Papa," Lizzie said.

"And where are you going? Come and greet someone."

"I'm just going to the bathroom."

"Good. Your hair is untidy. Neaten it," he said, his own hair overgrown, his nostrils flaring. She could smell the palm wine fumes emanating from all his skin's pores. "And none of your nonsense this time." As Lizzie was about to move toward the bathroom, she made out the suitor's shadow at the entrance. "Hurry up, eh!" Papa Yaw shouted, walking back to the shadow.

She strode along the thatch wall that enclosed the compound and passed by her mother's hut. She heard Papa Yaw laugh. Even though his voice was muffled, she couldn't miss its sycophantic undertones. Yes, she thought, it was now or never. Run now or be stuck. Stuck in some village, making babies for some old cocoa farmer. Cooking, cleaning and making babies. Surely, a woman had to be worth more than that. She ran by Mama Ama's hut and on to Mama Dufie's. There, she saw Papa Yaw's weak spot and her key to freedom—the fallen thatch fence that nobody had bothered to fix. She crept over it and stole a glance at the entrance.

This is it, she thought, her breathing raspier. Her heart pounded against her ribcage. Was she really doing this? Her stomach knotted over. She looked back at Papa Yaw's compound, turned and sprinted toward the Insu River.

Barefoot, she trampled over weeds, stones storm-tossed over wet laterite and dried twigs that pierced her soles. She heaved her body along the muddy path. Her breasts felt heavy as she thrashed her way on grass and wet soil. She arrived at the river, panting, her chest aching, feeling as if it would explode from sheer exhaustion. The stream bubbled on, gargling in its eternal song. She ran along it, looking for the wooden footbridge. The bridge seemed too far away. She didn't have the time to walk all the way to it.

She stopped running and studied the river. Its waters were like a bubbling brown soup. Several rapids rippled its surface. She looked around, hoping to find something she could use as a raft. Her eyes fell on the tree under which she'd fallen in love with Bador Samed. It stood there like a beautiful colossus. Its trunk, unmoving, solid, firmly planted, pushed up to the sky. Bador Samed, I'm coming to find you, she thought, and you have a lot of explaining to do.

She waded into the murky waters of the river, which rose up to her chest. Using both arms as oars, she swam through the rushing chocolate stream, slicing the water with her hands. In the middle the water level rose, hitting her chin. She raised her feet off the riverbed, moving them in frog-like strokes. Drenched in water and mud, she crawled out, dragging her body onto the green weeds along the river's bank. A lizard scuttled out of her way, paused, shook its head and disappeared. She inhaled and exhaled. No time to waste, she told herself.

She forced herself up from the grass and looked at Adukrom No. 2, masked by neem trees, plantain groves and cocoa farms. She broke into a run again. Not long after, a dull pain started from her left waist and slashed across her abdomen. After the Insu River, she didn't know how she was going to get to Suaadie Girls. All she was sure of was the school's northerly location. She looked up at thick clouds threatening rain, moving from right to left. She figured if she kept walking straight, she'd be going north.

After running for what felt like an hour, she'd covered enough ground to rest. She looked around the forest. The floor was covered with thick black loam, flecked with yellow leaves. The trees, sparse on the bottom, wide on top, blocked out the sun with their canopies. She saw an *iroko* tree with roots that looked like hands tilling the soil. She sat on the soil between two roots, resting her arms over the wooden solidness. This was much more impressive than her *khaya* tree. She held her side, exhaling fast, her heart crying out for respite. Using her wet blouse to wipe her face, she decided now was a good time to go over her options. One. Suaadie Girls. If she could only figure out how to get there through the forest. But Papa Yaw could easily find her there. Two. She could go to her mother's village, but that was south of Adukrom No. 2, so she was headed in the wrong direction.

"What do I do?" she screamed. She sat up. The convent! While at Suaadie Girls the Mother Superior of a local convent had been extremely friendly, telling her she could pass by for church services. A convent should be a safe haven, if just for a few days, she thought. If she wasn't imagining things, the convent was closer than Suaadie Girls. But where exactly?

Her stomach rumbled, reminding her that all she'd eaten since morning was a small bowl of *koko*, and not much of it. She'd lost her appetite two months ago. She heard rustling behind her. Startled, she sprang up and looked furtively around. She saw nothing, except for the deep green shrubs of the forest floor. The faint call of birds made her look up. She saw a patch of grey sky beyond the canopies. A group of birds were flying in the direction of Adukrom No. 2. The smallest lagged behind the others, turning around, twirling, taking its sweet time, oblivious to the urgency of the group. She felt sticky and damp. Her head and feet ached.

With no path in sight, she wasn't sure what her next step should be. She walked behind the *iroko* tree, sticking her right foot next to a cluster of cocoyam plants. She landed on a wet patch filled with pink worms. She lifted her foot in disgust and wiped it vigorously against a root. That was a bad sign, she thought and decided she wasn't going in that direction. She chose to go west—in a direction she thought was west.

After running for what seemed like hours, she felt she wasn't getting anywhere. All she saw was green, brown and black. She looked around again, and everything appeared the same whichever way she turned. Her chest felt heavy. Tears welled in her eyes as she regretted her rash decision. No, this was not the time to mope, she told herself, trying to stop the tears. Wiping her eyes with her muddy blouse, she decided to just keep running. She cut through spiky bushes, their branches scratching her already sore arms. A green snake slithered off in front of her. She froze, ready to turn around, when she heard voices. She walked toward them. They were children's voices.

"… jump like this," she heard. A clap followed. She walked closer. Parting tall blades of grass, she saw a group of children playing *ampe*. She strode toward them.

"Aie! Aie!" one of the girls cried out.

The other children turned to look.

"Mama *yiee*!" another girl shouted. They ran straight into a caramel-colored hut behind them. She looked down at her clothes. She was mud-strewn. I'd be afraid too, she thought. A child with clear bright eyes stayed behind, standing there watching as she approached.

A woman rushed out of the caramel hut, straightening the cloth she'd tied around her body. Half of her hair stood up in a bushy puff. The other half was corn-rowed.

"Your curiosity will kill you!" she shouted, grabbed the girl's left hand and shoved her into the hut. The other children peered out through the window. As Lizzie got closer to the woman, who was now standing with her hands on her hips, she saw goats and sheep in a thatch enclosure. Lizzie watched flies dance around the rump of a ram. It flicked its tail. The flies flew off, hovered above the animal for a few seconds and settled down again. The cycle continued. She looked back at the woman.

"Yes?" the woman said coolly to Lizzie.

"Good evening, auntie," Lizzie said, panting. "Sorry I scared your children. Please, I'm looking for the convent."

"Holy Sisters?" the woman asked, pointing over a plantain grove.

"Yes, I think that's it."

"It's not far, but first drink some water."

"Thank you so much," Lizzie said, plopping herself onto the grass by the enclosure for sheep and goats. The woman disappeared into the hut. One by one the children came out. They looked at Lizzie, keeping their distance. The woman came back out with a calabash of water and handed it to her. She walked back into the hut. Lizzie drank almost all the cool water in one gulp. She poured the remainder onto her face, trying to wash off the dirt.

"Mama, the madwoman has finished drinking," one of the children shouted.

Lizzie laughed at what she'd been reduced to. Madwoman! Being called madwoman was better than getting beaten with belt, pot, branch or whatever Papa Yaw found convenient. The woman came out of the hut. "Sister, here's your calabash," Lizzie said. "Thank you."

"My pleasure. After the plantain trees, cross the main road. You'll see the church."

"I'm really grateful," Lizzie said, lifting herself off the ground. As she passed by, the children scampered off. She turned around to wave at the woman and saw the children following her.

"Hey!" the woman shouted. "Naughty children! Come back here!"

Lizzie laughed as she passed through the plantain grove, striped with burgundy. She felt her knees laboring as she climbed up. At the top, she arrived at a large tarred road, lined on both sides with huge *khaya* trees. A large truck whizzed by, carrying enormous logs. She ran across to the other side of the street. She saw orange roofs down in a valley, a wooden cross nailed to one of them.

She looked behind her. The sun, hidden behind thick grey clouds, had left faint purple and orange traces. She inhaled deeply. Tumbling down the valley, she scratched her arms against the branches and stems of shrubs. Blades of tall grass cut through her shins. Her feet didn't provide enough friction over the stony path. She fell and landed at the foot of the hill. She picked herself up and wiped the dust off her already dirty clothes. Her elbow was grazed.

She saw the imposing, brilliantly white building of the convent. On its blue door a wooden cross was nailed above a bronze knocker. As she walked over, the gathered clouds started their own descent. She felt sprinkles of water land on her arms and face. She rushed to the door.

She lifted the knocker, banged it loudly and hurriedly. No one came. She leaned against the door, panting. She stood back and resumed her knocking. The rain was now pouring heavily. She couldn't hear anything but the steady pour of rain hitting leaves and roofs.

The door opened. A white woman and a black woman, both in white dresses and habits, stood side by side. The look on the white woman's face was one of horror.

"Hello," she said when she'd regained her composure. "Can we help you?"

"I am not mad," Lizzie said, panting. "Good evening, sisters. I ran away from home and have nowhere else to go. If I go back my father will beat me to death. Can I please stay here?" She hoped her words came out eloquently but expressed her urgency.

The nuns looked at each other. The dark sky fulgurated. Thunder boomed around them. The rain fell with increased vigor.

"Well, whatever your story is, you can't stay out here in this weather," the white woman said. "Come in." They led Lizzie into a dark corridor, closing the convent doors behind her. "We'll give you a room and we can talk in the morning."

Three
Nuns and Riots

When Lizzie opened her eyes the next morning, she saw bright light forcing through the slits of blue wooden shutters. The walls of the room were so white, they almost looked blue. She sat up, noticing a drawer underneath a desk. Her curiosity got the better of her and before she could stop herself she'd pulled it open. A black Bible and ivory rosary beads shuttled forward. She closed the drawer, settling back on the narrow bed—the only other piece of furniture in the room.

She thought about the sisters, Mother Constance and Sister Sarah, wondering if they would let her stay or if they would send her back. They had no reason to take her in unless she told them she felt what they called a vocation, a powerful desire to become a nun. But that would be lying. She looked at a cross nailed above the door. Could she give up everything she wanted in life? Could she dedicate her life to God? Just one night and she already felt lonely. The walls felt like they'd cave in and swallow her. Could she live in such isolation?

She thought of Bador Samed and smiled as she considered the choice she'd have to make. It was between Bador Samed and Jesus. Was she ready to have Jesus as the only man in her life? A part of her said yes, especially after Bador Samed's rude exit. Another part—the larger part—was still hopeful about Bador Samed. She had to find him. But how and where? She wanted to scream at the uncertain direction her life was taking. She hoped the nuns would let her stay till she figured what her next steps should be. She heard a knock on the door.

"Come in," she said.

Sister Sarah, the nun walked in. "Good morning," she said, handing Lizzie a cream towel. "I'll show you where the bathroom is."

Lizzie picked up a rectangular, sack-like, black dress Sister Sarah had given her the night before and trailed out behind Sister Sarah. They strode out into early morning brightness. The sun shone in full force. The concrete ground looked freshly scrubbed. Plants sprinkled with droplets of rainwater sprang from a small flower garden. Two sparrows landed in it, hopping around each other.

"That's where we'll be eating," Sister Sarah said, pointing to a building with a short wall and green mosquito-netting, looking new after the downpour. She walked to a small outhouse with two blue doors. "Well, here we are!" she said. "The bathroom is on the left. I've put a bucket of water in there and some soap."

"Thank you," Lizzie said. She walked into the bathroom. It was dark inside, but the light seeping in through the shutters helped her find the soap. Throwing water over her body, she rubbed the bar of soap on her arms. The soapy water stung as it passed down her legs. She passed her fingers over the cuts, wincing with pain. It was self-inflicted pain so it was bearable. If those had been bruises from Papa Yaw she was sure she'd be in more pain.

She washed and dried herself, pulling the black dress over her head and over her nakedness. She walked to the dining room and slowly opened its mosquito-proofed door. Five nuns sat on benches around a low wooden table, on which rested a large aluminum pot.

"Good morning," Lizzie said.

"Good morning," the nuns replied.

"Have some *koko*," Sister Sarah said, placing a metal bowl before Lizzie. As Sister Sarah dished out thick white gruel for her, Lizzie looked at the nuns. They ate silently.

This will be too difficult, Lizzie thought as she licked the porridge off her spoon. Complete silence. Is this the life I want?

As if reading her thoughts, Sister Sarah turned on the large radio that was on the concrete floor in a corner of the dining room.

Eighty-one expelled from the CPP. Kwame Nkrumah holds meeting in Kumasi.

Lizzie dropped the spoon in her bowl. It clinked loudly against the metal. She saw Sister Sarah flinch, cross herself and look at her, a tight smile across her lips.

"Let's go to Mother Superior," Sister Sarah said.

Mother Constance's office was small. Across from the door, a black and white picture of Pope Pius XII was mounted, the only adornment on the bare white walls. Manila files were strewn on the wooden desk. Two wooden chairs stood on opposite ends of the desk.

Lizzie felt the porridge stir in her stomach. Her palms were sweaty. This moment would decide what happened to her life. She looked at Mother Constance's round face. Here eyes crinkled with crow's-feet.

"Thanks, Sister Sarah," Mother Constance said. "Please sit, Lizzie." She placed her palm on Lizzie's shoulder and led her to a chair. She smiled and stared at Lizzie. Lizzie was trying to imagine what was going on in the woman's mind. Maybe she thinks I stole something, was all she could come up with.

"Lizzie," Mother Constance said finally. Her voice was soft. "I hope you slept well."

"Yes, thank you."

"Have you eaten? You must have been starving yesterday. I'm so sorry, I forgot to offer you food."

"I've eaten now. Thank you."

"All night I kept wondering where I'd seen you before. This morning it sank in. Suaadie Girls, right?"

"Yes, two years ago." Lizzie began to feel hopeful. Maybe, now she realized the connection, Mother Constance would be more willing to take her in.

"Last night, you said you ran away from home … and that your father beat you." Lizzie nodded. "Do you want to become a nun? You could have gone to other places. Is that what brought you here? Or are you just looking for temporary shelter?"

Lizzie was slow in responding. Should I lie? she wondered. "I'm seventeen," she started. "My father wanted to marry me off."

"But why?"

"To make money for his farm.

"Didn't he send you to school?"

"He did. But all his plants were infected with disease and he was convinced if he married me off to a rich farmer, all his problems would be solved."

"Interesting," Mother Superior said. "It's interesting that he sent you to school in the first place."

Lizzie chuckled. "When I was young, my father focused on preparing my older sister for marriage and sent me to school to learn a trade. But my sister passed on."

"May her soul rest in peace," Mother Constance said.

"Mother Constance," Lizzie said, slowly. "I want to make something of my life, besides belonging to someone," she paused, realizing that nuns belonged to Jesus. She had to take a different line of defense. "I want to take care of people. Nuns take care of people…."

"Yes …" Mother Constance said.

"But I can't go back home," Lizzie went on, her voice quivering.

"I'll make this easy for you," Mother Constance said. "We have a program for people who are thinking of becoming nuns. They stay for a year, two years … for up to three or four years. If you decide this interests you, it will be hard work from then on." She smiled, the corners of her eyes crinkling. "You have to renounce a lot of your old ways. You will learn the power of prayer and solitude. You will learn to serve the community. You will learn love."

Lizzie wondered about love. Was her love for Bador Samed the same kind of love Mother Constance said she'd learn? In that case, she already knew love and it hurt, but she had no other choice.

"I'm interested," she said, trying to convince herself and Mother Constance.

"Very well. We'll find you a place to sleep, and then we'll see how things go." Mother Constance got up. Lizzie heard the woman's bones cracking as a pained expression formed on her face. She straightened her back and smiled at Lizzie.

They walked out of the office, strode through the corridor and turned right into a narrow hallway which led to the church hall.

Benches were arranged in rows across from the altar. A table was covered with white cloth and adorned with two candleholders. Two nuns knelt on the floor in front of the first row of benches. Rosaries in hand, they prayed silently. Mother Constance bent down in front of the altar, stayed there for a minute and made her way back to Lizzie.

"You'll go there everyday to meditate, apart from Sunday when we have church service," Mother Constance said as they walked outside.

An orange-headed agama lizard with a broken tail scampered out of the shade cast by the roof of the dining hall.

"You ate breakfast here today," Mother Constance said. "Cooking is a group effort. The kitchen is behind the dining room. And that's the infirmary." She pointed at a white building on which a red cross was painted.

They entered the nuns' quarters. Mother Constance pointed at a door on the first floor. "That's Sister Sarah's room." She pointed an another on the right. "And, that's mine." They scaled the stairs, which led to a long corridor lined with five doors on either side. "Each room has a bed, table and a small wardrobe. Almost like the room you slept in. Nothing fancy." She smiled at Lizzie, her round face lighting up.

"It's more than I've ever had," Lizzie said.

Mother Constance unlocked the last door on the left. A brown mattress sat on a wooden bed frame and a film of dust had collected on the surface of the table. The casement window was closed.

"This will be your room."

"Thank you so much," Lizzie said, thinking of the room she shared with her sisters. This was heaven. She sat on the springy mattress. Mother Constance opened the closed window.

"Life here might get a little boring," she said. "But we sometimes go to town to sell the jam we make. I'm sure you'll enjoy those kinds of activities. Tell me if there's anything you want to help with." She paused and looked out the window. "God sent you here for a reason. I'm sure we'll find out why," she said. "Soon."

*

July 1954

Lizzie woke up at five in the morning. She rolled out of bed and reluctantly knelt on the hard concrete floor and bent her head for silent Morning Prayer.

Father, she prayed, thank you for a new day and a new life. Make my thoughts pure and holy…. Bador Samed crept into her mind. She only wanted to think of him. She'd dreamt of him and the day they made love—the day he'd disappeared.

That night, the moon full and bright blue, he sat under the *khaya* tree, smoking his sweet tobacco. The silence of the night was punctuated by the cries of crickets, and the gargle of the indifferent river. She sat by him, felt moisture seep into her clothes. He planted his lips on hers. She kissed him back. They lay down on the moist loam. He peeled off her cloth. She didn't resist. She heard him take off his smock. He kissed her lips, nuzzled her neck, suckled her breasts. She closed her eyes as he let himself into her. Sweet pain enveloped her body.

She tried to shake away the dream and the wetness lubricating her thighs. Father, she started again, I pray for my family. I hope I haven't caused them too much pain. Have them know I'm in a good place, and this is for the better. I pray for Bador Samed. Watch over him, wherever he is. I pray for Asantewa. She's starting school soon, please keep her healthy. And Mama Efua too. Please let Papa Yaw be kinder to her. Lord, help me find direction…. She couldn't think of anything else to pray for. Amen, she said.

She peeled off her grey sack-dress, replacing it with one of the two black dresses she now owned. She opened her door, walked out of the room, down the stairs and picked up a short palm-frond broom and a metal dustpan behind the staircase.

Outside, she stopped next to the little garden, where two butterflies danced around the flowers of an eggplant. She passed the fronds of the broom along the concrete floor, sweeping leaves that had fallen from the ubiquitous Indian almond trees in the convent. She cursed under her breath. In five minutes, she'd come back to find a new batch of green and brown leaves on the ground. Only good thoughts, she berated herself. After gathering a little pile of rubbish next to the bathrooms, she swept the area in front of the nuns' quarters. Cocoyam leaves glistened with morning dew, their heart-shaped faces reaching for the sun.

When she was done, she walked toward the dining room. She heard voices raised in the infirmary.

"… in her mouth."

"Don't let her die, oh!" another voice screamed. She heard the thud of some body part hitting wood. Her curiosity got the better of her, and she peered in through the open door. Goose pimples puckered her skin. She saw Sister Magda put a wooden spoon in the mouth of a little girl. The girl's leg kept hitting the foot of the bed. Lizzie was reminded of the day Owusua died. She moved closer to the infirmary, feeling a combination of nausea and curiosity. Sister Magda stuck a syringe in the crook of the girl's left arm, finally calming the girl.

"Amen!" Lizzie heard a woman say. "Thank you, sister. I thought my daughter was going to die."

"Just let her rest," Sister Magda said, noticing Lizzie, who expected to get told off. "Hello, Lizzie," she said softly.

"Good morning, Sister Magda," Lizzie said, preparing to walk back to the dining room.

"Is something wrong?"

"No…. Well, I was going … I noticed…. My sister was epileptic too," she said to stop her rambling. "She died even after the medicine man had treated her. I want to learn how to cure people … or at least take care of people like my sister…." Emboldened, she walked in. She finally saw the child's mother, who was sobbing quietly by her daughter.

"Jesus, thank you," the woman said between her sobs.

"Well," Sister Magda said, "we could always do with some extra help around here. Since you haven't gone through training, we can't let you take care of patients, but you can watch and learn."

"Thank you, thank you," Lizzie said, unable to contain herself. This would at least give her something to look forward to during the day. Something to take her out of her head and her lustful thoughts of Bador Samed. A reason to live. "When can I start?"

"I'll let Mother Constance know later today, and let's say you'll start tomorrow."

*

June, 1955

Lizzie whistled, a white apron tied over her black dress. She looked at the infirmary's only occupant—a little boy fast asleep on a twin bed. In the apron's pocket, she gathered plastic syringes, thermometers and a collection of scissors. She trudged back to the kitchen and dumped the instruments into a boiling pot of water. She really hated the silence in the convent. She used a wooden mortar to keep the kitchen door open, walked to the dining room and turned on the radio, which crackled to life. She heard shuffling behind her and turned around.

"Oh, good morning, Mother Constance," she said.

"There you are. I went into the infirmary looking for you."

"I'm sterilizing instruments," Lizzie said. "Do you want me to do something?"

"Oh, no. I just wanted to make sure you were all right," the old nun said, smiling and settling down on a bench. Lizzie heard the woman's bones crack. "The infirmary nuns tell me you've been working splendidly."

"That's kind of them," Lizzie said. She wanted to tell Mother Constance that she wanted more responsibility. That she felt confident enough to take care of patients, even if it was just cleaning them. After all, she'd been working in the infirmary for a year. "Mother Constance," she said.

"Yes?"

"When will I get to look after patients?" she asked, sitting down across from the nun.

Mother Constance laughed heartily. "Only trained nurses can take care of patients, Lizzie."

Lizzie's eyes widened. "Oh," she said. "I don't want to inject them or give them medicine. I can help clean them … and things like that."

"Lizzie, you've been here for a year. I know you quite well now. I'm going to ask you a question." Lizzie swallowed. She knew the conversation was about to take a serious turn. "Do feel being a nun is your calling?"

Lizzie paused. "I'd very much like to have a family one day. That's the only thing that makes me think I can't stay a nun. But first, I want to become a nurse."

Mother Constance smiled. "I'm glad you told me the truth. I have friends at nursing schools in Accra and Kumasi. I'll write to them, and we'll see what happens. You have to be patient, though. These things take time."

"Thank you, Mother Constance," Lizzie said.

The radio crackled in the background.

Ashanti National Liberation Movement demands a federal form of government ...

Mother Constance sucked her teeth. Lizzie didn't know the woman was interested in politics and especially, that of the Gold Coast.

"What's wrong?" she asked the old nun.

"I don't think this country is ready for independence," Mother Constance said.

"Why do you say that?" Lizzie asked.

"Trust me, I'm Irish. I know the value of independence, especially from those ..." Lizzie could have sworn the woman had been about to drop an expletive. "... from the English," she said. "But this country is divided. Kwame Nkrumah needs to talk to the NLM and quell the fire that is raging in people's hearts, before taking control from England. Baffour Akoto and the NLM don't want the kind of government Nkrumah is pushing for. He seems in such a hurry to free this country, but if he doesn't work with them, I'm afraid the Gold Coast will be torn apart. The last thing you want is a civil war."

From the kitchen, a large pop startled them.

"What was that?" Mother Constance asked.

"One of the syringes," said Lizzie, walking to the kitchen.

"Very well, then," Mother Constance said. "Keep your fingers crossed about nursing school. I'll let you work now." She shuffled out.

"Thanks, Mother Constance," Lizzie shouted. She poured the hot water off the sterilized instruments, carrying the pot back to the infirmary. As she used a pair of tongs to pick up the sterilized items, she thought of the possibility of a civil war. That would be dreadful. She supposed that was a wake up call for her to find out more about what was going on with politics in the country. The more exciting part of her conversation with the old nun kept trying to surface, so she let it. Nursing school! That was definitely her ticket out. If she went to Accra, she would find Bador Samed, and they might end up working in the same hospital. Her heart skipped a beat. This was a sign that they were meant to be together. All she had to be was patient. Even if it took the next five years, they would still be young, and that would be the perfect time to start a family. Nursing school, her own family, Bador Samed. A fat syringe and a pair of scissors slipped from the tongs, landing onto the concrete floor. She sucked her teeth.

*

May 1956

Lizzie, Sister Sarah and two other nuns stood outside the walls of the convent waiting for Mother Constance. Lizzie looked at her cane basket of pineapple jam and shifted her gaze to the blue van they were about to board. In front it their driver scrubbed his teeth vigorously with a chewing stick.

"Sorry to keep you waiting," Mother Constance said, coming out through the doors. She handed Sister Sarah three envelopes. "Here's money to pay the driver and for food when you get to Kumasi. Please drop this one off at the Polyclinic. And Lizzie," she turned to her, "this is for the Accra Nursing School. Sister Sarah, show her where the post office is. Be careful, ladies. I hear there's a big NLM rally in town."

"Thanks, Mother Constance," Lizzie said.

The nuns sat in the minivan, Sister Sarah in front, Lizzie and two others in the back. Lizzie heard the click of the key in the ignition. The engine started and sputtered to a stop soon after.

"Ei, you sisters are going to have to push," the driver said to the nuns, chuckling. Lizzie suppressed a snort. The other nuns remained silent. He started the engine again, and after the fifth attempt it revved up. He laughed loudly. "You're very lucky," he said. Lizzie smiled. She missed such exchanges.

The sky outside was dark blue, silhouetting the trees that towered above them as the driver sped on the bumpy road. The road ebbed and flowed. Lizzie's stomach rose and sank every time the car went downhill.

As the sun rose, coloring the sky a light shade of indigo, Lizzie made out *khaya* trees. Her heart ached with longing.

They got into Kumasi two hours later. At a roundabout decorated with red, yellow, pink and purple blooms and a signboard that read, GARDEN CITY, cars were stationed bumper to bumper.

"Sisters," the driver said, "Baffour Akoto, you know, the NLM's big man, is in town. All these cars you see, they're full of his supporters."

Sister Sarah mumbled something to him. Did she have to be so humorless? Lizzie wondered. If Mother Constance had been in her place, Lizzie was sure the woman would have been bantering with the driver.

Steering out of the thick of cars, the driver turned onto a narrow dirt road and parked in front of a blue general store. The narrow road buzzed with activity. Market women walked over with big pans hooked under their arms. Small boys clutched wooden boxes they were hitting with short metal rods.

"Shoe!" they shouted.

A thin woman with a matching red and yellow cloth balanced a bowl of oranges on her head.

"Yessss, orange," she hissed. Lizzie loved the energy.

"Let's go to the post office first, Lizzie," Sister Sarah said. "Sister Henrietta and Gloria, you two can start preparing our table in front of the Kumasi Polyclinic. They know we're coming. They'll give you a table. We'll be back soon." Lizzie handed her basket to Sister Gloria.

Sister Sarah grabbed Lizzie's right hand and they walked by a large open gutter, filled with plastic bags, orange peels, chicken bones and brown water. The filth didn't seem to bother the market women who were setting up their stalls.

As Lizzie and Sister Sarah were about to cross a road, Lizzie saw a group of young men walking towards them wielding machetes, shouting, "No CPP! No Nkrumah!" They chanted, whistled, stomped and brandished their machetes, creating a cloud of dust.

"Wait," Sister Sarah whispered to Lizzie, huddling closer to her.

"No CPP! No Nkrumah! Federal government only!" Their chants crescendoed, their machete-waving grew more frantic as they passed by Lizzie and Sister Sarah. One of them in tight blue trousers flourished his machete in front of them, his eyes popped out as he shouted their slogan, saliva squirting out of his mouth. Lizzie noticed he kept his feet in a trot. He set a precedent. After him, every one who passed by did the same. Lizzie wasn't scared. Somehow she was convinced they wouldn't hurt women, especially not women dressed in nuns' clothing. She felt

Sister Sarah's nails dig into her each time one of the marchers stopped in front of them.

The last person in the group, a boy who looked fifteen years old, stopped completely. He waved the machete close to Lizzie's face, sticking his nose on hers. He went on to Sister Sarah. Lizzie heard her whimper. Now she was getting worried.

"Repeat after me," he said, puffing his chest, slicing the air with his machete as if it were an orchestra conductor's baton. "Federal government!"

"Federal government!" Lizzie and Sister Sarah said.

"No Nkrumah!"

"No Nkrumah!" Their voices shook.

"No unitary government!"

"No unitary government."

"Hallelujah!" the boy said and crossed himself. He swung the machete from left to right, as if to fan the women. Then he ran off to catch up with the other men.

"These people will end up killing everyone in Kumasi," Sister Sarah said, composing herself. That was the strongest opinion Lizzie had heard her utter. She herself was strangely thrilled by the mob. The boy had scared her somewhat, but even that, she'd found exhilarating. She really needed to educate herself on what the Gold Coast was going through.

"Come," Sister Sarah said, pulling Lizzie close. "The post office is around the corner."

They sent off the letter to Accra. Now Lizzie could only hope for good results. They walked back to the Polyclinic, Sister Sarah striding with a new burst of energy. Lizzie figured the woman didn't want to run into the NLM twice in one day.

They found Sister Henrietta and Sister Gloria in front of the clinic, sitting behind a table piled with their jams.

"Sister Gloria," Sister Sarah said. "Can you please drop this letter at the reception?"

"No problem," Sister Gloria said.

Lizzie and Sister Sarah joined Sister Henrietta behind the table. Lizzie didn't even want to consider the Polyclinic as an option. Her goal was to get to the Accra Nursing School. She looked at Sister Sarah, who looked like she was still rattled. Why was she so worried? Lizzie thought. God was on her side, right? She looked at the nun, her skin dark and beautiful.

"Sister Sarah," Lizzie said.

"Yes?"

"Are you fulfilled?" Lizzie asked.

"I'm doing the Lord's work. That is the most fulfilling thing on the earth's surface."

"I know, but don't you want more from life? Like a husband, a family, children, money?"

"Lizzie, you're part of my family. Being a nun, everyone in the world is your brother and sister. I love the Lord and have a heart big enough to love everyone in the world. That's more fulfilling than showing love to just one or two people."

Lizzie knew she wasn't going to get very far with her. "Thanks," she mumbled. She wasn't fulfilled. She'd rested enough. It was time to get out of the convent. It was no place for her.

Four
Freedom at Last

Dawn tinged the sky purple. Lizzie, Mother Constance and Sister Sarah stood on the dusty curb of the road, Lizzie hugging a leather bag which Mother Constance had given her. Mother Constance watched the road with the eyes of a hawk, her hands clasped behind her back. All three women remained quiet.

A small wine minivan rattled up the road, a thick cloud of smoke trailing it. Mother Constance stuck her arm out and flagged it down.

"This is it," she said as the van sputtered to a stop. "Good luck, Lizzie!" She waved her hand in the air, as if that would get rid of the pervasive smoke.

"Thank you for everything," Lizzie said as she hugged Mother Constance.

"Write to me!" Sister Sarah said.

Lizzie looked at the van. It seemed as if someone had taken the time to smash his fist on every part of the car, even the windows. She looked up at the roof, where a sheep was trussed to the luggage rack. She lowered her eyes and saw the bodies of people squashed next to each other. She exhaled, took one last look at the sisters, the dense foliage behind them, and climbed into the van. This was it. The start of a new life.

She sat next to a middle-aged man who was topped with a straw hat. He snored by the window, his hands clasped over his distended belly. She wanted to shake him awake to ask him to switch places so she didn't miss a single thing on the way to Accra.

The van bumped as it hit a crater in the road. Lizzie felt her abdomen sink and rise. The man's head rolled from the window and landed on top of her head. The straw hat caught in her hair, which she'd combed into a puff. She tried to untangle the hat.

"Hmmm?" the man mumbled.

"Sir," Lizzie said. A snore escaped his lips. She shook his shoulder.

"What is it?" the man said, his left eye fluttering rapidly.

"Sorry to wake you up, sir, but your hat is stuck in my hair."

"Ho!" he scoffed. "That's why you wake me up?" He yanked his hat. Lizzie winced, sure he'd torn some of her hair but she didn't complain. She smiled at him, hoping she could cast her legendary charm on him.

"Sir," she squeaked. "I've never been to Accra. Can I please sit by the window?"

"No!" he said. "First you wake me up, now you want to take my seat. Impossible!"

"Sorry for disturbing you," she said.

"Accra?" the man mumbled as he went back to sleep. "There's nothing to even…." The sound of his snore floated up and settled like a thick cloud above him and Lizzie.

The sky brightened, turning turquoise, bringing with it birds chirping with morning energy.

"For the Independence Day celebrations, they say the Queen herself will be coming," shouted a man sitting in the back.

"Don't lie," a woman yelled back at him. Her voice was deeper than his. "The Queen won't be coming. Where do you get your news from? The Duchess of Kent is coming."

"Was I talking to you?" the man inquired. Lizzie turned around. She saw the man, dressed in a black and white cloth, his mouth shaped into a round pout, staring at a big woman sitting in front of him. The woman looked straight ahead, the skin on her forehead creased into a frown.

"Yes. You were," she said finally. "And even if you weren't, stop spreading wrong information."

"Look forward and mind your own business," the man shouted.

"This country is not ready," another man said. "Your Prime Minister doesn't want to work with his opposition, like the NLM. I smell trouble ahead for us. No peace."

"Keep your *toli* to yourself. Bush Ashanti liar!" the woman yelled.

Lizzie looked forward and smiled. This was what she hoped Accra would be full of—people with opinions, who weren't afraid to air them. Sure, Mother Constance was full of opinions, but she seemed apologetic for even owning them to begin with. Lizzie stretched her neck to see what was going on outside the window.

A fat mother rat scuttled along the roadside, its five baby rats in tow. The *khaya* trees that silhouetted the road earlier had disappeared, giving way to smaller narrower trees. She looked at her cantankerous neighbor. A silvery glob of saliva danced around his lips, threatening to fall onto his shirt. She closed her eyes.

The bus rattled violently and its engine petered out.

"Ei, driver!" a woman shouted. "I want to live till Independence!"

The driver tried the ignition. The engine's parts ground against each other but would not start. He mumbled to a man sitting to his left.

"Brothers and sisters," the driver said. "Please bear with us."

"Please hurry up!" the woman continued. "I want to get to Accra for Independence Day."

"Oh ho!" the man in the black and white cloth shouted. Lizzie recognized his whiny voice. "That is not till March."

"Was I talking to you?"

Two men got down from the van. Lizzie looked out the window. One man walked behind the van. The other stood by the driver's seat. She strained her neck to see him better. He bent his body and placed his palms on the door. His calves were taut. He arched his feet. She could feel his energy pulsing through his arms as he began to push. The driver started the ignition. She saw the man's feet lift off the ground. The engine started. People in the van clapped and the two men got back in.

Lizzie opened her bag and pulled out the letter the Accra Nursing School had sent her. She unfolded it. Her directions were spelled out:

Walk toward the Kumasi-bound buses, women selling watermelons usually sit near that exit. Walk out through that exit. I'll be waiting for you by a blue and white Volkswagen van …

She felt her neighbor's gaze, but thought she was imagining things. She looked at him and he was wide awake and gaping at her.

"Is this really your first trip to Accra?" he asked, licking the whitened corners of his mouth.

"Yes," she said.

"Then, my dear, the window seat is all yours," he said. Lizzie raised her brows at him, surprised at his change of heart.

"Thank you so much, sir!"

"There's not much to see, but since this is your first time…." He pointed at his crotch and smiled. Lizzie wondered how she was going to get over him, especially since he wasn't making any effort to move.

"How do we do this?" she asked.

"Climb over me."

She picked up her bag and stood up, pressing the metal roof with the palm of her right hand. She waited for him to slide over. He was riveted in place.

"Can you please move now?" she asked him, realizing that her buttocks were level with his face.

"Oh, yes, yes," he said. She saw him shift. She lifted her right leg over his legs. As she was about to sit, she felt him pinch the left cheek of her buttocks.

"Why did you do that?" she asked quietly, not exactly wanting to cause a scene.

"Do what?" he said, grinning. "You wanted the seat, or? I needed to get something in return."

She sat down in a huff and wrapped her arms tightly around her bag. The man chuckled. She looked outside the window wondering what she'd done to deserve this molestation. All she wanted to do was see Accra.

The streets became more organized, grid-like.

"Here's your Accra," her perverted cantankerous neighbor said.

The van drove through into a walled bus station. Vans reversed out of the station, taxis with fastbacks painted orange and yellow steered carelessly into tight parking spots. Voices floated above the din of automobiles.

"Kumasi, Kumasi, Kumasi!"

"Elmina, Elmina, Elmina!"

"Kpando, Kpando, Kpando!"

The driver stopped in front of a sign that read KUMASI. Lizzie got down. Women, younger than she, walked around balancing glass boxes filled with pies and stainless steel pans, hissing and calling out.

"Yesss, rice!"

Lizzie straightened her yellow dress and puffed up her hair. She saw a round market woman bend over to pick up two watermelons as large as her breasts. The woman carefully placed them on a mat. Next to her was an exit. Lizzie strode out and looked left and right. A white nun dressed in a white dress and habit came toward her.

"Elisabet Appiah?" she asked.

"Yes. You must be Mother Maria."

"Yes, I am. Welcome, Elisabet," the nun said. Lizzie thought her accent strange, much different from Mother Constance's.

"Welcome to Accra," the woman said.

Lizzie smiled at her new Mother Superior. They walked to a blue and white Volkswagen van. Marked on its flanks were the words ACCRA NURSING SCHOOL. They boarded the van.

"How was your trip?" Mother Maria asked.

"It was nice," Lizzie said, more interested in life outside the window. A woman roughly shoved a man away from her. The man tottered on one foot, but didn't fall. His arms swayed along his body as he tried to maintain his balance.

As they drove toward the school, Lizzie saw and marveled at the sea. This was the first time she'd seen the sea. The Insu River seemed to run on forever, but it was nothing compared to the sea. The sea stretched on forever, kissing the sky infinitely. They stopped at a pink building.

"This is the Accra Nursing School, Elisabet," Mother Maria said, pushing her door open.

"I like the colors," Lizzie said, admiring the pink walls, a welcome change, after the austere white walls of the convent. She picked up her bag, got down from the van and followed Mother Maria through an open blue gate.

"Elisabet," Mother Maria said, "this is the administrative building." She pointed to a two-story building they were passing by. "In it are the classrooms, my office and the offices of the teachers. Now, we're walking to the dormitories." They stopped at another two-level pink building with several wooden casement windows. Mother Maria opened a blue door. They climbed up a staircase to the second floor. She knocked on a door, stood and waited.

A girl Lizzie's height opened the door and grinned at Mother Maria.

"Hello, Mercy," Mother Maria said. "I've brought your roommate Elisabet." Mercy shook Lizzie's hand. "I'll leave you two." Lizzie stepped into the room.

"This is yours." Mercy pointed to a twin-sized, wooden bed next to the window. "Mother Maria told me this was your first trip to Accra, so I figured you'd appreciate the view of the sea."

"Thanks," Lizzie said. She stared outside the window. The sea's waves crashed against a small cliff just behind their building. "It's beautiful," she said quietly. She placed her bag on the bed and caught Mercy staring at her and grinning.

"You look so lost," Mercy said. "It's a good thing you're my roommate. There's no place in Accra I don't know…. You should unpack."

Lizzie didn't have much to unpack. She looked at the wardrobe with dread. A frameless mirror was mounted on its left door.

"Here," Mercy said, opening the wardrobe. Split in two parts, on one side hung white uniforms and dresses in blue, yellow, floral and checkered prints. On the side that would become Lizzie's, hung two uniforms. "You can make more uniforms," Mercy said. "My mother's seamstress is very good. She made me three more uniforms. That way I can wear one a day. Accra is so hot, you'll have to wash your uniform every day or every other day otherwise …" Wow, this girl can talk! Lizzie thought.

She opened her bag, extracted the two dresses she'd brought, took out her Bible and placed it next to her pillow.

"I'm so excited you're here," Mercy said. "You'll have to meet my Minister," she added, her eyes narrowing.

"A real Minister?" Lizzie asked.

"Yes."

"Is he your boyfriend?" She draped the dresses over her right arm and stood up.

"Yes, but he has a wife and three children." Lizzie was shocked, but not in a bad way. She was so tired of piousness. "He can take us out when he's not busy."

"Aren't the sisters strict?" Lizzie hung the dresses next to her uniforms.

"They try to be, but this is a nursing school, not a convent," Mercy said. Lizzie was quiet. "I'm so sorry. Sometimes I just say things. I know you just came from a convent." Mercy reminded her of Asantewa.

"I wasn't much of a convent girl," Lizzie said, trying not to lose her new friend.

"What were you doing there?"

"Buying time," Lizzie said, smiling.

"Buying time for what?"

"To come to Accra. To find my boyfriend."

"Oh, really, now?" Mercy said, putting on a British accent. "Listen, dear, you've met the right person. We'll find this boyfriend."

*

February 1957

Lizzie stood in front of the mirror, wearing a pink and white dress Mercy had lent her. Its full skirt was gathered at the waist, adding more voluptuousness to her already ample bottom and hips. Mercy stood behind her, fussing with a hem on the dress.

"I can't believe you managed to convince me to come out," Lizzie said. "I'm a good Catholic girl." She giggled and slipped her hands into white gloves.

"So am I, my dear Elisabet. So am I," Mercy said.

"Do you know how many times I've tried to get Mother Maria to say 'Elizzzabeth'?"

"She's a stubborn old Italian nun," Mercy said, "who should be the last person we should be talking about if we want to make a clean escape."

"Wait," Lizzie said. "I thought you had this all planned out. Haven't you already done this before?"

"Yes," Mercy said, about to slip her right foot into a white pump. "Actually," she said, "we should go barefoot till we're outside the gate."

"Unbelievable!" Lizzie said. Her heart started a trot. She knew that she, of all people, had to be careful. She couldn't afford to get caught. And yet she loved the thrill of breaking bounds. She was beginning to discover that this was who she was. A rule-breaker.

Mercy opened the door slowly, her shoes hooked over her left middle and index fingers. The door creaked. Lizzie stepped out after her.

"I hope I don't fall down the stairs," Lizzie whispered, feeling the dust on the floor sticking to her feet.

"Shhh!" Mercy said. "I'm on the first step down. Hold my shoulder," she whispered. Down they went, step by step, two round twenty-year-old rule-breakers. As Lizzie's foot hit the last step, the board creaked loudly. She was convinced she'd woken up the whole dorm. "Ah! Lizzie," Mercy whispered when they were outside, "you know that last board ..."

"Sorry," Lizzie said. "I forgot. And I thought this wasn't a big deal." Of course it was a big deal, but she wanted to shift all responsibility on Mercy. She was the innocent newcomer who was just following her experienced friend. As they tiptoed barefoot toward the gate, Lizzie saw the dark blue outline of a coconut tree dancing ominously in the night breeze. She was still adapting to the thickness and salinity of the Accra air. Mercy pushed open the gate and burst into a fit of laughter as she bent over to put on her shoes.

"I could have killed you when you stepped on that last board," she said, clutching her chest.

"Well, I could kill you now with all this secrecy. You haven't done this before, have you?" Lizzie asked.

"No," Mercy said, a grin on her face. Lizzie wanted to swipe it off her face. "But I'm an expert at running away from school."

Across the street a man stood in front of a silver car. He raised his hand limply at them.

"That's him!" Mercy said, grabbing Lizzie's right hand. Her nails dug into Lizzie's palm. They crossed the empty street, their shoes click-clacking on the tarmac. Mercy threw herself onto the man, not much taller than she and Lizzie.

"Selasi," she said, kissing his cheek, "this is Lizzie."

Lizzie shook his hand. After offering her a flaccid handshake, he almost dropped her hand. Lizzie was too caught in admiring his car with its sleek round lights to be offended.

"Nice car," she said.

"Thank you," Selasi said through his nose, his voice as lifeless as his handshake. "It's a 1955 Corvette." That meant nothing to Lizzie. Where on earth did Mercy pull this man from? He didn't seem interesting in the least bit. Then again, she couldn't say she really knew Mercy. She entered the back seat. Could she say she really knew Bador Samed? After he ran away, she couldn't say that she did.

"… so I told my mother that she has to talk to these nursing teachers," Mercy said. "They're so picky. I drew the digestive system and one of them said, 'all the food from this body will come pouring out, Mercy. Your pencil lines don't join.' It was just a drawing, for goodness' sake!"

Selasi grunted. Lizzie kept her gaze outside the window. Trees glowed in orange luminescence under streetlights. She felt like she was in a surreal dream. She'd wake up and be married to a suitor Papa Yaw had handpicked for her.

Selasi parked outside a deep purple building on which a wooden sign read, PINK IGUANA. The pulsating beats of highlife being played inside wafted outside. Cigarette smoke blown out of the mouths of men wearing dark glasses floated up to the roof of the club. Lizzie drew her eyes down from the swirls of vanishing smoke. She stared at the thin smokers, at their cigarette-holding hands and at their dried up mouths. She gawked at their thin women. They stood between the men, in tight dresses that traced huge backsides. Huge bottoms and breasts on sticks. She couldn't help looking. They oozed intoxicating sexuality.

Mercy hooked her arm in Lizzie's and in Selasi's. The Mercy-sandwich walked to the entrance, up to a man dressed in a black felt hat and brown suit.

Lizzie looked away from the entrance. To her right, she caught the stare of a man in an ill-fitting tan jacket, dark brown trousers and shoes that matched his jacket. And straightened hair. He smiled at her. Lizzie took her gaze away. What a creepy man, she thought. Maybe it was the matching jacket and shoes. Or the hair.

The Mercy-sandwich walked inside, where Lizzie saw sweaty bodies gyrating in the hot staleness of the room. Backsides bumped left to right, heads bobbed, arms flailed. Selasi unhinged himself from Mercy's hold. He walked up to the bar, whispered to the bartender and signaled for Mercy and Lizzie to follow him. They settled at a table with four metal chairs.

"Two cokes and one shot of whiskey," Selasi said, when the bartender came over. He hadn't bothered to ask Lizzie and Mercy what they wanted. He extracted a cigar from his pocket, lit it and puffed on it with all his energy. His cheeks inflated and deflated.

"John Quaye and his band," Lizzie heard a voice say over the music. "Ladies and gentlemen, hope you're digging our music."

The crowd roared in approval.

The bartender danced over with their drinks.

"Thanks," Selasi said, a small smile creasing the corner of his mouth. Lizzie picked up her coke.

"We're going to dance," Mercy said, pulling Selasi from his seat.

Lizzie wondered if the stiff Minister could even move. She kept her eyes on them, smiling as Mercy stuck out her buttocks and pushed left, right, back and forth. She was about to watch Selasi's moves when a shadow blocked her view.

"Would you like to dance?" the man with the tan jacket, tan shoes and straightened hair asked.

"No, thanks," she said.

"Please. It would be an honor. You're exquisite." As much as she thought he was creepy, flattery had its benefits.

"Only for one song," Lizzie said. He led her onto the dance floor. She tried to steer him close to Mercy and Selasi, but he had other plans. He wrapped his arms around her and caressed her back with his palms. He pressed her close to him, her breasts felt flat against his chest. His breath reeked of alcohol. She tried to pry herself from his grip. He held her tightly. Just for one song, she said to herself. He hummed into her ear, pressing her tighter. She felt a strange poke. It grew more persistent, pressed into her groin. She realized what it was. Disgusted, she used all the strength she could muster to push him away.

"That's enough," she said, walking back to her table.

"Baby, I want to see you again after tonight," he said.

"Sorry, I'm already taken," she said, looking in the throng of dancers, trying to find Mercy.

"It's a white man, eh?" the man said, his voice loud. "You Gold Coast girls! That's all you know. It's disgraceful! Independence is coming, but we will never be free because of you people. The Gold Coast will never be free!" His voice grew hoarser. She saw Mercy coming over with Selasi.

"What's going on?" Selasi said, his flat voice not at all menacing.

"Your little sister here only likes white men!" the man went on. "Tell her to change her ways!"

"Sir, please leave," Selasi said.

"We are stuck," the man went on. "Mentally. Brothers and sisters. We will never be free! The British might leave us in March, but in here," he hit his chest, "we will never be free!"

"All right, girls," Selasi said, "I think it's time to go."

They drove back in silence. Selasi parked next to the nursing school gate.

"Thank you," Lizzie said, getting out of the car.

"Wait for me at the door," Mercy said.

Lizzie took off her shoes. The man's words were bothering her now, even more than his prodding member. She would rather live in Accra than live in Adukrom No. 2. She wanted nice clothes and to ride around in shiny cars. Did that mean she liked the white man's ways? Did that mean she wasn't free?

As she walked toward the door, her leg knocked over a hard object which clanged loudly to the ground. As it rolled noisily along the concrete floor, Lizzie picked it up. It was a metal bucket. Lizzie heard the Minister's car whir and leave. Mercy tiptoed over, her shoes in her hand.

"What was that awful sound?" she asked.

"Somebody put a bucket smack in front of the door," Lizzie said. "It wasn't there when we were leaving."

"Who could …"

The door opened. Lizzie saw the ghostly face of Mother Maria appear behind the door.

"Aha!" Mother Maria said. "I thought I heard noise earlier. I put the bucket there to catch the thief! Elisabet, Mercy! Punishment in the morning!"

Back in their room, Mercy wasn't smiling. Lizzie grinned guiltily.

"She would have caught us, either way," she said.

"No. You knocked the bucket down," Mercy said. "I have good news."

"What?" Lizzie asked, surprised at the quick change in mood.

"Selasi said we can be escorts during Independence Day!"

"Really?" Lizzie asked. "But I don't know anything about Accra. What would I tell people?"

"Don't worry," Mercy said, unzipping her dress.

"Ooh! I'm so excited," Lizzie said.

Clutching a palm-frond broom, Lizzie bent over and swept an algae-filled gutter behind the administrative block. Mercy sidled up to her, carrying a bucket of soapy water.

"Mercy, I'm so excited about Independence Day!" Lizzie said. "On my way to Accra, everybody was talking about it and to be part of it now…. Thank you."

"Don't thank me! Thank Selasi." Lizzie remained quiet. That boring man! she thought. "What do you think of him?"

Lizzie thought about sugarcoating her real feelings. He's nice, she could say. Truth is she actually liked Mercy and she didn't think it right to lie to her. "I like his car," she said.

"He does have a very nice car, doesn't he? Apart from that?"

Lizzie bent over and swept a stubborn green patch. She stood up. "He's married."

"I know," Mercy snapped back.

"What do you see in him anyway? I think he's too selfish," Lizzie said.

"I didn't realize you were so honest. At least he took us out and bought us drinks." Mercy placed her hands on her waist and rounded her mouth into a pout.

"I know. I don't mean to sound ungrateful." Lizzie looked at Mercy. "Come on! Don't look at me like that. Would you rather I lied?"

Mercy shook her head. "It was a lot of fun, except for that crazy man," she said. "That your husband was something else! The first time you go out in Accra, and you go and pick the worst kind. Didn't you see how he was dressed?"

"I did," Lizzie said, "but I didn't want to sit down all night long. Can you please pour some water here for me?" Mercy dragged the bucket close to the gutter and tipped it. The soapy solution splashed on the green. "I'm sorry about what I said about Selasi. I guess I'm just feeling a little jealous, is all," Lizzie said, her voice lowered.

"Why? You shouldn't be, when you caught yourself such a fine husband?"

Lizzie laughed. "I've been thinking," she said. "Remember I told you I was looking for my boyfriend?"

"Yes! Finally, you reveal the details!" Mercy said.

"Elisabet! Mercy!" Mother Maria's voice floated from a classroom above. "You will do your punishment and stop talking!"

"Yes, Mother Maria," they chorused.

"He just disappeared after we had made plans to come to Accra together. I've been living to find him, not for myself. If he was a man, he would have come back for me. It's been three years and I still haven't heard a word from him."

"I'm sorry," Mercy said. "Well, there are so many nice men in Accra … we should find you your own Minister!"

Lizzie smiled. A muscle in her heart twitched. She'd made up her mind. She wasn't looking for him anymore. Even if she went in search of Bador Samed and found him, she was sure he'd be living a pauper's life and couldn't give her the things she wanted. She moved to another part of the gutter and realized she was the only one doing the scrubbing.

"Don't worry, I'll take care of you," Mercy said. She couldn't complain, especially not after that offer.

*

March 5, 1957

Lizzie, dressed in a red, yellow and green *kente* cloth, stood in front of the mirror in her room. She held her hair, now straight, in a pompadour.

Mercy told her she couldn't start independence with her hair coarse and kinky and had passed a hot comb through it to get it straight.

"Ready?" Mercy asked, wearing the same outfit as Lizzie.

"Yes," Lizzie said. They walked out of the nursing school and into Selasi's Chevy Corvette.

"Hello," Mercy said.

"Hello," Selasi said, his voice betraying no excitement about the coming festivities. "I'll drop you two off at the Arena. That was the arrangement, right?"

"Yes," Mercy said. She seemed less interested in him than she was the first time Lizzie met him. Lizzie hoped it wasn't because of her. As they drove, boys waving red, yellow and green flags blew whistles and wove in and out of the road.

The Arena, a small cream-colored building, buzzed with young people clad in the same cloth as Lizzie and Mercy. Inside, it was voluminous and high-ceilinged, not at all what Lizzie had expected, after seeing its exterior. Mercy dragged Lizzie to a corkboard. A long list of escorts in two parallel columns was posted on it. Lizzie looked for her name. She was paired with Charles Boateng and they were escorting John and Nora Johnson. How she was going to find Charles Boateng was beyond her.

"I'm with some Ntem guy. I'm going to look for him," Mercy said. "We'll see each other at the dance tonight."

"But ..." Lizzie started to protest. Mercy had already disappeared in the crowd. Lizzie stood there helpless, ready to go around asking every man if they were Charles Boateng. A young man walked up to the wooden stage.

"Ladies and Gentleman," he said. His hair was parted on the left. "Thank you all for coming. Please find a seat. I'll make this brief, especially since you all have to pick up your guests. You will not regret helping to make this great moment in Ghana's history a success. At the entrance we have the names of all the escort pairs. To help you, the men have been assigned cars and will be driving, so the women can search for the men outside. We've listed the car numbers." Lizzie felt relieved that there was a system in place. "Go out and make Ghana proud!" The room erupted in applause. "Oh," he said. "Before I forget! Everyone will get paid after the celebrations. Don't worry, you'll get your money. Also, dinner will be available here from six onward. Thank you."

Lizzie walked back to the list and memorized her car number: *ANR 248*. Outside, she started looking at all the number plates. She noticed the cars were parked in alphabetical order. One of the men stuck out his index finger and curled it at her, beckoning her over. She hurried away.

"Elizabeth Appiah?" a scrawny man—he looked more like a boy—called out.

"Yes?"

"Charles Boateng," he said sticking out his hand.

"Oh, good!" Lizzie said, shaking his hand. "Where's our car?"

"This way," he said, walking to an olive green open top Mercedes Benz. Lizzie sat in it, smiling from cheek to cheek. Where was Papa Yaw? He needed to be here to see her.

"We're going to the Sea Breeze Hotel," Charles said and clammed up. Obviously he wasn't interested in talking to her. His eyes were sunken, the skin under them baggy. She was sure Charles killed himself at whatever he was studying.

He steered into the Sea Breeze Hotel, a black and white multi-story hotel draped with a red, yellow and green Ghanaian flag. Lizzie got down, straightened her *kaba* and slit and walked into the reception.

A big AKWAABA sign hung over the reception area. *Kente* cloth covered all the walls. Lizzie walked to the unhappy-looking receptionist.

"Good afternoon," she said chirpily. "I'm here to pick up Mr. and Mrs. Johnson." The receptionist nodded at Lizzie, picked up the phone and whispered quietly into it.

The Johnsons walked into the reception, arm-in-arm. They looked like seventy-year-old siblings with skin the color of warm caramel. They were both so delicate.

"Hello," Lizzie said to the couple. "*Akwaaba*. Welcome."

"Thank you," Nora Johnson said. Her husband smiled. Lizzie walked them to the car, opening the backseat door for them.

"This is Charles Boateng," Lizzie said. "My name is Lizzie-Achiaa Appiah."

"Beautiful," Nora Johnson said. "Well, you probably already know my name is Nora and my husband's John."

"Pleased to meet you," Lizzie said.

"*Akwaaba*," Charles said, smiling for the first time that day. She had to admit he possessed a boyish charm underneath those baggy eyes. "We're going to give you a mini-tour of Accra," he said.

"That's my school," Lizzie said with the excitement of a four-year-old, pointing at the pink building as they passed by it.

"Such a pretty building," Nora said. "What kind of school is this?"

"It's a nursing school," Lizzie said.

"Wonderful," Nora said. Her voice was warm and buttery. It spread over the ears so gently. "What about you, Charles?"

"I'm studying physics at the University College of the Gold Coast," he said. That explains the bags, Lizzie thought, and ill-humor. Physics!

"Very impressive," Nora said, buttering Lizzie's ears.

Lizzie wondered why John was so quiet. She peeked at him and saw him extract a large camera from his bag.

"John has been dying to take pictures of your beautiful city," Nora said. Lizzie saw him gesture at Nora. "He wants us to stop a little so he can get some shots of the beach," she said.

"Of course," Charles said, pulling the car to the curb.

They stood by the roadside, a warm sea breeze flapping about them. John walked farther away, pointing and shooting his camera. He walked back, a smile on his lips. They boarded the car and Charles drove into Osu.

"Madam, sir," Charles said. "We can't drive over there now, but if you look to your back and to the right, you'll see the road that leads to the Castle."

Lizzie turned back. She saw the couple straining their necks.

"What's in the Castle?" Nora asked.

"That's where the British governor lives," Charles said. "The beautiful Independence Arch will be unveiled at midnight." It was covered with a black cloth. "It was built to remember the shooting of soldiers who were marching to send a petition to the British Governor. It's a symbol of our struggle."

"And struggle, indeed, we have," Nora said. "You know this day is just as important to us. With Ghana free, all of us can one day hope for freedom."

They drove into Accra. Lizzie left the tour-guiding to Charles, who seemed pleased with the role. His voice squeaked, crescendoed, ebbed and flowed with love and pride for the new country.

"That's the James Fort Prison," he said, pointing to a cream-colored fort to his right. "Kwame Nkrumah was imprisoned there."

Charles parked in front of the fort. As John took photos of the building, Lizzie sidled up to Nora. She didn't know what was pushing her, but she couldn't help it.

"Mrs. Johnson," she said.

"Yes?"

"Can I ask how you met your husband?" Nora smiled.

"We've known each other since we were three. I knew there was no one else in the world I could spend my whole life with."

"That's so nice," Lizzie said. Someone to grow old with—that was nice. Someone to die with—that was morbidly nice. If she loved someone so deeply she'd want to die with them. But now she loved no one.

"Oh, my goodness," Nora said. "That man could talk before he lost his voice! What am I saying? He still talks a lot."

"We have to drop you off at the pre-Independence Day dinner," Charles said, opening the car doors.

"Yes," Nora said. "You two have been so wonderful. Thank you. How do I say that in your language?"

"*Me da woase*," Lizzie volunteered.

"The people of Accra say *oyiwaladon*," Charles added.

"Beautiful!" Nora said. Charles drove them to the National Assembly Building. "*Me da wa si*," she said, hugging Lizzie and Charles.

John clasped his hands around Lizzie's, looked in her eyes and mouthed, "Thank you." He was such a charming man!

Later that night, Lizzie, Mercy and Charles and thousands of people gathered next to the National Assembly Building. Lizzie and Mercy drank cokes, while Charles gulped down a beer.

"Where's Selasi?" Lizzie asked Mercy.

"Do I know?" Mercy spat back.

"He's giving his speech at the Assembly," Charles volunteered, having clearly misheard them. Of course they knew Kwame Nkrumah was outlining the new government's policies. Lizzie looked at Charles. She wanted to laugh. He was a funny man but she was warming up to him.

Lizzie saw Kwame Nkrumah being carried through the crowd in his black and white smock. The din increased. Lizzie grabbed Mercy's hand, squeezed it. They were carried in the throng toward the Old Polo Ground. The bellows of people in the crowd grew louder. They screamed and clapped. A brass band of policemen in beige uniforms pumped the air with feisty highlife.

Nkrumah walked onto a stage that was bordered with wooden bars. He flung his arms into the air, waving a white handkerchief. He danced behind the stage. The crowd went crazy. Lizzie screamed her lungs hoarse. Three of his Ministers, similarly dressed, joined him.

"*Tsoooboi!*" Kwame Nkrumah shouted.

"*Weey!*" the crowd erupted.

"*Tsoooboi!*"

"*Weey!*"

"At long last ..." he said, "the battle has ended." The crowd's response was so loud, Lizzie could barely hear him. He held onto the wooden bars behind the microphones. "And then, Ghana, your beloved country is free forever." The crowd screamed. Lizzie shouted too. "From now on there's a new African in the world. That new African is ready to fight his own battle and show them that, after all, the black man is capable of managing his own affairs," he said, throwing his hand into the air. Lizzie roared along with the crowd. "... Our independence is meaningless unless it is linked up with the total liberation of the African continent."

Lizzie stood still as the band began the new National Anthem. She looked around, noticing the VIP area. She searched for the Johnsons. She saw Nora's face. It seemed so sad.

"Freedom!" Nkrumah shouted.

"Freedom!" the crowd shouted back.

"Freedom!"

"Freedom!"

"May God bless you," he said and walked off. The brass band continued playing their music. Lizzie couldn't move without bumping into someone. She didn't mind—all that mattered was that they were now a free people. Fireworks burst into the sky, fizzing, whizzing and whooping above Lizzie.

Ghana! Ghana is the name—Ghana! We wish to proclaim—we will be jolly, merry and gay, the sixth day of March, Independence Day …

*

May 1957

The nursing school exam results were posted on a bulletin board by Mother Maria's door. Lizzie was nervous. She felt that she could have studied some more, but with all the Independence Day celebrations there was only so much she could get done. Eliza Sam, a girl in her class stood by the list, running her index finger down the list. Lizzie rubbed her arms together, preparing for whatever the results would be. She had no choice, she had to see them. She looked at the white sheets, kept her eyes on them and strode resolutely toward them.

"Congratulations, Appiah!" Eliza said loudly.

"Huh?" Lizzie looked at her.

"You made top five!"

Mother Maria's door opened at the same time.

"Elisabet, a quick word, please," she said. Lizzie wondered what she'd done wrong. If she'd truly made top five, hopefully, the woman would be lenient. Lizzie stepped into the office. It was bare, except for a wooden desk, two chairs and a bookcase. The terrazzo floor looked cool and distant. "You did very well, Elisabet," Mother Maria said.

"Really?"

"Yes, second in the whole class. Listen, there's a nursing internship at Korle Bu," Mother Maria said.

"Yes?" Lizzie said, standing by the door.

"Here's the information about the program. It's too late to start this year's, but I want you to keep it in mind for next year. I think it would be very good for you," she said, smiling.

"Thanks, Mother Maria." Lizzie beamed.

"I have a meeting, so you have to leave now," Mother Maria said.

Lizzie stepped outside the office and looked at the handwritten sheet, just to make sure she wasn't being tricked. There her name was:

2. Elizabeth Achiaa Appiah: 85%

She sauntered up the stairs and burst into her room.

Charles jumped out of Mercy's bed, wearing only a pair of white shorts. He covered his chest with a green cloth.

"Jesus! Can't you lock the door?" Lizzie asked, not sure whether to stay or leave. Mercy was in hysterics. She lay on the bed in a light pink satin slip, cycling her legs in the air.

"Hello, Lizzie," Charles said sheepishly.

"Charles. Is this where you live now?" Lizzie asked, feeling a twinge of jealousy—not that she was even interested in him.

"I'll be leaving now," he said, grabbing his clothes and putting them on his lean frame. Mercy was still in stitches as Charles slunk out of the room.

"How did you get him in?" Lizzie asked.

"My secret. See how he can get out so easily?"

"Tell me!" Lizzie said, sitting on her bed. "And what happened to Selasi?" Yes, she was jealous.

"Of course, he's still there. I need some young blood every now and then," Mercy said, looking extremely pleased with herself. "I told Mother Maria he's my brother and he's helping me move some things," she blurted out.

"You're an only child!" Lizzie said, trying to focus on her recent success, instead of her rising envy. She was sure she'd meet someone special when the time was right.

"I'll teach you my tricks one day, if you're good," Mercy said.

Five
A New Beginning

March 1958

Lizzie had barely walked into the muggy general ward of Korle Bu, when a group rushed in, shoving her to the side. Bridget Mantey, the head nurse, a tall large woman with shiny black hair bobbed at her neck, followed the stampede.

"There," Bridget shouted. "On that bed."

They seated an old lady clad in a *boubou* on a metal-framed bed. Bridget took a pan from under the bed and placed it on the woman's lap. The woman retched loudly.

"God, don't kill me oh!" she shouted.

"Nana, breathe," said one of the men who'd brought her in.

Lizzie strode toward them.

"Elizabeth," Bridget said brusquely. "Go get a bucket. Come clean this lady."

This was only Lizzie's first week in the hospital and her first vomiting case. As she passed by a child who was stretching her neck to see the new arrival, she prayed that she herself wouldn't throw up on the woman. She didn't mind blood, but vomit, she couldn't stomach.

She went to the supplies room and picked up two white face towels, a pair of gloves, soap and a metal bucket filled with water. She grabbed another bucket and headed out to face the vomiting woman.

As she walked over she saw the woman lying with her buttocks up in the air. Her family was seated on the bed across from her. A strong smell wafted Lizzie's way as she got closer. As the lady let out coarse sounds from her throat, soft moist sounds, escaped from her posterior. It wasn't just vomit.

"Excuse us," she said, drawing heavy, faded, green curtains around the old woman's bed. The old woman sucked her teeth.

"Who are you?" she said. "I want the old nurse. No child is going to touch me."

"Please, I'm just cleaning you," Lizzie said.

"Don't touch me. I want the old nurse to clean …" The old woman vomited in the bedpan.

"Nana," said one of the young men, poking his head through the curtain. "Please cooperate with the girl."

"It won't take long," Lizzie added.

The old woman was placated. Lizzie helped her out of the *boubou*. Her breasts stood erect. Lizzie had expected them to droop, considering her age. She wet one face towel and wiped the woman's face. She helped her out of her huge white drawers, dripping with brown liquid. She stole a glance at the old woman and could tell that she was embarrassed. Lizzie threw the soiled panties into the empty bucket. She wet the other towel and wiped the woman's buttocks clean. She chucked both towels on top of the stained clothes.

From a wooden cabinet next to the bed, Lizzie took out a square piece of white terrycloth and safety pins. She folded the cloth in half and wrapped it around the woman's bottom and pelvis, like a baby's nappy. The woman had completely calmed down. Lizzie put on a green patient's gown on the woman.

"The head nurse will see you soon," she said, drawing apart the curtains.

*

May 1958

Cleaning blood, changing soiled sheets, being bombarded with insults. Rousing sleeping patients, being vomited on, calming worried mothers, holding down children throwing tantrums. Lizzie was beginning to question her choice of profession.

On a hot Saturday afternoon, she followed Bridget into a private room, expecting to get told to wipe the bottom of a diarrhea patient. Inside, a man was asleep, snoring lightly. Bridget shook his shoulder.

"Mr. Mensah, wake up," she said.

He opened one eye, took a look at them, and opened the other.

"Oh, hello. Good morning," he said, clearing his throat. He smiled and stole glances at Lizzie. He had a narrow, pleasant face, with skin the color of coffee beans. His bulbous nose gave him a friendly air and his hair was about an inch high with a parting on the right. Bridget turned him around, not gently.

"Elizabeth," she said. "He has assma. We are about to inject his botoss." She pulled down Mr. Mensah's pajamas. "You take cotton wool, dab with alcohol and wipe the area you want to inject."

Mr. Mensah giggled and wheezed, making Lizzie laugh.

Bridget shook a bottle of colorless solution, stopped and glared at Lizzie. She stopped explaining. She stuck a syringe into the bottle.

"Be gentle," Mr. Mensah said, winking at Lizzie, who was trying to keep a straight face. She held her breath. She didn't want to make the needle to go the wrong way with her laughter. Who was this man?

Bridget extracted the syringe from the bottle, inserted the needle into Mr. Mensah's left butt cheek, took it out and gave his cheek a quick slap.

"Ooh," Mr. Mensah cooed.

Lizzie looked at him from the corner of her right eye, trying to stifle her giggles. He must be about twenty-five, she decided.

"Next time you will come and inject the botoss," Bridget said, interrupting Lizzie's thoughts. "I'll watch and after that you'll be coming here by yourself to inject the patient." She had covered the injected area with gauze and plaster. "Less go," she said to Lizzie. "Mr. Mensah ..."

"Please call me Ernest."

"You need to ress," Bridget said.

"Yes, madam," Ernest responded, grabbed a newspaper on his side table and stole a fast wink at Lizzie.

*

Lizzie's hand shook as she prepared the adrenalin chloride injection solution. Bridget's breathing and Ernest's wheezing were competing with each other. Breathe-wheeze. Wheeze-breathe. They weren't really helping her concentration. She stuck the needle of the syringe into a transparent glass vial and drew up the liquid.

"Thass enough," Bridget barked, as the liquid rose above the two-milliliter mark. After flicking the syringe, Lizzie looked at Bridget for encouragement. "Yes, go on."

Ernest pulled down his pajamas. "Be gentle," he said.

"Please, don't make me laugh," Lizzie said.

"Inject!" Bridget snapped.

Lizzie dabbed a ball of cotton wool on his butt cheek and stuck in the needle.

"*Agyee*!" Ernest exclaimed.

"I'm so sorry. Did I hurt you?" Lizzie asked.

Ernest burst into a fit of giggles which became hoops of dry coughs. "I got you," he said, his eyes watery and red.

"Please, Mr. Mensah, behave," Bridget said. "You muss not get excited. You'll bring on the assma again." She looked at Lizzie, eyeing her. "Less go," she said. Lizzie was annoyed at Ernest because of the attention he was drawing to her. She really thought she'd hurt him.

*

Lizzie was convinced she wouldn't be let her near Ernest's room again. Not after the episode from the day before. She entered the nurses' room, almost running into Bridget, who held a mug in hand.

"… I'm sure it's those Ashantis who are causing the lawlessness in town. Because of them we have to suffer this curfew …" Bridget was saying.

"Sorry," Lizzie said. "Good morning."

"Elizabeth," Bridget said, "today, you'll go to the assma patient by yourself. When you're done move to the general ward."

"Yes, Mrs. Mantey," Lizzie said.

She walked into Ernest's room and found him standing by the window, looking out through the dusty netting. He was only a few inches taller than she was.

He turned around. "Where's your madam today?" he asked.

"Sit and let me inject," Lizzie said.

Ernest giggled like a schoolgirl.

"Please sir, you muss not get excited."

"I was praying you'd walk in here alone," he said. "Ernest Mensah, but you already knew that."

"Lizzie-Achiaa Appiah. Mr. Mensah, please, I have to inject," Lizzie said, smiling mischievously.

Ernest stood by the window and stared at her.

"Please let me inject you, before she comes in to check."

Ernest climbed onto the bed, stuck his bottom out and pulled down his pajamas. Lizzie held the syringe above his buttocks. As the needle broke through his skin, he said, "I know this is the least romantic position on earth, but would you like to have dinner with me?"

Lizzie smiled as she dabbed the spot she'd injected.

"That's kind of you, but I have to be professional," she said, helping him pull up his pajamas.

"Think about it," Ernest said. "It'd be a friendly dinner."

"I'm sorry, Ernest," Lizzie said, unsure why she was turning down his invitation. "I'd rather not mix work with personal life. Besides, I'm just an intern here ..."

Ernest smiled sadly. "What do you do when you're not interning, Lizzie-Achiaa?"

"Just call me Lizzie. I'm in nursing school," she said. She studied him. He was not bad looking. He could have been taller and there was this asthma business. "What brought on your asthma?" she asked.

"The Prime Minister organized an event for young businessmen, and here I was dancing away. Before I knew it, I was being brought in here. I haven't suffered an attack in a couple of years."

"Asthma has several triggers," Lizzie said. "You might have eaten something that set it off," Lizzie said, thinking all the while, he said "young businessmen." That was a plus. So what if he wasn't tall? At least he was making money. "Are you allergic to anything?"

"To shrimp, but I don't think I ate any," he said.

"You should be careful," Lizzie said, now standing by the window, looking at the hospital entrance as people walked in and out.

"When does your internship end?" he asked. She looked at him sitting up in bed.

"I'll intern here till I finish nursing school," she said. "After that, I hope they hire me."

"You seem very competent. I'm sure they will," Ernest said.

"Thanks," she said. She wanted to ask him what he did, but she stopped herself, hearing Mercy's voice. "The best thing," Mercy had said to her, "is to pretend you're not interested in the man. And don't reveal too much about yourself." Unwillingly, she found herself playing along. "I should let you rest," she said. "I have to check on other patients."

"Lizzie," he said. "Please, think about my invitation."

She walked out, closing the door behind her. In the hallway, she looked left and then right. A man approached, but wasn't close enough to see her face. She squeezed her eyes shut. Why did you say no? Silly, silly girl! As the man got closer, she gathered herself and walked to the general ward.

After work she arrived at the nursing school and walked into her room, where she found Mercy pressing a tube of red against her lips.

"Hello, my dear," Mercy said.

"Hello. Where are you running off to?"

"A date."

"With Charles?" Lizzie asked.

"It's a surprise," Mercy said, making Lizzie raise her brows. Mercy never held anything back.

"I got a date invitation today," Lizzie said.

"Hallelujah! I hope you said yes." Lizzie shook her head. "What's wrong with you? Please don't mention Bador Samed or I'll do something horrible to you, because you're the one who didn't want to find …"

"I think I like this man."

"So why did you say no?"

"I don't know, Mercy," Lizzie said. "He's a patient at the hospital. He makes me laugh. We make fun of the head nurse. But to go out with him all-alone…. He could be a rapist for all I know."

"You're too paranoid!" Mercy said. "I have an idea!"

"What is it?" Lizzie asked, prepared to pretend to listen.

"It's simple. When you're ready for your date, I'll call Charles. Tell this fellow to take you to the Ambassador Hotel. Charles and I will go there and pretend to be just another couple."

"You think your broke Charles can afford the Ambassador Hotel?" Lizzie asked, giggling.

"You mock me. Let me tell you, Charles has come into some money. He's taking me out tonight. That's the surprise."

Lizzie was now on her bed, in stitches. She held her sides.

"Well, if you two don't blow off all the money before I decide to give Ernest a chance, all you'll be having at the Ambassador Hotel is a bottle of coke and you'll be sharing it."

"Ernest is his name, eh?" Mercy said.

"Yes."

Mercy made her way toward the door, her white shoes hooked in her fingers. "Have fun, my dear. Give Charles a kiss for me."

*

Lizzie arrived at the hospital the next day, ready to accept Ernest's invitation. Bridget Mantey didn't assign her his room, but she passed by it. His door was ajar. She stuck her head in and saw a pot-bellied, middle-aged man fast asleep instead. She couldn't believe it. That was just her luck! He'd checked out. Why had she been so difficult the day before?

In the general ward, she walked to a child with malaria. She smiled distantly at the girl, who frowned when she saw Lizzie approach.

"I don't want chloroquine," the girl yelled, flapping her arms like a duck. "I won't take it!"

"Then you won't get any better," Lizzie said. "Aaam." She tried to pry the girl's mouth open with her fingers. It was clamped shut. She'd let a nice prospect slip through her fingers. "Open up," she said. "When you get better you won't have to take any more of this nasty medicine, but if you don't take it now, you won't get better."

Lizzie poured the thick red liquid into a tablespoon and placed it on the girl's lips. The girl opened her mouth, gagging as she swallowed.

"Good girl," Lizzie said absentmindedly.

All morning she worked in a daze, berating herself for being too hard to please, too proper, too stupid.

As she walked out of the ward, she still felt a cloud hanging about her shoulders. She passed by the Indian almond tree, leaves scattered around its roots. She looked up and saw Ernest walking toward her.

"And where are you going to?" he said, his right hand held behind his back.

"Back to school. I have a class this afternoon."

"I might have missed you. Oh, what a thought!" He clutched at his chest. "These are for you." He handed her bright yellow sunflowers. "Can I offer you a ride?"

"Only if it's not out of your way. Thanks. These are beautiful."

"Your school is right by where I need to go."

"You're too kind. Thank you," she said, as they walked to his car. She was trying to find a way to say yes to his invitation but didn't know how to bring it up.

"Lizzie, I'm going out of the country tomorrow," he said. "It's for my business. I would still really like to go out to dinner with you." They stopped at a red and white Pontiac. It shone like new and Lizzie, with her soft spot for nice cars, was won over. He opened the passenger door.

"When will you be back?" she asked, getting in.

"That's the thing…. Going to Germany means staying there for at least three months. I know it seems like such a long time," he said, starting the car.

Lizzie was annoyed. After all her excitement, to be told to wait another three months! See if I stick around, she thought.

Ernest smiled, noticing the look on her face. "I can't stop thinking about you…."

"I thought this was a friendly dinner," Lizzie said.

"It is. I want us to get to know each other as friends first," he said.

"Just so you know, I was with somebody before," she said, feeling the need to let him know right off the bat.

"I don't care about your past, Lizzie," Ernest said. "You haven't said yes or no to my invitation."

"Yes," she said and smiled.

"You have such a beautiful smile."

"Thank you." She looked outside at the Korle Lagoon, its black sulfuric waters shimmering under the afternoon sun.

They drove by an expanse of land filled with patches of overgrown grass being weeded by men in navy blue uniforms. Yellow ploughs turned over large clumps of loam.

"What kind of business do you run?" she asked.

"It's a small company. I import fine goods from Germany."

"But why do you have to go so urgently?"

"I'm expanding the business and meeting new suppliers."

"Don't business deals take a few days?"

"They do take a couple of days," he said. "Thing is, I currently have just one supplier and when I leave everything to him, the goods get sent to Gibraltar, Cape Verde or God knows where."

"Has that happened before?"

"Oh, yes!" Ernest said breathlessly. "Countless times! Now I make sure the goods are physically loaded in crates and placed on the right ship before I come back home. Picture me in overalls, packing, shoving and hollering."

"Don't overtax yourself," Lizzie said.

As he pulled up at the pink walls of the nursing school, he said, "Can I have your address?"

She scribbled it behind one of his business cards.

"Thanks for the ride," she said. "Safe journey."

*

June 9, 1958

My dear Lizzie-Achiaa,

I've arrived in Berlin, after a tiring weeklong trip. I swear we stopped in every single town in West Africa before the captain decided he'd had his fill of African beauties. Each time we stopped, women kept getting on and off. But, I promise, I didn't look at any of them!

The weather in Berlin is miserable. Rain and sleet are making me regret my decision to come and oversee my shady supplier. I meet with my possible new suppliers in two days. I'm trying to get as much beauty sleep as I can. When they see my calm, dignified self, they won't say no to supplying Ghana's ladies and gentlemen with only the finest of luxury goods.

Study hard! Look forward to hearing from you soon.

E.M.

*

July 1958

As Lizzie walked out of the nursing school for an afternoon shift at the hospital, a secretary in the administrative building accosted her.

"It's your letter from Germany," the woman said, smiling. "And another. He can't wait, eh?" Lizzie chuckled as she took the two letters. How the secretary knew her letters were coming from a man was anybody's guess. "Ei, have you heard?" the secretary said.

"What?"

"The Prime Minister has passed a new law. The Preventive Detention Act. If you say something against him, you end up straight in James Fort. Be careful."

"Thanks," Lizzie said, barely hearing the woman. She studied both letters. The first was from Ernest. The second she couldn't recognize. She tore that one open. It was Asantewa's reply to the first letter she sent home.

Everybody was happy to hear that Lizzie was alive, the letter said. Asantewa said their mother had been sick for two months, but Opanyin Nti's medicine helped. Papa Yaw was actually worried. That was the first time Asantewa had seen him show any emotion toward their mother. Asantewa then went on a rant about how she didn't know what to do with her life and was thinking of also running away.

Lizzie chuckled, thinking, Asantewa, you know you'll never do that. She opened Ernest's letter. He was coming back in a month, in the first week of August.

*

August 1958

After spending the whole day getting her hair prinked, combed and curled, Lizzie stood in front of the mirror in a black petticoat. Over it, she put on a long-sleeved silk green dress with paisley prints. She slid her fingers into short white gloves.

"We've changed positions today," Mercy said. Lizzie looked at her through the mirror.

"Where's Charles?" she asked, applying rouge to her lips.

"Don't ask."

"Let me guess, the money is all gone. I told you it would go like water. Where did he get it from?"

"He did some work for Nkrumah on campus and got rewarded quite well," Mercy said.

"Can we get some of that work too?" Lizzie said.

"I have a feeling he reported some people and they were imprisoned. I don't like Nkrumah's PDA. I told Charles that before I dumped him."

"You dumped him? Didn't he get paid before the PDA was passed?" Lizzie asked.

"I don't know," Mercy said and shrugged. Lizzie grabbed her black pumps and tiptoed out of the room. She still wanted to believe that Nkrumah could do no wrong.

Outside the nursing school, Ernest leaned against the passenger seat door of his car. He was dressed in a heather brown suit and a matching hat. Lizzie stuck her hand out, even though she wanted to hug him. Ernest shook it and opened her door.

They drove through Osu, on a street lit with the lanterns of nighttime vendors. *Kenkey* sellers arranged big metal pans with mounds of fresh *kenkey* and fried fish. They battled with *kelewele* mummies, whose large pans balanced precariously over Dutch ovens. The smell of sweet plantain soused in ginger and pepper wafted into the car. Around one *kenkey* seller a long line queued to buy her food.

"This is it," Ernest said. "We're having a romantic roadside dinner."

"Oh, yeah?" Lizzie asked.

"Yes. That's why I told you to wear your Sunday best."

Lizzie giggled. The food did smell good, though. As he drove on, the aroma of fried shrimp, grilled pork and mutton assaulted her nostrils. He turned onto a quiet road, which was lit by a two-story house in a cul-de-sac.

Lizzie heard the faint buzzing of a saxophone floating out of the building. Several cars were parked outside. They walked in, on a brick walkway lined with black flowerpots, which sprouted dwarf palm trees.

A tall woman clad in a full *kente* skirt and a white shirt led them to a round cane table surrounded by two cane chairs.

"Would you like to hear about our specials?" she asked.

"Please," Ernest said.

"For the continental dish, we have sole and a rich tomato sauce, served with white rice. For our Ghanaian dish, palaver sauce served with sweet boiled yams," she said.

"Lizzie, what would you like to have?" Ernest asked.

"I'll have the sole," she said. "If I wanted palaver sauce I'd have bought that on the roadside," she whispered to Ernest.

"You read my mind," he said and turned to the waitress. "Same for me. And a glass of Star beer. Lizzie?"

"Orange juice. And please make sure there's absolutely no shrimp in his food," Lizzie added.

Ernest looked at her tenderly. "Thanks," he said.

As the waitress strode away, Lizzie glanced around at the men and women in the room. Some of the diners were in their twenties, looking as nervous as she was feeling. Others laughed heartily, their mouths wide open, dripping with palm oil. A band of four in a corner of the room serenaded them.

"This is a lovely place," Lizzie said. "How did you find it?"

"One of my employees told me about it. I think he was more interested in the waitresses, though!" He stared at her. "You know, I really enjoyed our letter writing. I get so miserable when I'm in Germany. This time, you kept me going. I couldn't wait to come back."

"How come you chose to import from Germany?" Lizzie asked.

"It's a bit of a long story. I'll have to tell you a little about my life."

"I'm all ears."

"I grew up with my mother and sister. My mother said our father was a useless drunkard. She worked in the market trying to get enough money to pay for my education. My sister, she said, would work with her, but I needed to get a good education."

"It's sad that she didn't see the need for your sister to go to school," Lizzie interrupted.

"I know. She didn't have money, so she thought better educate the man so he'd take care of us. She paid my way through most of secondary school. When I was in my last year of school, I met a German import trader and begged him to make me his messenger. I loved the idea of selling products and making money and wanted to learn the skills of the trade. He gave me more than I'd asked for. I was good in math so soon I was handling his paperwork. I realized school wasn't bringing in money to take care of Naa Mensah and Adoley so I dropped out."

"Wasn't your mother upset?"

"No, she encouraged me to work really hard with Mr. Lutterodt. This was in 1947. Soon, I was the 'moneyman'. That's what he called me. I took care of his finances. In 1951, he fell really ill. He wasn't finding the right treatment here, so he had to go back home. Lizzie, he took me with him."

"That was kind of him."

"Yes. We went on a boat all the way to Spain, and then boarded a small plane to Berlin. It was a wonderful trip. Sadly, he passed away five months after we arrived. He left me his business in Accra, and gave me the right to do what I wanted with it."

"You're a lucky man."

"I suppose. I changed the name of the company, but in homage to Mr. Lutterodt, I keep everything German. Enough about me…. This food is taking too long. What's your story?" he asked.

"I'm still looking for my happy ending," Lizzie said.

"I thought there was something sad about you. Tell me more," Ernest said.

"My father, luckily, sent me to school, but only because I wasn't a pretty child."

"You grew out of it," Ernest said.

Lizzie laughed. "Thanks. I had bigger dreams than marriage at seventeen. To achieve them I ran away …"

The waitress carried their drinks and food over, not offering an explanation for the tardiness. She placed their plates in front of them.

"Enjoy your food," she said.

"Thanks. You were talking of dreams," Ernest said, taking a sip of his beer. "It's flat!"

"We won't come here again," Lizzie said, picking up a fork with her gloved hand.

"You'd want to see me again?"

"I'd love to, Ernest," she said. She didn't want to even think about Bador Samed, who'd been the driving force of her flight. She would steer the conversation away from that.

"When did you last see your family?" Ernest asked.

"Four years ago. I'll go back, but only when I have something to show for myself."

After dinner, Ernest helped Lizzie out of her chair.

"Do you want to go dancing?" he asked.

"I'd like to, but I didn't get permission to stay out late. Next time."

"You have to get permission to go out?"

"Yes. The school is run by Catholic nuns. The process is so long, it's easier to just sneak off," she said.

"What can I do to make it easier?" Ernest asked, opening the passenger seat door for her.

"Don't worry," Lizzie said.

"I can pretend to be your relative," he said.

"Thass sweet, Mr. Mensah, but you muss not tell lies." Ernest burst into his schoolgirl giggles. Inexplicably, that was one of the things that drew Lizzie to him.

"So," he said.

"So?"

"Would you want to go for dinner again, tomorrow?"

"You're not tired of me?"

"I don't think I'll ever tire of you, Lizzie," he said, steering his car by the nursing school gate. He helped her out of the car.

"Tomorrow it is, then," Lizzie said. He stuck out his hand. She hugged him. "Thank you so much for dinner, Ernest."

He took her gloved hand and kissed it. "My pleasure."

*

January 1959

Lizzie was staring at the chart of nerves in front of her. She heard three loud honks. The honking stopped and resumed. At first she thought it was just a passing car. But when it didn't stop, she, like the other students, got curious. Eliza Sam, the most *kokonsa* girl on the block, stood up and walked to the window.

"Elisa," Mother Maria said. "Only a little nosiness is good, but will you bring it back here?"

Eliza gasped and signaled for the other girls to come to the window. Lizzie went over.

A cardboard collage stuck to Ernest's car spelled out, "ELIZABETH ACHIAA APPIAH. WILL YOU MARRY ME?" He stood by the car waving frantically.

Lizzie laughed. This man is too funny! she thought.

"Girls, girls!" Mother Maria said as she walked to the window and then turned to look at Lizzie. Lizzie felt all eyes on her.

"Will you marry the man?" Eliza asked.

Lizzie nodded, tears now streaming down her face.

"Yes," she said quietly.

"Yes!" Eliza shouted down to Ernest.

Then all the girls started shouting "Yes! Yes! Yes!"

Lizzie screamed her lungs out, "Yes!"

"All right, girls, enough romance for one day. Back to the nervous system."

Six
Family

Lizzie, Mercy and Esther, Mercy's mother, were seated on a sofa. Across from them, Fiifi, Mercy's father, sat in his worn-out burgundy armchair, reading the *Daily Graphic*. Lizzie looked at the newspaper headline—Ghana: A Nation Reborn—and shifted her gaze to the wedding dress catalog spread on Esther's lap.

"This one is nice," Mercy said, pointing to a long-sleeved dress with a long train.

"It's too frumpy," Esther said, with a hint of an English accent. "The latest style is to have a puffy short sleeve, not to look like some old lady from the fifteenth century."

Lizzie caught Mercy rolling her eyes but Esther didn't notice. Lizzie wanted a dress that would make waves, but she couldn't really concentrate. Not now. Ernest was supposed to come pick her up in any minute. This was the first time Mercy's parents would be meeting him, and now they were as good as her parents. She was sure they'd be even harder to please than Papa Yaw and Mama Efua. Her heart rose and fell every time she heard a car engine whir to a stop. She looked at the wooden grandfather clock in the living room. It was now half past six. He was half an hour late.

She rubbed her wet palms on her yellow and green skirt, which Esther's seamstress had made for her. Esther turned over a page of the catalog.

"Now, that's the style!" Esther shouted. "Yes! I think Edinam Bucknor wore something similar for her wedding. My seamstress can make that easily."

Lizzie suppressed a laugh, after Fiifi looked over his newspaper and glared at his wife. She looked at the dress. It was high-collared, its sleeves short and rounded. She had to give it to Esther—her pretentiousness paid off.

"It's beautiful," she said. A honk at the gate cut through the air, startling her. "That must be him." She sprang out of her seat, her heart racing. Mercy followed her.

Outside the gate, in Ernest's Pontiac, Lizzie saw Ernest's large bespectacled mother stuffed in the passenger seat. Ernest got out of the car and hugged Lizzie and Mercy.

"So sorry for the tardiness," he said.

"Good evening, Naa," Lizzie said, curtseying.

"How are you?" Naa Mensah said curtly, her eyes magnified by the glasses.

"Very well, thank you," Lizzie said. "Ernie, come in and greet Mercy's parents and then we'll go."

"You should have warned me. I'd have brought some gifts," Ernest said.

"Mrs. Mensah," Lizzie said. "Please come in."

"No," Naa Mensah said. "That's all right." This was the third time Lizzie was meeting Ernest's mother and the woman was still distant. She was sure it was because she had broken the rules by asking Mercy's parents to give her away.

Inside, Esther was looking ravenously through the catalog. Mercy cleared her throat.

"Introducing … Lizzie's fiancé!" she sang.

"Oh!" Esther said, her voice an octave higher than usual.

Ernest shook hands with Fiifi.

"How are you doing, young man?" Fiifi asked.

"Very well, sir."

He walked to Esther, "Good morning, madam. Sorry to have come empty-handed."

"Oh, no problem. What a gentleman," Esther said, it seemed more to Fiifi than to anyone else.

"We're off then," Lizzie said. They both seemed pleased with him, so there was no need to spoil things by lingering.

"Have a good time," Esther said and glared at Fifi. "I was supposed to come myself, but someone says he's not in the mood."

Mercy whispered to Lizzie, "Take me with you. Don't leave me with those two! Please!"

"No Minister to take you out?" Lizzie asked, laughing.

"Shhh!" Mercy whispered. "Go! Before you get me into trouble."

As they walked out of the gate, Ernest said, "We're dropping Naa off at her cousin's. She made me late. I shouldn't have told her I was coming this way."

He lifted his seat for Lizzie to get in the back. She sat down and stared at the back of Naa Mensah's head. "Ernie," she said, pressing his shoulder. Naa Mensah stared at her hand, then at Lizzie and immediately looked away. "I was looking at dresses today."

"That's wonderful," Ernest said. "I can't wait for you to be my bride." Lizzie smirked.

"Is your family going to come for the engagement?" Naa Mensah asked, wiping off the grin that had formed on Lizzie's lips.

"Naa!" Ernest said under his breath.

"I've been telling Ernest that we don't know who you are …"

"Naa, please stop. Sorry, Lizzie."

"Who are these people? Do your parents know them?" Naa asked.

"Naa, please!" Ernest shouted. The woman clammed up.

They dropped her off in front of a rusty red gate. Lizzie moved to the front. She looked through the side mirror, watching Naa Mensah's large form get smaller and smaller. She was sure the engagement was more important to Ernest's family. But it was her marriage. She decided she would focus more on the church wedding.

At the State House, as Ernest and Lizzie walked toward the red, yellow and green-ribboned entrance, Lizzie began to feel a part of Esther's world. A poor village girl now mingling with Ghana's movers and shakers. She looked back at the people getting out of their cars decked in suits, *batakari*, *kaba* and slits, others bedizened in cocktail dresses. Ernest presented their invitation to an usher who led them into the banquet hall.

"These are my cronies," Ernest said, pointing to a group sitting around a long table covered in a white tablecloth. He led her over. "Comrades!" he shouted, bursting with gusto.

"Ernest!"

"Ernesto!"

"This is my fiancée, Lizzie," Ernest said. "Alhaji Andani, Akwasi Otchere, Philip Oni and Philip's wife," Ernest said. Lizzie was sure he'd forgotten Philip's wife name. When she got married to him, his friends had better not address her as just Ernest's wife. He pulled out a chair for her. "Alhaji is a sawmill magnate," Ernest went on. "Akwasi works in the Trade and Labor Ministry and Philip is our resident lawyer."

"And Ernest makes sure our gentlemanly needs are met," Alhaji Andani boomed, making everyone around the table laugh. He lit a cigar and turned to Lizzie, "Your husband ..."

"Fiancé," Philip's wife corrected.

"Apologies. Your fiancé brought this from Germany. Everything he brings is top notch." Lizzie smiled at Ernest. She turned to Philip's wife.

"I'm sorry I didn't catch your name," she said.

"Effie Oni."

"These men didn't have the courtesy to introduce us properly," Lizzie whispered. "What do you do?"

"Oh, I don't work," Effie said. Not another Esther Boye, Lizzie thought. No wonder, she was just known as "Philip's wife." "And you?"

"I'm a nurse."

"That must be tiring. When you start having babies, I'm sure you'll give that up."

"I don't think I will," Lizzie said. That wasn't even an option she'd considered.

"That's what I said too," Effie said. "I used to teach. Then I had three children. There was no way I could work and raise the children properly."

"Will you work after the children are grown?"

"I'm not sure," Effie said. "Children never quite grow!"

"... Ernesto," Lizzie heard one of the men say. "Don't worry, I'll take care of them."

"That will make my life so much easier, Akwasi. Those permits …"

Lizzie's eyes glazed over as Effie went on about how she was thinking of sending the children to school in England and moving there to look after them. That the woman possessed no dreams of her own, Lizzie couldn't understand. If being a mother was all she wanted from life, she'd have stayed in Adukrom No. 2.

"Don't worry, my brother. I'll see about it," Akwasi said. "Alcohol is always tricky, because the Prime Minister wants us to boost our own industries."

"Which, of course, we have to," Ernest said. "But I don't think we're close to making great single malts yet."

Loud percussion cut through the room. She saw men dressed in heavy, grey and white smocks drumming, their muscles taut. One of them reminded her of Bador Samed.

"Ladies and gentlemen," a portly man standing behind a microphone close to the head table shouted. "The President of the new Republic of Ghana. Osagyefo Dr. Kwame Nkrumah!"

Everyone in the room stood up, applauding. Lizzie smiled as Nkrumah walked in, followed by an entourage. She noticed that not all of the faces in the room wore smiles. Some people whispered, maliciously, it seemed, to others. Nkrumah, clad in a white suit and a black bowtie, strode to the head table and sat down. She didn't know the man, but she admired and adored him for what he stood for—freedom.

Ushers moved behind two long tables on which metal trays stood. They unveiled basted whole chickens, heaps of *jollof* rice, rice yellowed with curry, fish fried to crispness and *kelewele*. Lizzie, Ernest and his friends stood up to join a line that had formed next to the tables.

"Do you have a dress for the wedding?" Effie asked.

"Yes," Lizzie lied. Three months before the wedding she couldn't say she didn't have one.

"That's splendid," Effie said. "I loved my wedding dress. I've been dying for a chance to wear it again, especially because it was so expensive."

Lizzie loaded her plate with a grilled chicken drumstick and *jollof* rice. As they walked back to the table, she thought that as much as she wanted to be a part of this world, the women seemed so frivolous. And their poor children! Take Mercy. Obviously her mother had tried to raise her to be a perfect well-dressed little girl, and Mercy played the part. Outside her parents' home, though, she was rebellious and sleeping with men older than her own father. When she had children, she'd raise them differently, Lizzie decided. Of course, they had to be smartly dressed too.

"Did you see the presidential swearing-in this morning?" Alhaji asked Ernest.

"No," Ernest responded.

"It was beautiful," Alhaji said. "I didn't stay for long, but the President came in this rich *kente* cloth. The drumming was so loud, you couldn't hear anything else. When they started singing, 'Lift high the flag of Ghana,' my brother, I just got chills. You should have been there. We've finally made it." He scooped a piece of *fufu*, dipped it in soup and led it straight into his mouth.

The band started an up-tempo highlife song. Lizzie watched as Ruth Botsio, the wife of one of Nkrumah's Ministers, danced with the Duke of Edinburgh. Ernest pulled her up to dance.

"I forgot to tell you," she whispered in his ear. "The priest at St. Mary's Church has confirmed that we can have the choir and their wonderful soloist for the wedding. Ernie, you should hear her sing. I get goose pimples every time she opens her mouth."

"Good, good," Ernest said, leading Lizzie. "I know my mother was overly direct about it, but we can send for your family."

"Remember when I told you I wouldn't go home till I'd made something of myself?"

"Yes."

"Ernie, I'm living in my friend's house. I'm a junior nurse. That's hardly impressive. They can't come here and see me living like this. Where will I even put them up?"

"All right," Ernest said. "It's your decision."

Lizzie changed the subject. "Thanks for bringing me, Ernie. I'm having such a good time."

"No, thank *you*," Ernest said. "I would have been intimidated without you. All these big men and women …"

"You liar!" Lizzie said, chuckling. She didn't know what the lure of society was. She wondered if it was the cars, the clothes, the events or the glamour. She couldn't place her finger on it, but it was calling her so strongly and she was ready to heed its call, ready to make that her new goal. She'd just have to remind herself not to become like Esther Boye or Effie Oni. When she got there, then she'd reach back out to her family.

*

October 1960

Lizzie stood outside the St. Mary's Church, dressed in a high-collared, puffy-sleeved white dress. It was just like the dress Edinam Bucknor had worn to her wedding, though not ordered from Harrods. Esther's seam-stress made it, adding three white Bakelite buttons to the front to make it unique—Esther's idea.

"You're a beautiful bride," Mercy said, fussing with the high waist of her own dress.

"Thanks." Lizzie looked over at Fiifi, who didn't seem as scary as he did at other times. He smiled at her.

"You're beautiful, Lizzie," he said. "Smile." She did, but halfheart-edly as she thought of the conversation she'd overheard between Ernest and his mother at the rehearsal the night before.

"Why did you let that girl make you choose this church? We're Methodist, not Catholic," Naa Mensah had said. All night, those words had replayed themselves in her mind. *That girl.* Breathe, she told herself. This is your big moment. You've beaten your father, you've beaten Bador Samed and you can handle this old witch, even if you are marrying into her family.

"This is it," Mercy said, pulling down Lizzie's veil and walking ahead of her.

Fiifi hooked his arm in hers and together they strode down the red-carpeted aisle. She kept her eyes on the carpet, trying not to cry. She was thinking of all the choices she'd made to end up in this place. She was thinking especially of Bador Samed. This was the official end to any pos-sibility of a future with him. What if by some sick twist, he came into the church and disrupted the affair? How ridiculous, she thought, pushing the thought of him far back into the bottom drawers of her mind. As she saw guests in both aisles standing up, she smiled.

The church wasn't even half full, but she didn't expect it to be. On the left side, she saw her classmates from nursing school and her new friends at Korle Bu. On Ernest's side, which was definitely more packed than hers, she recognized family members she'd seen at the engagement. Naa Mensah was wearing her hideous glasses and what could only be a scowl on her face. She noticed Ernest's sister wasn't smiling either. She swallowed and looked ahead of her. She mightn't have to deal with them after getting married, she hoped.

Behind the lectern, the members of the choir had arranged themselves in four rows. A brown piano stood to their left. Before the lectern, Ernest and Akwasi stood in black tuxedos, staring at the approaching bridal party. Mercy stopped and stood at Lizzie's left and Fiifi placed Lizzie's arm in Ernest's.

Father Thomas stood above them, in a white frock. Lizzie looked up at him as he said a silent prayer and crossed himself.

"Welcome, Elizabeth and Ernest," he said. "Welcome, family and friends of the bride, family and friends of the groom. Let us pray.

"Father, we are gathered here today to bring together Elizabeth Achiaa Appiah and Ernest Mensah and their two families. We ask that you guide their lives and become the center of their marriage. Amen."

Lizzie watched Mercy walk to a pulpit set up to the left of the altar. She opened a huge Bible using a white bookmark.

"Our Bible reading is taken from Mark, Chapter ten, Verse six to nine," Mercy said. "'But from the beginning of the creation God made them male and female. For this cause shall a man leave his father and mother, and cleave to his wife; and they twain shall be one flesh: so then they are no more twain, but one flesh. What therefore God hath joined together, let not man put asunder.' Amen."

Lizzie wanted to see the look on Naa Mensah's face. Why couldn't anything be easy? she wondered. She met a man she liked very much, and his mother was a witch. Let not woman put asunder, she thought. No, she chided herself, focus on your future and your new husband.

The soloist stood up, her hair wrapped tightly into a beehive. As she sang *Ave Maria*, her voice pocked Lizzie's flesh with goose pimples and filled her eyes with tears. Father Thomas walked to the pulpit.

"I'm going to make this message short and sweet," he said. "I've known Lizzie for a few months now. She might think I didn't take notice of her before the wedding rehearsal, but every shepherd knows his flock. Lizzie and Ernest, you're about to start a family. Always have Christ at the center of your family, and raise your children in the Catholic Church …"

Lizzie's feet ached. Minutes passed and Father Thomas was still on his speech.

"Brethren, when I moved here from Ireland in the 1930s, I saw an oppressed people in your country Ghana. I saw people in subjugation who could not fight for themselves. I've served St. Mary's Church for many years and I've seen the Gold Coast become Ghana. Your founding fathers fought for truth and justice and at Independence your country rose from the ashes. Likewise, Lizzie and Ernest, you will go through trials and tribulations as a couple and as a family. There are times when you will wake up and wonder why you got married, but that is no reason for divorce. There are times when you will wake up and wonder why you brought children into this cruel world. But through the hard times, you learn more about each other …"

Lizzie heard people fanning themselves. Coughs punctuated the sermon. He ended his speech and looked down at Akwasi, who duly extracted the rings from his left tuxedo pocket. Lizzie stretched her left hand out and felt Ernest slide the warm band onto her ring finger. After she slid his ring on, Ernest lifted her veil. She beamed at him.

"God bless you both," Father Thomas said. The pianist began Elgar's *Pomp and Circumstance*, the recessional hymn. Lizzie grinned as she ran down the aisle holding Ernest's hand.

Seven
Biding Time

Above Naa Mensah's imposing house, speckled grey from lack of paint, clouds floated languorously from east to west. Lizzie lowered her gaze, taking in the greening steps she and Ernest were about to scale. Under her right arm, she clutched a snakeskin bag, a wedding gift from Mercy and her mother. She heard Ernest open the trunk of his Pontiac. She turned round and saw him struggling to yank out her suitcase. Strings of plastic from their wedding still clung to the car's bumper.

She was about to walk over to help him with the suitcase, but he seemed to gain control of it. She took a step up and studied the building again. The stairs led to a closed double door, painted a bright aqua. Four wooden shutters flanked the door. Those on the left were closed. On the right, the window farthest from the door was open. When she and Ernest got engaged, she hadn't had the time to study the building. It had been such a whirlwind of a day. She saw Naa Mensah's head bob in and out. Why am I moving in here? Lizzie wondered, toying with the idea of going back to Mercy's till the house Ernest was building was ready.

"Shall we, Mrs. Mensah?" Ernest asked, lugging her suitcase.

"Yes, we shall."

Lizzie held on to the grey concrete banister and trailed behind Ernest as he carried the suitcase up, his breathing labored.

"Fifteen steps in all," he rasped. "When I was young, I'd always get stuck on the ninth step and had to stop to catch my breath."

"Your mother should have moved to a place without stairs."

At the top of the stairs, he opened the door to a dark room. Lizzie peered around, making out two sofas facing each other and a radio atop a glass cabinet. She saw a warped dining table with four mismatched chairs next to an unpainted wooden door. The door opened just as Lizzie was about to continue studying her new abode.

"Welcome," Naa Mensah said, stretching out her hand. Lizzie took the hand and pulled the woman in for a hug. She didn't know what possessed her to do that. Adoley came through the same door, ignored them and walked out of the house.

"So, Mrs. Mensah …" Ernest started.

"Yes," both Lizzie and Naa Mensah responded.

"Sorry, Mrs. Mensah junior. To your left is the living room. Straight ahead is our dining area. My mother is an excellent cook, as you will soon find out. It's in here that we've sampled some of her finest recipes. And now if you will follow me…." He led Lizzie through the unpainted door, into a narrow verandah, which seemed to serve as a storeroom. On the right, two bookcases housed piles of aluminum pots. Ernest unlocked a grey door and pushed in Lizzie's suitcase.

A fishy smell rushed into the room as Ernest unbolted the wooden shutters. Trying surreptitiously to hold her breath, Lizzie looked around the room. She sat on Ernest's queen-sized bed and stared at the view of the dull grey sea.

"Are you all right?" Ernest asked.

"I love the view of the sea," she said. "I'd never seen the sea before I moved to Accra." She looked back around her immediate surroundings. Across from the bed stood a small wardrobe. The blue floor was linoleum-tiled. How long would they have to live here? she wondered. "Ernie," she said, "how far has our house gone? Can we move in if even one room is done?"

"Patience, darling," Ernest said and chuckled. "I want it to be perfect when we move in."

"All right," Lizzie whispered. Why were people always trying to make things perfect for her? She wasn't some delicate princess. Besides, the last time she'd heard that, the man had run away. She was sure this was a sign that they'd never move out of Naa Mensah's.

"Let's take a walk," Ernest said. "I'll show you the neighborhood."

"Ready when you are," she said.

They strode out of the house and found Adoley sitting on the banister talking to someone downstairs.

"They're here now," Adoley said and turned to Ernest. "Mama wants to see you."

"All right," he said. "You met Mama at the engagement. She's senile and very quarrelsome. Ignore her." He led her through a mildewed wooden gate. It opened into a small courtyard, enclosed by two perpendicular outhouses. Lizzie looked up and recognized the verandah she'd passed through earlier.

Ernest knocked on a door. Mama opened the door with her caramel-colored skin. She peered out, leaving just enough space for her body. She wouldn't let them in. She stared at Lizzie.

"Is this the girl?" the woman asked in Ga, which Lizzie was beginning to understand.

"Yes, Mama," Ernest responded and looked at Lizzie as if to say, "I told you so."

Lizzie stretched out her hand but the old woman wouldn't take it. She looked at Mama's features. Her eyes shone brightly with the mischief of a two-year-old, her four long white braids framed her round face.

"Hmmm," Mama said abruptly and banged her door shut.

"Sorry about that," Ernest said. "I warned you about her."

"Don't worry."

"She's crazy. She doesn't let anyone into that room. The last time I went in there, it was 1950. And she never leaves the house."

Ernest hooked Lizzie's arm in his and they walked out of the courtyard. They strolled on a paved road lined with houses with wooden casement windows.

"You have to meet these men," Ernest said, as they walked toward a pastel blue semi-completed house. Two middle-aged men sat by a board of checkers. They were silent except for the choppy sound of wood hitting wood. One of the men looked up.

"Ernefto!" he shouted, his tongue snaking out of the gap between his teeth.

"Archimedes!" Ernest screamed back. "Meet my wife, Lizzie."

Archimedes stood up and mimicked the removal of a hat. "Pleathure, mi lady," he said. "Hey, Charlie, thand and greet the lady."

"I'm showing her the area," Ernest said.

"Jamestown is very fine, you'll find," Charlie said.

"Peath be with you," Archimedes said.

When they were out of earshot Lizzie said, "Archimedes is funny."

"They've been here since I could remember," Ernest said. "They taught me everything I needed to know about street hustling."

"You, a street hustler?" Lizzie scoffed. "I'm more of a hustler than you."

"If you say so," Ernest said.

They passed by women pouring gallons of oil into metal pans and moved on to a building, which Lizzie recognized as the James Fort prison. She remembered how she and Charles had escorted the old African-American couple there on Independence Day. She remembered how she'd asked the woman about her husband, and the sadness she'd felt at being so alone. How life could change, she mused.

"I recall the day Kwame Nkrumah was released from here," Ernest said. "You can't imagine, Lizzie.... It was in February 1951. It was so thick, you couldn't move without stepping on someone's foot. The whole street was packed with people."

"You know what surprises me?"

"What?"

"That you're not a politician, the way you love being a part of such things."

Ernest scoffed. "Politics is not for me. I'm a simple man. You know what's funny, though?"

"What?"

"I remember how everyone out here was so happy. And today, they're trying to kill him."

"I know!" Lizzie said. "All these explosions and attempts on his life! But, Ernie, people are fickle." People, like life, could change at the drop of a hat. She'd learned that with Bador Samed, hadn't she?

As they passed by the Accra Lighthouse, he said, "Let's see if they'll let us up."

They walked up to a security guard slouched over in his wooden reclining chair.

"Master!" Ernest said as loudly as his lungs would let him. The man did not stir.

"Sir!" Lizzie yelled, shaking his left shoulder.

"What? What?" the guard said, wiping the drool that had trickled down his cheek.

"Will it be possible for us to go up the lighthouse?" Ernest asked.

"For what?" The man regained his security guard's confidence. Lizzie wondered why Ernest was being so polite.

"My wife just moved to Accra," Ernest said. "I'd really like to show her the view from up there." Lizzie caught sight of his hand moving stealthily into his pocket. He brought it out fisted and placed it over the guard's palm.

"Be fast," the guard said.

They ran up a narrow winding staircase, its wooden boards creaking. At the top, Ernest pushed open a metal door into the watchtower.

"Wow!" Lizzie exclaimed, rushing to the window. The sun was beginning its descent, making the sky a tie-dye of teal and orange. The waves of the still dreary sea frothed over, crashing on the shore that stretched up to a stony cliff on top of which sat the Christiansborg Castle. Coconut trees bent next to winding grey roads packed with cars. She looked at the city that was Accra. Parts of it undulated in little olive-green hills. Rooftops were scattered all over, no discernable pattern in sight. Lights began to go on. She looked back at the sea. Shipping vessels and canoes dotted the vast shimmering liquid. "It's beautiful," she said, kissing Ernest on the cheek.

"I'm glad you like it," he said.

After taking a cold shower, Lizzie put on a white nightdress, wrapped her hair in pink rollers to give her hair volume and slipped into bed. Ernest walked in, bare-chested, a towel wrapped around his waist. He locked the door behind him and turned off the light. A faint wisp of blue light filtered into the room. Lizzie saw him stride toward her. He climbed over her, stuck his mouth on hers and pushed his tongue against her teeth.

"Ernie," she mumbled. "Your mother will hear us."

"We'll be quiet," he said nuzzling her neck.

"I'm tired," she said, pushing his chest. "Tomorrow. Ernest, no. Stop," Lizzie said even though she was getting excited.

"What's wrong?" Ernest asked, rolling off her.

Lizzie pointed at the wardrobe.

"Oh," Ernest laughed loudly. "Don't worry. We'll make no noise at all." He kissed her ear. His tongue and teeth pulled on her earlobe. She gasped. He kissed her lips. She kissed him back, hesitantly. Her tongue began to shyly move into his mouth. She stiffened when she realized Ernest's towel had slipped off. She'd done this once already but she was petrified. She felt Ernest harden against her thigh. He tried to take off her nightdress. A mini-battle ensued as she struggled to keep it on. "I thought you told me you were skilled, Mrs. Mensah," he said.

"Well, I'm nervous, all right. With your mother next door and all.… Kiss me near my ear and make me relax." Ernest licked her left ear. His hands found the hem of her dress and pulled the dress over her head.

"You're beautiful," Ernest said, dotting kisses all over her body. He climbed on top of her again. She pressed her legs and her eyes together. Ernest pried her legs apart. It was invasive, troubling and yet excitingly sweet. She felt warm. Then she felt Ernest entering her. She screamed. It was a scream caught in a land between pain and desire.

"Did that hurt?" he asked. She nodded. "Sorry. I'll go slowly." She didn't know whether to cry or laugh as he pushed and pulled on top of her. The bed creaked. She could feel him in the depths of her body. She felt his muscles spasm. "I hope you're all right," he said, rolling off her.

"Yes," Lizzie said as Ernest wrapped his hands around her. Her eyes remained wide open. She thought of Naa Mensah. The woman would probably want proof that she was a virgin. She tiptoed to the wardrobe, took a tube of lipstick and smudged it on the sheet with her saliva. She'd flash the red at Naa Mensah and all would be well.

Bright morning light streamed in from the window, waking her up. She looked over at Ernest who was still sleeping. Three rollers had fallen out of her hair and lay by the pillow. Next to Ernest's buttocks, she saw the red lipstick stain on the yellow sheets. She tugged the sheet from under him. She bunched them up, put on her dress and left the room.

She ran straight into Naa Mensah. The bespectacled woman was looking for pots and pans just outside their room. Lizzie was convinced the woman had been there all morning, waiting for her to come out.

"Good morning, Naa," she said.

"You two couldn't keep it down yesterday," Naa Mensah said, a smile on her lips. "You better not be an empty barrel. I hope all that noise will give me grandchildren." Naa Mensah's eyes were fixed on the sheets.

Lizzie, embarrassed and annoyed, could only manage a forced smile. She walked down the stairs, pain searing between her legs. In the courtyard, Mama was talking and moving her hands up and down animatedly. Lizzie prayed they wouldn't ask her to show them the blood.

"Hmmm," Mama said loudly.

"Good morning," Lizzie said. She trudged to the bathhouse to pick up one of two metal basins placed against the wall. She started filling the basin with water.

"That's enough!" Mama yelled. "You don't pay our water bills."

Lizzie felt like crying. This reception was the last thing she'd expected when she married Ernest. It made her miss her own family. She held the sheet in both hands, rubbing it between her palms.

After taking a shower, Lizzie picked up a pen and paper and walked outside. Settling on the second step, she looked up at the cloudless blue sky. The air felt crisp.

October 21, 1960

My dear Asantewa,

I believe you owe me a reply to the last letter I wrote you. I have a surprise, though, so I relented. Remember, Ernest, I told you had been wooing me? Well, we got married! I'm sorry I didn't tell you earlier. I just wanted everything to be perfect and I didn't have the money to bring all of you here.

Ernest is a wonderful, caring man, but his family is, well, not very warm. At least they haven't thrown me out. Ernest is building a nice house and we'll be moving out soon, and then you and Mama Efua can come anytime you want.

I really love Accra, as I'm sure you would. I can walk to all these shops and find whatever I want, whenever I want. I can finally find my way around the city without getting lost. So how's the family? Has Papa Yaw been up to anything lately?

Say hello to all, especially Mama Efua.

Your sister,

Mrs. Lizzie-Achiaa MENSAH!

*

August 1961

The doors leading to Naa Mensah's house were flung wide open. Women clad in white and black cloth stood on the steps, shouting and cackling. Ernest's large aunt came in, arguing with Naa Mensah.

"Naa Mensah, this *kpodziemo* is not complete without Club beer," she said, biting into a piece of chicken.

"All they had at the depot was Star, Naa Tsoo. Why are you already eating?" Naa Mensah asked, adjusting her glasses.

Lizzie watched them from the sofa in the living room. She cradled her eight-day-old daughter. She'd never seen Naa Mensah so subdued and she was pleased. Mercy sat to her right. Ernest, dressed in a white *agbada* and matching white trousers, sat to her left.

Ernest's relatives came in and out of the room, shouting, and paying more attention to the food than to Lizzie and the new baby.

All the shutters stood open, so the room was eye-blinding bright. Across from her sat the cantankerous Mama, eyeing her suspiciously.

"Do you want to hold her?" she asked Mama.

The old woman stretched out her hands. Lizzie noticed her nails were long, like the talons of a hawk. Please, God, don't let her scratch the child, she prayed. She stood up and carefully placed the baby in Mama's arms.

"Baby little girl, don't cry," Mama started singing. Her bright eyes lost their look of war.

"Seriously, Naa Mensah, this Star beer won't do." Naa Tsoo came back into the living room. "And on top everything, you people want to give this child an Akan name. The father is Ga. Who is responsible for this abomination?"

"Auntie Naa Tsoo," Ernest said. "Lizzie and I agreed to give our first born Lizzie's grandmother's name. I promise you, our next girl will be named after you."

"It's just not done!" Auntie Naa Tsoo said, but seemed to be placated. "Naa Mensah, you have to send Adoley to get me Club," she went on. "Adoleeeey!"

Lizzie pressed Mercy's arm.

"You were telling me about your latest," she whispered.

"Lizzie," Mercy said, pursing her lips. "I think I've found the one."

"Seriously?" Lizzie didn't believe her.

"I'm going to get married like you."

"Who is the lucky man? Please don't say Charles."

"No, not that foolish boy. His name is Kwabena Ntim. He works in the government," Mercy said.

"You and your government men! I'm happy for you."

Boisterous Auntie Naa Tsoo came back into the living room. "It's time," she shouted, holding a bottle of Schnapps close to her breast, a little too lovingly.

Mama handed the baby back to Lizzie. Everyone walked down the stairs and gathered in the courtyard. Naa Tsoo stepped forward, her arms outstretched for the baby. She held the baby up in the air and brought her down. The baby yowled. Naa Tsoo lifted her up again and descended her. She did that three times. She dipped her fingers in a calabash of water that Naa Mensah was holding and sprinkled it on the baby three times. "Akua Afriyie Mensah," Naa Tsoo said. She opened the bottle of Schnapps and dropped a pearl of alcohol into Akua Afriyie's open mouth. She closed the bottle and returned it to the crook of her arm.

People clapped. Before the applause died down, Mama started praying, "May the parents of this baby live long! May Akua Afriyie never look back…. May she be pleased to always stay with us! May she respect her elders and be full of grace and honor …" As Mama went on, Lizzie looked at Akua Afriyie in Naa Tsoo's arms. That this person had come out of her, still had her in awe. She stared at Akua Afriyie's dark skin, at her wide white eyes as she took in her new world and at her tiny fingers folding and opening. She felt a rush of what she could only describe as love. Naa Tsoo handed her back to Lizzie.

Adoley started serving bottles of coca cola and Star beer. Lizzie smiled as she saw people in the neighborhood trickle in. Archimedes walked in with his draft-playing crew. He wore a faded tweed jacket, his hair combed and parted at the right side. He walked over to Ernest who brought him over.

"Madam," Archimedes said, bowing. "Congrathulations."

"Thank you," Lizzie said. "Have a drink, please."

He signaled for his crew to come over. They followed Adoley who was balancing a tray of green bottles on her right hand.

"Darling," Mercy said, walking over to Lizzie. "Esther is forcing me to go to some woman's wedding, so I have to leave now."

"No problem," Lizzie said. "I'm tired, myself, I'm going up to rest. Thanks for coming." She puckered her lips and grazed Mercy's cheeks. She went upstairs, leaving the revelers behind. She curled up around Akua Afriyie, hoping that life would be kind to her daughter.

*

December 1961

Lizzie trudged up Naa Mensah's stairs, after a shift at the hospital. She'd left an hour earlier than usual. She opened the front door, yawning as she made directly for Naa Mensah's room. She knocked. While she waited for the door to open, she looked over the balcony. In the courtyard she saw Naa Mensah. Her saggy breast was exposed, its nipple in Akua Afriyie's mouth. Akua Afriyie was wailing.

Lizzie flung her bag down and stormed into the courtyard. Naa Mensah shoved her breast back under her striped blouse. Lizzie snatched Akua Afriyie from Naa Mensah's clutches.

"What were you doing?" Lizzie asked.

"She was crying. You left her here. What did you expect me to do?" Naa Mensah said.

Lizzie made her way back toward the house. She heard shuffling behind her. The woman must be spoiling for a fight, she thought.

"We all have work, you know," Naa Mensah said, tapping her right shoulder. "I've stopped going to the market to take care of your daughter, and this is how you thank me?"

"I know what you're trying to do," Lizzie said, climbing up the stairs. "You want this child to turn against me, just like how you've poisoned everyone in this house."

"What are you talking about?" Naa Mensah asked.

"Why were you breastfeeding her? I gave you her feeding bottle."

"She was crying, that's the best way to calm the child," Naa Mensah said.

"Well, it wasn't working. She was still crying. And why did you hide your breast when I came? How long have you been doing this?"

"I was going to give her to you is why," Naa Mensah said.

"You're lying. You just don't like me, and you want to turn everyone against me. You're trying to do the same with *my* child." Lizzie's voice broke. She pushed the door open. They stood in the dark living room.

"I wouldn't have let you stay here for so long if I didn't like you," Naa Mensah said, her voice laced with sweetness. "And now we're on that topic. It would be nice, if you contributed more to household duties. Adoley is always cooking. You've recovered from childbirth now, it's time you helped."

"Naa Mensah, I work. I bring in money. Isn't that enough?" Lizzie said, patting Akua Afriyie's back.

"Everybody brings in money. For some reason, you think you're so special."

"I know you just want to get rid of me. You know what?" Lizzie started. She marched to her room and put Akua Afriyie on the bed. She opened the wardrobe, pulled out bundles of paper and strode out with them. Naa Mensah stood right outside her door. "Look," Lizzie said, brandishing the bundles under Naa Mensah's nose. "We'll move out soon. Our house is almost done. We'll move out and you can have the peace you want."

"That's the house my son is building. What money have you put in it?" Naa Mensah asked, adjusting her glasses.

"You're a witch!" Lizzie shouted, flinging the bundles at Naa Mensah.

"You must have no training, stupid girl," she said. "No wonder your own family wants nothing to do with you."

Lizzie grabbed the bundles of paper and hobbled back to her room, slamming the door behind her.

Two hours later, she woke up when she heard the door whine open. Ernest walked in. He picked up Akua Afriyie, who was sleeping. Lizzie rubbed her bloated eyes.

"What's wrong?" he asked.

"Ernie, when are we going to move out?" Lizzie asked, placing Akua Afriyie on her lap. She didn't want to talk about Naa Mensah.

"Soon, my dear. I just need to make a little money to buy the roofing and glass for the windows. You don't want to live in a roofless house, do you?"

"Ernie," Lizzie continued, "I think you should start importing from other countries. Not just Germany. England, for instance. You'll make more money that way."

"Lizzie, you know why I keep the products German."

"But that fellow has been dead for decades now …"

"Lizzie!" Ernest said. "Are you going to tell me what's wrong?"

"I'm fine," she said, looking out the window. The sea was still. She just had to bide her time. But for how long?

Eight
Wild Eyes

Lizzie sat at the foot of Naa Mensah's staircase while Akua Afriyie played with a tag on one of six suitcases next to her feet. She looked at Akua Afriyie's long legs and the ponytails on either side of her head. The girl was cute. Lizzie looked up, at the drone of a car. Ernest approached in a rickety, blue and white Volkswagen van.

"Bye, Afriyie!" Naa Mensah shouted down from her bedroom window, her head covered with a yellow scarf.

"Buh bye, Naa!" Akua Afriyie piped up, her ponytails ricocheting from left to right.

Ernest parked close to the curb, stepped into the street and lifted the trunk open. He strode toward them.

"Ready?" he asked.

"All set," Lizzie said. He picked up the heaviest suitcase, struggled to raise it onto his back and hobbled to the trunk. "Don't move," she warned Akua Afriyie, grabbed two suitcases and followed him.

"Oh, Mrs. Mensah," he said, breathlessly. "This is a man's job!"

Lizzie sucked her teeth. "You're wheezing and telling me this is a man's job," she said, as she lifted a suitcase into the trunk.

"*Finito!*" Ernest said.

"*Finito!*" Akua Afriyie mimicked her father.

Ernest picked up Akua Afriyie and dropped her onto the passenger seat.

"Papa, again!" Akua Afriyie said, giggling hysterically.

He placed his left palm on his chest. "Next time, Afriyie."

Lizzie climbed in after Akua Afriyie. She pushed aside a *Daily Graphic* with the headline, "We enter one-party state." She couldn't stop thinking about their new house. She hadn't felt this excited in a long time, probably not since the day she'd arrived in Accra. She felt like a child about to unravel a huge present.

Ernest opened his door and climbed into the car. As they nosed out of Jamestown, the road began to wake up. Market women trekked to their stalls. A bicycle rider passed by, a green, white and red scarf tied around his head fluttering into the breeze. They passed by the UTC Stores, in front of which people were unloading tubers of yams and bags of rice from boxes onto wooden tables. UTC seemed empty.

Akua Afriyie lifted her gaze toward her father. She looked at Lizzie and stared at Ernest again, her ponytails bouncing like tennis balls.

"Akua, you're making me dizzy with your pompy-joes," Lizzie said. Ernest laughed.

"Close your eyes!" he said. "Afriyie, cover your eyes."

"OK, Papa," Akua Afriyie said, plastering her tiny fingers over her face. Lizzie closed her eyes. She heard the engine die out. Ernest stepped out of the car, opened her door and led them out.

"Open!" he said.

A rust-colored gate stood in front of them. Lizzie saw the top part of the completed house. The crowns of two royal palm trees, their leaves bristling in the wind, flanked the house.

"Wow!" Lizzie said. "Is this really for us?" She'd seen the house go up, but to be standing in front of the completed thing ... her house ... her family's house.... She couldn't believe it. "It's beautiful, Ernie," she said, hugging him. A loud sob escaped her lips. "I'm sorry," she said, wiping the tears pouring from her eyes.

"And you haven't even seen all of it!" Ernest said.

"Why is Mamaa crying?"

"Afriyie, those are tears of joy," he said. The three-year-old shrugged and walked up to the gate, trailed by Ernest. Lizzie looked at them. Ernest dug in his trouser pockets, took out a key and unlocked the padlock on the gates, pushing them open. Akua Afriyie crept in, looking left and right.

"Akua," Lizzie shouted, finally getting a hold of herself. "You can run anywhere you want. It's our house!" She sauntered in toward the house. Ernest walked back to the van. Akua Afriyie tumbled on a patch of grass to the left of the house, which was dotted with royal palms, coconut, mango and guava trees. "This is paradise," Lizzie shrieked, running to join Akua Afriyie. She caught her and dragged her down onto the grass.

Akua Afriyie squealed. "Mamaa, again!" Lizzie smiled. She looked behind her. The ground was covered with more loam than grass. Beyond that stood a small outhouse.

Ernest drove in with the van and walked back to latch the gates. Lizzie noticed a watchman's room now that Ernest had closed the gates.

"You two seem quite content on the grass," he said, unlocking the front door. "You can sleep there all day if you like. I'm going inside."

Lizzie grabbed Akua Afriyie's hand and dashed into the living room. It smelled of paint, wax and wood. The dark panels of the floorboards gleamed.

"We'll have to go furniture shopping," Ernest said. "I decided to hold off on that, so your womanly touch would be on the house."

"Oh, Ernie," Lizzie said. Akua Afriyie extracted her hand from Lizzie's clutch and ran off. Lizzie had never been happier.

*

March 1964

Lizzie, Ernest and Akua Afriyie stepped out of the Pontiac and stood outside an unpainted wall. A woman sat against the wall, selling red and green kola nuts which she'd spread on a table in front of her. A child sat on wet sand, dipping a stick in a puddle and painting a leg of his mother's table brown. Lizzie caught Akua Afriyie staring at him.

"Madam, good afternoon," Ernest said. "We're looking for Abokyi."

"Abokyi!" the woman shouted at the wall behind her. "He'll come soon," she said confidently.

Lizzie saw a man poke his head over a small rusty gate and grin.

"Massa!" he said and let them in. His face was covered with drops of water. "I was just performing my ablution. Please come in." Lizzie bent her head backwards to look at his face. On his lanky body, he wore a long brown gown. Two scars marked either side of his temples and he had a pleasant, and it seemed permanent, smile.

He led them into a dark living room. Four armchairs with blue cushions were arranged so close to a rectangular table, Lizzie wondered if there would be any legroom.

"Please, sit," he said. Lizzie sat down and lifted Akua Afriyie onto her lap. Surprisingly her knees didn't touch the table. Ernest sat in the armchair adjacent to hers. "Do you want some water?"

"Yes!" Akua Afriyie said.

"No, we're fine," Lizzie said. She didn't want to take any risks, especially not for Akua Afriyie. "You were going to pray," she said. "Finish that first."

"Thank you, madam," Abokyi said and walked out of the living room through a side door.

"Tenk you, madam," Akua Afriyie repeated. Lizzie pulled her ear. She looked around the living room. It reminded her of Adukrom No. 2. The way the furniture had no breathing space. Next to the side door stood a dining table which had been covered with a plastic tablecloth. Abokyi walked back in and settled in the seat across from Ernest. His knees jutted out in front of him. He looked at them and grinned.

"Great," Ernest said. "Abokyi came by the house a couple of times when we were building."

"Have you worked as a watchman before?" Lizzie asked, wondering why Ernest wasn't getting to the point.

"Yes. You know the house with the blue gate close to your house?" he asked.

"Yes …" Ernest said. Lizzie hadn't seen it. She shook her head.

"I used to work for a man and his wife there."

"Why did you stop working for them?" Lizzie asked.

"They were from London. They went back."

"How long did you work for them?" Ernest asked.

"Eight years."

Ernest whistled.

"Is there any way we can check that?" Lizzie asked.

"Ah, yes, madam," he said. "A garden-boy goes there everyday to water the grass. Ask him."

Lizzie didn't need to be convinced. His height was intimidating. He seemed trustworthy. She looked at Ernest, trying to get him to read her approval through her eyes.

"All right," Ernest said. "My wife and I will have to come to a decision."

"Yes, massa." Abokyi scratched his head. "Eh, massa …"

"Yes?" Ernest asked.

"Massa, can we talk of my pay?"

"Oh, sorry. Yes, yes. I'm sure we can't pay you as well as the English couple. How is ten pounds a month?"

"Thank you, massa."

"Tenk you, massa," Akua Afriyie repeated.

"Stop it, Akua! Sorry about her," Lizzie said. "We need to talk about sleeping arrangements," she said to Ernest.

"You said this is your aunt's house?" Ernest asked him.

"Yes, massa."

"There's a watchman's room where you can sleep, in our house," Lizzie said. "You can move in there if that's more convenient for you."

"Oh, thank you, madam!" Abokyi exclaimed.

"Oh, tenk you, madam," Akua Afriyie repeated.

"Akua Afriyie, stop it!"

"Oh, madam, it's fine," Abokyi said. "She's small madam."

Lizzie let out a laugh laced with embarrassment as she stood up. Abokyi also got up.

"Come by the house tomorrow," Lizzie said. "We'll tell you our decision." Ernest looked at her, wide-eyed. Abokyi walked them to the gate.

"Tomorrow, then," Abokyi said.

As they walked toward Ernest's Pontiac, Lizzie whispered, "Let's hire him!"

"Wow, Mrs. Mensah. Are you sure?"

"Yes. He should start work tomorrow."

*

June 1964

Lizzie and Ernest's noses were buried in newspapers. Lizzie looked over hers, wondering if she should check on Akua Afriyie, who she'd just tucked into bed.

Ernest's breathing was, as usual, raspy. She rubbed her globular stomach and flipped a page of the newspaper.

"Goodness, gracious! Listen to this," she said.

"What?"

She noticed a hint of annoyance in his voice but went on. "Some Nigerian man is begging to be sent to jail because he doesn't have a job and if he doesn't go to jail, he'll be tempted to steal."

"Well, let's hope with Kwame Nkrumah's Seven-Year Plan, people like him will get jobs. With socialism, everyone should be covered, don't you think?"

"You don't sound too thrilled," she said.

Ernest sat up. "It's this socialism thing. Private business owners like me are suffering. Already they've started restricting imports of 'luxury items' into the country. That directly affects us. And all this one party business and jailing anyone who criticizes his government ..."

"Ernie," Lizzie said. "You know what will solve our problems?"

"What?"

"You need to run for MP or get a position in the Trade Ministry like Akwasi."

"Lizzie ..."

"That way, Ernie, either way you'll be covered. If government doesn't work, you have your own job. If your business suffers because of import restrictions, you have a job in the government."

"Lizzie, have you seen the lines that are forming outside stores? Times are hard and people aren't too happy with the government."

"But as a business owner in the government you'll be able to make policies that will benefit you and other business owners. I'm not saying you should be corrupt. No. Just be in a position to influence ..."

Ernest shook his head, clicking his tongue. "I don't want to go anywhere near politics."

"There's security in working for the government, then you won't have to go begging every time you need a permit."

"My dear, you have it all wrong. There's more security in working for yourself than for a government that someone can easily overthrow. Have you been following all these coups across the world?"

"You don't have to run for a big position …"

"Have you read how many bomb threats there have been on Nkrumah?"

"I know," Lizzie said. The man was being too stubborn.

"Besides, I'm always away for part of the year, that's no way for a politician to behave. Why don't you run for MP?"

"Maybe I will!" She folded the paper in a huff and turned over, her back facing him.

He chuckled. "Mrs. Elizabeth Mensah, MP for Labone South," he said. He was infuriating.

The next day Lizzie clasped Akua Afriyie's hand tightly as she crossed the busy road before the CPP head office. The two-story yellow building was buzzing with people coming in and out of it. Akua Afriyie pulled her hand out of Lizzie's grasp in the middle of road. A car was speeding toward them. Lizzie glared at Akua Afriyie, bent over and roughly grabbed Akua Afriyie's wrist. She raised her left palm up at the approaching car and ran across.

Akua Afriyie whined, making hiccup and crying sounds.

"Shhh," Lizzie said. "Did you want us to have an accident?"

They walked into the terrazzo-floored reception.

"… have been devouring all the pods. I don't even know what to do about them. Do insecticides kill bats?" said a voice to her left. Lizzie turned to look at him.

He was an old man in white and black cloth, talking to a younger man in a political suit. The way he kept on about his cocoa farm, Lizzie had to do a double take to make sure he wasn't Papa Yaw. She strode over to a woman sitting behind a wooden table. Above the woman was a framed picture of Kwame Nkrumah. "Good morning," Lizzie said.

"Good morning. Can I help you?" the woman replied, adjusting the wig on her head. Lizzie detected the hint of an English accent.

"I'd like to find out about how I can help with the Party," she said.

"Are you a member?"

"Yes, I am," Lizzie said. "But I'd like to become more active."

"All right," the woman said. "I take it to mean you'd like to volunteer."

"Yes," Lizzie said, thinking, I'm actually looking for a leadership role.

"We have the youth wing and the women's wing which are in dire need of help."

"The women's wing," Lizzie said. "That sounds promising."

"Would you be interested in a fundraising position within the women's wing, then? I'm part of the group and we need to raise money for our projects."

"Yes, yes," Lizzie said. Akua Afriyie whined. Lizzie ignored her. "I'm definitely your woman for the job."

"Great," the woman said.

"Grrreat!" Akua Afriyie repeated.

"I'm sorry about her," Lizzie said.

"Your daughter?" the woman asked.

"Yes," Lizzie said, pulling on Akua Afriyie's ponytails.

"She looks just like you. Tell you what," the woman said. "Our most pressing assignment is to raise money to buy school supplies." Lizzie thought of organizing the mother of all fundraisers. She'd invite all the Esther Boyes and other big people in Accra…. "Here's an application form. Please fill it out and our president will call you." Lizzie hastily filled in her information.

"Here," she said, handing back the form.

"Good. We'll call you very soon."

*

January 1965

It was one of those days when the air was thick with dry heat and yet the sun was hidden behind grey clouds. Huge market women clad in white cloth imprinted with the green and red cock of the CPP logo and the face of Kwame Nkrumah, jostled for space with teachers and nurses. Lizzie looked at the women gathered at the rally. She saw some of them mopping their brows, while the ashen faces of others would benefit from a good oiling.

She felt light. She'd been feeling that way since she'd delivered Naa Tsoo. She smiled, thinking of how she'd convinced Ernest to make the birth a small affair. She was a fan of grand outdoorings, weddings and funerals, but she didn't want to deal with Ernest's family, hence the small affair.

She nestled a silver whistle in her mouth. Coins danced around in the cane basket she cradled as she ran by the market women and back toward the nurses and teachers. Policemen flanked the crowd.

Up on a small wooden stage, behind a microphone, the woman Lizzie had talked to in the CPP office sat on a metal chair next to two others, one with a big round wig and glasses that covered half her face. Lizzie blew her whistle as the woman with the large hair made for the microphone.

"Ladies of Ghana," the woman said, her voice crisp. Her sassy white pearls swayed as she spoke, her large hair bouncing in agreement with her every word. "*Akwaaba*. Welcome. We're here today to help our children do better in school. Osagyefo Dr. Kwame Nkrumah's Seven-Year Plan, stresses the importance of free education for all Ghanaian children. His Plan spells out that primary, secondary and tertiary education be freely available to every Ghanaian citizen. Already, our primary schools and universities are free ..."

The women applauded.

"Amen!" a woman in the back shouted.

"As women, we know the value of educating our children. I hope you have all sent your children to school." She glared at the group.

"Yes!" the women responded.

"We have well-trained teachers instructing our children, but they need our help. Teachers need the students to have the right tools. Today, I beg you to give what you can so we can buy pens, pencils, notebooks and textbooks for our children. Ghanaian women, today, let us give for our children's futures. Nothing is too small. Ghanaian women for Osagyefo! Ghanaian women for CPP!" she shouted.

"Ghanaian women for Osagyefo!" the throng responded.

Lizzie wiped her brow and blew hard on the whistle. She was sweating.

"I'll be back," she said to Mercy, who stood with the crowd of nurses. She didn't think fundraising would be so physical. And to think she'd imagined standing in an air-conditioned room, throwing a ball! She wound her way around the first line.

"Madam! Watch where you're going," a woman with a bulbous nose shouted. "You're stepping on my toes!"

"Sorry, oh," Lizzie said and thrust the basket under the woman's nose.

The woman sucked her teeth. "You step on my feet and want me to give you money?"

"It's for our children," Lizzie said and smiled.

"CPP, CPP, *osee yiee*! Ghana, Ghana, *osee yiee*!" the women's voices rose in song. The woman joined in the singing, opened her eyes widely and made faces at Lizzie.

"*Yiee ayiee*!" she mouthed. Just say you don't have money, Lizzie thought and walked on.

The women's voices crescendoed as Lizzie wove in and out of the crowd. The air grew colder. A gust of wind blew leaves into the air. She looked up at the thickened clouds. She walked back to Mercy, looking at the coins in the basket.

"It's too hot," Mercy said.

"It looks like it's going to rain," Lizzie said.

"It won't, it's the harmattan."

Lizzie counted the coins in the basket. "Five pounds!"

"Only!"

"How far would that go for even one school?"

"I think most of these women need the money themselves."

"I know," she said, turning round to study the faces of the women singing happily. Singing like they knew no worries. Or were they singing, praying their voices will be heard? Their voices, celebrating the Party, celebrating Ghana, were they masking voices asking for change and for better times to come? She felt a drop of water on her face. "Mercy, it's raining," she said as more drops fell down.

The women shrieked and scattered in all directions as the clouds burst open. It was raining in harmattan.

*

Passing over a large pothole, the taxi Lizzie sat in bumped up and down. Lizzie clutched Naa Tsoo, who was half asleep in her lap. Akua Afriyie sat to her right, jumping up and down each time the car went in and out of a pothole.

"Madam," the driver said, "there are no goods in Makola, I tell you."

"So what should I do?" Lizzie asked.

"Add a few more shillings and I'll drive you to the UTC. I swear you'll find what you want there."

"Fine," she said. Naa Tsoo gurgled. Lizzie rocked her. She hung her right breast over her blouse and inserted her nipple into Naa Tsoo's mouth. She looked out the window. Accra was becoming a difficult town to live in. Before, she could get everything she needed cheaply at Makola and now….

The road ahead was choked with cars. From the distance, Lizzie heard the chugging of a train on its tracks.

The driver turned off his ignition as the train dawdled by. Hangers on held precariously to doors and windows. She shifted her gaze back to Naa Tsoo. She pushed her breast back into the blouse as the last car of the train passed by. The driver started his engine.

In front of the UTC building, Lizzie saw a queue leading to a table piled high with goods. She stepped out of the car. Akua Afriyie wasn't budging. She grabbed her wrist and pulled her out.

"How much?" she asked, peering at him through the passenger seat window.

"Two pounds."

"Eh? I thought you said I should add a few shillings. I feel like you've added a whole pound!" He was eating into the little money she was going to use to buy her goods.

"Madam, from your house to Makola is one pound, twenty shillings. From Makola to here—ask anybody—is one pound, fifteen shillings. I've given you a special price. In all, two pounds."

"You can see I have children, I have to feed them and you're taking all my money," Lizzie said, sucking her teeth.

"Madam, it's not like that. I gave you a good price. We all have to eat."

"Here, here," Lizzie said, flinging coins onto the passenger seat. That's all they knew, those taxi drivers—how to cheat people!

She went to the end of a line, carrying Naa Tsoo on her left hip, holding Akua Afriyie's hand and dangling her purse over her right shoulder. Just in front of her, stood an old wrinkled woman in thick glasses.

"Have you been here long?" Lizzie asked her.

"Thirty minutes," the woman squeaked.

"Whoa!" Lizzie exclaimed. She stretched her neck and looked at the people distributing food.

The line was not moving. A thin man peddling plastic combs, balms in small green, yellow and orange receptacles and pens on a wooden tray walked close to the line. She looked back down at Akua Afriyie.

"Excuse me," she heard a male voice say. She thought it was the peddler.

"No, thank ..." She almost dropped Naa Tsoo.

"Is this you?" he asked. She didn't know how to react. He stood there, tall, red-skinned, dressed in tight chestnut trousers that had been patched at the right knee and that were too short on him. His smock, black and white, hung loosely about his lanky frame. Was that the same smock? Lizzie wondered. His hair was kinked into tiny balls. His tiny eyes looked wild and red.

"Yes," Lizzie said, keeping her expression stoic. "It is."

"I've been looking for you," he said.

"Bador," she said. "If you were looking for me, why didn't you ..." Her voice broke. "... you couldn't write? You just left.... I've moved on. And so should you."

"Lizzie," he said, "not one day has gone by when I haven't thought of this day. I've been waiting for you. Lizzie, it's time." Time for what? He's mad! Lizzie thought. "Oh my! Can you believe it? The number of years ..." He clasped his mouth.

"It's too late now, Bador," Lizzie said, shaken. She was shaken by his appearance. Shaken by his presence. Shaken by his existence. It might have been better if he were dead.

"It's not too late," he said, his mouth curving down. "It's not too late. Lizzie, you're the only woman I've ever loved. I've been going crazy without you. Now that I've found you, we can work things out and get married." Lizzie snapped out of the trance he was weaving her into. She looked at Akua Afriyie and Naa Tsoo and suddenly felt that they might be in danger.

"We have to go," she said, dragging Akua Afriyie's hand.

"Lizzie, wait!" he said, running to catch up with her. "Tell me where you live. Lizzie, let's finish what we started."

"I'm sorry," she repeated. "I have to go." Tears welled up in her eyes, a thick lump lodged in her throat. The man that she'd once been building her dreams around was mad! Thank God, Ernest had come into her life. She would have to send Abokyi for the food. She couldn't stay there—Bador Samed might do something to her. She stuck her arm out for a taxi.

"Lizzie, please. Please! I don't drink, I don't smoke. I've saved myself for you."

Naa Tsoo wailed. Lizzie felt like wailing too.

"Please go away," she said. "You're upsetting my baby." She pursed her lips and bounced Naa Tsoo on her hip.

"Mummy, who's that?" Akua Afriyie asked. One never knew whom the girl would blab to. She hadn't told Ernest, who was away in Germany, about Bador Samed. And she wanted to keep it that way, especially now.

"A madman," Lizzie said, looking him square in the eye. His eyes watered and reddened.

"Lizzie, please!" he said, his hands stretched out in supplication. "All these years, I've been waiting to see you again."

A green and yellow taxi drove to a stop by them. Lizzie fumbled with the door handle, opened the door, pushed Akua Afriyie into the backseat and slid in by her. She slammed the door shut and felt tears welling in her, but thought of Akua Afriyie and pushed them down. He looked terrible. As she suppressed the sobs, her emotions took root in another form—she shook violently.

At home, she left Naa Tsoo and Akua Afriyie in the living room and walked outside.

"Abokyi!" she shouted, banging on his door. He didn't answer. She yanked open the door and found him sprawled on his bed, snoring. She shook him awake. He jumped up and spread a smile on his face.

"Madam!" he said, wiping the corners of his eyes. "Good morning."

"Abokyi, what if somebody came to steal from us? Heh? What if somebody came in here to do something bad to us? What if…. Accra is not safe these days."

"Madam, I'm sorry. Yesterday, I had to stand in line for five hours for my aunty …"

"I don't need your excuses, Abokyi."

"I'm sorry, madam."

"Chew kola or drink coffee, because you can't just be sleeping like this. I need you to go stand in line. Will you come back, sleep like there's no tomorrow and say I made you stand in line?" Lizzie realized she was taking out her frustrations on him. She calmed down and said, "We have no milk, corn or baby food. There's food at the UTC. I went there but I couldn't stay … because of the children."

"Yes, madam."

"Here's money for the food and this is your fare. Don't let the *trotro* mates cheat you."

"Yes, madam."

The lanky Abokyi stretched his long limbs and walked out of the room. She watched his head bobbing away and latched the gate shut. Strangely, he reminded her of Bador Samed.

Nine
Digging for Dirt

February 1966

Lizzie walked straight into the nurses' room when she arrived at work. The radio was blaring loudly. Another nurse sat in a black armchair looking shell-shocked. She was about to ask her why when she heard the announcement.

... Armed Forces in co-operation with the Police have felt it necessary to take over the reigns of power and to dismiss the former President, Kwame Nkrumah ...

Lizzie was dumbfounded. What was going to happen to the country? What was going to happen to them? She clasped her mouth.

All Members of Parliament are to report at the nearest police station to be incarcerated for their own good.

"I'm going home," the other nurse said. Yes, me too, Lizzie thought. She couldn't speak. They were first going after MPs. Who would they go after next? Party members? She picked up her bag. The other nurse was putting on a grey sweater over her green uniform. Lizzie stared at her, dazed. Only when the nurse walked out did she follow, her body, leaden. What was going to happen to them?

"Christie," Lizzie said, her mouth dry. "Where do you live?"

"Dansoman. Why?"

"I thought ... I thought we could share a taxi."

"Where are you going?"

"Labone."

"But that's in the opposite direction."

Yes, I know, Lizzie thought. She didn't know whether to laugh or cry. They walked through the general ward. An old man sat up in bed, his eyes fixed to the wall.

"They say the king is no longer! No one is immortal!" he said, repeating his eerie chant as the nurses passed by him. His voice got louder the farther they moved from him.

Outside, doctors and nurses milled about in a sea of greens and whites speckled with oranges, yellows and blues. One of the doctors threw his hands up in the air, above the mass of people, clapping.

"No more Satan! No more Satan!" the crowd shouted.

Lizzie's stomach lurched. She didn't realize so many people were anti-Nkrumah. She looked at the faces of the gathered crowd. One or two people seemed to share in her confusion, but most, like the doctor with his hands in the air, were hooting.

Lizzie walked toward the road where taxis waited. Most of them sat empty. In one taxi, Lizzie found a man sleeping behind the wheel.

"Brother!" Lizzie shouted, startling him awake.

"Eh?" He stretched his arms. His fist hit the roof of the car.

"Can you please take me to Labone?"

"I'm not going there."

"Where are you going?"

"Nowhere." He wiped the corners of his mouth.

"Brother, I beg you. I'll pay you extra." He clicked his tongue and shook his head. Lizzie yanked open the door and sat in the car. "I'm paying you. Now, please take me to Labone."

"Madam, it's not by force."

"Brother, please. I have two babies at home in Labone. If I leave them, they'll die. Brother plea…" Her voice broke. She stared through the windshield.

"You will pay me plenty, madam."

"Thank you," she said. The crowd outside the hospital was getting more heated. The driver reversed so fast, Lizzie thought he'd crash into an Indian almond tree at the side of the road.

"Madam, I am going to speed so get ready."

Lizzie pressed her hand against the glove compartment. She looked out the window. Greens blended into browns, browns into whites, whites into greens again. The driver turned off the Old Winneba Road onto High Street, where cars were stuck bumper to bumper. Crowds of people wove in and out of the traffic.

"Can't you go another way?" she asked, turning round to see if they could still leave the road. Four cars had already pulled up behind them. The driver sucked his teeth.

"No Nkrumah! No CPP! No Satan! No PDA!" Lizzie heard people chant.

The driver opened his door.

"Where are you going?" she asked, her voice shaky.

"I'm coming. Stay here. Don't go anywhere!" he said, jumped out and left the door hanging open. She saw him meandering between cars. Soon he was out of sight. The driver's door slammed shut. A man with brown teeth wedged his head through the window, wielding a broken green bottle in his left hand.

"Are you CPP?" he asked. She was quiet. Her heart was drumming loudly. She sat still. "If you're CPP, report yourself!"

The driver pushed the man out of the way. "Go way you! Leave my sister alone. She's not CPP."

"No CPP!" shouted the intruder, running to the car ahead of them.

"Thank you," Lizzie said.

"My sister, we'll be sitting here all day. There are so many people in front of James Fort and Ussher Fort. They want all the people Nkrumah detained freed right now."

Cars honked, the chants crescendoed and Lizzie grew more nervous. In the distance, she saw a man pick up a stone and smash it against a store front.

"How are we going to get out of here?" she asked, her voice tremulous.

"I'm coming," the driver said.

"Where are you going now?"

He walked behind the car. She looked through the rearview mirror. He was sprinting down the road. She didn't know what to do. She put her index finger in her mouth and bit her nail. Is that how easily loyalties shifted? She was sure all these people had once supported Nkrumah.

The driver came back. "We're lucky. People are turning around," he said. "You see why I said I wouldn't take you?" He waited for the car behind him to move. Once it did, the driver reversed the car a few meters and angled the car to the right. He honked and stuck his hand out at a red car in the right lane. "Massa, I beg, wait small," he shouted.

"No way!" the other driver shouted, closing the already tiny gap between his car and the one in front of him.

"*Shiii*," the driver said. "People are wicked!" He honked at a taxi, whose driver stalled for him. The driver nosed the car into the gap, changed gears, reversed, steered strenuously, the steering wheel click-click-clicking. He backed up, rotated his steering wheel clockwise and maneuvered the car into the right lane. Just as he was mopping his face with his shirt, Lizzie saw a stone strike the glass of the side mirror, shattering it into a million pieces. She screamed and ducked.

"It's fine, sister," he said, speeding down the street. "It's fine."

Her head still bent, she rummaged through her purse. She'd give him all the money in there. She hoped it would be enough to fix his mirror. She heard chants and whistles blowing all over the city.

"Sister, you can relax," the driver said.

Lizzie sat up and saw clouds of smoke rising everywhere she looked. When they arrived outside her gate, she handed the notes to the driver and got down hurriedly.

"Thank you, my brother," she said. He drove off as she banged on the gate. Abokyi stuck his head over it.

"Ah, madam. Back so soon?"

"They've overthrown Nkrumah and nobody is CPP anymore. Haven't you heard?"

"No, madam."

"Is uncle back?" Abokyi shook his head. Ernie is not afraid for his life, she thought. "Abokyi, if anyone comes asking for me, tell them I'm not in. Don't let anyone in."

"And uncle?" Lizzie wanted to slap him.

"You can let only uncle in. Nobody else, you hear? It's not safe."

"Ok, madam."

Lizzie ran into the house and up into her bedroom. She would stay in there all weekend if she could help it. She fell asleep and woke up with a start when she heard a car drive in.

Ernest walked in.

"Are you all right?" he asked.

"Someone threw a stone at my taxi, but I'm fine. How about you?"

"Lizzie, I have to go to Germany as soon as possible."

"Why?"

"Until things die down. They're going hard after people who contributed to the CPP."

"Then we should all come with you," she said.

"Lizzie, we don't have enough money."

"I'm pregnant," she said. "You can't leave us here!" she blurted out.

"We'll hire extra help for you and Abokyi will be here for security."

Lizzie said nothing. Too many thoughts ran through her head. There was the threat of Bador Samed. The new government might come after her for being in the CPP, she was bringing yet another child into an uncertain world and, Ernest was going to Germany again.

*

April 1966

Lizzie watched Ernest fix on his purple and yellow striped tie in front of a mirror pinned to a brown armoire. He tied a knot and untied it. He tried again.

"Are you nervous?" she asked.

"Wouldn't you be?"

"I would be, which is why I don't understand why you insist on going. You'll only be calling attention to yourself," she said, picking herself out of bed. She pulled on her shorts, wedged between the cheeks of her buttocks. Her round stomach jutted out as she picked up and folded the paper she'd been reading.

"544 are in custody," the headline read.

She walked up to him, pushed his hands off his tie and fixed it for him.

"There! Why are you going out there when you're the same one who told me people are out there hunting CPP supporters?"

"Akwasi is my good friend. He's helped me with all sorts of things over the years. Like with those import permits. Visiting him in prison is the least I can do."

"We should both keep a low profile is all I'm saying."

"Lizzie, I'm a low-profile man," he said.

"Well, if you must do this … I'll check if the food is ready," she said. Maybe she was being cowardly, but they had two children and a third on the way. This was not the time for him to try to get himself locked up, or worse, killed.

She looked back at him combing through his hair and drawing a line from his forehead to make a right parting. She sighed and hobbled out of the room.

Akua Afriyie, in a long yellow nightgown, sat on the floor playing with her dolls and talking to herself. She paid no attention to Naa Tsoo, who was crawling on the floor, picking up objects and sending them straight to her mouth.

Struggling to bend over, Lizzie patted Akua Afriyie's head. "Sweets, how are you?"

Akua Afriyie ignored her. Lizzie picked up Naa Tsoo and rested her on her left hip. She stuck her finger into Naa Tsoo's mouth, dug and probed, hoping she could remove any dirt the girl had lodged in there.

"Akua, it's rude not to respond when someone talks to you," Lizzie said. The girl didn't look up once to acknowledge Lizzie. What have I done to that child? she wondered. Balancing Naa Tsoo on her hip, she descended the stairs and walked by the dining room into the kitchen.

Senam, her new help, stirred a pot of stew. She was taller than Lizzie with square shoulders marking off a boyish frame.

"What have you packed so far?" Lizzie asked.

"The *jollof* is done. It's in the basket." She pointed to a small brown basket sitting on the counter.

"Good. Make sure to add lots of oranges and bananas."

Lizzie stared at a hole in the net door that led outside, she looked back at Senam who reached for a plastic bowl and scooped out steaming red sauce into it.

"Mamaa, banana," Naa Tsoo said.

"OK, sweets. You'll get a banana when it's time to eat," Lizzie said. Senam covered the plastic bowl and put it into the basket. She picked up five bananas and struggled to make them fit in the basket. She rearranged them at least three times. She gave up and covered the basket with a red and white napkin. Everyone was so jittery.

"Banana!" Naa Tsoo screamed.

"You won't get one if you shout. And say please." Lizzie grabbed the handle of the cane basket. Senam opened the door for her. Ernest walked downstairs.

"Is everything ready?" he asked.

"Yes," Lizzie said, placing the basket on the dining room table. "What will you do if they throw you in?"

"They won't."

Lizzie grabbed his wrist. "I'm serious."

"You know me. I don't like trouble."

"I'm coming with you," she said.

"Huh?"

"You heard me. Either I come with you or you don't go at all."

"No! There's no need, Lizzie. I have this all under control."

"I'm coming," she put Naa Tsoo down.

"Don't worry, my dear, it will be well." He picked up the basket from the table.

Lizzie shooed Naa Tsoo into the kitchen. "Senam, I'm going with uncle. Keep an eye on Akua upstairs."

"OK," Senam said, a loud pot crashing to the floor. Lizzie winced.

"Lizzie, you don't have to come."

"I'm just going to wear something decent," she said, bounding up the stairs.

Outside the moss-streaked walls of the Ussher Fort Prison, a fishy smell thick in the air, Ernest steered the car into a parking spot.

"Will you wait in the car?" he asked.

"No," she said. He hopped out of the car, and rushed over to open her door. She stepped out, her pink and purple *boubou* fluttering in the breeze.

Ernest picked up the basket and they walked to the entrance. Three soldiers in green fatigues were stationed in front of the fort's gates, a portcullis half-drawn.

"State your purpose," a thick soldier said, pointing a gun at Ernest.

"Good morning, gentlemen," Ernest said. He looked at each of the soldiers. "I've brought some food for one of the prisoners." Lizzie was surprised he was so calm. Such diplomacy! He would have made a fine MP! A sad smile formed on her lips. She'd been pushing him right into a jail cell.

"No visitors allowed," he said, now looking at Lizzie.

"Please, we'll be fast," Ernest said.

"No visitors allowed."

"Sir," Lizzie said. "Can we at least leave this …"

Ernest cut her a stern look. "His name is Akwasi Otchere. I'd like to see him. Is that possible?" he asked.

"No visitors allowed." The other soldiers chuckled at their fellow officer's obstinacy.

Ernest dug into his trouser pocket. "Please, it will be very brief. I just want to make sure he's all right," he said.

"And who are you?" the soldier asked.

"I'm his cousin."

"No visitors."

Ernest took his hand out of his pocket and balled it into a fist. "Sir, can I please talk to you?" He handed Lizzie the basket. The soldier followed him. They walked away from the entrance.

Lizzie watched them. Ernest talked, the soldier shook his head.

"… you should have seen him," one of the soldiers behind her said. "Big man like that asking me for toilet paper." He cleared his throat and spat.

"He didn't ask you to clean his buttocks for him?"

"Those days are over!" Lizzie heard another splat of saliva.

Lizzie saw Ernest stretch out his hand and graze the soldier's palm. The other soldiers went quiet. The one who spat broke the silence. "And these ones, I smell Nkrumah all over them."

Lizzie froze. Ernest walked back with the soldier. He wasn't smiling. His face hung a little lower. He reached into his pocket, pulled out a white handkerchief and wiped his face.

"Apparently they have a strict no-visitor's policy," Ernest said. "He said he'll make sure Akwasi gets the food."

"Is that the best we can do?" Lizzie asked.

Ernest nodded. "Thank you, my brother," he said to the soldier. He held Lizzie's back and they walked back to his Pontiac. Lizzie knew the food wasn't going to get to Akwasi.

As Ernest opened the car door, she asked, "How much did you give that pig?"

"A whole ten cedis."

"The fool will spend it on drink and women."

"I just hope Akwasi is OK."

"Let's pray he is."

*

July 1966

Naa Mensah, bursting out of her outfit, sat in a cane armchair in Lizzie and Ernest's living room. She was clad in a green and white patterned *kaba* and slit, her neck bedizened with a heavy gold chain. Lizzie had never seen her this dressed up.

Naa Mensah loosened her skirt, as she downed a glass of beer. Lizzie was trying to keep a straight face. To stop herself from laughing, she took a sip of coca cola and as a floating ice cube hit her teeth she suppressed a snort. She looked at Kwame sleeping on a white cloth on the sofa.

"As I was saying," Naa Mensah said, holding on to her glasses. A faint trace of red lined her lips. Was she wearing lipstick? Lizzie wondered. "Ernest told me to keep checking on you. Especially with all this CPP witch-hunting going on. So, the long and short of this is that I'm moving in to take care of my grandchildren."

"Oh, Naa, I'm managing just fine," Lizzie said.

"I'll go home to pack my bags and I'll be back in a week."

"Naa, really, we're fine. You can come in every so often to check on us, but you don't have to disrupt your life. The market ... I'm sure...."

"Adoley will take care of selling at the market."

"It's only three months. Naa, don't worry."

"Yes, three months. I'll stay till Ernest gets back from Germany."

"Naa, don't overburden yourself."

Naa Mensah didn't say anything. She finished her beer, got up and said, "In a week or two, I'll bring a suitcase over."

"Naa, I beg you, don't worry yourself. I've got a lot of help here."

"Do you not want me around my grandchildren? Eh? Is that it?"

"No, it's not that. I said you could come visit whenever you want. You don't have to move in."

Naa Mensah opened the door. "This is my son's house. I can move in to take care of my grandchildren."

"Naa, we might not be here. I don't want you to waste your energy. I'll let Senam help you get a taxi." She followed Naa Mensah outside the house. "Senam!" she shouted.

Senam came out through the front door.

"Please help Naa get a taxi." Lizzie turned to Naa Mensah. "Thanks for coming."

Naa nodded at Senam and walked out of the gate. "So, next week," she shouted.

Abokyi, smiling brightly, closed the gate behind Naa Mensah and Senam. Lizzie held on to the gate and tried to stick her head over it. She was too short. "Abokyi!" she whispered.

"Madam," he said.

"Abokyi, that old woman is going to come back here in a week. Please, every time she comes, tell her I'm not in."

"OK, madam."

"Don't let her in. Be hard on her. Can you?"

"Yes, madam."

*

Lizzie heard loud banging on the gate. The knocks were loud enough for her to hear above the mechanical drone of the air-conditioner. That could only be one person, she thought. She turned off the air-conditioner and lowered the louver blades. She looked out the window. Naa Mensah! All she saw was the woman's grey hair, braided in a bun.

Lizzie scanned the garden and spotted Abokyi dozing under one of the royal palms. Naa Mensah banged again. Part of Lizzie was happy Abokyi was sleeping, the other wondered what would happen to them if someone—soldiers, thieves or Bador Samed—someone stormed in. Would Abokyi sleep through that?

The banging intensified. Finally, he woke up and stretched his lanky body. He wiped his face and skulked over to the gate, opening it slightly. Lizzie strained her ears. She wanted to hear every word. Abokyi had blocked the opening, so she still couldn't see Naa Mensah's full figure.

"Is this what my son is paying you to do? To sleep? Open the gate for me," Naa Mensah shouted.

Naa Mensah pushed Abokyi in. Lizzie caught a piece of her red and yellow cloth. It disappeared as Abokyi blocked her, preventing her from coming in.

Abokyi's voice was too soft. All Lizzie made out was, "… sorry … can't go in."

"Let me in. Your madam knows I'm coming. Open the gate."

"… anybody in. … go and come back."

"Nonsense!" Naa Mensah bellowed. "My child and three grandchildren live in this house. You can't tell me not to come in."

"… sorry, madam. … safe."

"Do I look like I'm carrying a gun?"

"Please wait for my madam to come home."

"You will be sorry for this! You and your madam," Naa Mensah shouted. Lizzie smiled. "Open the gate!" The woman tried to force her body in. Abokyi pushed her back outside and latched the gate. Naa Mensah banged furiously, her voice getting hoarser. "Open the gate!"

Abokyi walked back into his little house. Lizzie heard Kwame sneezing. She moved away from the window to look at her baby. Five minutes later, the banging ceased.

*

August 1966

Lizzie lay flat on the cane sofa. The room smelt strongly of polish. When she wasn't thinking about how the smell was bothering her, she wondered what Ernest was doing. What kept him occupied for three months in Germany? When would he come back?

She sat up and saw Naa Tsoo sitting on the carpeted floor, playing with one of her hand-me-down dolls. Naa Tsoo cupped the skirt of her green dress and lay the doll in the pouch she'd created. She rocked it.

Lizzie remembered the day Akua Afriyie had offered the doll for adoption. Naa Tsoo had gratefully taken the doll, promising it just as good a home as its first owner. Two hours later, Akua Afriyie had stormed into her room, crying that Naa Tsoo had decapitated the doll. Even after she'd stuck the head back onto the body, Akua Afriyie couldn't be appeased. She wanted the doll back. She didn't know how Naa Tsoo had ended up getting the doll again. Talking of Akua Afriyie, where was she? She hadn't heard from or seen her since lunch.

Lizzie walked to the white cot standing next to the cane armchair on the left. Kwame was sleeping, his buttocks humped in the air. A white cloth was bunched in a ball at the foot of the cot. She picked it up and spread it over his rump. She climbed up the stairs.

"Sweets," Lizzie said, as she pushed open the door. She saw Akua Afriyie standing in front of Alex Quansah from next door, her striped pink and blue panties at her ankles, her dress tucked under her chin. Alex's eyes were fixed on the mound of flesh under her dress, his finger, poised, ready to stick into the unfamiliar, intriguing organ he didn't have. "Oh my goodness!" Lizzie shouted. "What are you two doing?"

"Nothing," Akua Afriyie said.

"Alex, go home! Bad boy!" She hit Alex's back as he ran out of the bedroom. "And you! Akua Afriyie!" She smacked her buttocks and looked up. She gasped. Akua Afriyie and Alex had doodled crimson half-formed flowers, strange animal shapes, smiley faces, eggs, apples and all sorts of objects on all the possible wall space they could reach. Akua Afriyie started crying.

"Shut up!" Lizzie shouted. "You know you've been naughty. Stretch out your hand." Akua Afriyie shook her head. "Your hand!" Lizzie said again, sticking out her index and middle fingers. Slowly, Akua Afriyie offered her hand. Lizzie spanked Akua Afriyie's wrist. Akua Afriyie retracted her arm. "One more. Stretch …"

"No," Akua Afriyie said and tried to run to a corner of the room.

Lizzie caught the bottom of her skirt and pulled her back. She twisted Akua Afriyie's left ear and dragged her downstairs.

"You will stand in the corner till you learn to be good. What were you doing with that boy?" Lizzie said, shoving her into the corner by the stairs. "Stop crying! You'll wake up your brother." Lizzie sat on the couch. To paint that room, she'd have to save up so much money. Why was this girl becoming problematic with age? She thought it was the other way round—children were less trouble as they grew older.

Ten minutes later the bell rang. Great! More nuisances, she thought. She sucked her teeth. "That better not be your grandmother," she said to Akua Afriyie.

There was a knock on the door. Lizzie opened the door slightly.

"Madam, please a woman at the gate says she's your sister," Abokyi said.

"What woman?"

"She's very small."

"She said she's my real sister?"

"Yes, madam."

"Ask her what our father's favorite meal is. Don't let in."

Abokyi smiled and walked back to the gate. Lizzie closed the door and turned to look at Akua Afriyie who was no longer caged in the corner but was standing on tiptoes, trying to peek out of the window.

"Do you want me to beat you?" Lizzie asked.

Akua Afriyie shook her head and shrank back into the corner.

Abokyi knocked on the door rapidly. Lizzie opened it.

"*Ebunu-ebunu*," he said, all smiles. "'He always saves the biggest snail for last,' she said."

Asantewa! "Oh, let her in! In fact, I'm coming with you."

Lizzie ran out, leaving Abokyi behind. She unlatched the gate and enveloped Asantewa in a huge hug. She stepped back to look at her sister, tears coursing down her face.

"Eh, Asantewa! You're a woman!"

"And what about you?" Asantewa asked. She was still small, but had filled out in womanly places. Her hips could sway if they had to. She was dressed in a blue button-down blouse and a skirt that reached her shins. A small blue leather suitcase sat at her feet.

"Why didn't you tell me you were coming?" Lizzie asked. "I would have prepared a feast. Come in. Abokyi, please take her luggage to the guest room."

"You look very good. And this your mansion is simply beautiful."

Lizzie laughed. They walked into the living room. "Akua, Naa Tsoo, come hug your Auntie Asantewa."

Akua Afriyie strode apprehensively toward her aunt.

"Has someone been bad?" Asantewa asked, hugged Akua Afriyie and wiped the stains her tears had left on her face.

"The child has cost me."

"How?" Asantewa asked, hugging Naa Tsoo who was clutching her doll.

"I'll show you when we go up." Lizzie didn't want to talk about what Akua Afriyie had been doing with Alex. She felt it would reflect badly on her. She was happy to see Asantewa, after twelve years. But she wished the woman had warned her. These were not the best of times to be in Accra. "What would you like to drink? I'd have offered you some nice juice, but all we have is coke and water."

"Eh, my sister! Times are hard and you can offer coke! Water is fine."

Lizzie went into the kitchen and came back with a glass and a bottle of water on a metal tray. "So you found this place, from my description in the letters?"

"Yes. I asked the *kelewele* seller at the junction for Mr. Ernest Mensah's house and she knew exactly where you lived. You are big people!"

"No, no," Lizzie said as she placed the tray on a side table by the cane sofa, reveling in Asantewa's wide-eyed appreciation of her life. She poured a glass of water. "Catch your breath and after that you have to tell me all about the gossip from Number 2!"

"You first. Where's the man of the house?"

"Ernest is in Germany. He'll be back next month."

"Your husband travels a lot. Are you sure there's no lady out there? Some special *obroni*?"

"You really haven't changed! No tact at all!" Asantewa, I've been wondering the same thing, she thought. "I don't have that many updates. Kwame is the last baby now. He's in the cot."

"I didn't even see him," Asantewa said, sipping from her glass and getting up. "He's awake!"

Lizzie walked over and picked him up. "He looks just like his father, especially when he's grumpy, like now." She cupped her right hand and bumped his ample buttocks. "Let me show you your room." She saw Akua Afriyie standing between the living room and the stairs not sure what to do with herself. "Play with Naa Tsoo," she said. "And if you're naughty your punishment will be worse—no dinner for you."

Lizzie carried Kwame as she and Asantewa scaled the stairs.

"This is a nice house!" Asantewa said.

"Thank you. Let me show you the crime scene before we go to your room." She opened the door to Akua Afriyie's room, and Asantewa chuckled.

"Papa Yaw would have roasted her," she said.

"I know!" Kwame started crying.

Lizzie opened the door to the room next to Akua Afriyie's.

A queen-sized mattress lay on a wooden bed frame. Asantewa's suitcase stood next to the bed. At the foot of the bed was a green upholstered stool. "This is your room," Lizzie said, walking to the mahogany-paneled wardrobe across from the bed. She removed a floral pink bed sheet set.

"This is wonderful," Asantewa said.

Kwame's crying grew louder. Lizzie patted his back. She put him on the stool. She and Asantewa spread the sheet across the bed. Asantewa put a case over a pillow. Lizzie tucked the sheet under the mattress. Picking up Kwame, she sat on the stool, raised her T-shirt and suckled him. "So, tell me what happened when I left."

Asantewa sat on her bed. "Hmmm! That day! I remember it like it was yesterday. When you left the room, I heard your conversation with Papa Yaw. When you told him you were going to freshen up."

"I'm telling you that came to me on the spur of the moment."

"You won't let me tell my story!"

"Sorry."

"You left and it was quiet for about fifteen minutes. Papa Yaw came to our room. He asked me where you were. Of course I had no idea. He screamed at me, saying the visitor had other things to do. I told you were probably still in the bathroom. He left the room in a huff. I followed him. He knocked on the bathroom door. He knocked over and over and when he got no response he pushed the door with his finger. When it yielded so easily, he knew something was amiss. He scratched his head.

"He turned around to me. 'Where's Lizzie-Achiaa?' he asked. I shook my head in confusion. He went to Mama's room. You weren't there. He went to Mama Ama's, Mama Dufie's. You were nowhere to be found. He started to shout your name. He screamed and screamed till we couldn't hear his voice anymore. He walked back to the visitor …"

"Did you see the man?"

"Some old man! Lizzie, you made the right decision. He looked even older than Papa Yaw. So, Papa Yaw went to the man, stooping. His whole body seemed smaller than the usual Papa Yaw size. The man left, but not without telling told Papa Yaw off for wasting his time. That did it! Papa Yaw stormed back. He called Mama Efua out. 'Where's your daughter?' he asked and hit her before she could respond. He called me. 'Where's your sister?' He slapped me. He went down the list of all us— Mama's children. He swore he wouldn't waste his energy trying to marry Mama Efua's children anymore. The man said he wanted nothing to do with Mama Efua."

"Poor woman."

"She didn't mind, though. He was the one who crawled back into her arms after a week."

"I'm sorry you went through so much for me."

"Mama Efua was so sad. She—we all thought you were dead, until you wrote to me."

"I had to do that, Asantewa," Lizzie said, saddened that Papa Yaw didn't put any effort into finding her. "It's good to have you here."

Lizzie woke up the next morning, bothered. She'd dreamt that Ernest was seeking Asantewa's hand from Papa Yaw. She sat up in bed but couldn't rid herself of the feeling that the dream had a deeper meaning. Asantewa's words the day before had probably fed the dream. Was Ernest cheating on her?

She sprang out of bed and walked straight to his wardrobe. She sorted through his suits and shirts. She moved down to a group of three drawers. The first drawer contained his briefs and socks. Nothing else.

The second, his T-shirts and undershirts. Nothing that exposed a philandering husband. In the third drawer, Lizzie found clothes Ernest didn't wear anymore. Among these was an old CPP T-shirt, which she made a mental note to destroy in case soldiers raided their house.

She walked to his bedside table. The surface was crowded with inhalers and business cards. She was ready to stop her hunt and admit defeat, when she saw his wooden shoe rack. She looked behind it and pulled out a thin briefcase.

She put the dusty black briefcase on her lap and sat on his side of the bed. It had a three-number combination. She tried his age with a zero: 3-6-0. Nothing. She tried different permutations of his birthday, 5th September 1930. 5-9-3, 3-9-5, 5-3-9, 3-5-9. Finally, 9-5-3 clicked into place. I am a genius, she thought.

Inside were a plethora of papers: import permits, an old driver's license, an old passport, his birth certificate and his sister's birth certificate, both browning and another birth certificate. Gertrude Mensah. She didn't know Naa Mensah was called Gertrude. She wasn't going to give it a second thought, but realized it was written in German and Gertrude was born in 1956. She looked at it again. Father: Ernest Nii Mensah. What? She put the papers back, trying to make them look exactly the same way she'd found them. She closed the briefcase. Ernest had some serious explaining to do.

*

September 1966

Lizzie and Asantewa stood at the top of the staircase watching Abokyi carry up a suitcase. They made room for him. Ernest was behind him carrying another. Lizzie pressed Kwame close to her chest. Abokyi placed the suitcase by Lizzie and Ernest's bed and walked out of the room. Lizzie put Kwame on the bed and lay on her stomach. Asantewa sat at the foot of the bed.

Ernest opened one suitcase and took out boxes of chocolates, tiny T-shirts, two floral-print dresses.

"For the *kinder*," he said.

He pulled out a striped orange and white dress. He stood up and spread it over Lizzie's back.

"*Danke schön*," she said. He handed Asantewa a box of chocolates and unpacked his own clothes, folding them in a pile.

"Thank you," Asantewa said, getting up. "I'll let you two catch up. See you at dinner." She closed the door behind her.

"What's the latest? Any luck bringing any items?" Lizzie asked.

"I don't think it's going to happen."

"Why not?"

"The new government—those NLC people—has outright banned all imports."

"And you thought Nkrumah was bad."

Ernest shrugged. "I kept hoping something would change. Now I don't know what to do. My clients will be looking forward to getting their products."

"You don't know anyone in the NLC?"

"You want to just cross carpet like that?" He shook out a brown suit jacket, placing it on a metal hanger.

"That's not what I meant. A little help goes a long way …"

"We'll just have to cut down a lot in this house. With so many mouths to feed, we'll just have to learn to ration better."

"Ernie, I know you're talking about my sister. And you're the one who keeps making me pregnant!" Lizzie was annoyed. All she could think about was Gertrude Mensah. If he was looking for a fight, she would give him one.

"Your sister can stay here for as long as she likes. It's just that you turn my mother away not once but countless times."

"What are you talking about?"

"She said you and Abokyi plotted to keep her out."

"I wasn't here when she came … I told Abokyi to not let anyone in. That was all."

"But Abokyi knows she's my mother."

"Ernie, she was imposing herself on us. We were really fine, but she wasn't taking no for an answer." She picked up Kwame.

"Allowing her to stay wouldn't have killed you."

"Ernest, you know I don't get along with that woman."

"She's my mother." His expression was more sad than angry.

"I'm sorry." They were both quiet. She wished the other children were up in the room to fill in the silence. She put down Kwame.

"How are things in the house, though?" Lizzie ignored him. How about I ask the questions? Who is Gertrude? Are you married to her mother? When were you going to tell me? Ernest looked at her and clicked his thumb and middle finger in her face. "What's wrong?"

"Nothing. I'm just tired."

"I hope it wasn't too bad dealing with three young ones." Lizzie still ignored him. Ernest climbed onto the bed and lay on top of her. "I'm sorry if I was harsh," he said. "It's just that Naa Mensah has been through a lot, so I thought you'd just humor her a little." He kissed her left cheek. As he made for her other cheek, Lizzie heard his wheezing and smiled.

"I'm sorry, Ernie. By the way, you won't believe what your favorite did while you were away."

"Afriyie?"

"Yes, I'll show you."

Ten
An Unfortunate Accident

April 1971

Plates crashed loudly against the floor. Lizzie winced as she removed bottles of whiskey and gin from the alcohol cabinet by the dining room table. This girl and her butterfingers, she thought. She placed the bottles on the dining room table and walked into the kitchen.

"Is everything all right?" she asked Senam, who was kneeling down, picking up white shards of glass from the floor.

"I'm so sorry," Senam said, on the verge of tears.

Lizzie rubbed her forehead. She wasn't sure she'd made the right decision, having the party today. The day was really not going well.

"Clean up and carry one plate at a time, since four or five are too much for you to handle," Lizzie said and walked out.

"Yes, ma."

Asantewa came down the stairs, carrying one-month-old Tsotsoo. She was trailed by Akua Afriyie, Naa Tsoo, Kwame and Ernest Jr. How did I manage to have all these children? Lizzie wondered. She was harried and seeing her brood wasn't helping. And why did they all look so skinny and long? She fed them well....

"What happened?" Asantewa asked. "We heard a loud crash."

"It was Senam. She broke five of my best plates."

"Goodness!" Asantewa said.

Lizzie went back into the kitchen. Senam wasn't in there. She caught a whiff of stew and walked over to the stove where a pot sat. She raised its lid and stirred the sputtering red sauce. On the floor lay a frying pan with oil. On the counter, a saucepan with chicken stock looked like it would tip over. Everywhere she looked pots and pans idled. Senam hadn't done anything with the lettuce and carrots on the cutting board. Next to them were four plucked whole chickens. Flies flew around them, buzzing in ecstasy. She clasped her fingers behind her neck. Will all this be ready before six? she wondered.

She went out through the tattered net door—she still hadn't replaced the net and the hole had widened. A black Dutch oven stood poised, ready to be lit, with pieces of glistening charcoal. She sighed. Senam should have been grilling the chicken kebabs by now. She trudged back into the kitchen, washed her hands and searched through a drawer under the counter for a knife. She realized that somebody had broken the can opener's handle and taped it. She picked up one of the whole chickens and was about to saw its legs off when Senam came back in.

"Oh, ma," Senam said. "Please don't worry, let me do that."

Lizzie put down the knife. She felt the beginnings of a migraine. She walked out of the kitchen, upstairs to her room. She saw her unmade bed. Clothes were dispersed all over it. Everything was a mess. She pulled forward the first drawer of her mahogany dresser, pushed aside old buttons, CPP badges, camphor balls, syringes and thermometers. She sucked her teeth. She walked into her bathroom. The pale blue walls shone in the afternoon light. She opened the white medicine cabinet and extracted a sachet of aspirin. She took out two tablets, put them gingerly on her tongue, placed her palm under a silver faucet and sucked up water to down them.

When she walked back downstairs, Ernest Jr. ran up to her crying. Where was Asantewa? Their deal was she didn't have to think about the children just this once.

"What's wrong, Junior?"

"I want chips," he said.

"Who has chips?"

"Wame."

"Kwame, Junior. Kwame."

"Yes, Wame."

Lizzie smiled. "Why does Kwame have chips?" she asked, picking him up. She walked outside, where they'd set up a long table, covered in a white cloth printed with the *akoka nan* symbol—it looked like two sickles fused together—a hen's foot. Kwame stood behind the table, his bushy head barely visible, his fingers clawing through a plate of plantain chips. "Kwame!" she yelled, striding toward him. He tried to run, but a flowerpot directly behind him blocked his escape. He held his right hand behind his back. Lizzie put down Ernest Jr., yanked Kwame's hand and smacked it. He started howling. She wanted to pull her hair out. Asantewa appeared from the garden. "Where were you?" she asked.

"Akua and Naa Tsoo want to wear the same dress. I just went to wash Naa Tsoo's."

"You shouldn't let these children bully you." Kwame was still caterwauling. "That one was stealing food…. Asantewa, please deal with them! I'm going back to the kitchen."

The kitchen with all its bubbling stews, rawness and incompleteness was surprisingly the only place she could be calm. Senam was still carving the chicken. She went straight for the drawer under the counter. Picking up a knife, she declared, "I'm making the salad."

"But, ma …"

"Finish the chicken. Have you even marinated a single piece?" She sucked her teeth.

"Sorry," Senam mumbled.

Lizzie grabbed three heads of lettuce and rinsed them repeatedly. Peeling apart each leaf, she tore them into bite-sized pieces and put them in a big brown Pyrex bowl. She felt her headache abate as she sliced onions into rings and diced carrots. She quartered tomatoes. "Where are the baked beans?" she asked Senam.

"Ma, I didn't find any. I looked in all the stores."

"Why didn't you tell me?" Lizzie sucked her teeth again. "Now, what am I going to use? The salad is not complete without baked beans. How's that a salad? Tell me." All right, Lizzie, she said to herself, calm down. She put four eggs in a small green pan, filled it up with water and set it on the stove. Opening the fridge, she extracted bottles of salad cream and ketchup. She saw a tin of tuna by the bowl of lettuce. She walked to the drawer, took out the can opener and pressed its legs together. It broke into two pieces in her hand.

"Senam," she said.

"Ma?"

"Why didn't you tell me about the opener?"

"I'm sorry," Senam whispered.

"How am I supposed to open this?" she asked, pointing the can at Senam. Senam took it, banged at it with a knife and handed the opened can back to Lizzie. "You're going to have to start speaking up, my dear. If you break something, don't let me catch you before you tell me. I'm sure if I hadn't heard those plates you would have pretended nothing happened."

"No …"

"How long has this opener been like this?"

"Ma, I just didn't want to bother you. You've been busy. And I know things have been expensive."

"I'll decide what's too expensive," Lizzie said, looking at the net door. "Just don't hide things from me," she said, softening her tone.

"Yes, ma," Senam said as she doused the chicken in a garlic and ginger marinade.

Lizzie took the eggs off the stove, unshelled them and sliced them into round pieces. She arranged them with the tomatoes, tuna and onions in a colorful mosaic. She spread healthy amounts of salad cream and ketchup over the vegetables and put the bowl of salad in the fridge.

Two hours later, Lizzie was on her way to the kitchen to make sure Senam had finished the chicken, when Ernest came in through the front door, wheezing. Cradling a red crate of beer toward the kitchen, he smiled at Lizzie. He looked weary.

"Are you all right?" she asked, rushing forward to open the kitchen door.

"Yes, I'm fine," he said. Lizzie could tell he wasn't

"Tell me, Ernie," she insisted.

"Oh, it's nothing," he said, lifting the freezer door.

Lizzie shrugged, realizing she wasn't going to get anything from him. "What took you so long?"

"I searched the whole of Accra for a place that had enough coke and beer." She didn't believe him. Ever since finding Gertrude's birth certificate, she couldn't believe anything he told her. Abokyi walked in with a crate of coca cola. She walked toward the stove. A pot of rice was stewing in sauce. The red hotplate under the pot turned grey. She turned the knob of the hotplate. The hotplate stayed grey. She dialed another knob and placed her palm over the matching hotplate. It stayed cold. No, not this now, she thought. She pressed on a switch by the stove. The bulb above her didn't light up.

"Jesus Christ!" she screamed.

"It'll come back," Ernest said, holding up the freezer door. Abokyi was unloading the bottles from the crate into the freezer.

"I can't deal with this!" Lizzie said, storming out of the kitchen. She walked up to Asantewa's room where Akua Afriyie was twisting her dress over her head. Naa Tsoo was copying her sister. "They haven't bathed yet?" she asked Asantewa.

"No."

"OK, then I'll take the girls ..."

"I want to bathe in Auntie's bathroom," Akua Afriyie said.

"Fine!" Lizzie said. This was not the time for one of Akua Afriyie's antics. "I'll take the boys and Tsotsoo." She picked up Tsotsoo from Asantewa's bed. "Come, Kwame. Come, Junior."

They walked into her bedroom. Lizzie placed Tsotsoo on her bed, undressed Kwame and Ernest Jr. She pushed the bathroom door wide open and fetched a bucket of water to bathe both boys. Then she bathed the baby. When they were all washed and clean, she powdered them. Opening a drawer in her armoire, she pulled out new shorts and shirts Ernest had bought them on his last trip to Germany. She took the children back to Asantewa's room. Akua Afriyie and Naa Tsoo were wearing their matching green and yellow dresses.

"I'm going back down to check on things," Lizzie said.

"Relax! Things will go smoothly," Asantewa said.

"I hope so," Lizzie said, putting Tsotsoo in Asantewa's arms.

Downstairs, the photographer had arrived. He stood by the food table, his large camera slung around his neck. He held a plate of chicken in his right hand, a bottle of beer in the other.

"Hello," Lizzie said to him.

"Evening, madam."

"People will start showing up soon," she said, more to reassure herself than the photographer. He was getting paid whether people came or not. What did he care? She walked into the living room and flicked on a switch. The power was back. She went into the kitchen where she found Senam dishing out heaps of rice into a brown Pyrex bowl.

"Thank God that's done," Lizzie said.

"Ma, everything is ready," Senam said.

"Good. Where's uncle?"

"I think he went upstairs."

She hadn't seen him go up. She trudged back up. Ernest stood in front of a mirror, studying his face.

"Are you sure you're all right?"

"Yes, Lizzie. Don't worry."

By seven everyone in the Mensah household was ready for the party. Lizzie, dressed in a long white dress, stood by the food table. It was piled with plates, Pyrex bowls, translucent glasses, cutlery and white napkins.

"Everyone!" Lizzie shouted. "Gather round."

Ernest held Kwame and Ernest Jr.'s hands. Lizzie took Naa Tsoo's hand and balanced Tsotsoo on her hip. Akua Afriyie had draped her long arms around Asantewa's waist. They stood in front of the house. Abokyi and Senam stood by each other, behind the photographer, smiling at the family. Abokyi, towering over Senam and the photographer, wore a black suit, its trousers hanging at his shins. Senam was smartly dressed in a *kaba* and slit.

"Abokyi! Senam!" Lizzie said. "What are you standing there for? Come over!"

After they had moved over to join the family, the photographer bent his torso and held his camera to his face.

"Ready?" he asked them.

"Yes!" they shouted.

A flash of white light blinded Lizzie. For a split second, everything she saw took on indigo and white hues.

"OK, Abokyi and Senam, let's give them their Mensah family photo," Asantewa said, dragging Senam and Abokyi to stand by the photographer. Another flash of blinding light went off.

"Yay!" Naa Tsoo shouted. Asantewa took the children and seated them in the garden.

Lizzie walked around checking that they'd hired enough chairs. She brushed off a mango leaf that had fallen onto one of the metal table-tops. She walked back to the food area and opened a cooler. It was filled with beer and coke surrounded by blocks of ice. She was about to join Asantewa when Ernest walked out with a cigar in his mouth, a glass in hand. A golden liquid floated around a rock of ice in the glass. She glared at him. Whatever was ailing him earlier must have evaporated.

"I hope you're not smoking that," she said.

"No, no," he said. Lizzie heard the gate whine open. She turned around. Mercy and her husband, Kwabena Ntim, were the first to arrive. Kwabena wore a tan-colored suit, Mercy, a simple yellow dress.

"Music!" Lizzie whispered to Ernest. She walked to the gate. "Mercy!" she said, hugging her. "Kwabena! Welcome. Thanks for coming."

"Congratulations, Head Nurse!" Mercy said.

"Thank you, thank you." She led them to Asantewa's table.

"Hello," Asantewa said to the newcomers.

"What will you have?" Lizzie asked.

"A coke," Mercy said. "Do you need any help?"

"No, no! Sit. And for you, Kwabena? Gin? Whiskey?"

"Whiskey," he said, gruffly. What did Mercy see in him? she wondered. He looked stiff, stuffy and like something was stuffed up his…. Oh, the whiskey! she remembered, walking toward the food table.

Ernest strode out of the living room, bopping his head to the trumpet and drum beats of the music he'd just put on.

"Ernie," Lizzie said, "Kwabena wants whiskey. Can you get that for him?"

She picked up a glass and a bottle of coke and danced her way back to Mercy and Kwabena. Ernest walked over with a bottle of Johnnie Walker and two glasses, one brimming with ice. He set the bottle down in the middle of the table.

"Ice?" he asked Kwabena, handing him a cigar he took out of his suit pocket.

"Please. Many thanks for this. Cuban Davidoffs, eh?" he said, admiring and sniffing the *Panetela*. Lizzie wanted to roll her eyes.

"Yes, yes," Ernest said. "It's a No. 2."

Kwabena sucked in his cheeks in approval.

Akua Afriyie, Naa Tsoo and the boys were running around in the garden. Lizzie didn't have the energy to tell them to calm down. She decided to let them have a little fun. She heard the gate open and looked back as two nurses from Korle Bu walked in.

"Be right back," she said, getting up. "Hello! Christie! Hawa!"

"Hello," they chorused back.

"Welcome. Did you find the place easily?"

"Yes," Christie said. "After the *kelewele* seller, it was easy to find."

"We're sitting there," she said, walking back to the others. "This is Ernest, my husband, Asantewa, Mercy and Kwabena," Lizzie said, pointing at each of them. "Christie and Hawa."

"Hello," everyone said.

"Who's singing?" Kwabena asked Ernest sternly.

"Osibisa. You haven't heard of them?" Kwabena shook his head. "They are phenomenal."

"Yes, they are," Kwabena said dryly. "I don't follow highlife much. Give me a good Schubert any day." Lizzie wanted to throw something at him. Mercy giggled.

Half an hour later, a handful of people from Ernest's office showed up. Lizzie stood up. She walked to the food table. She touched the bowl with the *jollof* rice. It was lukewarm. She took it back into the kitchen where Senam was chewing on a chicken bone.

"We have to heat the food again," Lizzie said.

"OK, ma," Senam said, putting down the bone, washing her hands and dashing out of the kitchen. Lizzie went back outside.

"... these students need to stop their 'We want Nkrumah back' whining," Kwabena was saying when she got to the table.

"I'm inclined to agree with the students," Ernest said. "Since Nkrumah was overthrown, our lives have gone downhill."

Lizzie walked to the children. "Akua, Naa, Kwame and Junior!" she shouted.

"Yes, mummy," they screamed, running toward her.

"It's time for dinner!" She walked ahead of them like a mother hen, her brood of four in tow. They went into the living room. Lizzie walked into the kitchen.

"Is everything ready now?" she asked Senam.

"Yes, ma."

"OK, I'll take the food out. Please give the children their dinner."

Outside, only the seats around two tables were full. Lizzie had expected more people. She straightened her dress and strutted over to the tables.

"Food is served!" she announced. "Please help yourselves."

Back at the table, Kwabena bit into a golden-brown drumstick. "Nkrumah, with all his one-party politics, preventive detention acts and socialism, would have turned this country into communist Russia!" he said, pieces of chicken dancing around his teeth.

"But ..." Ernest tried to protest.

"Good heavens!" Kwabena bellowed. "Was he expecting to be president for life?"

"Kwabena, Kwabena ..."

"Somebody had to let the fellow know the country did not belong to him."

"I was no fan of Nkrumah's socialism," Ernest finally managed to say, "but he had a plan for this country. Nobody since him has come up with any ..."

"This is coming from a man who was a critic of Nkrumah when he was in power," Lizzie said, pointing her thumb at Ernest. "You should listen to him!"

"Ho!" Kwabena said. "A plan? It was a plan to make all his ministers rich. He set the precedent for all coming governments of Ghana, I tell you."

"Listen, Kwabena," Ernest said, trying to get a word in, straining his neck. "I had lots of qualms about the one-party state, but what it comes down to is the fact that people voted for the CPP to be the only party in the country. A whole nation of people decided." He took a sip of his whiskey.

"We didn't know what we were doing! In fact, we'd have been better off staying with the British." He pushed his plate back and sniffed the cigar. He reached for a lighter in his suit pocket and held its flame to the cigar. He puffed on the cigar and wispy smoke came out of his mouth.

Ernest choked on his whiskey. "I can't believe you'd say that. The British were sucking us dry, and you'd rather *they* kept doing that?"

Kwabena chewed on the cigar. "Busia, I feel has a …"

"Busia? The man is destroying all the foreign relationships we have. My business is suffering …" Lizzie could see the muscles taut on Ernest's neck. He loosened his tie.

"Ernie, are you OK?" she asked him.

"It's just a little hot, isn't it?" he asked, clutching his chest with his left hand. "I can't breathe …" he said, standing up.

"Ernie!" Lizzie shrieked. Ernest stroked his neck. His eyes watered. "He's having an attack," she said. "Kwabena, can you drive us to Korle Bu?"

"Of course."

"Asantewa, if more people show up, tell them we'll be back soon."

Mercy, Kwabena and Lizzie rushed Ernest to the back seat of Kwabena's car.

Lizzie sat by him. "Breathe in slowly," she said. Lizzie took off his suit and unbuttoned his shirt. Kwabena sped to Korle Bu.

In the hospital, Lizzie steered the group through the emergency ward. She knew she should have gone through the reception, but she wasn't taking any chances. They might say there was no room. Besides, she was head nurse, wasn't she? She pushed open the door to a private room. A man was asleep in there. She went to the next room.

"Are you here to give …" a weak voice said.

"No, sorry," Lizzie said and closed the door. She opened the door to a third room. It was empty. She led Ernest to the bed. She rushed to the nurses' room.

"Good evening, Lydia," she said.

"Ei, Lizzie," the nurse responded, putting down her knitting, "how come you're here tonight?"

"My husband is in room three. He's having an asthma attack. He needs a drip." The nurse followed Lizzie to Ernest's room.

"Did you get assigned this room?" Lydia asked, her brow raised.

"No. But, don't worry. I'm going to fill out his hospital card."

When Lizzie got back, Mercy and Kwabena were seated on a bench outside Ernest's room.

"I hope none of this was my fault," Kwabena said. "With the cigar and all …"

"No. Don't worry," Lizzie said. "Any changes?"

"The nurse said we should let him sleep," Mercy said. "Lizzie, Kwabena was telling me that one of his cousins was asthmatic. The only way they cured it was to go to a traditional healer." Lizzie shook her head. "It won't hurt to try them."

Still shaking her head, Lizzie said, "We've been managing fine. I don't know what happened today but I don't think traditional medicine has the answer to our problems."

"Just think about it," Mercy said.

"You two don't have to stay here all night. We'll take a taxi home."

"Nonsense!" Kwabena said. "We'll stay here with you."

Lydia walked to Ernest's room two hours later. She poked her head out of the room. "He's fine now," she said.

Lizzie, Mercy and Kwabena walked in. Ernest sat up, grinning. An IV drip stood by his bed, its tubes plastered to his hand. He doubled over in laughter and ended in a fit of coughing.

"Remember, this is how I met you," he said to Lizzie. "Only, you were injecting my ..."

"That's what you get for mixing alcohol, politics and cigars," she interrupted. Ernest was still laughing. "Ernest you're not going to Germany this year. We're going to go to Adukrom No. 2, to find out about this asthma of yours." She looked at Mercy who was beaming.

"What about the business?"

"Do you want to die running back and forth between Germany and here?"

"No, boss," Ernest said. "You always get so bossy in the hospital."

"I'm serious," she said. We're going to find a cure once and for all. You have Mercy and Kwabena to thank for getting you here before you passed out."

"Many thanks," Ernest said. Lizzie looked at him. She didn't understand how he got so giggly in the hospital. And a grown man too! This year she was taking him away from his Gertrude and whoever her mother was.

Eleven
Adukrom No. 2

August 1971

Ernest sat in the driver's seat of the Pontiac tapping his fingers on the steering wheel. Lizzie packed Akua Afriyie, Naa Tsoo, Kwame and Ernest Jr. onto the back seat. She looked back at Abokyi who was grinning, holding on to the open gate. She sighed. It was a sigh filled with nostalgia. It was a sigh swathed in fear so strong, she was ready to cancel this whole trip.

"Aren't you ready?" Ernest asked her.

"I am," Lizzie said as she opened the passenger seat door, surprised at his testiness. She sat down, rested Tsotsoo in her lap. All their suitcases were packed in the trunk. Tsotsoo's baby food was safely stored in the snakeskin bag at her feet. She'd taken enough clothes for the children. "Ernie," she said, "at the gate, let me have a word with Abokyi."

"Make it snappy."

"All right." And what is wrong with this one? she wondered. Abokyi stuck his head through the window. "Abokyi," she said, drawing her own head back. "We'll be away for two weeks. As usual, don't let anyone in. And don't tell them we've traveled. Just tell them we've gone to work."

"Is this necessary?" Ernest asked. Lizzie eyed him.

"Yes," she said.

"Abokyi, if my mother comes by you can let her in."

"Yes, massa!"

Lizzie eyed him again. "OK, that's it. Senam will give you your food. Make sure to water the plants! Bye!"

"Safe trip!" Abokyi said, smiling.

"Bye, Abokyi," the children chorused from the backseat.

"And what's ailing you?" Lizzie asked.

"Have you looked at the time? We're going to get stuck in that Nsawam Road traffic. And we still have to pass by Asantewa's. Do we have to?"

"Yes, I have to give her the keys." She sucked her teeth and looked out the window. She was nervous enough as it was, and now Ernest was acting strangely.

They drove through Mallam Attah's gated entrance. The market bustled with women slinging baskets around their arms, market women haggling and calling for customers. Ernest slowed down. In front of them walked a woman in a blue and green cloth, her head wrap held high, her buttocks swaying to the beat of the morning.

"This one. Stop!" Lizzie shouted and pointed at an oily blue store-front.

"Give me the keys," Ernest said.

"I was going to ..." Lizzie actually liked this side of Ernest. She'd never seen him take control of any situation like he was doing now. He strode into Asantewa's store. In his peach-colored shirt, slightly flared burgundy trousers, he exuded a somewhat cocky air. His hair was over-grown with its parting on the right. Straining her neck to look into Asantewa's store, she noticed a lot of the shelves were empty. Boxes sat on the floor. Lizzie waved at Asantewa from the car.

Asantewa walked over with Ernest. "Thanks," she said.

"I put the money for Senam and Abokyi under your door."

"OK," Asantewa said.

Ernest was back in the car.

"Let's see, what else?" Lizzie said, trying hard not to notice Ernest glaring at her. She was sure he was seething now. A part of her was trying to delay this trip as much as possible. "You might have to keep an eye out for Abokyi and those plants. Either he doesn't water them or he floods them with water. Any messages for Papa Yaw or Mama Efua?"

"Give them my love. Safe journey!"

"See you in two weeks!" Lizzie said.

Ernest muttered something under his breath. "Ready?" he asked loudly.

"Yes."

He drove to an Agip filling station close to the market. All four of the transparent petrol dispensers were empty. A bored attendant sitting under the awning of the station's mart lazily waved at them.

"No petrol!" he shouted.

Ernest sucked his teeth. They drove to two other filling stations and heard the same story. The only place with petrol was at the Kwame Nkrumah Circle, an attendant told them at the last place.

Lizzie saw a line of cars snake out of the station. It wasn't even a line. It was chaos as taxi drivers tried to cut in. Lizzie felt ashamed. But only fleetingly. Every minute they spent in the queue delayed the moment of arrival in Adukrom No. 2.

"This is exactly what I was trying to avoid," Ernest said.

"Sorry," Lizzie said. She turned round. She made sure the children were well dressed especially for today—Akua Afriyie and Naa Tsoo in their matching yellow A-line dresses and the boys in their button-down white shirts and tan trousers. "You all look lovely," she said to them.

"Thank you," they chorused.

"I still don't understand, Mamaa," Akua Afriyie said, "why I had to wear the same dress as Naa Tsoo."

"Because she likes you and wants to be just like you," Lizzie said.

"But she's eight and I'm ten. We can't wear the same things."

"Akua, it's too late to complain now." Lizzie looked forward, avoiding Ernest's eyes. She could feel the hostility emanating from him, like the heat in the air on a harmattan afternoon. The car ahead of them inched forward. Ernest closed the gap. Tsotsoo gurgled. Lizzie rocked her. She felt the muggy heat rising the longer they stayed in the queue. "Maybe there'll be petrol along the way," she said.

"I'm not taking any chances," Ernest snapped at her.

By the time they'd filled up it was a quarter past ten.

"All right, gang," Ernest said, "to Adukrom No. 2 we go!"

Lizzie looked at him. She was amazed at how fast his mood switched. Maybe it was her fault, taking him away from Gertrude.

He drove along Nsawam Road, parts of which had been washed away by the recent flooding in Accra. The Pontiac bumped in and out of a huge crack in the earth. Tsotsoo wailed.

"Shhh!" Lizzie said, rocking her in her arms. She tried to imagine what Adukrom No. 2 had become. She was sure it looked the same. Papa Yaw's house must not have changed. She hoped they hadn't cut down the *khaya* tree. The air rushing in was blowing the curls on her head into her face. As she rolled up the window, she was fascinated at the number of new houses being built along the Nsawam Road.

As if he'd read her thoughts Ernest said, "In a few years, this area will be considered Accra."

They drove for an hour. Fear gripped Lizzie's tongue.

"You're quiet today," Ernest said.

"I'm nervous. Wouldn't you be?"

"It'll be fine."

"And why are you being nice to me now? At nine this morning you were behaving like a certain German person I shall not name."

"I just wanted us to leave on time."

"German temperament coming in, huh?" Lizzie said, looking at the roadside, a continuous sea of green. The farther they drove from Accra, the higher the grass grew. The more the road undulated, the taller the trees became. A thick cloud Lizzie hadn't seen coming burst open, sending down a flash of rain, wetting the tarmac, washing their car and leaving droplets on all the windows.

"Wow," Akua Afriyie said. "It only rained on that part of the road."

"Mummy, I want to weewee," Naa Tsoo said.

"Me too," Kwame said.

"Me too," Ernest Jr. repeated.

Lizzie looked at Ernest. "Can we stop?" she asked.

"We're almost at the Nkawkaw Rest Stop," Ernest said.

"Everybody count to ten and hold your weewee. Let's go, one, two …"

The children counted with Lizzie. The loudest voice was Ernest Jr.'s and he didn't even know how to count. His two-year-old babble floated above the other children's voices.

"Waa, waa, ten!"

At Nkawkaw, a little town buzzing with *trotros*, private sedans and taxis coming and going, passengers milling about, hawkers screaming their wares, Ernest pulled up behind a white mammy lorry.

Lizzie took the girls, Ernest, the boys. A narrow gutter ran through the women's urinal. The shallow depression reeked of urine. Two women squatted, the rush of their released waters flowing through the gutter.

"Don't wet your panties," Lizzie said to Akua Afriyie and Naa Tsoo. She watched Akua Afriyie spread her legs over the gutter, pull her panties down, raise her A-line dress, show her pudendum to the whole world, and then sit on her haunches. Her urine splashed into the gutter, spraying her white sandals. Lizzie shook her head. Naa Tsoo looked ready to copy her older sister. Lizzie wondered when the mimicry would end. Akua Afriyie, in her opinion, was hardly a suitable role model. She passed Tsotsoo to Akua Afriyie. "Don't drop her, Akua," Lizzie warned. She squatted, hiked up her pink *boubou* and unleashed a torrent of liquid she herself had been holding in. She took Tsotsoo from Akua Afriyie's arms, studied her girls to make sure they were still presentable. Why they don't build these places with sinks, I don't understand, she thought. "Let's go get Papa and the boys," she said.

The boys were already at the car.

"Maybe we should eat now," she said.

"Now?" Ernest asked.

"I don't want us to stop again after here," Lizzie said. Her current state of mind reminded her of her nursing school days. After exams she was always gripped with the worst feeling that she'd failed. She wanted nothing to do with the results. Soon after, rising above the fear, she felt a surge of excitement, a sadistic yearning to see what her results were, no matter how good or bad they were. Now her sadistic yearning for Adukrom No. 2 was surfacing. She wanted to show off her new family. Show off who she'd become. If they accepted her, fine. If they didn't, fine. Ernest popped open the trunk. She strode over to his side and took out a bottle of water and the basket Senam had prepared with tuna sandwiches.

With Ernest leading the way, the family walked toward the main rest stop building. Lizzie handed him the basket.

"Everyone over here! Time to wash your hands." She crowded the children around her and poured the water in the bottle over their fingers.

They walked into a concrete open space swarming with travelers, drivers and young women hawking oranges and bottled drinks. Ernest stood by a grey bench and table. The children slid along the bench.

"Sssss," Ernest called out to a girl balancing a silver tray of oranges on her head as she peeled an orange in a spiral. "Six oranges, please."

"One new cedi," the girl said, slicing the tops off the oranges.

"Thank you," Ernest said, handing her a rumpled note.

Lizzie picked out paper plates from the basket and placed one in front of each child. She distributed the sandwiches on the plates.

She caught Ernest Jr. stuffing his mouth with his sandwich. "Junior! A bite at a time," she said.

"Wame did some," Ernest Jr. said.

"Kwame, don't stuff your mouth!" She looked around the enclosure. Two men were smoking. They kept studying their cigarettes before lifting them to their lips.

"… these made in Ghana cigarettes are really no good," one of them said.

"I know, man. What is Busia going to ban next? Fresh air?" They burst into peals of laughter. She looked at Ernest.

"It's true," he said. "The government is not letting us bring anything in. Not even pens! If I'd gone to Germany, I could have found a way."

"Sorry," Lizzie said. She felt bad, but not entirely. Germany was now a sore spot. Germany was Gertrude. Lizzie bundled the children back into the car.

As they drove on, her stomach knotted over. She couldn't remember the turning to Adukrom No. 2, especially coming from this direction. In her Suaadie Girls days, she'd come from the north down. Now they were coming up from the south. There was a cedar tree close to the entrance with one colossal branch pointing down. That was her landmark. She stared intently at all the approaching trees.

It was in the search for the one-armed cedar that she saw the accident.

"Close your eyes, children," she said.

A huge timber truck had indented half of a white mammy lorry and blocked off half of the road. Ernest drove slowly by the accident. People were pulling out wounded persons from the windows of the lorry. Lizzie could feel her insides scraping, as if she was the one being rescued. She looked back at her children. They were gawking out the window.

"Didn't I tell you to close your eyes?" she shouted. "Close your eyes! Ernie, drive carefully," she said. She looked back through the rearview mirror. "That was horrible."

They drove in silence, Lizzie's insides still itching. Fear rose in her again. Now she wanted to delay their arrival. She thought about everything Adukrom No. 2 stood for: Bador Samed. Papa Yaw. Her past. How was this all going to go down? she wondered. Looming in the distance, to the left of the road was the one-armed cedar. It stood grey, its bark gnarled, its crown completely leafless.

"Turn right," Lizzie said. The road to Adukrom No. 2 was now tarred. Most of the trees that had covered the entrance had disappeared. The village looked small, sparser than she remembered it. Corrugated tin roofs had replaced the thatch on most of the homes. A few new houses were in places she didn't remember and were built of cement. "You can park by that tree," she said, pointing to a neem tree. Emotion rose up in her, swelled in her chest. She didn't want to cry. She opened the door for the children to pour out. They ran forward as if they knew the place. "Behave yourselves," she shouted, regaining her composure.

She looked back at Ernest who was unloading their suitcases, placing them on the laterite ground. She walked over, balanced Tsotsoo and the snakeskin bag in one hand and picked up a suitcase with the other.

The children cantered about.

"Stop running!" she said, striding forward.

The neem tree just outside Papa Yaw's compound was still standing. Lizzie looked at the tree, its leaves rustling. Its lemon-green neem fruits hung like little pearls from the branches. She shivered.

She stared at the entrance. The last she'd seen of it was when Papa Yaw walked back to her shadowed suitor. She walked into the compound trailed by her family.

Two girls, about Akua Afriyie's age, sat across from each other, their legs spread out, empty tomato paste cans gathered between their thighs. They were now staring at Lizzie and her family.

"Is Mama Efua in?" Lizzie asked.

They didn't respond. One of the girls, in a yellow checked dress, stood up. Cans fell from her dress and clanged against the ground. She ran into Efua Serwah's hut, behind an orange-print curtain. Lizzie looked back at Ernest. His eyes were encouraging. Even the children were standing still, as if they too understood what this moment meant.

Dark chocolate fingers parted the curtain. Out stepped Efua Serwah. She stood tall, her frame still slender. Her skin was tauter against her bones, yet in that tautness age was spelt like the growth rings in the bark of a tree. Her eyes seemed tired. Her hair was tied with black thread that didn't mask her grey tresses. Efua Serwah seemed to be studying the group in front of her. She looked at Lizzie, her eyes flashing briefly with recognition. She went on, studying each member of the family. Her eyes reddened, tears ran from the corners of her eyes. Lizzie turned to give Ernest the baby. She walked toward her mother, who had now placed her right hand over her mouth. Lizzie wrapped her arms around Efua Serwah's waist.

"Thank you, God!" Efua Serwah said quietly. She now embraced Lizzie, her arms rubbing her back. She leaned back, kissed Lizzie on both cheeks. Lizzie was also crying.

"Daddy, why is mummy crying?" Lizzie heard Naa Tsoo ask Ernest.

Ernest shushed her. Lizzie turned around, waving her hand in front of her face. "Come say hello to Mama Efua," she said. All four children ran forward and wrapped their arms around Efua Serwah's legs.

"They are beautiful," Efua Serwah said, sucking the phlegm that was stuck in her throat. "And this must be your husband." She beckoned him toward her. Ernest gave Lizzie Tsotsoo. Efua Serwah hugged Ernest. "Welcome, my son," she said.

"Where's Papa Yaw?" Lizzie asked, looking around the compound.

"He's out somewhere," Efua Serwah said, taking Tsotsoo out of Lizzie's arms. "What will you drink? Some palm wine?" she asked Ernest.

"Yes, please."

"Bring stools," Efua Serwah said to the girl who'd called her out.

"Akua, go help her," Lizzie said. Akua Afriyie reluctantly trudged behind the girl who could be her cousin or auntie. "Who's the girl?" she asked Efua Serwah.

"Owusua?" Lizzie felt a sharp pang. She wished she hadn't asked. "That's Mama Ama's granddaughter," her mother said. Of Papa Yaw's other wives, Mama Ama was the one Lizzie liked the least. She was always competing with Mama Efua, who was first wife. "I've been dreaming about this day since April 1954," Efua Serwah said. "The only way I could survive was knowing you were fine from the letters you wrote Asantewa. How is she?"

"She's started a business. She's doing very well." Lizzie wasn't going to tell her about the empty shelves. That life in Accra was hard. That getting people to spend money was what both Asantewa and Ernest were battling with. Tsotsoo yawned widely. Her mouth had barely closed when she reopened it in a loud cry, showing ridged pink gums.

"She's hungry," Efua Serwah said, handing her back to her mother.

Lizzie pulled her breast over her *boubou*'s low neckline and put her nipple in Tsotsoo's mouth.

"Owusua," Efua Serwah said. "Go buy one bottle of palm wine and six coca colas."

"Yes, Mama Efua," Owusua said, dragging Akua Afriyie by her wrist. Naa Tsoo stood up and ran behind Akua Afriyie and Owusua. The boys sat on the ground by the other girl playing with cans.

"Wame, Wame!" Ernest Jr. said. "I want some." He pointed at the cans.

Lizzie laughed. At first she wanted to tell them to get off the filthy floor. But, she remembered this is where her beginnings were. She had played on that same ground. This was who she was.

Ernest unzipped one of the smaller suitcases and lifted its flap. It landed in the dust. "Something small," he said, removing boxes of chocolates, tea, soaps and fabric. He handed Efua Serwah a box of tea.

"This is too much," Efua Serwah said, her eyes clouding over with tears. "Thank you."

When Lizzie had fed Tsotsoo, she stuffed her breast back under her *boubou.* "What's new in Adukrom No. 2?" she asked.

"A lot! Remember Koo Manu?" Lizzie nodded. "He died last year," she said. "His family didn't have the money to have a proper funeral. Papa Yaw had to loan them money." Papa Yaw had enough money to lend to someone? "All the young girls are married," Efua Serwah went on. "Remember the Aduhene's last wife?"

"The young one?"

"Yes. She left him. I think she moved to Accra too." Efua Serwah touched her aquiline nose, rubbed the pointed end with her thumb and index finger. She always did that.

"What did the Aduhene do?"

"The man is a fool!" Efua Serwah whispered. "He married again! And he beats the girl like no one's business." Lizzie winced. Papa Yaw beat you too, she thought. "And you? How's Accra?"

"The pictures," Lizzie said to Ernest, who took an album out of a pocket of the suitcase. He gave them to Efua Serwah.

"Oh, beautiful," she said.

"This was the first picture we took together as a family," Lizzie said. "We were having a party that day and I had a professional photographer come over."

As Efua Serwah flipped through the photos, Lizzie heard shuffling at the entrance. She looked up and saw Papa Yaw. His hair was completely grey, except for a bald shiny spot above his forehead. She didn't remember him being bald.

"Ei, you're still alive," he said, his eyes darting from Lizzie to Ernest to the boys playing on the ground.

"That's no way to welcome your daughter," Efua Serwah said.

"Sorry, for my rudeness," he said. "Welcome." He walked to Ernest and shook his hand. He shook Lizzie's limply and walked into his hut.

"We can drive to Kumasi to stay in a hotel if we'll be a bother," Lizzie said.

"Ah, Lizzie-Achiaa! Don't tell me that because you live in Accra, you're now an *obroni.* Family stays here."

Papa Yaw came back out. "Your husband can sleep in my room." Lizzie's eyes popped open. She looked at her mother and wondered if Papa Yaw wasn't hatching some evil plan.

"Thank you, sir," Ernest said.

"What a proper family," Papa Yaw said, chuckling. "Sir! Lizzie-Achiaa married an *obroni*," he said to his wife. He chuckled back to his room.

During dinner, the family sat on stools in three groups, around the three wives. In Mama Efua's circle, Ernest sat by Papa Yaw, the boys to his left. Owusua had hijacked Akua Afriyie, and of course, Naa Tsoo sat by her. Lizzie didn't know half the faces in the other circles. She caught Mama Ama looking over every so often. Lizzie licked the spinach stew off her hand. Kwame and Ernest Jr. were bound to get palm oil on their shirts. Stop worrying! she told herself. She looked up. The sky above, already indigo, darkened.

After dinner, she took the children into Efua Serwah's room. It wasn't like she remembered. A queen-sized bed had replaced the mat Efua Serwah used to sleep on. On top of a dresser she'd placed dusting powder, shea butter and little bottles of perfume. They didn't seem to be struggling.

The next day, after their *koko* and bread, Papa Yaw who'd been whistling since he came out of his room, offered to take them to Opanyin Nti's.

Papa Yaw, Lizzie and Ernest walked by young girls sweeping through dust with palm frond brooms. The girls stopped as the trio walked by.

"Have you lost something?" Papa Yaw asked them, sucking his teeth. Lizzie wondered what her father had against young girls. He just always seemed to be inordinately rude to them.

They arrived at Opanyin Nti's hut. It was exactly the way she remembered it—woven from palm fronds and strong branches blown off trees during thunderstorms. She remembered running there when Owusua fell to the ground, writhing. How she'd met Bador Samed for the first time. How she was instantly intoxicated in his strangeness and foreignness.

"Opanyin!" Papa Yaw shouted.

The medicine man walked out. Like his home, he hadn't changed. Sure, his hair was entirely grey, but his face looked, if anything, younger than before. He moved about stridently, with verve and with a vibrancy that none of the older people in the village possessed.

"Who is this?" he said, smiling broadly. "When did you come back?" He looked at Lizzie, shaking Papa Yaw's hand. He moved on to shake Lizzie and Ernest's hands.

"Yesterday," Lizzie said.

"Come in, come in," he said, arranging four stools in his cool hut. "So?" he asked.

"Opanyin," Lizzie said, "this is my husband Ernest. He's been asthmatic for so many years. We've tried all sorts of drugs, but nothing's worked …" She looked at Ernest.

"Yes," Ernest said, "two months or so ago, I had a really bad attack. We were hoping you could help," he said, fiddling with the top button of his shirt.

"All right," Opanyin Nti said, "I'd like a word with Ernest here."

"We'll wait outside," Papa Yaw suggested.

"No, no. We'll just go into my inner room." Opanyin Nti said, springing up from his stool, leading Ernest into the darkened room.

Papa Yaw and Lizzie hadn't been alone yet. Now he looked at her, a smirk raising the right corner of his lips.

"Lizzie," he whispered, "who is this Ga man who can't breathe properly? Is this the best you can do? Some man with some disease?"

Lizzie bit her tongue. The man always had to find a way to dampen her spirits. "Papa Yaw, please don't start," she said. This man with a disease has built me a house you'll never see, she thought. "We have five healthy children. We live comfortably. He has a good job," Lizzie said, wondering why she should be making any excuses. Ernest was better than any suitor Papa Yaw would have offered her.

Opanyin Nti and Ernest came out fifteen minutes later.

"We've talked about Ernest's health history," Opanyin Nti said. "I have a remedy."

"Good," Lizzie said, clapping her hands, even though she was doubtful.

"I have to make soup, though, and it will take time. Come back this afternoon."

After they'd gone back to the compound, Papa Yaw went into his hut and came back out.

"Can I have a word with you, Lizzie?" he asked, while Efua Serwah played with her grandchildren. Ernest sat by her. Lizzie wondered what that could be about, hopefully not about Ernest.

"Of course, Papa," she said. "I'll be back," she said to her mother and husband.

Papa Yaw didn't say anything as he strode ahead of her. She looked around as they passed by houses that stood on ground that used to be bush. She realized they were walking toward his farm. Was he going to ask her for money? That would be her ultimate victory. When she saw his farm, she was even more convinced. It was a shambles. Long dried grass covered most of the area. Only half the number of cocoa trees that they'd planted in the fifties seemed to be left standing.

"What happened here?" she asked him.

"Oh, don't worry about the farm," he said.

"But, Papa Yaw, how do you get money?"

"I've retired," he said. "My children take good care of me." He knew how to get her goat—she hadn't sent him a pesewa since she left. "But that's not why I brought you here. I have something to get off my chest."

"What's this about?" Lizzie asked, beginning to get worried the man might start beating her, even though this time she would definitely have the upper hand. She could smell palm wine on him. He'd probably imbibed so much of the stuff that it coursed through his veins now.

"You've managed to do well for yourself," he said. Lizzie looked at him incredulously. Had she heard him right? "I have to tell you ..." he faltered. "All those years ago," he said, his eyes distant, "I wanted you to marry someone I chose, but you made the right decision. Even though your husband can't breathe well, he seems like a gentleman. *Mo!* You have a beautiful family." She couldn't believe that her father had actually uttered those words. This moment was what she'd come back to Adukrom No. 2 for. They walked back to Papa Yaw's compound, where Ernest stood at the entrance, looking out for them.

"There you are!" Ernest said. "I'm sure Opanyin Nti has finished brewing his soup."

Lizzie smiled. "I was catching up with my father." Papa Yaw seemed to have a sad expression on his face. How could saying something nice about her make him so sad? Lizzie wondered. He was too proud.

They walked to Opanyin Nti's. Lizzie walked in a daze—having her father's opinion of her be so high was, really, what she'd been living for. Now, there was only one problem left for her to solve.

In Opanyin Nti's hut, the medicine man offered them seats. He brought out a steaming pot of soup. It smelled delicious. She watched as he took a tortoise shell, turned it over and ladled the orange soup into the shell.

"There's turtle oil in the soup," Opanyin Nti said. "Drinking from this bowl will cure you." He passed the shell to Ernest, who took a sip and gagged. "Drink up," Opanyin Nti said, as if Ernest was a child refusing dinner.

Ernest gulped down all the soup in one go. After barely a minute, he retched violently. He waved his hand under his chin. Lizzie and Opanyin Nti helped him outside the hut where he threw up all the soup, the *koko* he had eaten that morning, as well as bits and pieces Lizzie couldn't make out. What had he been eating in her absence?

"Is this working?" she asked the medicine man.

"Exactly like it should," he said. "Take him home, let him rest. He's going to vomit the entire day. Tomorrow bring him back for more soup. We'll do this for three days."

"Yes, Opanyin," she said. Ernest continued to heave, his whole torso shaking. This better work, Lizzie thought.

*

On the fourth day after the turtle soup treatment, Ernest walked out of Papa Yaw's hut, beaming. It was the first day since imbibing Opanyin Nti's concoction that Lizzie had seen him smile. He wasn't retching or holding onto his abdomen. She was amazed at how this was also the first time a healer had subdued his spirit. She remembered all the times in Korle Bu, when he'd just end up in giggling fits.

"You look well," she said.

"Have never felt better," he said. "I can breathe without a wheeze getting in the way." Wonders never cease! Lizzie thought. She had been convinced Opanyin Nti's medicine wouldn't work.

"Let's take a walk then," she said. She walked into her mother's room, where she found Efua Serwah lying on her bed, surrounded by her grandchildren. "Junior!" Lizzie shouted, as she saw him twiddle his grandmother's big toe.

"I'm their nana," Efua Serwah said.

"If you're not firm with these children, they'll bully you," Lizzie said. "You should see how they walk all over Asantewa. I'm going for a walk with Ernest."

"All right," Efua Serwah said.

"Bye!" the children chorused.

She hooked her arm in Ernest's as they left Papa Yaw's compound.

"Where are we going?"

"I'm going to show you my favorite place in the whole world." And we're going to have a tête-à-tête, Lizzie thought. She was going to deal with her other problem.

"I'm honored, Mrs. Mensah," Ernest said.

They walked behind the compound, on a laterite path.

"All this used to be grass," Lizzie said. "They get rid of the grass and leave sand that just stains your feet!" She sucked her teeth. She could hear the gargle of the Insu River before they got to it. Nostalgia swam about her.

There it stood. The *khaya* tree. Her *khaya* tree. Hers and Bador Samed's.

"This is it!" she said, pointing up and down the tall trunk. The Insu River bubbled by. It was smaller than she'd imagined it.

"Wow!" Ernest said. "This tree goes up to heaven!"

They settled at the base of the tree, where she and Bador used to have their long conversations, where Lizzie had experienced love for the first time. Of course, Ernest didn't need to know that.

"Ernie," she said, "is there anything you want to tell me?"

"Like what? You're the best wife a man could ask for? Thanks for bringing me here, showing me how great your family is, and for clearing my chest!"

They remained silent. Lizzie hoped Ernest would break down and confess, but he had no idea that she knew, so why would he? A forest bird cuckooed.

"I'm such a city man," Ernest said. "I love being here, but I miss the smell of pollution and the sound of taxi drivers honking insanely. You must miss the sounds of the forest living in Accra. *Trotro* mates shouting, market women haggling …"

"Ernest, I have a question and please don't lie to me," she said. Ernest looked at her with such a sad look, she wished she wasn't about to say what she was. "Who's Gertrude Mensah?"

Ernest choked. "How do you know about Gertrude?"

"Accra is a small place. People talk."

Ernest scratched his head.

"No playing around, just the truth," Lizzie said.

"That's strange. Only one or two people know about her," he said quietly. Lizzie wasn't going to tell him she broke into his briefcase. "She's my daughter."

"That much I knew. When were you planning to tell me?"

Ernest, now looking at the damp loam, said, "She was born before we met. Her mother is German. I just didn't want to mix flavors."

"Mix flavors? Ernest, you should have told me before we got married. I wouldn't have said no just because you already had a child. A part of me thinks that you haven't told me because you're still seeing her mother."

"No, no," Ernest said, still looking down.

Lizzie wasn't convinced. "You are divorced from her mother, aren't you?"

"Oh, yes, before we got married. She was my boss's daughter."

"The Lutterodt guy?"

"Yes."

"Did you feel like you had to marry his daughter because of all that he'd done for you?" Lizzie asked, thinking that if Ernest said yes to that question, Gertrude and her mother wouldn't be as important in Ernest's life. They were just there to return a favor.

"No. We genuinely loved each other. When I met her in 1951, she was the first white woman I was ever attracted to. But you know, you might love someone dearly, but you just can't live together. You just don't work. That's what happened to us." That was far from the answer Lizzie was hoping to hear.

"Do you still love her?"

"Lizzie!"

"Answer me!"

"It's not easy to stop loving someone. Especially when you have a bond like a child. But I love you so much more," he said. She was not happy.

"So you were planning on keeping your daughter a secret forever?"

"Honestly," he said, exhaling, "I was. I thought I could keep both worlds separate."

"Ernie," Lizzie said, "I hate to say this, but she's going to want to know where her father is from. Everyone has two histories. And keeping her away from here is depriving her of half her life story. She has all these crazy sisters and brothers. One who cannot pronounce a single word properly, but insists on talking. Another who insists on fighting with me every opportunity she gets."

"What you say is true…." Ernest said, smiling.

"If you want to bring her to Ghana ever, she can stay with us." Ernest looked at Lizzie. They hugged each other, under the *khaya* tree, the tree that seventeen years ago spelled a different destiny for Lizzie.

*

Lizzie was mentally and physically exhausted. As they left Adukrom No. 2, too many thoughts were running through her mind, some good, like Papa Yaw's approval and others not so great, like Ernest's other daughter. She had to start sending money to Papa Yaw and she wanted to build a clinic in Adukrom No. 2. She had to tame Akua Afriyie's wildness and make sure the other children stopped mimicking her. She turned to look at her.

"You start boarding school next year, Akua," she said. "You're going to have to stop playing with your little brothers and sisters and start behaving like a big girl." Akua Afriyie glared at her. "What do you want to be, when you're as big as your Papa and me?"

"An artist," Akua Afriyie said, looking out the window again.

"You won't make any money," Lizzie said. "You should think about becoming a doctor or a lawyer, OK?"

"You're not a doctor. Papa's not a lawyer. Why can't I be an artist?" she asked, pouting.

"Because artists are poor," Lizzie said, her conclusion final.

***

PART TWO

Twelve
Silver and Gold

October 1978

Akua Afriyie liked to think she was a simple girl living a simple life. She sat in the passenger seat of Eunice's father's silver BMW, hugging an orange raffia bag. She looked at Eunice clasping the steering wheel with her left hand, her fingernails bright red, tapping her thigh with the other.

Akua Afriyie stared out the window. Grey clouds hung low in the sky, kissed occasionally by groves of coconut. Every so often blocks of houses being constructed came into her view. She shifted her gaze to the side mirror through which she saw Dede's round face pressed against Fati's shoulder. Akua Afriyie loved road trips. She was looking forward to lying on the beach, sketching and being entertained by her crazy friends.

"Charle, the sun better come out," Eunice said, rubbing her cheek, the color of a ripe mango.

"I know," Akua Afriyie said. Yes, it was the simple life.

"I hope there are cute boys around," Eunice said.

"That's all you think of. You're so boy crazy. And to think you have a boyfriend."

"I was thinking of you," Eunice said and tapped her steering wheel. "Since you broke up with what's-his-name eons ago, you've become this old maid."

"Kwakye."

"Yeah, yeah, I know."

"What about those two sleeping beauties?" Akua Afriyie asked nudging her head toward the backseat. "They don't have boyfriends either."

"I won't even get started on them. I'm talking about you. You're my accomplice and I miss you being fun and boyfriended."

"I have better things to think about," Akua Afriyie said.

"Like what?"

"Like what I'm doing with my life. Now, if you don't mind, I'm going to read. I've seen enough of Accra's urban sprawl," she said, reached into her bag and pulled out a Wonder Woman comic book. She did feel alone, but she was tired of immature boys who didn't know who they were and who only did things to prove themselves to their immature friends. And all they did was complicate life.

"You're driving back to Accra, just so you know," Eunice said. "And I'll ignore you while you drive."

"If you want your father's car to return in one piece you'd think twice about that," Akua Afriyie said, opening the page she'd bookmarked with her father's forest green business card. *Ernest's fine goods.* Her thoughts drifted off. She had a few months of secondary school left, after which she wanted to go to art school. Her father's business friend told her to consider the Rhode Island School of Art and Design. She'd have to get pictures taken of her work, find out about studying in America…. So much to do so little time, she thought, as her eye lids drooped, lulling her into a doze.

"Oh, ho!" Eunice shouted, startling her awake.

"What?" Akua Afriyie asked, wiping the corners of her mouth. Dede and Fati also woke up.

"Another checkpoint," Eunice said. "This is the fourth and we haven't even left Accra. Akua Afriyie, please give me ten cedis."

Fati sucked her teeth. "You know what? This is ridiculous," she said. "Corruption in this country is out of control. If the bloody SMC paid these bloody policemen …"

"I think they're soldiers," Dede volunteered.

"Well, if they paid them properly, we wouldn't have to do their bloody job for them," she said. "You take over in coup, you better take care of your bloody people!"

"They're planning on handing over to a civilian government soon," Dede said. "Maybe things will get better then."

"Ever the optimist, aren't you?" Fati said.

"I'm sure half these people aren't even real soldiers," Akua Afriyie said.

"So true!" Dede said.

Eunice drove to the checkpoint, a horizontal wooden bar that blocked two-thirds of the road that was nailed to a small concrete building on the right. Two men in green military fatigues with AK-47s strapped around their arms stood by the building. The shorter of the two walked to the car.

"Yong laydays," he said, leaning into Eunice's window. "Where to?"

"The beach," Eunice said.

"Your license. You laydays want to take us with you?" Akua Afriyie was trying to keep a straight face. She looked in the side mirror. Dede had pursed her lips into a fish face. Akua Afriyie snorted and Dede burst out laughing.

"Why are your friends laughing?"

"Don't mind them," Eunice said, handing him a green booklet.

"Your friends are not respectful. Eh, Bright, come. These laydays are laughing at us," he said to the other.

"Sorry," Eunice said, her skin now tinged red. "They're laughing at a joke we were sharing before we got here."

"We're really not laughing at you," Akua Afriyie said as she tried to set a frown on her face to appear serious. She peered in the side mirror. Four cars were stalled behind them. She looked at Dede who was still trying to suppress laughter. Fati seemed peeved. Akua Afriyie realized she had to get them out of the mess they were weaving themselves into. She took out a twenty-cedi note and crumpled it into Eunice's palm. That was more than the standard bribe.

"Sir," Eunice said, "we're really sorry. Here's something small …" She stretched out her hand.

"For your afternoon *kenkey*," Fati said from the back. "These girls are very silly. Please don't mind them."

The soldier took the money. "You laydays better learn to respect your elders," he said and signaled for the car behind them to move forward. Eunice drove on, her face beet red and her brow furrowed. Akua Afriyie and Dede cackled.

"'Yong laydays,'" Dede said.

"Honestly, you two are very silly," Fati said. "Imagine what would have happened if he had refused the bribe. We'd have been in deep shit."

"Language!" Dede said.

"You know that would never have happened," Akua Afriyie said. "An impoverished soldier refusing a bribe! Ha!"

"Dede, your aunt is a High Court judge," Eunice said, calming down. "If we run into any more soldiers, we'll let them know that."

"Hopefully there'll be no more policemen before Kokrobite," Dede said.

Akua Afriyie looked out the windshield. The road, ridden with potholes, was flanked by undulating hills and blocks of uncompleted houses. They sped by a spread of lake, the grass around it wild and verdant.

"Turn left after that signboard," Akua Afriyie said, pointing to a Coca-Cola billboard.

Eunice swiftly turned left onto a laterite road, making the car bump up and down. Akua Afriyie's head hit the window. Eunice steered right and then left. Akua Afriyie looked back and shrugged at Fati and Dede, who looked terrified. Dust rose up in a red cloud behind them. A horde of girls strolled on the side of the road with bundles of firewood on their heads, babies strapped to their backs.

They drove along the red road, passing by mud hut villages shadowed by coconut groves. In the distance, the sea loomed, a deep aqua. "We're almost there, girls!" Akua Afriyie shouted.

"I can't wait," Dede said.

The laterite gave way to white sand, which led to a row of five bungalows painted teal, salmon, yellow, lemon green and orange against a backdrop of the sea.

"Breathtaking," Dede said. "You should paint this, Akua Afriyie!"

"I'd say thanks," Akua Afriyie said, "but I can't take any credit for it. It's my parents'. Eunice, it's the second house."

Akua Afriyie unlocked the brown door to the house. The girls shuffled in behind her. The wooden floor was covered with the carcasses of moths. Rays of light forced themselves through the slits of the wooden shutters.

"Sorry for the appearance, girls," she said, placing her bag and an ice chest on the counter in the kitchen. "You can leave your things here for now. Let's take a quick tour." She walked toward a room painted a light turquoise, decked with furniture covered with blue and white fabric. "This is the living room," she said. "It's the kids' bedroom when my parents are here."

"It smells a little musty," Dede said, walking to a window. She unlatched the shutters and pulled them toward her, waking up a moth that fluttered right up to her nose. She shrieked. Eunice and Dede snickered.

Akua Afriyie pushed aside a red and orange curtain.

"This is the bedroom," she said. A queen-sized mattress on a cane bed frame filled up most of the orange room. A small table stood next to the bed.

"I love the colors," Dede said.

"Thanks," Akua Afriyie said, as she pushed open a door that led to a dark room. "That I contributed to. My parents have no artistic taste." She pulled down a metal light bulb switch. "No power."

"Good thing we brought candles," Dede said.

"There's another mattress under the bed," Akua Afriyie said. "Two people can sleep in here, two can take the living room."

"I know where I'm sleeping!" Eunice said.

"Now can we move on to my favorite view?" Akua Afriyie asked as she strode back into the living room. She unlocked a double door and shoved it open forcefully. A mini-balcony with three short steps led onto the beach.

"*Magnifique*," Eunice said.

"I'm sorry the house is a mess," Akua Afriyie said, turning around.

"We'll clean it," Dede said, smiling.

"OK, Dede. You can start cleaning and I'll fix myself a drink," Fati said. "Who wants one?"

"Charle, I could do with one," Eunice said.

Fati and Eunice walked to the kitchen, Akua Afriyie trailing behind them. They unpacked the boxes they'd brought in. Eunice took out a bottle of Bacardi rum. Akua Afriyie opened a cabinet and extracted two mugs. She left them on the counter and walked over to Dede who lifted a cloth off the cane furniture.

"We won't have to dust too much, thank goodness," Akua Afriyie said. "Party people, hit us up with some music. There's a radio on the kitchen floor."

Everybody do what you doing, smile will bring a sunshine day.

Akua Afriyie danced her way back to the kitchen, where Fati was pulling out bottles of coke. She opened the ice chest. "This ice isn't going to last past this afternoon," she said.

"If it gets really hot, and we get desperate, there's a hotel around here we can go to," Akua Afriyie said.

Dede walked into the kitchen.

"Why does it suddenly feel too crowded in here?" Fati asked.

"Who's hungry?" Dede asked, ignoring Fati.

"I am!" Fati said. "I knew you were useful for something."

"Don't mind her, Dede," Akua Afriyie said, extracting a packet of *gari*, black pepper paste and sardines. Dede grabbed them and poured the white granules of *gari* into a plastic bowl, added a dollop of pepper paste and mixed in the sardines. She added handfuls of water and whisked the ingredients together. "*Voila!*" she said. "You drunkards will need this to line your stomachs."

After the girls ate, they sat in the cane chairs playing a game of cards well into the evening. Eunice and Fati worked through the bottle of rum, getting rowdier as the night wore on.

Akua Afriyie woke up the next day to the smell of fried eggs wafting in the living room. She picked herself off the mattress on the floor, stretched her limbs and stared out the window. She shuffled over to the kitchen, where Dede, dressed in a white halter neck top and hot pink shorts, stood behind the two-burner stove, spatula in her right hand.

"Good morning," she said, her voice chirpy.

"Morning," Akua Afriyie rasped.

Dede put the spatula under a round yellow omelette speckled with red bits of tomato. She masterfully turned it over without breaking it.

"I always destroy omelettes," Akua Afriyie said. "They break into two or into tiny morsels…. You know you'll be catering my wedding."

"I'll be honored," Dede said. "The trick is to use really low heat."

"That sounds easy and I feel stupid! Where are the others?"

"Still sleeping."

"After all that rum they drank, of course they'll sleep the weekend away. I'm going to bath," Akua Afriyie said. She walked into the dark bedroom. She made out Fati and Eunice's forms on the bed. They looked so serene. "Fati Alhassan and Eunice Attoh! Wake up!" she shouted, jumping on the bed.

"Stop! Stop!" Eunice said. "My head hurts."

Akua Afriyie laughed and walked into the bathroom. After her shower, she put on an orange bikini and a pair of blue shorts she'd made herself. She picked up a sketchbook and a pencil from her bag.

The living room was brighter than before and Eunice and Fati sat shielding their eyes from the light. Akua Afriyie snickered. Dede walked to her with a plate covered with a quarter of the omelette. A fork sat at the edge of the plate, threatening to fall.

"Thanks, darling," Akua Afriyie said. "You drunkards want some food?"

"You think you're funny," Eunice said.

"Ugh, don't talk about food," Fati said.

Akua Afriyie opened the double door and sat on the first step. She put the plate on her lap and looked out to the sea. The waves rolled lazily toward the shore. The white sand hadn't been marked by a single footprint. Coconut tree leaves bristled in the sea breeze. She wolfed down the omelette.

"I'm going to do some sketches," she said, as she took the empty plate to the kitchen. "There's a hammock under the bed you can bring out if you want."

Akua Afriyie strolled out onto the white sand, barefoot. It felt warm. She looked back at the prints she was leaving and felt bad for destroying the pristine surface. She loved nature virginal and unspoiled. She sat in front of two coconut trees. They looked like two lovers, their crowns locked in an embrace. Perfect, she thought as she opened the sketchbook. She traced in pencil the arc the trees formed.

Eunice, Dede and Fati walked onto the beach not long after. Eunice clasped newspapers and magazines in one hand and the hammock in the other. Dede and Fati, clad in bikinis, made for the water.

"Eh, you can draw!" Eunice shouted over her shoulder. "But this is the hammock spot now."

"I knew someone was going to destroy my perfect afternoon. And it had to be you!"

Eunice tied the hammock's strings to the stems of both trees. She sat in the hammock and opened up *True Confessions*. Akua Afriyie looked at the sea. Dede stood in the water holding her waist. Fati was running back to them.

"That," she said, pointing at the sea, "is too cold." She sat down under the coconut tree on the left. "Miss Attoh, please entertain us with some Auntie Abena stories."

"Soon. First let me finish this page of *True Confessions*."

"You're addicted," Akua Afriyie said.

Dede walked back and sat by Fati.

"OK, here's your Auntie Abena for the day," Eunice said opening a newspaper. "'Dear Auntie Abena. I'm a fifteen-year-old girl. I just found out I am one month pregnant. I want to keep the child, but my uncle, who got me pregnant, wants to abort it. Please advise. Yours, Worried in Teshie.'"

"Poor girl," Dede said.

"What was she doing having sex at fifteen?" Fati asked.

"Didn't you start earlier than that?" Dede asked.

"I was mature," Fati said. "People like you, Dede, have to wait until you're twenty-five before doing such ..."

"Fati!" Dede shouted as Eunice snickered loudly.

"Leave Dede alone," Akua Afriyie said, almost adding that Eunice was a virgin too, but she kept quiet. "We should talk instead of what we're we going to do after the A-levels. I don't mean to put a dampener on our holiday spirit, but come on ..."

"What about your art school in America plans?" Eunice asked.

"Yes, but I need something else in case that doesn't work."

"Join me at Tech," Dede said. "They have a good art program. That way you can eat all the experiments I cook up."

"Why aren't you saying anything, Miss London School of Economics?" Akua Afriyie asked Fati.

"What do you want me to say?" Fati said. "Yes, find a school here as a backup, but if you get the American program, don't stay. You're not going to make anything as an artist in Ghana. Besides, the way soldiers are ruining the country …"

"Thanks for the vote of confidence," Akua Afriyie said.

"Don't look back," Eunice said quietly. "Three pieces of fine chocolate are approaching."

"You're lying," Akua Afriyie said, as she, Dede and Fati spun their heads around. Three bare-chested men in swimming trunks were walking their way. The one in the middle was dark, tall and muscular. The others were shorter with lighter complexions. Akua Afriyie looked back at the one in the middle and turned round quickly. "They *are* fine!" she said.

"You people are embarrassing!" Eunice said. "And why are there only three of them?"

"Don't you have a boyfriend?" Dede asked.

"Thanks, moral compass. But there's nothing wrong with a little entertainment now and then," Eunice said, fussing with her hair.

"Where are they going?" Akua Afriyie asked. "Are they still com…"

"Hello, ladies," a deep sonorous voice said behind her. "We thought we'd come say hello."

"Hello," the girls chorused.

"Rashid," said the dark one. His eyes were large and Akua Afriyie thought them beautiful. On his right hand, a ring gleamed against his dark skin. "Setor and Michael," he pointed at his friends.

Eunice sat up. "Eunice," she said. "Fati, Dede and Akua Afriyie."

Rashid smiled. "You're all very beautiful."

"Thanks," they said. Akua Afriyie saw Fati roll her eyes.

"Well, it looks like you're all busy," Rashid said. "We'll let you…. That is a beautiful sketch, Akua Afriyie."

"Oh, this? It's still rough," Akua Afriyie said. He remembered my name! No one remembers my name.

"A beautiful sketch done by a beautiful lady," Rashid said. "We're in the Diamond Hotel over there," he pointed behind him. "You should come over for some drinks later."

"That's kind," Fati said. "But, we're spending our evening here."

"You guys should come by," Eunice added quickly. "We'll be making a fire."

"OK, we'll come then. Cheers, ladies."

"Bye," Dede, Akua Afriyie and Eunice sang. Fati rolled her eyes as they walked away.

"I didn't know we were making a fire," Dede said.

"Well, we are now. And you too," she turned to Fati, "you were about to ruin a nice evening."

"They are men, Eunice. How do you know they're not married with six children running around their wives while they chase small girls on the beach?" Fati asked. "I know those types very well."

"I don't care. They were good looking," Eunice said.

"Akua Afriyie, I think you have a fan," Dede said.

"He liked the sketch is all," Akua Afriyie said. She felt sweat form in her armpits. An older, mature man—just what she'd been looking for. No. No men or boys. She wanted to keep her simple life going on.

The sky was pitch black and spotted with bright stars when the girls walked back to the beach. Eunice searched for fallen coconut tree branches.

Akua Afriyie walked into the house. She was excited about seeing Rashid again. He was interested, wasn't he? Going on about beautiful sketches and beautiful ladies. He had to be! Her palms sweated. She wiped them on her flared red skirt. She strode to the kitchen, picked up newspaper and a box of matches. She strutted back out, adding the paper to a heap of dried coconut branches Eunice was building. She lit a match and set the heap on fire. They gathered round it.

"We should sing or tell stories," Dede said.

"Stories, please," Fati said. "And I'll start. You know how dark it gets in Achimota School when there is no moon?"

"Don't scare me," Dede said.

"On a night like this, no moon in sight," Fati went on, "a girl in Clark house ..."

"And you had to pick my hall! Fati, you're cruel," Dede said.

"What? That's what the girl told me. Let me finish my story, ah! This girl was walking back to the dorm alone. She had been gating and after her boyfriend left her, she didn't want to get noticed. So," Fati's voice deepened, "she started tiptoeing. Up the stairs she went. Suddenly, she heard clicking behind her. *Kronchia, kronchia, kronchia.* She looked behind her. No one. She passed through the corridor. She stopped and the clicking stopped. She started again. The clicks came back. *Kronchia, kronchia, kronchia.* When she got to the glass door, she saw ..."

"Whooooo!" a deep voice howled. The girls screamed.

Rashid guffawed, fell and rolled in the sand by Akua Afriyie and Dede. "Even the story teller was scared," he said, holding his sides. Setor and Michael sat between Fati and Eunice. "It was Lady High Heels, right?" he said. "You girls have made my night. I haven't laughed like this in so long." He sat up.

Setor pulled out a packet of cigarettes and passed it around.

"They don't smoke," Fati said, pulling out a cigarette. She gave the box to Michael sitting next to her.

Rashid held the tip of his cigarette in the fire. "By the way," he said. "Great bonfire you've got going here."

"Thanks," the girls chorused.

"Didn't think women were capable of such ..."

"Please," Fati said, taking a hit of her cigarette, "if you know what's good for you, you'll retract that statement."

"Duly retracted," Rashid said. Dede, Akua Afriyie and Eunice held their cigarettes to the fire, like Rashid had done. They coughed loudly as they inhaled them. Rashid laughed again.

"I'm glad they're entertaining you," Fati said. She turned to Michael. "Where do you work?" she asked.

In a low quiet voice, Michael said, "I'm a clerk in the Ministry of Finance."

"Good," Fati said, linking her arm in his. "Tell me, what is happening to this country? Your people are killing us."

Rashid waved at Akua Afriyie, trying to get her attention. She ignored him. She glanced at him and then looked at Eunice and Dede who were fascinated with their cigarettes. Between coughs, they were trying to get the smoke to come out of their nostrils.

"Hold it for two seconds," Setor said, a white wisp of smoke escaping his nostrils.

"Wow!" Eunice said.

"Akua Afriyie," Rashid whispered. "Want some chocolate?"

"Sure," she said. Out of his pocket, he pulled out a bar of Nestle chocolate. "I thought these were banned," she said, tearing apart the paper and opening the foil. She took a bite and passed it on to Fati, who was staring at Michael so intensely, it looked like she wanted to eat him up. "Fati!" she shouted.

"Oh, thanks," Fati said.

"We have drinks inside!" Eunice shouted suddenly. "Let's go in!"

"Can we talk for a little before going inside?" Rashid asked Akua Afriyie who watched the group move inside. She felt him boring into her with his eyes. She wanted him to stop staring, yet loved the attention.

"Where do you work?" she asked, trying to lessen the tension that sat in the air.

"In a bank," he said. "Where do *you* work?"

"Me?" she laughed. "I'm an airhostess." She didn't know why she was lying, but it sounded better than saying she was still at Achimota.

"For Ghana Airways? I've never seen you. An airhostess who draws so well?"

"Drawing—that's just a hobby," she said, waving her hand which still held the cigarette stub.

"You're lying," he said. "I know all the Ghana Airways hostesses and none of them is as pretty as you."

"Well, thank you," she said, wiping her forehead. The bonfire and Rashid were heating her up. She liked his forwardness. "But I didn't say I worked for Ghana Airways," she said. She noticed him toying with the ring on his right hand. "Can I see your ring?"

"Only if you tell me the truth."

"Why do you think I'm lying?" she asked. He stretched out his hand. The ring was a band made of silver and gold woven together. "This is beautiful," she said, rubbing the ridged surface of the ring.

"*You're* beautiful." He cupped her hands in his.

She pulled her hands away. "I'm getting tired," she said. "I think we should go in."

"I don't mean to be so bold," Rashid said pulling out a card from his top pocket. "I feel really drawn to you and can't explain it. Trust me, this never happens to me. All day I've thought about you. Call me, OK?"

She nodded. She didn't know whether to believe him. She was wary of love at first sight, even though she was also strongly attracted to him. If he tried to do anything, she knew she would yield completely.

"OK, Miss Achimota! You can go get your beauty sleep," he said. "I'll head back to the hotel."

"What? How did you know?" she asked him, giggling.

"Only school children tell Lady High Heels stories and wear cute little afros," he said.

She laughed. "Goodnight, Rashid."

"Goodnight, beautiful. Please call."

She walked back toward the house, not sure if she'd call him. She slipped the card into her brassiere. Inside, the girls, Setor and Michael were on the floor smoking and taking swigs from the bottle of rum. A white candle sat on one of the cane chairs.

"Where's Rashid?" Eunice slurred.

"He's gone back to the hotel."

"Why, what happened?"

"Nothing," Akua Afriyie said. "He said he was tired."

"Join us!" Fati said.

"Yes!" Dede said, her arms around Setor.

"Charle, I'm tired! Maybe later," Akua Afriyie said. She moved the candle to the floor. She went behind the door curtain and lay on the bed. She thought of Rashid and his expressive eyes. He seemed mature and she figured that's what attracted her the most. But she wasn't going to call him, she decided as she drifted off to sleep. The last things she heard was the sound of a bottle hitting the concrete floor, loud laughter, Dede's high-pitched voice saying, "I did it! See, smoke came out!"

Thirteen
King Solomon Hotel

December 1978

Akua Afriyie's eyes darted over frames of Wonder Woman and Steve Trevor almost exploding after Trevor tried to kiss her. She heard chairs scraping the concrete floor impatiently. She closed the thin comic book, which she'd hidden in a voluminous art history textbook. She looked up to find a class staring at her, waiting for her to say the words. She could feel their thick impatience in the air.

"OK, go back to your dorms," she said. "And no gating!"

The students chatted noisily, threw their chairs over their tables and milled out of the classroom. A girl and boy lingered behind stealing glances at each other. Ah, young love, she thought. As they strolled out, she felt a mix of nostalgia and sadness. Wonder Woman and Trevor's heroics hadn't exactly helped her state of mind. She rued the missed chance with the man she'd met at the beach. She didn't know why she hadn't called him and now it was too late. Wasn't it?

Eunice burst in through the door, her cheeks working themselves up and down as she chomped on gum.

"Hello," she said, her hair patted into a little afro. "Are you done?"

"Hi, darling," Akua Afriyie said, stuffing her books into her green satchel. She slung it over her left shoulder, turned off the lights and closed the classroom door. "How are you?" she asked.

"I've been cramming for my government exam tomorrow."

"I have to tell you something ... and you're going to kill me when I say what," Akua Afriyie said.

"What? You have home chow and you've been hiding it?"

"No! You like food too much!" Akua Afriyie said and laughed. "Remember what happened in October?"

"Yes, how could I not? Dede almost losing her, you know what, to that guy…. And you, not giving that hunk of a man a chance." Eunice smacked her lips together. "What is wrong with you? He was so interested in you. Why did you just blow him off?"

"I have his business card," Akua Afriyie said.

"Huh?" Eunice stopped, clasped her hands on her hips and rounded her mouth. "No. You're lying! All the way from your parents' beach house you pretended you didn't care if you never saw him again."

"I needed to think about if I wanted something to develop."

"I see. And it's taken you two months? We're writing to him."

"We?" Akua Afriyie's raised her brow. "Besides isn't it too late?"

"Yes, we. Apparently when I leave you to your own devices you don't know what to do with them. And no, it's not too late. It's actually the perfect time! You've stretched him enough."

"But what am I going to say to him?"

"Leave it to me," Eunice said.

Akua Afriyie had thought of writing to Rashid every day for the past two months. Each time she'd worked up the nerve, she managed to stop herself. It was something in his smoothness and the whole instant attraction thing that had blocked her.

They arrived at Kingsley House. It was quiet and painted white on the outside, its blue shutters thrown wide open. They climbed up a set of burgundy-colored stairs and strode through a corridor that opened into the main hall. The hall buzzed with girls changing into their nightgowns, talking nineteen to the dozen and dusting their faces with powder. It was a marketplace with gossip being peddled.

"And that Mrs. Ankrah can't stop mixing her r's and l's," said a girl with a face dotted with acne.

"Erections are part and parcel of the democratic system," another said. A loud uproar of laughter ensued.

"Poor woman," Eunice said as they walked by the girls. "She'll have the last laugh tomorrow, when she hands out that exam." She dragged Akua Afriyie to her bed, the last in the farthest corner of the room. She reached under her bed, opened her trunk and extracted a writing pad bordered with yellow and pink roses and a silver cannister of perfume.

"What's that?"

"Mary Quant's *Havoc*," Eunice said.

"But I don't smell like that," Akua Afriyie protested.

"Smell it," Eunice said, popping the cap from the can. She shoved it under Akua Afriyie's nose.

"It does smell nice. But a pad with flowers? Come on, Eunice, that's not my style."

"Shut up and let's write this letter," Eunice ordered. "The only thing I'll let you do is pen it. Write exactly what I tell you."

"I'll be editing, just so you know. This letter is coming from Akua Afriyie Mensah not Eunice Attoh."

"Start! Dear Rashid …"

"How about 'Hello, Rashid'? It's not a love letter. It's just a reaching-out-letter."

"Don't interrupt me," Eunice said.

Akua Afriyie wrote 'Dear Rashid.' They went on, one interrupting the other, Akua Afriyie usually ceding power to Eunice, till they had written and rewritten half a page:

December 14, 1978

Dear Rashid,

Sorry it took me so long to contact you. I'm in my last year of school and preparing for my A-levels has kept me occupied. I thought I'd lost your card, but found it this morning. How are you doing? How's life in the bank? It must be hard being a banker with so many people in the country desperate for money. I hope you're safe.

Life in school is pretty uninteresting, especially with exams looming. Once that is done, I hope to apply to art school in a country where artists are appreciated. I don't think Ghana is ready for me, yet.

I look forward to hearing from you.

Akua Afriyie.

"Guess what?" Eunice asked chirpily. Akua Afriyie felt drained.

"We're rewriting it again?"

"No," Eunice said. "It's good to go. But I'm posting this letter."

"Why?"

"Just give me Rashid's card." Eunice's light brown eyes shone. "And some pesewas."

Akua Afriyie sucked her teeth. She took out Rashid's card and three coins from her satchel and handed them to Eunice.

*

January 1979

Eunice had done the math—so, she told Akua Afriyie. She figured the letter would get to Rashid just after least New Year's Eve. He would take a week to write back and mail the letter. His reply should be in the post office by the third week of January. She dragged Akua Afriyie there on the twentieth of January. Nothing had arrived. The second day was no different. Finally, on the third day the postmaster handed Eunice a white envelope with Akua Afriyie's name on it.

"Can I have it?" Akua Afriyie asked, snatching it from Eunice and tearing it open.

"And all this while I thought you weren't interested."

The note was written in a neat cursive hand on a Ghana Commercial Bank letterhead. It was brief. Rashid said he'd been waiting to hear from her and was glad she'd written. Instead of writing letters, which took too long to get to him, he suggested going to the housemaster of Guggisberg House, who would let her use his phone. He'd written to the housemaster, who'd been his mate when they were at Achimota, and he was sure Mawuli Ayeh wouldn't mind. P.S., he'd added, the perfume drove him crazy.

"Let's go now!" Eunice said.

"Why are you so impatient?" Akua Afriyie asked. "Mawuli Ayeh probably hasn't received Rashid's letter yet." She paused. "Now, you have to give me that bottle of perfume."

"You can borrow it when you want," Eunice said.

Three days later when Akua Afriyie couldn't take any more of Eunice's nagging they met in front of Guggisberg House. She walked toward Eunice who stood with her arms folded across her chest, her caramel skin looking freshly scrubbed.

In front of the wide house, boys bent over, sweating, pulling out weeds, slashing through overgrown grass. Another group—sixth formers—stood by supervising. Among them, Akua Afriyie recognized Kwakye, with his bony frame, and hoped she could pass by without getting noticed.

"Eh, Kwakye!" a guttural voice shouted. "It's your girlfriend." Akua Afriyie felt all eyes turn to look at her. Their gazes moved to Kwakye.

"Hello, Akua Afriyie," Kwakye said and waved. Akua Afriyie waved back. He looked like he was about to come talk to her but Eunice pulled her arm and dragged her into the dorm. Akua Afriyie felt horrible. They'd gone out from form two to five, but she'd dumped him, because he just didn't have a backbone and was too childish. He was still trying to get her to change her mind. Suddenly, Rashid seemed even more attractive.

They strode through the hall and out into a backyard. Eunice knocked on a blue door, which was answered by a young man in khaki trousers and a grey shirt. His dark mahogany skin did not have a spot or blemish in place. Akua Afriyie hadn't registered that he'd been Rashid's mate. She'd been imagining a middle-aged, pot-bellied housemaster.

"You must be Akua Afriyie," he said. "Come in. I was expecting you days ago." Eunice eyed her.

"Yes, I am. This is my best friend Eunice," Akua Afriyie said.

He shook their hands, "Mawuli. I'm sure you're both busy with exam preparations, so we can make this fast. Rashid told me you're in upper six."

"Yes," Eunice said, gaping carnivorously at Mawuli.

"The phone is in this corner," he said.

Akua Afriyie took out Rashid's letter and dialed his number. She looked around the room, which was sparsely furnished. Across from her were two brown upholstered armchairs, in which Mawuli and Eunice were now seated.

"Ghana Commercial Bank," a woman's voice screeched.

Akua Afriyie held the phone away from her head. "Yes, good morning. May I please speak to Mr. Rashid Adams?" The crackling returned. A solid voice said hello. "Hello, Rashid? This is Akua Afriyie," she said.

Akua Afriyie looked at Eunice.

"Afriyie! You must be at Mawuli's. It's great to hear your voice! How are you?" Rashid asked.

"Very well, thanks," Akua Afriyie said. Eunice was now sitting at the edge of her seat, wide-eyed, her lips pink and wet. Akua Afriyie wanted to laugh at her eagerness.

"Good," Rashid said. "It will be nice to chat with you in person. Can we meet? Can you leave school anytime soon? I can come for you."

"This weekend I can leave school," Akua Afriyie said, smiling.

Eunice's eyes twinkled. They seemed to say, "My job is done."

"Wonderful! I'll come to your house on Saturday. At ten. What dorm do you live in?"

"Kingsley."

"I hope you remember what I look like."

"Of course I do. See you then."

The girls thanked Mawuli and walked out. A lilac cloud shaded the orange sun. Akua Afriyie felt her heart pummeling her ribcage.

"Mawuli," Eunice said, as they strode into Kingsley House.

"Huh?" Akua Afriyie said, distracted.

"Nothing," Eunice responded.

*

Akua Afriyie was seated on Kingsley House's burgundy steps, watching cars arrive and leave. A Datsun drove up and she recognized Rashid's round head. She picked up the bag she'd stuffed with her clothes and walked up to his car.

When she saw him, she felt a tad disappointed. In regular clothes, he looked different from the tall confident man who'd swaggered up to her on the beach. He seemed to have aged more.

"Hello, stranger. Hop in," he said, leaning over the passenger seat to open her door.

"Hello," Akua Afriyie said. When he smiled, she remembered that it was his smile and large expressive eyes that had caught her attention.

"I hope you brought the sexy bikini I met you in," he said. She wasn't sure if going out alone with him was a good idea—the first thing he talked about was her swimsuit! To her it spelled that he wanted one thing. "We'll have lunch by the poolside, is why I asked," he added, as if he'd read her thoughts.

She was relieved. "Oh no. I didn't," she said. "You should have told me to bring it." She studied his profile. His jaw was strong, his teeth straight and his nose aquiline. He wore a snug polo-neck shirt and brown trousers. Akua Afriyie decided that he was attractive, but was probably being overworked at the bank. He hummed while he drove, tapping his fingers against the steering wheel. The silver and gold ring on his right hand glistened under the Accra sun. "I told you I also went to Achimota, right?" he asked.

"Yes, you did in the letter. When did you finish?"

"Oh, ages ago," he said. "1965." That was more than ten years ago! Akua Afriyie thought. He's ancient! Once again she wondered what she was getting herself involved in. "I remember those days like they happened yesterday. I came all the way from the north," Rashid said. "Most people were from the coast and they were all so snotty. Mawuli was one of my first friends. We bonded because he also came from far away."

"Where did he come from?"

"From the Volta Region. He was just like me. Family far away, green in Accra."

"Is your whole family from the north?"

"Yes," Rashid said.

"One of my maternal great-grandmothers was from the north," Akua Afriyie said, looking out the window. The roads were traffic-free except for the occasional taxi.

"Really? What was her name?"

"Sugri."

"I knew we were connected," he said, palming his ring-bearing hand on her left hand which she'd placed by her left thigh. She wanted to retract her hand, but thought it rude. She kept her gaze outside the window. As he turned left at a junction that led to a row of semi-completed houses, she saw people going in and out of the houses, even though their brick walls stood with no netting or roofing. Clothes were hung where there should have been windows. People were really suffering in the country and she was going goodness-knows-where with a man she barely knew. "Can I call you Afriyie?" he asked. "I think it's so beautiful."

"Thanks. Yes, you can. That's what my father calls me."

"And your mother?"

"She calls me Akua. When she's angry with me, she uses my full name. Sometimes she scares me."

"She'd probably kill you if she knew where you were," Rashid said and smiled.

"Which is why she'll never find out," Akua Afriyie said definitively.

Outside what looked like an Accra man's three-story dream house was posted a large white signboard that read KING SOLOMON HOTEL. Rashid steered through the open black gates and onto the gravelly driveway. The hotel's whitewashed walls were more green than white. Big climbing elephant ears started from the ground, wound their way around a terrazzo-engraved jutting and ended at the top of the building.

They stepped out of the car and walked to the reception, where a young girl was bent over sweeping the parquet floor. The walls were made of mahogany panels. A fluorescent bulb above had been turned on, but did nothing to illuminate the dark, woody room.

"Ei, Mr. Rashid!" said the receptionist, a thin woman. "How are you today?"

"Can't complain, Abena," Rashid said.

He must bring all his girlfriends here, Akua Afriyie thought. And these people are complicit in his affairs. She looked at the young girl who had been sweeping. The girl was gawking at her, her mouth open. The receptionist handed Rashid keys. Wow, he doesn't waste time, does he? Akua Afriyie thought.

"I'm sure you want to change into your regular clothes," Rashid said. "Here are keys to a room upstairs. I'll wait for you by the poolside. Abena will bring you there when you come back down."

"Hey," Abena addressed the girl who was sweeping, "take the lady up."

They climbed up two concrete flights of stairs to the third floor. The girl, singing to herself, turned right and stopped in front of a wooden door that seemed recently polished. On it the number twenty-seven was painted in gold. The girl stretched out her hand for the keys, took them and unlocked the door.

In the room, a double bed was covered with bright white sheets etched with the words "King Solomon Hotel" arched around a moon and star.

Akua Afriyie changed into a pair of red flared trousers and a white peasant blouse. She trudged back downstairs.

"Abena," she said. "Where did Mr. ... where did Rashid go?"

"Come, I'll show you," Abena said. "How do you know him?"

"He's a friend," Akua Afriyie said.

They walked away from the reception through a narrow corridor that led outside. The pool was moon-shaped and turquoise. Rashid sat at the other side of it. Akua Afriyie walked toward him not sure whether to look at him, or whether to look down. Not sure whether to keep her hands by her side or on her waist. Not sure how to walk. Not sure what she was doing there with him.

"What can I get you?" he asked, his voice booming.

"A coke, please," she said, sitting down by him.

The waiter, dressed in a short-sleeved white shirt and black trousers, came over.

"Can we have a coke and a Club beer?" Rashid turned to Akua Afriyie. "We might as well order some lunch now ..." he started.

"Sir, I hope you know that coke is now four cedis and the beer, five cedis," the waiter volunteered.

"That's ridiculous," Akua Afriyie said. "That's twice the price of coke you buy from a store. You know, Rashid, I don't have to have a coke ..."

"Yes," Rashid said to the waiter, "I am well aware of the increases in the price of things. Just bring us our drinks and some chicken. That's the hotel price," he explained to Akua Afriyie.

"All the same," Akua Afriyie went on. "Prices are just skyrocketing. What's going on?"

"It's simple. It's the story of Ghana. People come in advocating change. They get into power, usually by force, get comfortable and forget about everyone else."

Akua Afriyie really couldn't care less about politics, but something in Rashid's passionate speech piqued her interest. "Explain further," she said.

"You don't want to get me started! Six years ago, Acheampong and the National Redemption Council came to power, preaching economic reforms. The man literally drove to the castle in a battered old Datsun. He started the Operation Feed Yourself program. We were all happy, thinking we could finally learn to produce for ourselves, but that got nowhere. Along the way, the NRC became the Supreme Military Council. Somehow the Datsun became the good old Mercedes Benz. And where is the ordinary man left?"

"But," she said, "people have been blaming our problems on ordinary people—on traders and hoarders."

"Of course our dear market women don't help. They sell goods at insanely high prices, but they're not the main problem. They are forced to do that because of decisions the government makes. Change is coming, though." His eyes popped open, lending him a slightly manic look.

"What kind of change?"

The waiter brought their drinks and pieces of chicken the size of Akua Afriyie's little finger.

"I can't really talk about it," Rashid said. "The idea is still simmering. Let's call it a political shake up of the country … especially now that the ban on politics has been lifted." He bit into a piece of chicken.

"There's a lot I don't know about you," Akua Afriyie said.

"I would like to become Finance Minister some day. That's my dream."

"I'm in the company of a big man then," she said, wincing at her words. Big men, Ghanaian politics, money—all that bored her. "Are we going to stay here all day? Can we go shopping?" she asked.

"I just want to talk to you. Get to know you. Next time—that is if you want to do this again—we'll go shopping."

"I do," she said, unsure what had driven her to say that. There was no Eunice to egg her on. That was entirely her doing.

After they downed their drinks and swallowed the miserable pieces of chicken, Rashid suggested they go up to watch a film, as he placed twenty cedis under the bottle of coke. He walked ahead of her into the reception.

Up in room twenty-seven, Akua Afriyie noticed that he'd left the door unlocked when they walked in. She smiled. He was a gentleman! He opened a cabinet below the television set.

"Do you live here?" she asked.

"Because I know where the videos are?"

"Yes and everybody knows you."

"First, please sit," he said to her. "I hope you don't mind sharing the bed with me." She sat at the foot of the bed wondering why he was being evasive. "Don't laugh at my collection" he said. "I have *The Sound of Music*, *The Wizard of Oz*, *Mary Poppins*. And of course, porn, if you're interested."

Akua Afriyie snorted. "So you have a soft spot for musicals, eh?"

"Yes," he said, his big eyes darting from her face to the floor.

"There's nothing wrong with that," she said, laughing. "I have a weakness too."

"Porn?" Rashid asked.

"Ah, you've uncovered my secret!" She chuckled. "No! Comic books."

"I'll remember that," Rashid said.

"Let's watch *Mary Poppins*," Akua Afriyie said.

Rashid put the video tape into the VCR and plunked himself on the bed. "Afriyie, relax," he said. She pushed her body up the bed till her back was against the wooden headboard. "So, why did you take so long to write to me?" he asked.

"I misplaced your card. I emptied my trunk one day and it was staring at me," she said, trying hard not to blink.

"I'm glad you called me," he said, his voice getting huskier.

Just a spoon full of sugar makes the medicine go down …

"I'm enjoying this. Thanks for inviting me," she said.

He put his arm around her, bent his head and planted his lips on hers, all in one smooth move. She didn't flinch. It was a sweet kiss. She was grateful he hadn't tried to shove his tongue into her mouth. Kwakye was such a bad kisser. Even before they kissed his tongue would be hanging out, pink, moist and ready to probe her tonsils. Akua Afriyie shuddered at the memory.

"Everything OK, Miss Afriyie Comicbooks?" Rashid asked, rubbing her cheeks with his thumb.

"Yes, Mr. Rashid Musicals," she said. "Now, we have to watch Mary Poppins because the governess wouldn't be pleased if we ignored her."

Somewhere after *supercalifragilisticexpialidocious* they fell asleep. Akua Afriyie woke up with a start, looked at her watch, panicked and shook Rashid awake. "My exeat ends in thirty minutes!" she screamed.

"No worries, Musicals will save the day." He got up and strolled to the bathroom.

As fast as she could, Akua Afriyie sloughed off her trousers and blouse and changed back into her school uniform. He was so calm and mature! And he hadn't tried to pull any fast moves.

He came out of the bathroom. "Shall we?" he asked.

"We shall," she said, walked to him and kissed his lips.

"I see you're friskier in your uniform," he said. "Next time, you shan't change into your own clothes. And that's an order."

"Yes, sir!" she said, giggling.

They walked down the staircase. Abena stood behind the reception counter, her lips shining. Akua Afriyie caught a whiff of palm oil and salted tilapia.

"You're invited," Abena said, wiping the oil dripping from her lips with the back of her hand.

"Oh, thank you," Rashid said, leaving a ten-cedi tip on the counter top.

"God bless you," Abena said. "Next time."

In the car Rashid screamed, "Good heavens!"

"What?"

"You're late! You missed your curfew. The only solution is to spend the night here with me," he said, breaking into peals of laughter.

Akua Afriyie hit him playfully. "Don't give me a heart attack."

On the main road back to school, Akua Afriyie saw a line of women and children carrying metal basins and plastic buckets, pushing and shoving to fetch water from a black tanker. Old women pushed over young children. Young children shoved over pregnant women. Boys cantered to the front trying to get their buckets filled before everybody else.

"I hope there's water in the taps in school," she said. "Last time there was a serious shortage, we had to fetch water from the swimming pool. Can you imagine?"

"I guess I was lucky I went to Achimota in Nkrumah's time," Rashid said.

"Yes, you were. The SMC is killing us."

He drove by the thick green Achimota forest and turned right through the school's main gates, where a small traffic jam had built up with parents dropping off their wards, and lovers, their loved ones. He pulled up in front of Kingsley House.

"Thanks for today," she said.

"No. Thank *you*. Can we repeat this in two weeks?" he asked as Akua Afriyie stepped out of the car.

"Definitely, but we're going shopping first! Bye!" she said.

"Bye," Rashid said, driving off.

*

February 1979

Akua Afriyie stood dressed in uniform on the second floor of the Kingsway building. She stared at the racks of clothing and didn't feel like buying anything. When she'd suggested they go shopping, she'd forgotten about the possibility of running into her father, or even worse, Lizzie. She glanced furtively around. Rashid also looked shifty.

"I'm hiding from my parents," she said. "What's your story?"

He laughed, but not with his usual pomp. "Afriyie, I'm supposed to be working today. I was told yesterday, but I didn't want to cancel on you. I checked in at the office, and have my secretary as an alibi. I'm hoping I don't run into any of my supervisors."

"Let's go somewhere else then," she said.

"Yes. Are you sure you don't want anything?" Rashid asked. "We'll go back to the hotel."

"Sure," Akua Afriyie said, disappointed. She was hoping he'd take her to his bachelor pad. "Where do you live, Rashid? Last time I asked you, you conveniently forgot to answer me." They walked out of the department store.

"In a dump," Rashid said. "Trust me. You don't want to see it. It's worse than Nima."

"You work in a bank. I don't believe you," she said as they walked to his car.

"OK, I lied," he cackled and unlocked the doors of the car. "I live with my parents. Grown man like me, it's embarrassing, all right?"

"No, that's adorable." She dug into her bag. "Here," she said, handing him an envelope.

With one hand on the steering wheel, and the other tearing open the envelope, he extracted a card. In the front she'd painted a yellow moon and star enclosed by a small blue square. In the background was the grey silhouette of a mother with a child by her side.

"Thank you. It's beautiful. But you haven't signed it, Afriyie."

"I like to remain anonymous," she said.

"What do you call it?"

"King Solomon, I guess. The hotel inspired me."

"You're very funny, Afriyie," Rashid said, steering into the hotel driveway.

In room twenty-seven, he'd barely closed the door, when he pounced on her, thrusting his tongue into her mouth. "I love a school girl, in uniform," he said, catching his breath.

"Lecherous old man."

"One minute," he said.

"What?"

"We need to talk about something first." What-the-hell-about? Akua Afriyie wondered. Thanks to him, she was worked up and ready to go. "Afriyie, I'd really like to make love to you …" He paused, seemed to be studying her. "… that is if you're not a virgin, Chrife or opposed to pre-marital sex …"

"None of the above," she said, wishing they'd get right down to business. She slunk toward him and unbuttoned his polo shirt.

"Afriyie," he started again, sitting at the foot of the bed. "Another thing. I really don't like condoms. They're too uncomfortable …"

"You should thank God for the pill and a thing called presence of mind."

He smiled and drew her close to him so she was sitting on his lap. She held his head back, placed her lips on his. He clutched her buttocks and snaked his tongue into her mouth. All she heard was their heated breathing and the lapping of their tongues. She pulled his polo shirt over his head. He drew her panties down to her ankles. She stepped out of them as she unbuckled his belt, unzipped his trousers. Easily, smoothly, he eased himself into her. She let out tiny gasps as they rocked back and forth at the foot of the bed. Passion welled up in her, flooded her veins, filled her every pore and bound her with Rashid in a forceful eruption.

After their tryst, they climbed onto the bed.

"I'd love to have more of you," he said.

"My insatiable Rashid," she said, surprised at how intense they were together. Explosive. Like Wonder Woman and Steve Trevor.

*

March 1979

Akua Afriyie and Eunice sat in Mawuli's living room, sipping on cold glasses of Fanta. Eunice went into the kitchen and came out with a tray of biscuits.

Akua Afriyie was amused at how Eunice had managed to start a fling with the housemaster. Apparently she hadn't slept with him—she was saving herself for marriage. Akua Afriyie didn't believe her.

"I'm calling Rashid now," she said as she dialed the bank's number, sure they hadn't heard her.

"Hello," the secretary answered. "Ghana Commercial Bank."

"Can I please speak to Rashid?"

"Rashid who?" the secretary asked bluntly.

"Sorry, Rashid Adams."

"Who's this?"

"Akua Afriyie."

She heard a click and then Rashid's voice. "Afriyie, how are you?"

"Fine, darling. Just making sure that I'll be seeing you tomorrow."

"I'm so happy you called me. Afriyie, I have to disappoint you. I'm sure you heard that on Monday we're going to be issuing new bank notes. I have to work all weekend …"

"Oh," Akua Afriyie said. "Right." She'd heard about that, but had forgotten that Rashid would be roped into such things.

"In fact, from now till the end of the month, I'll be working everyday. I will make it up to you, I promise. Did you get the comic books I sent you?"

"Yes," she responded quietly. "Thank you. Let me not disturb you then. Work hard."

"Greet Mawuli for me. Bye."

"Bye," Akua Afriyie said, pulling a face. Mawuli and Eunice were staring at each other, disgustingly, in her opinion.

"Why so glum?" Eunice asked.

"Rashid canceled on me. I'm going to go back to the dorm. Thanks, Mawuli. Eunice, later," Akua Afriyie said as she walked out. As she strolled on the laterite shortcut back to Kingsley House, she wondered why she was so upset. She must really like him. Well, if she wasn't going to see him for a while, she could get off that bloody pill. She needed a break too.

*

Akua Afriyie and the Kingsley House form one girls dug up the dark brown loam from which anthuriums sprouted. Akua Afriyie was in charge of the grounds and made sure that Kingsley House always won the award for Most Beautiful Gardens.

"Good morning," a high-pitched voice yelled. "I'm looking for senior Akua Afriyie."

"That would be me," Akua Afriyie said, turning around to see a scrawny boy. Behind him, dark pregnant clouds gathered, casting a halo around his head.

"Senior, Master Mawuli said I should give you this note," he said, handing her a piece of lined paper that had taken the form of an old over-circulated note of money.

"Thanks," Akua Afriyie said, opening it up. Rashid was coming to pick her up in an hour. She was excited about seeing him, but was unprepared with such short notice. "Harriet," she called her favorite student, who was bent over, pruning a plant.

"Senior," said Harriet.

"I'm going on exeat. Can you make sure that the tools are put away when everyone's done with the garden? Make sure they do a good job."

"Sure," Harriet said. "Bring me something nice."

"OK, sweetie. Thanks for being in charge."

"Anything for you. You're the only senior who treats us like human beings and even works with us."

Akua Afriyie dashed into the dorm, took a shower, changed into a fresh uniform and pulled out her red and black trunk. She dug deep, under a stack of comic books and found her birth control pills. She popped a pill into her mouth and walked back down to the bathroom. She swallowed the pill. She looked in a mirror. In her reflection, she saw a ripe red pimple jutting out of her chin. How convenient, she thought. But there was nothing she could do about it. She didn't like popping them.

Outside the hall, she saw Rashid's Datsun stalled. She opened the car door and wet his cheek with a kiss.

"This has been our longest separation," she said.

"Yes, it has been," Rashid said, his eyes bloodshot.

"I'm even surprised you were able to take a break to come for me. I hear the currency change has been horrendous."

"Well, I need this break otherwise they'll have an inefficient banker on their hands."

"Coming to think of it, I have lots of old cedis. You can probably help me change them," she said.

"Don't remind me," Rashid said. "The problem is Ghanaians don't keep their money in banks. People have been coming in with millions of cedis to change into the new notes."

"Where do they keep their millions?"

"Under their beds or in theirs shoes. I don't know. But if they kept that money in banks, it would have been a seamless change. Oh, it's been a nightmare. Enough about that. Let's talk about you. How are you?"

"Three more months till the A-levels!"

At the hotel, only the girl who swept the floor was in the reception area. She checked them in. They ran up the stairs impatiently. In the comfort of their love nest, neither waited for the other to make the first move. They grabbed each other's clothes, clutched each other's body parts, tore, pushed, pulled, pinned to the wall, flung, rose, peaked and fell in an exhausted heap on the sheets.

"I needed that," Rashid said, his naked body splayed on the bed.

"Yes, me too." Akua Afriyie said, getting up to put on her uniform.

"Where are you going?"

"Today, my dear Rashid," she said, "I'm treating you to drinks and food."

"Call for room service," Rashid said.

"I don't want that Abena snooping around. I'll be back soon."

Akua Afriyie walked down and found Abena now behind the reception counter.

"Ei, Afriyie," she said. "Long time no see."

"I know. School's keeping me busy. Can I order some food please?"

"You shouldn't have come all the way downstairs," Abena said. "Tell me," she went on. "Mr. Rashid used to bring his wife and children here, but he stopped. The children loved the swimming pool. Do you know why they don't come anymore?"

Akua Afriyie choked. Wife and children? Not just a wife. Wife and children? "You should ask him when he comes down," Akua Afriyie said, wondering why Abena had offered that piece of information. Probably out of pure spite. But Rashid had a wife and children?! "Don't worry about the order," she said.

She stomped upstairs and burst into the room. She stood by the bed, collecting her thoughts, thinking of how she should confront him.

"Where's the food," he asked.

"Have you been lying to me?"

"About what?" Rashid asked.

"You have a wife and children.".

"Calm down, Afriyie." He picked up his shirt and pulled it over his round head.

"Take me back to school. I can't breathe," she said, pulling on the collar of her uniform.

"Who told you?" Rashid asked his eyes popping open.

"Rashid!" Akua Afriyie screamed. "Take me back to school!"

"OK. Fine. Just don't trust every rumor you hear."

She stormed out of the room, down the stairs, by Abena and into the car.

They drove back in silence.

Akua Afriyie looked out the window. The thickened clouds seemed ready to break water. If it rained, it would be the first time that year.

"Is it true, Rashid?" she asked him softly.

"Yes. I'm sorry," he said.

"Then I can't see you anymore," Akua Afriyie said. "I can't be with a married man."

"You're overreacting—my wife and I are having problems," he said. "We'll be divorcing soon."

A flash of lightning scattered across the sky. A thunderous rumble ensued.

"Well, right this moment you're still married and I can't see you till after your divorce," she said. She felt numb, heavy, drained, as if she'd just fought in a boxing ring. He dropped her off in front of her dorm.

"Call me if you change your mind," he said. As he drove away the heavens split, pouring down buckets of water. She loved the rain. It always put her at ease. This time, even the rain couldn't wipe out the disillusion that was wracking her heart.

Fourteen
Snatched Dreams

Akua Afriyie crouched over a toilet bowl in the Kingsley House bathroom, retching. She looked at the porcelain bowl, at the sinewy mess she'd left in it, stood up and wiped her moist eyes. She reached out for the blue plastic handle and flushed her vomit away. She couldn't believe her luck. The doctor's report proved she was well and truly pregnant. She trudged by the shower stalls, out to the sinks, where she stopped. As water trickled down her hands, she stared at her reflection. Her eyes were hued scarlet. What am I going to do? she wondered. This was not in my plan.

She climbed up the dormitory's burgundy stairs. The market place was deserted. Everyone was in class. No one was in sight to ask, "Oh, are you not feeling well?" She was grateful—now was not the time to incur pity or suspicion from anyone or feed into the market place gossip.

Fighting back tears, she reached for her trunk from under her bed, unlocked it and ferreted through her neatly folded clothes and comic books. She picked up a brown envelope. The tears she was trying to dam, broke over her eyelids and rushed down her cheeks. She dabbed her eyes with a blue sweater she picked up and trudged downstairs.

Outside, a photographer, obviously trying to finagle a few cedis off poor students, was pointing his camera at a group of girls. Akua Afriyie quickened her steps to avoid being seen.

"Senior Akua, come take a picture!" she heard Harriet call out sweetly. Oh no, not now, Akua Afriyie thought, but obliged. She tied her sweater around her green and white uniform and strode toward the gaggle of girls. "Senior, where are you going?" Harriet asked after the camera man's flash went off. "I want to come too."

"Trust me, you don't want to come with me," Akua Afriyie said. "I'll tell you later. I have to run." She put on her sweater, hunched her thin upper body and walked toward the school's gates, without as much as a glance back. Such brazen rule breaking, she thought.

She knew where she was going. Straight to Rashid's. What she wasn't sure of was how she would announce that she was with child. She stared at the dark green impregnable Achimota Forest as she crossed the road that stood before it. She flagged the passing taxis, eventually stopping a battered red and yellow one.

"Circle. Dropping," she told the driver, a middle-aged looking man with a wide gap between his front teeth.

"Twenty cedis," he said.

"That's so expensive," Akua Afriyie said. She'd cough it out—she had bigger problems than trying to bargain with the driver.

"My sister, you're running away from school, eh?" he said. He reeked of stale perfume covering male musk. His scent wafted her way in waves, making her stomach heave.

"I'm not running away," she said, trying to quell her nausea. "I'm not feeling well. I'm going to my father's office." She hoped her tone was curt enough to discourage further probing.

"Oh, sorry. But my sister you look very healthy," he said, staring at her.

She felt he was keeping his gaze more on her than he was the road. She looked out the window at passing neem trees, Indian almond trees and newly constructed houses. Street hawkers stood idly by as the taxi zoomed by. As the driver turned onto the Nsawam Road, she felt the car bump in and out of large craters in the earth. She prayed she wouldn't throw up in his car.

At a traffic light she saw a girl, not more than ten, with hair beaded into a thousand little balls balancing a metal bowl of bananas on her head. A few meters ahead of her, a boy who couldn't have been much older than the girl sold dog chains. Her eyes were then drawn to a man sitting on the curb dressed in a black and white smock and burgundy trousers that hung at his ankles. His red skin seemed sunburnt. His eyes shone with ferocity as he stared intensely into space, his lips moved to their own beat. She felt as empty as she imagined he felt. Yet, she was filled with a new life.

"These hawkers are becoming serious," the driver said. "I blame it all on Acheampong. He came to spoil Ghana."

"Ghana has been spiraling out of control for a long time," she said, feeling her own stomach spiraling out of control.

"Let's wait for elections this June and all these soldier people will leave us alone," the driver said, sucking his teeth.

"Soldiers, civilians. They've all ruined this country," she said.

"I like your complexion and your slimness," the driver said. Akua Afriyie didn't react. "Your skin is so black. You don't bleach like these women have been doing," he went on, taking Akua Afriyie's silence as license to keep talking. He steered sharply around a bicycle rider. "Your mother!" he cursed at the rider. Akua Afriyie felt her insides rising. She exhaled, closed her eyes. Breathe, she told herself. "Will you be my wife?" the driver went on.

"I already have a husband," she said.

"Oh, no! Poor me! I don't believe it. In fact, you look very sweet, succulent and ripe," he said, staring at her.

If only you knew how ripe I am, Akua Afriyie thought. She hic-cupped. "I need to vomit," she blurted out.

"Don't do it in my car!" he screamed. He leaned over and pushed open her door. She hurled out a salivary mess onto the grey road that flashed rapidly by.

"Thank you," she said, holding on to her stomach.

"Eh, my sister, you're really sick," he said, as he parked in front of the Ghana Commercial Bank, a multi-story building with flaking grey walls and exposed white and yellow base colors.

"Yes."

"Get better," he said. Akua Afriyie paid the fare and walked to a glass double door guarded by a man in an olive green uniform. He pulled the door open for her. In the main banking hall, she walked straight into an elevator whose door had been thrown wide open.

Inside the small grey elevator, Akua Afriyie felt her fear rise. She'd broken up with Rashid. But he'd said he and his wife were divorcing, so things might work out in her favor. But did she want to get married to someone who'd lied to her? She looked at the buttons. Their numbers had rubbed off. She counted from the bottom and pressed the seventh button. As the elevator ascended, it rattled and squeaked, reminding her of the story of a woman who died in a lift in a Ghana Commercial Bank building when the power failed. She died as she was being rescued—she slipped and fell five floors down. The idea of death, for the first time in her life, seemed like a comfortable escape. If she died in the elevator, she wouldn't have to deal with the repercussions of her pregnancy. She could see the headline already:

Pregnant Achimota student dies in elevator on the way to see her paramour.

On the seventh floor, she stepped out of the lift, looked left and then right. She wasn't sure which way to go. She banked on left. She read the blue and gold plaques posted to grey doors.

Georgina Asare, Regional Director; Eric Avah, Operations Manager; Rashid Adams, Assistant Manager ...

She knocked on his door and opened it. Inside a slim attractive secretary sat under a framed map of Ghana and behind a pale blue typewriter. She quickly stuffed a magazine under her desk and looked at Akua Afriyie.

"Yes, can I help you?" she asked and pursed her lips, a deep shade of red.

"I'm here to see Mr. Adams," Akua Afriyie said. "Please tell him it's urgent."

"He's busy, but I'll see. And your name is?" The secretary looked up and rolled her eyes.

"Akua Afriyie."

The secretary did a double take. Her eyes opened and then slanted. She seemed to disapprove of Akua Afriyie. After what seemed like an eternity, she picked up her phone.

"Sir, there's one Akua Afriyie here to see you," she said, nodding and smiling into the phone as if Rashid were sitting in front of her. Akua

Afriyie thought the woman's job must be so boring. They were probably trained to smile every time the phone rang. "He'll see you now," the secretary said.

"Thank you," Akua Afriyie said, walking into Rashid's office. She closed the door behind her. She really wasn't sure how to broach the dreaded subject.

"Sit down, Afriyie," Rashid said, filling up his large cream swivel chair. "Are you sorry you broke up with me? You're here to say you love me?" She already felt that nothing good was going to come out of her visit. She placed the envelope on Rashid's desk. She stood there waiting for him to pick it up. "Please, Afriyie," he said, pointing to a black swivel chair across from him, "Sit!" She sat down. He opened the envelope, pulled out the sheet it contained. His protuberant eyes danced over the words on the sheet. He put it down, clasped his left fingers in his right and then toyed with the gold ring, which was now on his left hand.

She looked at the wood-paneled walls and shifted her gaze to his desk. Two in- and out- metal baskets bursting with papers sat on the black desk next to photographs of his wife and two daughters in wooden frames. The girls had both inherited his bulging eyes. She noticed the card with the abstract painting she'd given him in January next to the photos. Somehow she felt comforted. Somehow she felt that there was hope, after all.

"My dear," he said after the silence was becoming unbearable. "Good morning to you. Are you sure ... about this?" he asked calmly.

"Why would the doctor's report lie?" The more she looked into his calm face, the more convinced she was that this mess was hers alone.

"Afriyie," he started, "a baby is an occupation. I know, I've had two. This job has been forced down your throat, but you don't have to accept it.... I know someone who's very good with this kind of thing," he stopped. His fingers worked the back of his neck.

"What are you suggesting?" she asked, her voice thick with mucus. "This is not the time to get cryptic on me. Are you suggesting that I get rid of the baby?"

"I'm just considering our options."

"And the first one you consider is abortion? What happened to your divorce?" Tears ran down her cheeks.

"Oh, that," he said, twirling his ring. "We've decided to iron out our problems for the sake of our children. But if we're thinking on the same page, you know, I'm Musl…"

"That's out of the question," she cut him off. "I'm not going to be anyone's second wife." A loud sob escaped her lips.

"You know I can't divorce my wife," Rashid said. "Not after our decision to try to work things out."

Akua Afriyie was trying to think. She didn't know what to do. If she got rid of the baby, she could go back to school, finish her A-levels and carry on with her life. But she'd be tormented with the guilt forever. She knew herself. Things bothered her. They ate her insides, till her innards were sore. She heard the steady click-click-click of the secretary's typing outside. She looked at Rashid's navy-blue suit, his black face breaking into beads of sweat despite his calm. Her eyes were drawn back to the photos of his wife and children. His wife seemed so happy. What have I done? she asked herself. It was obvious he wasn't taking any responsibility for the child growing in her—unless she married him.

"You aren't saying anything," Rashid said, breaking the silence.

"What is there to say? You've laid down your options. Were you being serious about the second wife option?"

"Eh," he started. "It is a possibility, but not one I can spring on my wife now, considering our situation and you know, I have to seek her consent."

She rose from her seat, nauseated. The man wanted her to get rid of the baby, is what everything boiled down to. "I was told you were busy," she said. "Sorry to have wasted your time." She marched for the door.

"Afriyie," he shouted. "We can deal with this rationally."

"Obviously you've made up your mind about what *you* want to do, so I'll let you be and deal with things my way," she said, her voice quivering. She walked out and slammed the door behind her. She felt queasy. She thanked the secretary and went down the elevator. She felt too sick to go back to school. She was sure she looked sick enough to fool her mother. She caught a taxi and went home.

She banged on the rust red gate outside her parents' house. After five minutes, Abokyi's head appeared over the gate.

"Eh, small madam," he said, wiping his eyes. He bent over to open the gate. "Is it Easter already?"

"No, it's not. I'm not feeling well. Is any one at home?" she asked.

"Your mother and father haven't come back from work."

She thanked her stars and walked into the house. In the living room, she saw her parents had acquired a new thirteen-inch television set. She looked at it and climbed up the recently polished wooden stairs to her room.

Tsotsoo had taken over the room since she and Naa Tsoo had left for school. Her black and white pictures of Jimi Hendrix and The Temptations were still up by her bed. She walked to the fish she'd drawn on the wall when she was six. It had become one of those family stories that were repeated over and over again to every visitor. That was one of her first acts of rebellion. Would her pregnancy join the list of embarrassing family tales?

Confused, tired and angry, she lay on her bed, which was covered with an orange and white sheet. She'd go back to school after the weekend. She could probably hide the pregnancy for the next three months, write her A-levels and then she'd disappear and have the baby. Yes, that was her plan. It sounded good. She closed her eyes, replaying images of Rashid's face, his complacent smile and gold and silver hybrid ring, which was probably his wedding ring. She reached for her tattered lime-green teddy bear—one of her father's gifts from Germany—looked at its cold brown eyes and flung it at the wall. She closed her eyes again, trying to will sleep to make her thinking cease. She heard honking at the gate. Her stomach flip-flopped. The metal gates whined open.

"Abokyi, good evening," she heard her mother's voice say. She was sure Abokyi would blow her cover. She couldn't hear his voice. "Akua!" her mother screamed as she opened the front door. She cursed Abokyi. Why couldn't he just be quiet? She hoisted herself out of bed and walked to the yellow-bordered full-length mirror posted to the bedroom door. She looked at her reflection. Her eyes were crimson and wet.

As she descended the stairs, she saw her mother coming up, dressed in her green and white uniform.

"There you are! What are you doing here?" Lizzie asked.

"I think I'm coming down with something," Akua Afriyie said. "I get these temperatures at night and have been throwing up."

"Why didn't you go to the school hospital?" Lizzie asked.

Akua Afriyie felt her mother studying her whole body. She took cautious steps down the stairs. "You know they don't know anything," she said. "They prescribe aspirin for everything." She hoped her nonchalant act was working. Lizzie gestured for Akua Afriyie to turn around and go back up.

"Let me take your temperature and we'll go from there," Lizzie said.

Mother and daughter walked into Lizzie's room. The thick olive green curtains bordered with floral embroidery were drawn, making the room dark and cozy. Lizzie turned on the air-conditioner. Akua Afriyie sat on the impeccably laid bed. Lizzie pulled open a drawer. Akua Afriyie heard her mother push aside papers, plastic bags, stone-like objects.

Akua Afriyie fixed her eyes on her mother's shoe collection. This woman has shoes she hasn't even worn, she thought. Such waste! How much of one thing did a person need? she wondered. She knew she was avoiding the problem, but she thought the farther she shoved it from her mind, the less suspicious her mother would be of her.

"Aha!" Lizzie said and walked toward Akua Afriyie. "Raise your arm," she instructed, sticking a thermometer in Akua Afriyie's armpit. She pressed the back of her hand against Akua Afriyie's forehead. "You're warm, but it's not yet a fever. I'll take your temperature again later." Lizzie handed her a sachet of aspirin. Akua Afriyie smiled at the irony, walked into her mother's bathroom and downed the tablet. "You should go rest," Lizzie said.

Akua Afriyie went back to her room, convinced the worst was over. She'd go back to school on Monday, and ride out the first three months of pregnancy. She closed her eyes and drifted off into sleep.

When she woke up, she saw her mother's face hovering over hers.

"Have you eaten?" Lizzie asked.

"No," she said rubbing her eyes.

"Akua Afriyie," Lizzie started. Akua Afriyie swallowed. Oh, Lord, she thought, here we go. "Are you pregnant?" Akua Afriyie shook her head, unable to speak. "Don't lie to me," Lizzie said. Akua Afriyie stared at her bed sheet. "Oh my goodness," Lizzie exclaimed. "I knew it! As soon as I saw your face, I knew you were going to give me bad news."

"I'm sorry," Akua Afriyie said. She couldn't deny it. Maybe now that her mother had figured out she was pregnant, she could tell her how she planned to deal with it.

"Who did this to you?" Lizzie yelled. "Were you going to just pretend all along?" Akua Afriyie remained silent. "I don't know what to say to you. Your father … he'll be so disappointed. Eh, Akua Afriyie, you didn't think of any of us? You're going to give the man an attack." Her father's asthma had been cured, hadn't it? Her mother was too melodramatic. She stared at the orange and white stripes. Why did I think I could outsmart a nurse? she wondered. "Speak! Who did this to you?"

"I can't tell you, Mamaa," Akua Afriyie squeaked.

"This is not the time to be protecting anyone," Lizzie said, mopping her eyes. She lowered her voice, "Was it an Achimota teacher?"

"No, Mamaa."

"You don't know who got you pregnant?" she asked, flaring up. "Or are you such a … such a prostitute that you don't even know who put his thing in you to do this to you?"

"Thank you," Akua Afriyie said. Her mother had just called her a prostitute. Her own mother. Lizzie stormed out of the room. Akua Afriyie was stunned. It had been a bad idea to come home. She should go back to school. She stood up and was about to put on her shoes when the door opened.

"Pack a bag," Lizzie said. "You're going to your Auntie Asantewa's till this cools down. I don't want to give your father an attack."

"It's fine, Mamaa," Akua Afriyie said. "I'm going back to school."

"To do what? You're having a child. School is nowhere for you to be. Besides that art you're studying is not going anywhere…. Asantewa said she'd take you in, so pack a bag. Be quick before your father gets here."

Akua Afriyie looked at the bottom of her wardrobe. She picked up a snakeskin bag her mother had given her. "Are you kicking me out?" she asked, just to get the facts right.

"No, I just don't want to upset your father. I'll find a way to break the news to him and then you can come back home."

"I can tell him myself," Akua Afriyie said. "I'd rather tell him myself."

"Fine, whatever. I can't deal with you, now …"

Akua Afriyie picked up two dresses and stuffed the bag with them. "I see how it is," she said. "You'd rather kick your daughter out than send away a man who everyone knows is cheating on you. The man spends every year in Germany and yet you stick by his side."

Lizzie leaned forward and slapped Akua Afriyie's cheek. It felt like the first shock of cold water when she was taking a shower in the Achimota School bathroom.

"I'm sorry," Akua Afriyie said, a tear coursing down her face.

Lizzie snatched the snakeskin bag from Akua Afriyie and walked out of the room.

"Abokyi!" Lizzie shouted when they were outside. "Please open the gate. Please don't tell Uncle that Akua was here."

"Yes, madam," Abokyi said, grinning. "Small madam, next time."

"Yes," Akua Afriyie said. Her mother had just snatched away all her dreams. She had disparaged what she was studying and hadn't allowed her to finish school. It was now clear to her that her mother never wanted anything good for her. She wiped the corners of her eyes, realizing that she'd have to be strong for her child and be a better mother than hers was.

Fifteen
Northern Babies

May 1979

Akua Afriyie could feel the rays of sunlight seeping into the bedroom even with her eyes closed. She opened them and looked up. The corrugated-iron roofing glistened. She brought her gaze back down to the clock on the wall across from her. 10:15. Hoisting herself out of bed, she looked out the window. She saw a white wall so close, she could touch it. She bent down to open the snakeskin bag that sat by the bed's wooden frame and pulled out a black and gold scarf. She tied it around her uncombed hair and removed her nightgown, replacing it with an orange *boubou* Asantewa had given her.

As she trudged out of the bedroom she saw a note sitting under a cluster of keys on the plastic table in the middle of the living room. She picked it up:

No water. Didn't have time to fetch any. Tanker comes to compound at ten. Gone to the market. Auntie.

Should pregnant women be doing such heavy labor? she wondered as she made her way to the bathroom. The putrid stench of urine that had been sitting too long in one place rose, assaulting her nostrils. With no window in this place, it's no wonder the place smells like a public toilet, she thought. Asantewa's landlord is a conman!

Next to the toilet bowl was a shower. A metal bucket sat under a bronze tap, which she twisted open. Not a drop trickled out of it. She began to feel as if the acrid urine fumes were being absorbed into her skin. Disgusted, she picked up the bucket, hung it in the crook of her arm, grabbed her keys and walked out of Asantewa's house.

Just outside the door, she was startled by a tall man in burgundy trousers and a black and white smock. His uncombed hair had taken the form of a million little round balls. She'd seen him somewhere before.

"Morning," he said quietly.

"Good morning," she replied.

"Where's the woman who lives here?"

"She's not here today," Akua Afriyie responded, avoiding the man's intense stare. She still couldn't remember where she'd seen him.

"Thank you," he said, glaring at her, as if he were also trying to place her. He turned round and walked away. The morning sun bounced off his red skin, making it look aflame. She walked on a narrow laterite path between an uncompleted house and a bright pink house.

She came to a clearing and saw a large, black metal tanker parked on a patch of grass and dried clay. A long line of people snaked its way around the truck. She rushed to the end of it and stood behind a woman in glasses.

"Good morning," Akua Afriyie said.

"Good morning, Akua," the woman said, her wet jheri curls shaking. Her plastic glasses filled up more than half of her oval face.

"How do you know my name?"

"It's a small compound and your aunt told me you're staying with her. She's my very good friend. Gloria Kugblenu," she stuck out her hand. "I live in the house over there." She pointed at a blue house with a coconut tree in front of it.

"Oh, OK," Akua Afriyie said. She studied the queue. Some women were sitting on metal basins they'd stacked together. They'd also strung several buckets around their arms. I'd be foolish to fill just one bucket, she thought. "Sister Gloria," she started.

"Yes, my dear?"

"Can you please keep my spot? I'm going to get another bucket."

"No problem. This shortage could go on for days, and nobody knows when the tanker will come again. Bring as many containers as you can."

Akua Afriyie sprinted back to Asantewa's, all the while holding on to her belly. As the days wore on she became more aware of the life growing in her.

Asantewa's house was a small bungalow with rounded white walls. Her doors were unvarnished and unpainted. Akua Afriyie walked straight into the bathroom. She picked up a paint bucket they used to store water. She hurried back to the kitchen, looking around it for a basin. Everything in Asantewa's house was small and cute. Now that she needed a large pan, she couldn't find one. She looked at a wooden shelf stacked with aluminum pots, pans and plastic plates and gave up. Besides, two buckets was all she could carry.

Back at the tanker, Akua Afriyie noticed the line hadn't moved much. Three women now stood behind Gloria.

"She was here before," Gloria explained to the women just as one of them sucked her teeth loudly.

"Thank you," Akua Afriyie said.

"Anytime," Gloria said, a wide smile spreading her cheeks apart. Akua Afriyie caught her breath and put the white bucket down by the metal one. The ground, a sickly shade of brown, was caked and dry.

"Where are you coming from?" Gloria turned round to ask her.

"My parents live in Labone."

"So you're coming to keep your aunt company? That's good. She gets a little lonely."

"Why I'm here is a little complicated…. I'll be staying here for a while," Akua Afriyie said.

"Good. Now that I know you'll be here for some time, let me invite you to my church. The Christ Apostolic Church. We meet at the Trade Fair. It's not far at all. If you want, I can take you with me this Sunday." Akua Afriyie wanted to roll her eyes and ask Gloria where God had been all this while. Be nice, she scolded herself, she held your spot.

"Oh, thank you," Akua Afriyie said, preparing herself for a bold-faced lie, "but I go to my mother's church."

Gloria smiled. "Praise be to God that you go to church."

Akua Afriyie returned the smile but was trying to think of what she could say to the woman to make her get off the church topic. She toyed with the idea of telling her she was pregnant. I'm preg… It was on the tip of her tongue.

The line inched forward. Akua Afriyie pushed her buckets forward.

"My dear, feel free to come by my house anytime you want to eat or visit," Gloria turned round and said. "Also, I have bible study every Tuesday night. I like to encourage the youth of the compound to come. You'll make some interesting friends."

"Thanks," Akua Afriyie said, praying that the woman would just shut her trap. Her stomach was gurgling. She hadn't eaten a thing. But she couldn't leave the line. Why am I having this baby? she wondered. I don't know how to take care of my own self … how I'm going to look after it? Why was I so stupid?

Minutes passed, the line was still serpentine. Akua Afriyie felt faint. Gloria twirled around. Her jheri curls swished from left to right.

"My dear, what's wrong?" she asked. "Your eyes are very red. Have you eaten?" Akua Afriyie shook her head. "You don't look well at all. Go ahead of me. In fact, I'll tell the people in front you're ill."

"Thank you," Akua Afriyie said, licking her cracked lips.

Gloria walked to the front. Akua Afriyie saw the woman roll her hands, one over the other and point to Akua Afriyie. One woman shook her head vigorously. The other two nodded. Gloria signaled for her to come over. Akua Afriyie bent over, her head a heavy load and used all the energy she could muster to pick up the buckets. She strode to the front of the line.

"God bless you," Gloria said to the people now behind Akua Afriyie.

"Thank you so much," Akua Afriyie said weakly.

The tanker operator cranked the large faucet open and water gushed out of a huge pipe into Akua Afriyie's buckets. She'd never been so happy to see water pouring out like it was. When her buckets brimmed over with water, she strained her muscles and moved them out of the way.

"You don't look like you can carry those," Gloria said. "Go and eat and I'll bring your buckets over."

"Oh, sister, you've done a lot for me already. Don't worry," Akua Afriyie said.

"It will be my pleasure to help. I'll bring them to you. Go." She waved her hand at Akua Afriyie, who felt like a caged bird. She didn't know if she could trust the woman. She trudged back to Asantewa's house, hoping she hadn't been foolish.

The room was spinning when she got in. She limped to the kitchen and wolfed down cold leftover rice and beef stew. As she bit into a piece of meat, she heard a knock on the door. She walked over. Gloria stood at the door with the two buckets.

"I don't know how to thank you," Akua Afriyie said.

"No problem at all, my dear." Gloria walked into the living room and put the buckets on the concrete floor. "Remember to come to our bible study," she said and walked out.

Akua Afriyie carried the metal bucket to the bathroom. As she bathed, the sharp odor of urine rose up in waves. She held her breath to stifle her nausea.

She dried herself off and thought of Gloria and how the woman had selflessly helped her. She'd been as good as rude to her, thinking the thoughts she had. She hardly came across such people. Her own mother couldn't find it in her to help her. She put on the same orange *boubou* and retied the scarf. She walked into the living room and dialed the silver knob of the radio.

"... today's headlines. Flight-Lieutenant Jerry John Rawlings named as the leader of last Tuesday's attempted coup attempt," a woman's voice read.

Akua Afriyie spread herself on a cane sofa and dozed off. She was startled awake by a pot crashing loudly to the ground. She sat up and saw Asantewa milling about in the kitchen.

"Sorry," Asantewa whispered.

"Good afternoon, Auntie," Akua Afriyie said, wiping the sleep out of her eyes. "I didn't hear you come in."

Asantewa laughed. "How was your day? I see you were able to get some water."

"I almost fainted at that tanker. One of your neighbors, Gloria, helped me carry the buckets. She really saved me."

"When she's not doing her Chrife things, she's very sweet," Asantewa said, putting onions next to the sink. "We're all Christians but people like her take it too far."

"She said I should come for Tuesday night fellowship or something," Akua Afriyie said.

"You can go if you want. Just know what you'll be getting yourself into." An onion rolled off the sink counter and fell onto the floor. "I need a table for the kitchen."

"You should get lots of things, Auntie," Akua Afriyie said. "Ceilings, tiles in your bathroom, tiles on your floor ..." She counted off her fingers.

"I know," Asantewa said, sucking her teeth. "There's no money in this country. Everyone is hoarding goods at the market. Today, I decided I had to do the same. Now I'm selling a tin of milk for twice the price and pretending it's the last tin on the earth's surface."

"Ei, Auntie!"

"I know. But I'll lose if I don't do that."

"I suppose you have to do what you can to make a profit. Otherwise we'll starve. Ei, I almost forgot! Some man came here today. He looked a bit off."

"Oh, that's Babasam!" Asantewa said. "He's harmless. He comes around once in a while. Everyone in the compound helps him with food. Sometimes he does tasks when he's lucid. I think I humor him because he reminds me of someone."

"I thought the same thing too!" Akua Afriyie said. "Well, as long as he's harmless, next time I'll feed him."

*

Akua Afriyie was bored of sitting in Asantewa's living room with nothing to do. She relented and ended up at Gloria's house. The woman brought out two chairs, placed them under the coconut tree and went back inside. Akua Afriyie didn't know what she'd talk to Gloria about. She stared at the numerous houses squaring the compound, thinking of what to ask the woman.

Gloria came back out with a man who looked Akua Afriyie's age. He was dressed in olive green combat trousers and a matching T-shirt.

He spread a wide grin on his face. He looked like Gloria without a jheri curl.

"… don't worry, sister," he said to Gloria. "It's all for the good of the country. The SMC has toyed with us enough and they've thrown a good man in jail …"

"Just remember that Jesus never used violence," Gloria said, moving her glasses farther up her snub nose. "Akua, this is my younger brother, Wisdom."

"Hello," Akua Afriyie said.

"Hello," Wisdom said, gripping Akua Afriyie's hand in a solid handshake.

"He's a junior officer and as you know one of their people was thrown in jail recently for the attempted coup."

"Yes, yes, I heard. The last thing we need right now is another coup and another military government," she said. Wisdom's smile disappeared and he marched with a haughty air, toward the compound's exit.

"See you later, sister," he shouted.

"Oh, I probably shouldn't have said that," Akua Afriyie said. Gloria sat down.

"No, I agree with you. But these young soldiers, that's all they understand. All everyone needs is Jesus in their lives. I mean look at that man," she said, pointing to Babasam who'd wandered into the compound and was knocking on a red door. "I once asked him what his story was."

"Is he all right?"

"He has moments of lucidity. He told me he's looking for someone. I said to him everyone is looking for someone and that person is Jesus."

"What happened to him?" Akua Afriyie asked, intrigued.

"That, my dear, no one knows."

"That's so sad," Akua Afriyie said, staring at the man's back. He was in his burgundy trousers and smock uniform. "Does your brother have any clothes he doesn't wear anymore?" She didn't know why Babasam moved her so much, but she'd help him, however she could.

"Yes, he does."

"Please collect them for me," Akua Afriyie said. "I'll give them to Babasam."

"God bless your heart," Gloria said, her eyes wetted up. "In fact, I'm glad you came." She placed a bible on her lap. "God moved me to read a Bible passage to you."

Akua Afriyie groused internally. Hadn't she already done her good deed for the day?

"I'm reading from James, Chapter one, Verses two to four. Are you ready?"

"Yes."

"'Consider it pure joy, my brothers, whenever you face trials of many kinds, because you know that the testing of your faith develops perseverance. Perseverance must finish its work so that you may be mature and complete, not lacking anything.' Amen."

"Amen," Akua Afriyie said.

"You should read the whole chapter. You'll find it helpful."

*

June 4, 1979

Akua Afriyie wobbled on a bench in Asantewa's store that had become her throne. She clutched a Wonder Woman comic book in her right hand and had placed the left hand on her belly. She'd started insisting on going to the market with Asantewa because she was tired of Gloria's proselytizing. She looked at the pages of the comic, but her mind kept going back to the coup that had been announced that morning.

Posted on the aqua walls were two wooden shelves. They were stacked with plastic bottles of frying oil, powdered milk, bars of soap and packets of ginger toffees and yet, seemed half empty.

Asantewa stood behind the enamel counter, punching the keys of a calculator and making notes in a long ledger notebook. Crackling on the far left of the counter, by a plastic bottle of oil cut in half, was a small radio. Every so often, an announcer's voice said, "There has been a change of government. We are performing a house-cleaning exercise."

The radio blared louder. "Members of the general public should rest assured that we have taken care of an uprising which occurred earlier this morning. Armed Forces Officers should return to their respective units immediately."

Commotion and raised voices made Akua Afriyie strain her neck to look outside. She saw big market women waddling by as fast as their thick legs could carry them. She shifted her gaze to Asantewa who was looking up from her calculations.

"… soldiers!" Akua Afriyie heard from the store next door.

She jumped off her seat and leaned forward, placing her palm on the wall. Soldiers marched in and out of stores. One woman stood outside her shop, pulling her hair out as soldiers stomped out of the blue storefront, chucking boxes to the ground.

"Maybe we should close the door, Auntie," Akua Afriyie said. Asantewa was riveted in place. "Auntie!"

"Hmmm?" Asantewa said, distractedly. "I knew I shouldn't have kept those goods in the back." Akua Afriyie looked at the back of the store, at a closed bluish-grey door. She got up to start drawing the doors closed when two men in green army fatigues ran in, AK-47s slung around their shoulders.

"Who is the owner?" one of them demanded.

"I am," Asantewa's voice quivered.

The soldier penetrated the store. His boots cast angry thuds against the concrete floor as he inspected the shelves. The other stayed at the entrance, his eyes on Akua Afriyie.

"What's in there?" the first asked, pointing at the bluish-grey door.

"Nothing," Asantewa murmured. "Just extra goods I couldn't put on the shelves."

"Open it!" he barked. Asantewa, her shoulders hunched, walked to the door. Akua Afriyie heard it click open. "Get rid of all these things you've hoarded!" the soldier shouted and swiped Asantewa's cheek. Akua Afriyie heard the slap. It was quick and clean. "You market women have been hoarding all these goods. Look at the number of boxes in here. Throw everything outside! Throw them out!" He spat.

Asantewa obediently carried a box, walked by Akua Afriyie, and tossed it out onto the street. Cans of milk powder burst out.

"Sir," Akua Afriyie started, "don't you want to take these? Instead of …"

"Shut up," the other soldier sputtered in her face. "If you don't want trouble, you will comply with the rules. We're cleaning up. You market traders have been working with the SMC to destroy our country." He pointed the rifle at her. Its muzzle was level with her nose.

Akua Afriyie held her breath as she felt drops of spittle landing on her face. She glared at the soldier and wiped a drop that landed next to her lip. Asantewa was now standing in front of the counter, trembling.

"We'll be coming back to inspect. If you don't hoard, you'll have no trouble. If you hoard, you will pay!" They marched out.

"… no cause for alarm. The civilian population shouldn't panic," the radio droned.

Outside, soldiers paced up and down. Akua Afriyie saw one of them roughly push a girl to the ground. She heard the dull thudding of boxes hitting tarmac, the sharp clinking of metal cans against each other, frightened feet scurrying up and down and soldier's boots pounding with impunity. Despite all the noise, she sensed a quiet fear that had risen above the immediate din. Accra was shaken.

"We have to go home," Asantewa whispered.

Akua Afriyie nodded, her hands still on her belly. She couldn't erase the image of the gun that had been thrust in her face. "No," she said, changing her mind. "Let's stay in here till this dies down."

Quickly, the two women, one tiny, the other pregnant, pulled in the metal gate of the store. Asantewa locked them in. Akua Afriyie turned down the radio. They sat in the now dark room. Akua Afriyie heard her stomach growl.

"Eat something," Asantewa said.

Akua Afriyie shook her head. "Too scared, Auntie."

"Nonsense, you're having a baby. Eat milk powder, at least." Asantewa went to a shelf, fumbled along it and trudged back to Akua Afriyie. She popped open the metal cover open, scratched at the metal protective covering and thrust the can at Akua Afriyie. Akua Afriyie took the can, poured a heap into her hand and lapped at it.

When the sound of running abated, Asantewa opened the metal door. Akua Afriyie got up, picked up her comic book and took the tin of milk along with her. They stepped out of the shop. Asantewa locked up, and they made their way out of the market. Little boys scurried by picking a can of Milo here, a tin of sardines there, bars of soap—it was their day.

*

Asantewa leafed through the *Daily Graphic*.

"I don't understand why Limann's new government can't distance itself from Rawlings and his junior officers," she muttered under her breath. "They came to do their house-cleaning and some people were happy—I wasn't—but now that Limann has been voted in, they don't want to disappear and allow the man to rule in peace."

"Uh huh," Akua Afriyie said. She was lying on her back, her head cushioned by Asantewa's lap. Her mound of stomach jutted out. She'd been having contractions all morning but hadn't told Asantewa because she was sure the woman would overreact. Now, they were increasing in intensity. She felt her belly muscles contract. The discomfort disappeared and came back, stronger than before. A spastic pain traveled down from her abdomen, slicing its way down her lower back. She shrieked.

Asantewa dropped the newspaper on Akua Afriyie's face.

"I'm sorry. I'm sorry," Asantewa said, picking up the paper. Akua Afriyie howled again and sat up in the cane chair, holding her belly. Asantewa jumped and clutched her heart. "OK, we're going to the hospital now. No sitting around." She ran out of the house, leaving Akua Afriyie on the couch.

She ran in five minutes later, dashed into Akua Afriyie's room, came out with the snakeskin bag and helped Akua Afriyie out of the chair. They walked out of the house, on the narrow laterite path and onto the clay and grass clearing. Akua Afriyie saw a red and yellow taxi parked close to Gloria's house.

The driver got up to open the back seat. Pain coursed down her spine again. She bit her lip to stop herself from screaming. She lay on the seat. The driver closed the door. She looked above at the roof of the taxi, covered with a green paisley cloth. She kept staring at the patterns, trying not to think of the pain that was tearing through her body. She felt as if her womb was being torn open. As she exhaled, she felt the car gaining speed. The driver kept his finger on the horn, providing a soundtrack to her pain.

"Eh, sister, don't spoil my car," he said.

"The woman is in labor, please just drive," Asantewa said. Akua Afriyie sat up. They were already at the Liberation Circle. 37 Military Hospital was at the turning just after the circle, but traffic choked up circulation. The driver was now pressing the horn in staccato.

Akua Afriyie felt another wave of contractions. She suppressed the scream that was making its way out and it ended up sounding like a sneeze. A policeman at the circle looked at the taxi and walked over.

"Massa, the woman is in labor," the driver said.

"All right," the policeman said. He blew his whistle and made way for the taxi driver to go through.

"Thank you," Asantewa screamed at the policeman, her voice louder than Akua Afriyie had ever heard it.

Outside the hospital, Asantewa paid the fare and helped Akua Afriyie walk into the general ward. Akua Afriyie didn't feel like standing or walking—all she wanted to do was sit and stop the pain. Her knees buckled in agreement.

"Sit on a bench," Asantewa said, pointing to one of many drab grey benches in the reception area. "I'm coming." She walked away and returned with a nurse in a green and white uniform pushing a wheelchair. They helped Akua Afriyie into the wheelchair and carted her through the pale green corridor. Asantewa lagged behind. From the corner of her eye, Akua Afriyie could tell she was jumpy. They walked through a grey double door. In the ward, beds lined both left and right walls of the room. On the right most of the curtains were drawn. The nurse pushed Akua Afriyie's wheelchair to the end of the ward and helped her sit on a bed on the left.

"Breathe slowly. Like this," the nurse said, puffing and deflating her cheeks.

"I'm coming," Asantewa said again.

"Where are you going, Auntie?" Akua Afriyie asked, her eyes popping open.

"I'll be back."

Akua Afriyie stared at the bed just across from her. It was empty. The room was green. She continued breathing. Why was everything so green? From her last art history class, she'd learned that the word green stemmed from the word growth—that was an auspicious sign.

Asantewa came back to Akua Afriyie's bed.

"Where did you go, Auntie?"

"Shhh! Breathe," Asantewa said.

Akua Afriyie stuck her right hand in the air and gestured rapidly for Asantewa to hold it. Asantewa's calloused hands grazed Akua Afriyie's. Akua Afriyie puffed her cheeks in and out.

"Sweetie," she heard her mother call.

"What's she doing here?" Akua Afriyie asked Asantewa.

"Breathe, just breathe," Lizzie said as she came over.

"No, please leave. I don't want you here."

"Akua, she has to be here," Asantewa said.

"Sweetie, don't talk. Just breathe," Lizzie said.

"No!" Akua Afriyie said. Asantewa had looked after her through the entire pregnancy. She was the only person who deserved to be in there with her.

A nurse with flaky skin walked toward them.

"No, no, no," Akua Afriyie said, shaking her head.

"Why is she saying no?" the nurse asked.

"I don't want that woman here," Akua Afriyie said, pointing at Lizzie.

"Breathe!" the nurse said. "Madam, I'm sorry, but you're aggravating the patient. You have to leave. Or at least wait in the reception. But you can't be in here."

"She's my daughter."

"Oh, sister, why are you treating your mother like that?"

"Please. I don't want her here," Akua Afriyie said almost in tears, writhing in pain on the sheets.

"I'm a nurse. It's fine," Lizzie said.

The nurse now smiled smugly, as if to say that was more reason for Lizzie to leave. "Sorry, madam," she said. "I suggest you wait in the reception area. Right now you're not helping. Please …"

"This is ridiculous! Akua Afriyie, you're being utterly ridiculous."

Akua Afriyie screamed in pain.

"Breathe," Lizzie said.

"Go away!"

Lizzie marched out in a huff, trailed by Asantewa. Akua Afriyie just wanted the pain to stop. The nurse mopped Akua Afriyie's brow with a face towel.

Asantewa came back by her side. "You really hurt your mother," she said. "She was in tears."

"Auntie, I'm going to die!" Akua Afriyie said, crying out.

"No, you're not. Just breathe."

Another woman walked over to Akua Afriyie's bed.

"Hello, my dear," she said. She was tall and heavyset. "I'm your midwife. Just inhale and exhale but don't push till I say so." The midwife parted Akua Afriyie's legs and pulled down her panties. Akua Afriyie squealed in pain and discomfort.

"It's all right …" Asantewa said.

"Breathe," the midwife said, her voice menacing. She stood up and left Akua Afriyie with Asantewa and the nurse. After what felt to Akua Afriyie like hours and hours of contractions, she came back.

"She's fully dilated now," she said to Asantewa as she looked at Akua Afriyie's crotch. "All right, my dear, we're going to do this together." Akua Afriyie nodded. "Push slowly."

Akua Afriyie pressed her aunt's hand, pushed and stopped, and pushed and stopped. She felt as if her vaginal muscles would split and release all her innards. At some point the pain tearing through her body made her feel numb. When she thought she should give up she heard the baby cry. She was drained, but strangely excited.

"Congratulations! You have a girl!" the midwife said. Akua Afriyie already knew what the baby's name would be. She took the child and held her in her arms.

Sixteen
The Curfew

June 1980

With Sugri wrapped in an orange and red cloth on her back, Akua Afriyie locked the door to Asantewa's house. She trudged toward the clay opening. It was one of those days when grey clouds hung ominously low, seemingly ready to burst open with rain. She saw Gloria talking to another woman under the coconut tree. She walked toward them.

"... I went to buy corn yesterday. I couldn't find any," the woman was saying.

"All this is happening for a reason," Gloria said to her, adjusting the frames of her large glasses. "It will be well."

"Where is this country going?" the woman asked.

"God is in control," Gloria said.

"Hello. Good morning," Akua Afriyie said to the two women.

"Morning," they responded. Akua Afriyie gazed at the flowerpots lining the front of Gloria's house—by far the nicest looking building in the crowded compound. She peered through an open window and saw a framed picture of Jesus hanging in her living room.

"I have some clothes for you," Gloria said.

"Oh, thank you. I'm going for a walk, I'll take them with me."

Sugri made gargling noises behind Akua Afriyie.

"Ooh, princess," Gloria cooed.

"She cried all last night," Akua Afriyie said. "I didn't sleep one bit. And when I put her down she starts crying ..."

"I'm coming," Gloria said and went inside her house. She came out with a big white plastic bag. "Akua, I can take care of Sugri for you," she said, handing her the bag. "You look like you need a break."

"Don't worry. She'll probably start crying."

"It's no problem. I'll take care of her."

"Thank you," Akua Afriyie said, untying the cloth around Sugri. She patted Sugri's bottom and handed her to Gloria.

"Don't worry about the crying," Gloria said. "It will stop soon. They grow up so fast. In just a few years you'll be wishing she was still this tiny human being. It's wonderful."

"I can't wait for her to grow up," Akua Afriyie said. "I have to visit the doctor to find out when she can start eating solids."

"It must be impossible buying baby food, with the way things are expensive," the other woman said.

"It's only by His Grace that we survive," Gloria said.

"I was just telling her about how I went to the market and could only buy one thing. One thing!" the other woman said.

"I know what you mean," Akua Afriyie said, folding the cloth. "I'm so lucky my aunt has a store. She brings all this baby food and she gets good foreign brands too."

"Go ahead for your walk," Gloria said.

"You're a lifesaver," Akua Afriyie said. As she strolled out of the compound she passed by Gloria's brother in full military fatigues. "Hello, Wisdom," she said.

"Hello," he said coolly and bounded off. Since the handing over of power from Rawlings to Limann, he seemed to have become restless. She always saw him going and coming, each time dressed in soldier's garb. She was convinced he was plotting something.

She passed by the general store outside the compound. Babasam stood in front of a barred up tailor's shop, his look pensive. He seemed to possess the wisdom of time. She walked up to him and handed him the bag of clothes.

"Thank you," he said and stared off into space again.

She strode by a string of closed shops. What was going on? That area should have been buzzing with life and commerce. She saw the Trade Fair Site looming with its arched roofs, pavilions, high gates and white walls. Only about ten years old, it already seemed derelict. Instead of using the road in front of the Trade Fair, she decided to try the graveled path behind it. Mangrove trees stuck out of swampy murky waters.

White birds flitted in and out of the grove. The air stank of excrement. She rushed along the path till it opened out to the wide Labadi road. Cars whizzed by with reckless abandon. She crossed the road and passed through a small fence that led to the beach.

She slowed down, dragging each foot in the sand, pondering the wide expanse of grey sea. Its rough waves hit the shore, receded and continued their everlasting going and coming.

She sat on the brown sand and thought about Gloria. Her proselytizing aside, the woman exuded inner peace. Akua Afriyie couldn't put her finger on what exactly that was, but the woman was always calm. Maybe that was what came with believing wholly and completely in Jesus. But she didn't want to go that route. Even though she had Sugri, her life felt empty, pointless, compass-less. And she felt she was encroaching on Asantewa's space. And Sugri. What was she going to teach her? She was still a child herself. What would she say when her child wanted to know who her father was? It was time for her to get a job. That way she could be more independent. But what would happen to Sugri? No.... She'd take care of Sugri till she was old enough for nursery school. She'd start working and pay Asantewa some rent. She stared at the sea—at the point where it kissed the sky. The line was so faint; sea and sky seemed one continuous stretch of grey.

"Whooo!" a deep male voice shouted, rousing her from her daydreaming.

She looked over to her left. A group of boys and girls, just about her age, were setting up umbrellas and mats. The one who shouted was prancing about in the water, throwing his arms up and down. Akua Afriyie smiled sadly. That used to be my life, she thought.

The man with the deep voice dragged a girl into the sea and was trying to drench her with brine. The girl shrieked and tried to run from him. He pulled her back, successfully ducking her whole body into the water.

"Kwasi, you're a stupid fool, OK?" she shouted, laughing and squeezing the water out of her clothes.

They seemed so carefree. She was sure life would never allow her to possess that kind of freedom again. Her time had passed.

*

Sugri sat by Akua Afriyie's feet, on Asantewa's well-worn cane sofa. Akua Afriyie watched Sugri, whose hair was held in three little puffs, pick up a plastic doll and chew on its fingers.

The door opened forcefully. Startled, Akua Afriyie jumped out of her seat. Sugri broke into a loud howl. Asantewa stormed into the room, locking the door behind her.

"Oh, Auntie," Akua Afriyie exhaled. "It's you! You gave me the biggest fright. What are you doing here?" Sugri's wailing grew so loud, Akua Afriyie couldn't hear anything else. "It's OK," she said, hoisting Sugri from the seat.

"You haven't heard?"

"Heard what?"

"Rawlings has taken over in another coup."

"What?"

"Oh, yes. As soon as I heard it on the radio in the store, I locked up as fast as I could and caught a taxi back here. No, I wasn't going to be bullied again. No, not this time. No ..."

"Auntie, calm down. We should turn on the TV ... or the radio. This man is tireless, isn't he?" Akua Afriyie said, walking across from the sofa. She twisted a round knob jutting out of the brown-paneled TV.

"He announced a holy war," Asantewa said, settling on the sofa, catching her breath.

"A war?" Akua Afriyie asked. "Is that what we need?"

A greenish-grey image mottled itself into focus. "... B. Parliament is dissolved," Rawlings read out. His hair was shaped into a short afro and through the TV screen his skin took on a pale green hue. "C. The council of state is abolished. D. All political parties are proscribed. It is therefore illegal for any person or persons to belong to or operate under any party ..."

"What does this mean for us, Auntie?"

"Akua, I don't know. The way these soldiers like harassing us in the market, I'm sure we'll be forced to reduce prices again, just like in 1979." Sugri pressed her head against Akua Afriyie's chest. Akua Afriyie felt her child's mucus and tears seep into her clothes.

"Are you hungry?" she asked Sugri.

Sugri nodded, tears staining her face. Akua Afriyie placed her by Asantewa and walked to the kitchen. She popped open a tin of Cerelac, scooped out two spoonfuls and dropped them into Sugri's pink bowl.

"Is this going to keep going on?" Asantewa asked. "Coup after coup after coup? Why? I'm sure when Nkrumah and others were sweating for our independence, they never dreamt that this would happen to us."

"You know, Auntie, I've even lost track," Akua Afriyie said, stirring the cereal with water. "Nkrumah was overthrown by …"

"Akua, you're going to have to become less apathetic. First, Ankrah's NLC overthrew Kwame Nkrumah. Then Afrifa took over from Ankrah …"

"In a coup?"

"Ankrah was involved in a bribery scandal with a Nigerian businessman, so they made him resign. When Afrifa took over he lifted the ban on political parties."

"So that's when Busia was voted in?" Akua Afriyie plodded back to the cane chair, pink bowl in hand.

"Yes, Busia was elected after that. Acheampong's NRC overthrew Busia. I think that was in 1972."

"That I remember! Papa had to stay in Germany for almost a whole year because they banned all imports. OK, so after that, Acheampong changed the NRC to the SMC."

"Right, then Akuffo took over from Acheampong in a palace coup. Rawlings's AFRC overthrew Akuffo and then handed power to Limann."

"And now he's overthrown him again! This country is a mess! Sugri, open wide." She led the spoon into Sugri's mouth. The history lesson reminded her of Lizzie, who she'd managed to avoid for a year. She hoped she was well. With military governments it was impossible to know who they'd go after. Former die-hard Nkrumah supporters? "Have you heard from my mother?" she asked.

"Yes, she came by the shop to bring Sugri baby food." Asantewa's right hand clasped her mouth.

"I knew it! I had a feeling all this was coming from her." She pointed at Sugri's bowl. "Next time she comes by please thank her for me."

"You should call her, Akua." Her aunt was right. Maybe she should call to thank her. But that was just like Lizzie to be so sneaky. She couldn't bring herself to start a rapprochement just yet.

"I completely forgot to tell you," she said, changing the subject. "Last week I went to find out about getting Sugri into the Little Flower Crèche. The coming new year, I'm going to start working and help you with rent."

"How did that go?"

"She has an interview next week."

"An interview for a crèche?"

"Yes, oh, Auntie."

"Eh, is this what it's come to? In my time, you stood in front of the headmaster like this," Asantewa stood up and stretched her right arm over her head to touch her left ear. "If you could do that, you went to class one. There was no nursery school."

"That's funny," Akua Afriyie said. "The girl is hardly talking. I'd be interested to see how they have an interview with her."

"Well, Sugri is a smart one-year-old, I'm sure she'll get in."

"Yes," Akua Afriyie said absentmindedly. She looked at Rawlings's face. In 1979 he executed the previous heads of state. Who was left for him to shoot at gunpoint?

*

July 1983

The living room of Abigail Mulbah took on a blue ambience. Soft early evening light poured into the room through light blue curtains. Decked with Victorian-style furniture, the room wasn't as stuffy as one would have thought. Akua Afriyie figured the white walls softened the feel of the room. Armchairs in floral fabric were arranged around a low table piled with newspapers.

Splashed on the front page of a newspaper was a photograph of a swarm of people packed on the deck of a ship, their arms dangling from its side. Some of them lowered suitcases into a throng at the base of the ship. The headline read, "Deportees arrive."

Akua Afriyie looked at her watch. It was just after five. Hopefully the interview would take half an hour. She'd be a little late in picking up

Sugri from school. Who scheduled meetings this late anyway? she wondered. She hoped that this, unlike the countless fruitless interviews she'd been to in the past two years, would work out.

Forty-five minutes passed. Akua Afriyie was still sitting in the floral armchair. A girl not much younger than she brought her a glass of water. She stared at the curtains and the armchairs so many times, they were etched in her mind. Tired of being in the same position, she got up. A cupboard with cabrioles stood pushed against the wall. She walked to it and studied the three picture frames on it. A woman with caramel-colored skin stood next to ousted president Limann. In another, she was surrounded by a young man and woman who looked like her.

"Hello," she heard as she was about to look at the third frame. She turned around. The woman she'd seen in the photograph stood there with a young man. "Sorry that took long," she said slowly. "Thank you," she said to the young man. "I will call you tomorrow with my decision. Please come with me," she said to Akua Afriyie. The woman strolled ahead of Akua Afriyie, dignified, unhurried. She pushed open the door to a small room. "Please sit," she said.

The office was covered in pink floral wallpaper. She saw a black typewriter on the desk and swallowed. Was this going to be a test? she wondered. The woman extracted a white folder from a cupboard to Akua Afriyie's right. It was filled with thick books.

"What is your name?" the woman asked, enunciating every word.

"Akua Afriyie Mensah."

"Abigail Mulbah. I'm working on a number of books. I travel a lot these days, so I don't have the time to type up my books." She opened the manila folder. "What I do get to do is handwrite them." She gave Akua Afriyie the sheets. Her penmanship was careful, deliberate, legible. "I need an assistant who can read my notes, transcribe them and edit the text where necessary."

"All right …" Akua Afriyie started.

"I want you to type the first page," Abigail said. Akua Afriyie's eyes bulged open. She should have learned how to type all this while, but she hadn't found the time to. When she wasn't interviewing, she was looking after Sugri. "Page one is marked at the bottom. Let me see …" Akua

Afriyie gave her the sheets. "Yes, 'Women and the Revolution.' That's page one." She handed the page back to Akua Afriyie.

Akua Afriyie stared at the typewriter, a blank page jutted out of it. She'd seen people use typewriters. Then they seemed like easy-to-use machines. Now, faced with the task of proving herself, she found this one seemed larger than life. She was thankful she didn't have to insert the paper, because that would have disqualified her, right off the bat. She looked at the keyboard. Where was W? Ah! There. She pressed the key with her right index finger. Her hand hovered over the keyboard, looking for each letter. When she typed in all of the title, she felt as if she'd accomplished the biggest feat. She didn't want to see Abigail Mulbah's face. She was sure it would be contorted into an expression of pure disgust. She ventured a look. The woman looked confused. Her eyes were fixed on Akua Afriyie's fingers.

"All right," Abigail said, after Akua Afriyie had slaved through one paragraph. "The work I do is highly sensitive, so I need to know your background from the first school you went to till now."

Akua Afriyie glanced at her watch, with its frayed leather straps. It was a quarter past seven. The curfew started in forty-five minutes!

"Up to class seven I went to St. Mary's School. After that I went to Achimota School."

"Fine schools. What did you study in Achimota?"

"Visual Arts." Akua Afriyie wondered why the woman was keeping her there. It was obvious she couldn't type. She was sure the woman wasn't going to hire her.

"How do you think your Visual Arts training will help you be my assistant?"

Akua Afriyie didn't feel like answering. All she wanted to do now was go pick up her baby and go home. "I have an eye for detail. I'll apply that to working on your transcripts," she said.

"Good. Did you go to university? If no, why not?"

"I had a baby." And I need to go get her.

"Where have you worked prev…" Abigail cut her own questioning short as she looked at her watch. "Oh, dear," she said. "What time does the curfew start?"

"Eight." Where have you been living, woman?

"It's already 7:30. I shouldn't keep you then," Abigail said.

"Thank you," Akua Afriyie said getting up quickly.

"All right, Miss ..."

"Mensah."

"Miss Mensah, I'll give you a call."

Akua Afriyie didn't care if she got this job or not. She shook Abigail's hand, dashed out of the building and flagged a cab.

She arrived at the nursery school just before eight. She knocked on the door hurriedly. A teacher answered the door. "Eh, Miss! What happened?"

"I'm so sorry. I got caught in a situation. I hope you don't live far away," she said feeling bad that she'd get the woman into trouble.

"Oh, I live behind here. Sugri! Your mother is here."

"Mummy!" Sugri said, running to hug Akua Afriyie's long legs.

"Hi, sweetie. We have to hurry home. Thank you," Akua Afriyie said, taking Sugri's lunchbox from her and clasping her right hand.

They marched to the main road. Akua Afriyie, realizing Little Flower was in the Burma Camp area—soldier and military police heaven—started worrying. Christ! she thought, I'm definitely going to get in trouble. The cars on the street had disappeared. Dead silence hung over the city, punctuated only by the cries of bats. The sky was now pitch black. Akua Afriyie stretched her neck to see if any cars approached. She made out a soldier, AK-47 in hand.

"Hey!" he shouted, crossed the street and ran toward her.

Akua Afriyie burst into tears.

"Mummy, why is that man running here?" Sugri asked.

"Because we're not supposed to be ..."

"What are you doing here?" the soldier shouted.

Akua Afriyie was getting hysterical—it was a mix of theatricals and unadulterated fear. "I'm so sorry," she said, her words getting stuck in her throat.

"You know you shouldn't be out here," he said, his voice softening. "Especially not with your child. It's not safe."

Akua Afriyie sobbed. "I know. It's really not my fault. I ... had an interview and the woman went on and on.... She was still in school." She sucked in phlegm.

"It's all right," the soldier said. "We'll find you a car."

The road stayed deserted. A stray mongrel walked on the other side of the street.

"Woof!" Sugri shouted. Akua Afriyie shushed her.

"How old is she?"

"Three years."

"I have a two-year-old son. What interview did you have?"

"I'm looking for any type of work," Akua Afriyie said. "The woman told me to come in at five."

"I hope you get the job."

Akua Afriyie sucked her teeth. "I won't get it."

"My sister, there are no jobs here," the solder said. "My brother was a big man in Nigeria. They sent him back on the ship with all those people they sacked from their country."

"I'm sorry."

"He has nothing to do here."

"It's sad," Akua Afriyie said, clicking her tongue.

A navy blue *trotro* sputtered up the street. The soldier stuck his arm out. The car stopped in front of them. The driver looked visibly stressed when the soldier stopped him.

"Massa," the driver started, "I took the car to the shop. Just now, they finished working on it."

"You know you shouldn't be out," he said. "Everybody can say they were visiting their grandmother—that's not my concern. You have broken the curfew!" He poked his head into the van, studying the faces of the people in the car. "And all these people were in the workshop?"

"Massa," the driver scratched his head. "I ..." He reached for his glove compartment.

"I will let you go today. Please take my sister home. Next time I catch you, I swear...."

"Thank you so much," Akua Afriyie said to the soldier. "God bless you."

"Thank you, my sister," the soldier said, helping Akua Afriyie and Sugri board the minivan. He banged on the side of the car.

Inside the *trotro* Akua Afriyie looked at the silhouettes of three women in the back.

"Where to?" he asked Akua Afriyie.

"Labadi."

"Yes, it's really sad, the way they just sacked us from their country," one of the women said.

"Oh, but don't worry. I know Jerry John Rawlings will make things right. They don't know what they've done. J.J. will put pepper in their eyes!"

"My sisters," the driver shouted, "but we did that to them already."

"Huh?"

"When?"

"Busia sacked Nigerians in the seventies. They were only getting revenge. *They* needed to put pepper in our eyes."

"Mummy," Sugri said, "what is putpepperinoureyes?"

"I'll tell you later," Akua Afriyie said.

"Rawlings is so handsome, don't you think?"

"He's skin and bones! And he's a murderer! He kidnapped and killed those High Court judges."

"Don't say that! Those people deserved to die! They spent all Ghana's money!" Akua Afriyie shuddered as she recalled that one of those judges was Dede's aunt. A year ago, the charred bodies of three kidnapped judges were discovered outside Accra. The man behind the murder was a member of Rawlings's government.

Akua Afriyie and Sugri got off in front of the stores that were now completely closed up. She held Sugri's hand and sprinted to Asantewa's house.

*

December 1983

Abigail Mulbah never called Akua Afriyie back. She'd interviewed in ministries, with private companies, in libraries, in bookstores. Maybe she'd set the bar too high. She was at her wit's end. Maybe she should call her parents. No, she had to do this without their help. Rashid! He was connected. She had to swallow her pride and call him. She walked to the general shop in front of the compound. They charged cheap rates for phone calls.

"Hello, Ghana Commercial Bank." It was the same secretary!

"Hello. Can I speak to Rashid Adams?" Akua Afriyie said.

"Who's speaking?"

"Akua Afriyie." Akua Afriyie was convinced she heard the woman suck her teeth. After a minute, Rashid's voice boomed into the phone.

"Afriyie! Afriyie!"

"Hello, Rashid." Akua Afriyie looked at the shop assistant. The girl was ogling her.

"I am so happy to hear your voice."

"Rashid, I need to see you," she lowered her voice.

"Oh, good. Usual place?"

"Yes. Can we meet on Saturday?"

"Perfect!" Akua Afriyie hung up, feeling like she'd sold a part of her soul. Even though it was the last thing she wanted, she was sure they would end up sleeping together. She was desperate, though.

Akua Afriyie arrived at the hotel first. The receptionist who had blabbed on Rashid's marriage still worked there.

"Eh, sister, we haven't seen you in a long time," she said, her hands touching her wet jheri curl.

"I traveled," Akua Afriyie said, amazed at how lying was becoming second nature to her.

"I hope you brought me a present."

"I'll bring it next time. Can I please have the keys?"

"Of course."

She walked up the familiar stairs. Faded red carpeting along the corridors—that was new—ushered her to door number twenty-seven. She walked into their love den. The sheets were pink, not the usual white. She sat on a wooden chair instead of the bed, like she would have in the past. Better not give him any ideas.

After half an hour, the door opened and he walked in. He looked rounder than the last time she saw him. He wrapped his arms around her, hugging her, kissing her left cheek tenderly.

"Afriyie, why did you abandon me?"

"You know why."

"How are you? You look good." He's just flattering me, she thought. She felt old.

"You're the one who looks good. People are losing weight all over the country, but Mr. Adams isn't."

"I'm really glad you called me. I've really missed you. But how are you? Last time I saw you, you hit me with big news. What happened?"

"I'll tell you later. I need a little help, Rashid."

"You haven't changed," Rashid said, chuckling. He sat on the bed. "Always springing things on me." Akua Afriyie frowned. "OK, ask for anything."

"I need a job. If there's an opening at your bank, or with any of your friends.... I'm looking for secretarial work." She added jokingly, "If you sack that your secretary, I'll take her place."

"Nadine?" he cackled. His laugh rippled through the room. "She's irreplaceable!"

"How's your wife?" Akua Afriyie asked.

"Do you really want to know?"

"Yes."

"She's fine. But Afriyie, I've really missed you." She smiled. "Shall we relive some old times?" he asked. She wasn't in the mood, but maybe this way, he'd help her with the job. Before she could give her consent, he whipped out a pack of condoms. "Taking precautions this time."

She didn't smile. He got up from the bed, walked to her and pulled her onto the bed. He kissed her. She realized she didn't quite like his smell. She hadn't noticed it before. Maybe it came with the weight he'd put on. She closed her eyes and let him wet her face with kisses. She felt no excitement, none of the rush that she'd experienced when she'd first met him. This was a job and the sooner it was over with, the better. She pulled her blouse over her head. Sugri had done minimal damage to her breasts—they were still perky. He sloughed off his T-shirt and trousers. His belly was growing rotund, his chest hairy. What had she seen in him? Where was his boyish charm? He kissed her, suckled on her breasts. She thought of Asantewa and Sugri. They were at Asantewa's shop for the day. She heard him grunting. She moaned, pretended to be enjoying his prodding of her body. She felt like crying as she realized that her mother had, in a way, been right about who she was.

He rolled off her. The sex was disappointing. A heavy awkward silence ensued until Rashid said, "You know, I'll really like to help with the job thing. My people do need some help, so if you're interested you could help us out."

"People?" Akua Afriyie asked.

"The PNDC."

"The PNDC?" she spat out. She thought of the gun that was pointed in her face and the fear that had gripped her stomach when the soldiers raided Asantewa's store. How she thought she and Sugri would have been lashed the night they were stuck out after the curfew. She thought of Dede's aunt's maggot-infested, burnt corpse. No. They came to power by means she simply didn't agree with. Rashid was buttoning his trousers. "I'm sorry. I don't see myself working with you and Rawlings's people." She sat up and pulled her panties up her legs.

"I haven't told you what kind of work it'll be and you're jumping to some kind of conclusion."

"I don't think there's any part of the PNDC I'd want to be involved with."

"Listen! There are women's movements you could join. They need a lot of help."

Akua Afriyie put on her clothes. "Rashid, I really can't be a part of any movement that uses violence to achieve its aims. The 31st December Women's Movement isn't any different. I know that's what you're suggesting."

"Women all over the country have been empowered thanks to them."

Akua Afriyie shook her head. "Why can't they be empowered with words? Or some thing else? But guns?! Imagine, getting handed a gun during an inauguration ceremony. Why would I want to belong to an organization like that?"

"If that's the stance you're going to take, I can't do much for you," he said. Akua Afriyie could tell he was annoyed. She looked at him, disgusted with herself—with him. She walked to the door.

"Thanks for nothing," she blurted out, feeling tears welling up in her. "And Rashid, I had a miscarriage." She slammed the door behind her, smoldering. She was shaking. When would all her troubles cease?

Seventeen
Breaking Out

"Sister, sister! Fine, fine tomatoes for you," shouted a woman sitting behind a short table, pointing to plump red tomatoes.

"I have nicer onions," another said, getting up to pull Akua Afriyie.

"Thank you," Akua Afriyie said, quickening her steps as she walked through the sweating bodies of market women and shoppers. The afternoon sun, high in the sky, was unrelenting.

She saw Asantewa sitting just outside her shop, her back turned to Akua Afriyie. She was talking to a woman nibbling a chewing stick and wearing a hairnet. As she approached, the woman spat out a big glutinous glob of saliva.

"… the Movement I've been doing really well. The soldiers have stopped harassing me," the woman was saying. "And also I get more products to sell."

"Good afternoon," Akua Afriyie said.

Asantewa turned around. "Akua!" she said a little too enthusiastically.

"All right, I'll leave you two," the other woman said.

Asantewa rolled her eyes as the woman walked off.

"She's always here," Asantewa said. "And is always talking about being part of the 31st December Women's Movement." She pulled out the wobbly bench for Akua Afriyie.

"It's becoming very popular," Akua Afriyie said, fussing with the shoulder pads on her pink and blue blouse.

"Especially with women in this market."

"Why don't you join, Auntie?"

"Me?" Asantewa sucked her teeth. "Because if I join them I know you'll be the first person to disown me."

"True, Auntie. But if you feel they'll protect you from the soldiers, go ahead."

"I'm fine. The soldiers have stopped harassing us since a lot of the market women are now members. And where are you coming from all dressed up like this?"

"I just dropped Sugri off at school. I was too nervous about the interview tomorrow to stay at home."

"You'll be fine, Akua Afriyie. I'm almost one hundred percent sure you'll get it."

"Amen, Auntie!"

"You know, you're my second visitor today," Asantewa said as she placed tins of sardine on the shelf.

"Who came to see you? Some suitor I should be aware of?"

"No, Akua! Your mother."

"Oh, OK," Akua Afriyie said. She didn't want to talk about Lizzie. Now she was feeling bad about not going to see her. "How's business?"

"Slow as usual. I really don't know if I can pay rent for the store this month."

"Auntie, I'll get that job and help you."

A woman with a big yellow head-wrap walked into the store, clutching a shiny brown basket. "Afternoon," she said. "Do you have Super Lux? The rose-scented one."

"You're lucky. There are only two bars left," Asantewa said. She put down a stack of sardine tins and walked to a shelf piled with soap and detergent.

"How much?"

"Ten cedis."

"Eh?"

"Ten cedis. That's the control price," Asantewa said.

The woman sucked her teeth. "For one bar of soap! Ei, Ghana!" She extracted notes from a piece of cloth tied around her waist.

"Thank you," Asantewa said. The woman kissed her teeth and walked out. "You see? Prices are too high."

Akua Afriyie looked at her aunt. Worry had creased itself into lines on her forehead. "Auntie," she said. "I'm off now."

"See you at home. Don't worry! That job is yours."

"Thanks, Auntie."

She walked out of the store and down the stall-lined streets of the market. Two soldiers wearing aviator sunglasses strode by her, laughing as they shared a joke.

*

All through her taxi ride, Akua Afriyie was convinced she was going to botch the interview. She stepped out of the taxi, paid the fare and strode toward a salmon-colored building. She straightened her black knee length skirt and puffed up her hair. Her hands were sweating. Her thighs were rubbing against each other, between them, a thin film of sweat lubricating her nervousness.

She walked up to a bungalow behind the first building, with two doors painted a deep maroon. The front of the building was lined with flowerpots bursting with green vines. She couldn't remember if she should use the door on the left or the one on the right. Left, right. Left, right. She decided to go for the door on the left.

Inside, two men were crouched over a large piece of white paper spread on a table. They stopped talking and looked her way. The one on the left adjusted his horn-rimmed frames and said in a sprightly voice, "Yes, can we help you?"

"Yes. I'm looking for Mr. Barnor's office," Akua Afriyie said.

"It's next door."

"Thank you. Sorry to have disturbed you."

"I'll walk you there," the one in glasses said.

The other man coughed loudly. "Eh, be careful of this man," he said.

Akua Afriyie wanted to laugh, but her nerves weren't allowing her to. All she managed was a smile. The bespectacled man stood up straight, adjusted his trousers and walked ahead of Akua Afriyie.

"Why are you looking for Barnor?" he asked.

"I have an interview with him."

"To work here?"

"Yes."

"Oh, good, good," he said, adjusting his glasses. "Good luck."

"Thank you. I need it."

"John Barnor is tough, but if you have a good CV, he'll hire you." Akua Afriyie swallowed hard. She was wasting her time then. Her CV had nothing on it to begin with.

The man opened the door and led her into a room with a desk, a standing fan and a typewriter covered with a film of dust. Her escort knocked on a door behind the desk. A gruff voice said, "Come in."

"Sir, good morning. This lady is looking for you," the man said.

"Thank you," said a balding portly man sitting behind a glass table. An air-conditioner droned loudly in the background. The bespectacled man left, shutting the door behind him. "Hello, Afriyie," the balding man said enthusiastically. "Sit, sit." Akua Afriyie sat in a brown swivel chair. "John Barnor," he said, stretching his arm toward her.

She shook his hand. "Akua Afriyie Mensah," she said. He already knows your name. What was the point in repeating it? she asked herself.

"Great, Afriyie," he said. "I have your CV here. I see you went to Achimota. Wonderful school!" He smiled widely.

Akua Afriyie wondered why he was calling her 'Afriyie'.

"You got just your O-levels, though. What happened?"

"I had a baby," she said, her jaws aching from the grin she'd forced on her face.

"Have you worked for anyone else?" John Barnor asked.

"No. But I learn fast."

"How are your typing skills?"

"I'm a little slow, but I've been learning." This is the moment when he tells me he needs someone with more skills, she thought.

John Barnor studied her resume for a long time, a deep frown furrowing his forehead. "Excellent," he said, after a while.

What could possibly be excellent? she wondered.

"I am looking for someone bright I can train. A lot of people have come in who have many skills, but too many bad habits. You seem intelligent…. And you're a clean slate." Akua Afriyie was stunned. She was still smiling sheepishly and didn't know if he was joking or being serious. What did he just say to me? She opened her eyes wider and looked at him. Barnor seemed to notice the confusion on her face and said, "My dear, you're hired."

"Really?" Akua Afriyie asked. "I mean, thank you." She rubbed her palms against her skirt. "When do you want me to start?"

"You can take the rest of the week off and come in on Monday," Barnor said, clasping his hands under his round face. "On Monday come straight in here. Your office is just outside."

"Where the desk is?"

"Yes. If I'm not in, just wait. We'll discuss salaries and all that good stuff then. Welcome aboard." He stood up to shake Akua Afriyie's hand. He was half her height.

"Thank you, sir."

"Please, call me John. This is a relaxed working environment." He grinned, his face took on the shape of an American football.

"Thanks, John. See you on Monday."

Akua Afriyie walked out, wondering why her luck had changed, feeling extremely light. Now she could give Sugri everything she needed and pay Asantewa for all she'd done for her.

*

December 1984

Akua Afriyie's fingers danced over the white typewriter as she typed a document for John Barnor. She'd made a lot of progress with her typing. For one, she didn't type with two fingers and she didn't look at the keyboard. Enough ego inflating, she thought.

The head of old fan orbited in front of her, clicking at the end of each rotation. She stared at the red plastic chairs across from her and wondered if she should go Christmas shopping. There'll be too much traffic in town. Maybe I should look for the flat today instead. As she battled over what to do, she heard a feeble knock on the door.

"Come in," she shouted.

The door opened and in walked Ernest wearing a grey political suit. His hair was greyer than Akua Afriyie remembered it.

"Eh, Afriyie! Is this where you've been hiding?"

Akua Afriyie felt ashamed, but thought his coming there was too much of a coincidence.

"Papa, how are you?"

Ernest smiled, which took away any suspicions she was harboring. "Can't complain, Afriyie. Ghana's difficult, but somehow we're surviving."

"Papa, how come you never came to visit me?" she asked.

"I was told that you weren't seeing any visitors," he said. "How's my granddaughter?"

"She's fine. You should see her. She's this tall," Akua Afriyie held her fingers by her head. "She turns five next month."

"Already? When are you two moving back home?"

"I'm looking for a place. I think it's too late to come home now."

"My girl's grown up. You should come visit us. We miss you."

"I miss you too, Papa." Five years had aged him, but he looked well. "You look happy," she said.

"Thanks, Afriyie. So do you." They remained quiet.

"You came here for John?" Afriyie asked.

"Yes. Funny I should find you here. He's a very good friend of mine. Is he in?"

"Yes. What do you need to see him for?"

"I'm working on opening a few more locations and I think he can give me a good deal. Cement prices are so high."

"What isn't expensive these days, Papa?" she said, now playing with her hair. "Let me check if he can see you now." She pushed away the papers which were covering the phone, picked up the handset and pressed a button. "Hi, John. Ernest Mensah here to see you."

She watched as her father walked into John Barnor's office.

"Ernie, old boy!" she heard John Barnor bellow. Her father was always gentle, yet she'd kept him out of her life, when he'd done nothing to her. She'd go home that weekend to call a truce.

Sugri bounced up and down on the bed. A brown cabbage-patch doll dangled precariously from her right hand as she worked the springs of the mattress. She squealed with each jump. Akua Afriyie had opened the *Daily Graphic* and was hunting intently for flat openings. She circled the only one she'd seen so far. One bedroom, bathroom outside house. Less than ideal, she thought.

"Sugri!" she said. "That's enough."

"Mummy, one more. Please."

She heard a knock on the door.

"Yes?"

Asantewa walked in. "Hello, ladies."

"Hello, Auntie."

"Hello, grandma," Sugri said, falling in a heap on the bed.

"Ei, life! Since you started working, I don't get any attention. And you!" she turned to Sugri. "Because you've started class one, you show no love to grandma."

Akua Afriyie laughed, "Oh Auntie, don't say that. Working women and school children just get tired, is all."

"How was work?"

"It was fine. Guess who I saw today?"

"Who? Babasam?" Asantewa asked, sitting on the mattress.

"No, I didn't see your husband," Akua Afriyie said. "Papa. He came to the office today."

"That's nice."

"Yes. Barnor called Papa, 'Ernie old boy'!" Akua Afriyie folded the newspaper. She hadn't told Asantewa that she was searching for flats. She was sure Asantewa had grown used to having them around and wouldn't take kindly to the news that they'd be leaving her.

"It's so sad that if you have no friends you don't get anywhere," Asantewa said. Akua Afriyie looked at her aunt, who was staring at the concrete floor, the corners of her mouth bent downwards.

"What do you mean, Auntie?"

Asantewa covered her mouth with her right hand. She said, "Did I say that out loud?"

"Yes, you did."

"This my mouth," Asantewa said. "I was just thinking about how John and your father have helped each other out …"

"Auntie, I don't think you would have covered your mouth if that was the only thing you were thinking about. And how did you know that John Barnor and Papa have helped each other?" Akua Afriyie knew the interview had been too easy. She was doing well at the job, but every so often, she'd get the nagging feeling that someone had worked a magic trick behind her back. She knew exactly what Asantewa meant by that. She stared at her aunt.

"You won't get annoyed if I tell you?" Asantewa asked.

"No."

"Your parents put in a good word for you."

"How did they know where I was interviewing?" Asantewa was quiet. "You had to have told them something. Why? What business of yours was it?" Akua Afriyie stopped herself.

"I'm sorry," Asantewa said. "I was trying to help. And you know Ghana—if you don't know somebody, you don't get anywhere."

Why couldn't they leave her alone? Akua Afriyie wondered. There goes the truce, she thought.

"Let me leave you," Asantewa said, getting up.

"Auntie," Akua Afriyie said when Asantewa was at the door. "I'm looking for a place."

"Oh! Because of this?" Asantewa said.

"I've been looking for a while. You need to have your space back."

"Akua, this is your home too. It's not much, but ... the girl needs to have more than one person around. Especially, with no father ..."

"That's enough, Auntie!"

Asantewa pursed her lips. Her eyes watered. "I'll leave you two then," she said, closing the door softly behind her.

Akua Afriyie's own eyes were clouding over with tears. She pulled Sugri toward her and held her tightly.

"We'll survive on our own," she said.

"OK, mummy," Sugri said.

*

March 1985

They walked over dusty wooden floors. The living room had big windows that overlooked a bare flame tree. One of the glass panels was broken. It looks like a dump now, but I can fix it, Akua Afriyie thought.

"Who are the people who live downstairs?" she asked, clutching Sugri's hand. Mr. Quartey, dressed in a bright blue suit and a red tie, was kneeling down by a wall, fiddling with a phone that sat on the dusty floor.

"A man and his young wife," he said. "I'm sure you'll get along very, very well." He picked himself up and brushed his knees.

"Do you handle painting or can I do that myself?"

"If I paint, I charge you extra," he said, now holding his tie, which Akua Afriyie thought he should loosen.

"I'll paint myself then," Akua Afriyie said, thinking of the colors she could splash on the walls to make the place warm and homey.

"Mummy, can I see my bedroom?" Sugri asked.

"Can we see the bedrooms now, Mr. Quartey?"

"This way," he said, walking though a small corridor. "This is the master bedroom. You have a very nice view." He looked through the window. Akua Afriyie and Sugri walked toward it. It was the same view as the one from the living room.

"Whose room is this?" Sugri asked.

"Mine."

"Do I also see that tree in my room?"

"She is sleeping in the other room?" Mr. Quartey asked.

"Yes," Sugri said. "Mummy, do I see the tree?"

"Isn't she too young?" he asked.

"I don't know, Sugri," Akua Afriyie said, ignoring Mr. Quartey.

They walked into what would become Sugri's room if Akua Afriyie decided to take the place. It was L-shaped and had a window that over-looked a backyard.

"I have plantain trees and corn!" Sugri said. "Mine is better than yours. Your tree had no leaves." Akua Afriyie stuck her tongue out.

Mr. Quartey looked at them with a face twisted in what Akua Afriyie could only describe as disapproval. What is your problem? she wanted to ask him. Are you also going to tell me how to raise my child?

He walked out of the room. They followed him. He flicked a switch. Akua Afriyie peered into the bathroom. The floor was tiled black and white. The bathtub looked new, the sink, not so much, with rust stains around the faucet. Above the sink was posted a wooden medicine cabi-net with engravings of leaves on it. Akua Afriyie loved it.

"Mr. Quartey, I'll take the place," she said.

"Very good. Do you have your deposit?" Mr. Quartey asked, shift-ing his shoulders under his suit. She felt hot, just watching him.

"You said we should add fifty percent of the rent to take care of cleaning the apartment. I want to do that myself, so I don't need to pay you …"

"Madam, there's a lot of work to be done. I suggest you let my boys take care of that."

"Why, isn't it just sweeping you'll be doing?"

"Madam, we have to wax the floors, fix holes in the ceiling, repair all the sinks, replace the mosquito nets, change the skirting boards, seal that broken window, paint—oh, you said you will do that—a lot of other things." The man kept hitting his left palm with his right index finger. She got the point.

"So that's twelve thousand cedis?" she asked.

"Twelve thousand five hundred," he said, straightening his suit jacket.

"I'll write you a check." She opened her orange purse and fished through it for her checkbook. "Sugri! Our new house!" she said excitedly.

"Our new house! Our new house!" Sugri chanted. Akua Afriyie remembered one of her earliest memories—moving into Ernest and Lizzie's new house. She recalled her mother shouting, "You can run anywhere you want! It's our house." She was wearing a white dress. She wasn't sure how accurate the memory was, but she felt just as giddy with excitement.

***

Eighteen
Babasam

July 1990

Lizzie-Achiaa was where she wanted to be in life but a lot of things bothered her—Ernest's excursions to Germany, Akua Afriyie's stubbornness and that she still hadn't met her first grandchild. Since Akua Afriyie had moved out of Asantewa's, Lizzie wasn't able to keep tabs on her, which was why she was going to the Tea House—a shady den of politicians, journalists and pseudo-revolutionaries. Mercy walked by her side, as they approached the thatch-roofed enclosure. She wondered why John Barnor had chosen this venue. They could have met in broad day light, in a place where older, calmer people met. Lizzie looked above the thatch roof. The sky was a dark purplish-blue speckled with light pink clouds. As they entered the Tea House, they were welcomed with rising voices laced with alcohol and boisterous guffaws cutting through the sound of glasses clinking and drinks fizzing.

Lizzie fixed her bag under her left arm and hooked her right arm in Mercy's. She saw familiar faces. A beautiful woman who broadcasted the news on Ghana Television was bent over a plate of *jollof* rice, twiddling her fork, not once lifting it to her mouth, while a portly man spoke sweet nothings into her ear. She looked out for Barnor but couldn't find him.

"Isn't that Fred Tetteh?" Mercy whispered and pointed at a young man clad in a white long-sleeved shirt.

"The anti-Rawlings journalist, right?" Lizzie asked. While she was no fan of Rawlings, she was living decently and didn't want to be associated with these incendiary types.

"He writes so well and yet is so young."

"I just want to see Barnor and get out of here," Lizzie said.

233

Next to Fred Tetteh was a scrawny man, wearing a yellow and brown tie-and-dye shirt that looked too big on him. Fred's jaws moved up and down without stopping, his hands formed shapes in the air and clutched at invisible objects.

"Mrs. Mensah," Lizzie heard a gravelly male voice say to her right, startling her. She'd been staring at the orbs Fred was molding out of air. She turned around saw John Barnor with his round face and rotund belly walking up to her.

"Oh, John! There you are! Long time no see." He smothered her in a hug. "You know, Mercy Ntim?" she asked.

"Yes," John Barnor said. "I believe we've met," he said, shaking Mercy's hand. "Do you want to join me at my table?"

"Sure," Lizzie said.

"You know what?" he said. "My table is rather unexciting. I brought the people who work for my newspaper out for drinks. They're being so boring. I think they're afraid of being themselves around me."

"That happens," Lizzie said. "Is Akua there?"

"No!" John Barnor exclaimed and laughed, as if Akua Afriyie's being there would have been out of the ordinary. She worked with him, didn't she? "Let's join Fred Tetteh over there."

"Whatever you want," Lizzie said.

Barnor, clasping a bottle of Guinness, led Lizzie and Mercy to Fred and the scrawny gentleman's table. Lizzie noticed that several large wet rings had marked the pink and white tablecloth. The men had probably been sitting there all evening.

"Fred old boy! Alai," John Barnor bellowed. "Can we join you, or will we be interrupting the secret workings of your cabal?"

"No, no, no," Fred said, picking up a sweating mug of golden beer. "Please sit."

"Lizzie Mensah, Mercy Ntim," John Barnor said. "Fred Tetteh and Alai."

"Nice to meet you," Fred said. "I was just telling Alai about how difficult it is editing a newspaper with this military, or should I say revolutionary government sitting on our necks."

Lizzie pulled out a cane chair, sat on it and rested her bag on the table and looked at Fred. His energy was intoxicating.

"How hard is it?" she asked him.

"You know, we're lucky we're even allowed to print. For everything we write, there's somebody in the PNDC crying libel. The *Daily Graphic* is the only paper that goes by unscathed."

"Don't you love how the *Graphic* shifts their message depending on who's in power?" Mercy asked.

"Yes!" Fred said. "That's why we need an independent press, but Rawlings's people are simply not letting us be."

"I loved that editorial your paper carried today," John Barnor said, shaking Fred's hand vigorously and cackling.

"Watch us get jailed for that," Fred said, waving his hand in the air. His eyes were beady and when he was making a point, which was all the time, he tried to open them widely but that only ended up highlighting how small they were.

"What was the editorial about?" Lizzie asked.

"It was in response to the Nigerian High Commissioner's speech yesterday. He said Africa shouldn't accept western styles of government," Fred started. "The editorial said when African governments stop going cap in hand to the IMF and World Bank, that's when they can choose their own forms of government."

"That's not the point," Barnor said. "The editorial said Rawlings came into power crying, 'Die imperialists!' Now he's a 'World Bank puppet'." Then as afterthought, he added, "Those were their words."

"I agree," Lizzie said quietly. She looked at Alai. He'd been silent since they came. His silence was unnerving. He seemed to be examining each and every one of them. "My question is," she went on, "when is the military going to let go? We ordinary people are simply tired of being under soldiers."

"When they squander all Ghana's money and have nowhere else to turn to," Fred said, "then they will hand over power to some poor civilian government they'll end up overthrowing in fifteen days."

"This country is living in a vicious circle," Mercy said, toying with the gold band on her left hand.

John Barnor sat forward and signaled for the others to lean in close. "I'm starting a party," he whispered and then pursed his lips.

"What about the ban on political parties?" Alai asked.

"Political party ban?" John Barnor said loudly and sucked his teeth.

"Are you serious about starting this party?" Lizzie asked.

"Why would I be joking?"

"You want to be overthrown by the military after being in power for fifteen days?" she asked him, chuckling. This man needs to stick to one thing, she thought. He dabbled in too many things for anyone to take him seriously. He had that construction company, the newspaper and now a political party?

"I'll tell you about it," he said. "First, can I treat you all to some guinea fowl kebab?"

"Definitely."

"I won't say no to that."

"Good," John Barnor said.

"What are we celebrating?" Fred asked.

"The future of Ghana," John Barnor said. He whistled for a woman wiping the counter to come over. She put down her rag and swayed over, robed in a long black dress. Her braided hair swished from left to right. "Woman! Some of your kebab man's best guinea fowl."

"Barnor!" she shouted. "That's no way to talk to the owner of this establishment. And above all, to treat a woman!"

The people around the table laughed.

"I don't know why I take such abuse," the woman said.

"Ignore the man's rudeness," Lizzie said.

"My sister, say it again. When Rawlings's commandos come and raid this place ..." She pointed at Barnor and Fred. "... just know I'll be coming to each of your houses, especially yours, Barnor. Guinea fowl, eh? How much?"

John Barnor looked at the faces of the people around the table as if studying them would reveal how much each would eat. "Give us five hundred cedis worth, for the moment. Ladies, what are you drinking?"

"Club beer," Lizzie said.

"Same," Mercy said.

"Madam Evelyn," he said, flourishing his hand in the air, "guinea fowl, two Clubs and one more Guinness."

"All right, sweetie-darling," she said and walked away.

Barnor looked around suspiciously and then said, "You all know how Busia's my hero?"

"Nkrumah! He's the one you should call your hero," Fred said.

"Hear! Hear!" Lizzie said, sticking her right hand in the air. Alai smiled at her and took a sip of his beer.

"Nkrumah?" John Barnor scoffed. "When Kotoka and his people took over the country, that was the only time I thought the army had done a good job. The man was a despot!"

Evelyn walked to their table balancing a metal tray with three mugs, two green bottles and a brown one in her left hand.

"That's where I disagree with you," Fred said. "He was surrounded by people who inflated his ego. Otherwise he had great ideas for the country and for African unity."

"But, Fred, you're a small boy. You don't know what you're talking about," Barnor said, pouring a thick stream of foaming Guinness into his mug.

"I might have been born after Nkrumah but I have eyes. I read! No other government since his has been able to, for instance, provide free education or healthcare ..."

"You know," Lizzie said. "I was a CPP girl back in the day."

"And what are you now?" John Barnor asked.

"Let me finish," Lizzie laughed. "As a woman in those days, I felt empowered. Running to rallies here, setting up a village school there. Nkrumah was a wonderful man. Now everyone gets into government just to get rich."

"What about the 31st December Women's Movement?" Alai asked.

"If they were operating under a proper civilian government, I would accept them as a powerful women's organization," Lizzie said.

"Uncle John," Fred said. Lizzie chuckled. "I want to hear about your party."

"Why am I even talking to you? I have a newspaper. I know you journalists. Like this." He hit the back of his left palm.

"This is off the record," Fred said.

"Hang on," John Barnor said, sipping from his glass. Froth caught in his moustache. "Where's our kebab? Evelyn!" The table erupted in laughter. Evelyn sashayed over with another metal tray heaped with grilled guinea fowl wings and drumsticks covered in a healthy mound of red pepper. John Barnor grabbed a wing and bit into it.

"I hope you're happy now," Evelyn said.

"Thank you, madam," he said, still chewing the meat. "I'm still working on the party framework. It will follow the Danquah-Busia tradition."

"You mean it will be a party of elites?" Alai asked.

John Barnor stopped and gawked at Alai. "My man, who exactly do you support? I know you've been a regular here for quite sometime, but don't think we're not on to you. You come here to just play devil's advocate for Rawlings. Really, who do you support?"

Alai slunk back in his seat. Lizzie was hoping for a serious fireworks-infused argument, but Alai wasn't going to defend himself, she could tell. She bit into a drumstick. The pepper burned her lips.

"Uncle," Fred said. "Let the man be. He has a point. One of the reasons I really like Nkrumah was that he reached out to the ordinary man, while Danquah and co. focused only on educated people and the big men of the Gold Coast."

"You are crossing uncharted waters, small boy," John Barnor said. "What I mean by a Danquah-Busia tradition is one that supports democracy without using one-party tactics, fear or force to rule. A tradition where people like you, Fred, can publish as many newspapers as you want without fear of being detained for saying the truth."

"Why didn't Busia succeed?" Lizzie asked.

"The military simply didn't let him," John Barnor said.

"You think the military will let you?" Mercy asked.

"Let history be the judge of that," he said.

"Hear! Hear!" Lizzie said, pushing her chair back. She looked at Mercy and nodded slightly. "Fellows," she said. "My husband is coming back to town tonight. John, thanks for the treat. Can I talk to you for a second?"

"Sure," he said.

"Aunties," Fred said. "Next time."

John Barnor sprang out of his seat, his right hand covered in oil and red pepper.

"How's Akua really doing?" Lizzie asked John Barnor, hoping the lilt of her voice carried no desperation. She wanted it to carry a mother's nonchalance, if there was such a thing.

"Afriyie?" he asked. Lizzie nodded. "Afriyie is very smart. I don't know what I'd do without her. She's organized my paperwork, and even helps with the newspaper. She's not here because of her child. I'm hoping she'll help with the party planning."

"Just be careful, John," Lizzie said, glad Akua Afriyie was spending time with the child, instead of coming to the Tea House.

As they made their way out of the enclosure, a tall gangly man in a light blue shirt and beige trousers walked toward them. Lizzie gasped. Bador Samed. Even though he looked neat, she could tell he was still lost in his own world. This was the first time she'd seen him since their encounter years ago. She bent her head, praying he wouldn't recognize her.

"Babasam, old boy!" John Barnor said. Lizzie could have killed him. "Coming for some guinea fowl, eh, old boy?"

Lizzie felt Bador Samed's eyes on her. He shifted his gaze to Mercy and walked into the Tea House. Lizzie's heart was tick-tocking. Those eyes. Those ageless eyes.

"John," she said, breathlessly, "why is he called Babasam?"

"Nobody has a clue," John Barnor said. "People say that's what he calls himself. Fellow doesn't talk much!"

"What happened to him?"

"They say he's looking for somebody," John Barnor said.

"Who says?" Lizzie asked.

"My children told me," John Barnor said, his eyes narrowing, making him look mysterious.

"How do children know these kinds of things?" Mercy asked. "And Mrs. Mensah, why have you taken such a keen interest in this madman?"

"Oh, nothing," Lizzie said quickly. He wasn't fully mad, was he? He just seemed lost. "All right, John," she said, hugging him and kissing his cheeks. "Thanks."

"Regards to Ernest," he said, turning round and plodding back to the Tea House.

"Mercy," Lizzie said hesitantly, her eyes fixed to the place the Bador Samed had disappeared through.

"Yes?" Mercy looked at her. Lizzie felt numb and saddened that the man who'd once been her raison d'être was now wandering the earth with a constant glaze over his eyes.

"I think that …" she started. She wanted to tell Mercy about who Babasam really was, but the woman would probably be convinced that she herself was mad.

"Lizzie, what?"

"Never mind," Lizzie said. "I forgot my train of thought." What happened to him? She felt guilty when she thought of how she'd tried hard to avoid being seen. Then she realized that she was probably the person he was looking for. No, this wasn't the time for him to declare his love for her in front of Mercy and John and all those people who looked up to her as a sophisticated woman. She sighed, thinking about life and how sometimes certain people just had to be forgotten. Coming to the Tea House had only compounded her worries. John Barnor had confirmed that Akua Afriyie was well, but now she had a fourth problem: a potential stalker on her hands.

***

Nineteen
Preachermen and Political Parties

January 1991

Akua Afriyie stood on a block in front of John Barnor's newspaper office, finishing off a meat pie she'd bought for a late lunch.

"Oh! Light off!" somebody inside shouted.

"Obviously!" she heard Salamatu say. She heard her suck her teeth deeply. These people aren't ready, Akua Afriyie thought.

She wiped her mouth and pushed the door open. James, a young reporter was crouched over a typewriter, his finger hovering above the keyboard, eyes glued to the keys, but unsure where to plant the finger. She laughed when she remembered how a few years ago she'd been in his shoes.

On the large table in the middle of the room, Lloyd, Salamatu and Ekow were pasting typed columns onto a tabloid-size sheet. Akua Afriyie squeezed herself between Lloyd and Ekow, whose hand shot up to his horn-rimmed glasses.

"You aren't ready, are you?" Akua Afriyie asked.

"Not with the power failure, no," Salamatu said, not bothering to look up. She rubbed a bottle of glue behind a strip of paper. Ekow looked at Akua Afriyie, shrugged and cut up a sheet with words in block letters.

Incompetent newspaper people! Akua Afriyie thought as she walked to James. She placed her palm over his shoulder, startling him. He dropped the handwritten notes that had been nestled in his lap.

"So sorry," she said, bending down to pick up the sheets. "Can you please call me when they are ready with the paper?"

"Yes. OK," he said, flustered.

They weren't even trying to hurry up, she groused. They would take their sweet time, bring her the proofs after five, and she would be the one rushing to the printers. She was so annoyed she didn't notice the block outside the door and tripped over it. She caught herself, wondering why she was having such a bad day. As she made for her office, a tall man in a white shirt and black trousers walked toward her.

"Excuse me," he said, his voice sonorous. "I'm looking for the marketing manager of the *Morning Guide.*"

She studied his face. What nice eyes! she thought. And dimples! Who did he just ask for? "Nkansah?"

"Yes, I think that's his name," he said, his hands in the pockets of his trousers. "There was no signboard, I wasn't even sure if this was the right office."

She pointed at the door to the newspaper office. "Nkansah works in there."

"Thank you," he said. "How about John Barnor? I'd like to see him as well."

"Mr. Barnor's in a meeting now. His office is in here," she pointed at the door she was about to pass through. "When you're done you can wait in my office for him."

"Thank you very much," he said.

Akua Afriyie walked back into her office. Who was that good looking man? His style was clean and simple. She looked at the low newspaper table in front of two red plastic chairs and suddenly it seemed too messy. She picked up the newspapers, rushed back to her desk, pulled out a torn T-shirt, skipped back, vigorously wiped the glass table, stacked the newspapers and placed them back on the table.

She moved back to her desk, knowing that in any minute, he would walk in. She arranged the manila folders on her desk in alphabetical order.

The door opened and in walked the tall dimpled man. He smiled at her and said, "Thank you. I met Nkansah. Is Mr. Barnor available now?"

"No, not yet. Please have a seat." She wondered why John Barnor was keeping so long. One of the models they used for the newspaper print ads had come in half an hour ago.

The man picked up a *Daily Graphic.*

Fifteen minutes passed. Akua Afriyie cleared her throat. "What's your name? I'll check with him."

"Edem Adomza," he enunciated.

Akua Afriyie picked up her phone and dialed in Barnor's exchange. "Yes, Afriyie," he said.

"John. Edem Adomza is here to see you."

"All right. Send him over in ten minutes."

Akua Afriyie put down the phone. "He'll see you in ten minutes."

"No problem," Edem said. He folded the newspaper and put it back atop the pile. "How do you like working with Mr. Barnor?"

"He's a good boss," Akua Afriyie said. No, he works me like a donkey.

"How long have you worked here?" Edem asked.

"I've been here for, what, seven years. Wow! Yes, seven years. Why do you ask? Are you looking for a job?"

"Oh, no. I was just wondering. I met him recently and he seemed like someone I could collaborate with."

"On what?"

"Well, I'm building a church ..."

"A church? Are you also into construction?"

"No. That's where Mr. Barnor comes in. I told him how I was having a hard time finding building materials for reasonable prices. He said he'd be able to work out decent rates for me. He also told me to immediately advertise in his paper to spread word about the church."

"Are you a priest?" Akua Afriyie asked.

"I prefer the term pastor."

"I see," Akua Afriyie said. That was just her luck. All the men she was interested in were always taken. Taken by other women and taken by God.

"You should come by the church," he said. "It's still under construction, but at least fifteen people show up every Sunday."

"What kind of church is it? Methodist, Catholic?"

"It's non-denominational. You should come."

"Maybe one of these days."

Finally, Barnor's door pushed open. John Barnor came out first, dressed in an embroidered short-sleeved shirt hanging over his trousers. The young model trailed out behind him, clad in a black skirt suit, her heavily-ringed right fingers clasping a cream manila folder. The suit ended at her hips and the skirt not long after that, high above her knees.

"Thank you," she said to John Barnor.

"Thanks, Lucy. See you at the shoot on Saturday." She walked out of Akua Afriyie's office. "Hello, Edem old boy, do come in."

"Thank you," Edem said to Akua Afriyie, following John Barnor into his office.

"Afriyie," John Barnor said, "before I forget, I brought some clothes for you."

"Thanks, John."

He handed her a big Harrods bag. Just as his door was closing, James walked into the office.

"The proofs are ready," he said, handing her a large white folder.

"Thanks," she said, picking up her orange purse, the folder and the Harrods bag. She strode out toward her car. A long grey streak of bird feces stained the windshield of her newly-bought, second-hand Fiat. I better be coming into some money, she thought as she got into the car. She looked at her watch. 5:20.

She reversed out of the car park, and drove toward the Kwame Nkrumah Circle. As her luck would have it, cars had choked up the large rotary. All she could see was the spike of the fountain that never worked in the middle of the circle.

That pastor was so easy on the eyes, she thought. She forgot to take down his information! How was she going to get to his church? There was no point anyway, she mused. He wouldn't be interested in her.

A taxi driver pulled up next to her on the laterite sidewalk of the road.

"Be patient!" she shouted. "It's because of you taxi and *trotro* drivers that there's such a jam."

"Go way you! Your mother!" the driver spat back, driving on.

Akua Afriyie groaned.

After thirty minutes in congestion, she parked by a large open gutter in front of the In God's Time printing press. A small wiry man was locking the door to the blue kiosk. She jumped out of the car, grabbing the plastic bag.

"Oh, Osei!" she shouted.

"Eh, Afriyie. You're very lucky," Osei said. "I was going to eat my dinner."

"There was so much traffic in town," she said, jumping over the gutter filled with black polythene bags, groundnut shells, newspaper and banana peels. "Thank God, I caught you. I don't know what I would have done."

"No problem," he said, taking the bag from Akua Afriyie.

She walked back to her car, feeling relieved and light. Now, it was time for her to go home and spend the weekend doing nothing. She drove through almost no traffic until she got to Nima.

On the left side of the road, a Benz van had broken down and blocked off half the road. Cars behind it were using the right side. People in Akua Afriyie's lane had to wait till those cars had gone by. Christ, why? Akua Afriyie thought. She looked at her watch. 6:26.

Sugri! She had completely forgotten to pick her up from school. And there was no way out of the jam. She pressed her horn. The driver of the car behind hers also started blowing his. Flat honks, perky beeps, heavy bellows all mixed together in the early evening breeze. Above the cacophony floated the Muezzin's evening call to prayer.

Once she was out of the jam, she sped down to Sugri's school. The school's white walls were now cloaked in a sea of bluish darkness. The gates were closed. She parked in front of the gate that usually led into the school. A watchman, an old man in a long white smock, shone a flashlight at her as she walked toward him.

"Good evening," she said.

"Evening," he said, standing up.

"Is there nobody in there?" she asked. He clicked his tongue and shook his head. "How come? I didn't pick up my daughter."

"I did my rounds, there's nobody there."

Akua Afriyie thought she would cry. Where was Sugri? "Where do students go if their parents pick them up late?"

"I don't know," the watchman said.

"What do you mean you don't know?" Akua Afriyie asked, her voice unsteady.

"Sister, I don't know. If students are left after six o' clock, they sit out here with me. Today I didn't see anybody inside the building. Everybody's gone."

Akua Afriyie bit her lower lip. Her mind raced. Recently, stories had been circulating about people coming to schools, pretending to be the relatives of students. What if that had happened? It could have. Sugri didn't know half the people in their family; anyone could pretend to be her aunt or uncle. The watchman was back in his reclining chair. "If a girl this tall comes back," Akua Afriyie said, holding her right hand at her shoulder, "tell her to call home immediately."

"All right," he said.

She drove back home, cursing herself, cursing the newspaper people for being late with a paper they'd had the whole week to work on, cursing God. She wiped her eyes, wet with tears. Should she file a police report? she wondered. Will those inept policemen even do anything? She turned at the last junction to her house.

A white Nissan Patrol was parked in front of her gate. Why were people so inconsiderate? she wondered as she honked. As if she didn't have enough problems. The back door of the car opened and Sugri stepped out, not in uniform—in pink shorts and a yellow T-shirt—and carrying her schoolbag.

Akua Afriyie parked in front of the white car, trying to wipe any traces left behind by her tears. She stepped out and marched to the Nissan. She looked through the car window. An older woman sat in the driver's seat, her head wrapped with a black scarf. A girl Sugri's age sat in the passenger seat, chomping on gum. The older woman waved at Akua Afriyie.

"Hello, madam," she said.

"Hello," Akua Afriyie said, hoping her voice came out cold.

"I hope you weren't too worried. Sugri is a friend of my daughter. I picked up Rose an hour late. When I got there, they were both starving, so I took Akua Afriyie home with us."

"That's kind," Akua Afriyie said. "I wish you'd left a message with someone, though. I was worried."

"I told one of the office administrators. He must have left before you got there."

"Thank you," Akua Afriyie said.

"What's your name?" the woman asked.

"Akua Afriyie."

"Dzifa," she said. "We should coordinate a system, so if one of us has to work late the other can pick up the children."

"That's a good idea," Akua Afriyie said, handing Sugri the key to the gate. No, thanks, she was thinking. Thanks for taking care of my child and thanks for almost giving me a seizure.

"Have a good weekend," Dzifa said. "We should talk."

"Thanks again."

"Bye, Auntie Dzifa. Bye, Rose," Sugri said. "I'll bring your clothes to school on Monday." She walked to the gate.

Akua Afriyie stormed back to her car. She still felt like crying—no, like hitting someone really hard. She drove into the compound, seething.

Inside their flat, after locking the door behind Sugri, Akua Afriyie set her purse on the table in the living room.

"Sugri."

"Yes, mummy." Sugri sat on the cane sofa.

"Next time, just wait for me."

"OK."

"Do you know how worried I was?"

"I'm sorry, mummy. Auntie Dzifa said she told ..."

"I've never heard you even talk about Rose."

"She's in my class."

"Sugri, you can't go around trusting just anybody. I mean, it was kind of that woman to take you home, but what if you ate something that made you sick?" Akua Afriyie knew all this was her fault, but she had to have the upper hand.

"Mummy, I'm really sorry," Sugri said. "Next time you're late, I'll just wait at the school."

This girl always finds a way to be rude, Akua Afriyie thought. "I suppose you've already eaten dinner, so you're not hungry."

Sugri shook her head. "I'm not hungry."

*

Akua Afriyie drove into the driveway of North Ridge Lyceum. Children
in brown and beige uniforms milled from the terrazzo-walled buildings
to their cars. Sugri was in her usual spot, under the white awning that led
to the administrative offices. She waved at her friends and rushed to the
car.

"Good afternoon," she said, throwing her schoolbag on the back
seat.

"Hi, sweetie. How was school?"

"You didn't forget me today!" Sugri said.

"Don't be rude. I forgot you because of your Uncle John's incompetent newspaper people."

"Exams are killing me!" Sugri said.

"You've never had a problem with school."

"Math today was so hard. I left two questions blank."

"Only two questions? You'll be fine," Akua Afriyie said.

"I hope I'm first this year. The exams are extra difficult."

"You're Miss Smarty Pants, you'll be fine," Akua Afriyie said, driving out of the school. As she nosed the car toward the Ring Road, a taxi
cut in front of her from a junction on the left. She braked suddenly. The
car jerked forward. "Idiot," she muttered under her breath. "These taxi
and *trotro* drivers are aggravating. They don't know how to drive."

Sugri fiddled with the knob of the car radio. "… PNDC is ready to
end its work …" She turned the dial.

"Go back, I want to hear that," Akua Afriyie said.

"This one?" Sugri asked after rotating the dial.

"Yes, shhh!"

"… Chairman, in a speech given at the *Palais des Affaires Etrangères*,
the Palace of Foreign Affairs in Paris, said the work of the Revolution,
which was to lay a sound foundation for a socially just and sustainable
economy, is nearing completion. The next step, he said, is in the hands
of the people …"

Akua Afriyie groaned.

"Isn't that a good thing?" Sugri asked.

"Oh, it is. It's just your Uncle John …"

"John number two?" Akua Afriyie laughed. "His name is John and Rawlings's name is John too. That's too funny!"

"I know. The thing is, your Uncle John has been dreaming of starting a party since ..."

"Uncle John wants to be president?"

"Yes! Now, he's going to go insane with joy, and guess what? I'm the one who's going to suffer." Akua Afriyie wondered if she would vote for John Barnor. She worked for him, but did she have to vote for him? She just couldn't imagine him as president. But he was better than Rawlings any day.

*

August 1991

The newspaper office was converted into the meeting place for the first brainstorming session for John Barnor's party. John Barnor himself leaned against the large table, clutching two hand-written sheets of paper, his rotund belly distended.

It seemed as if everyone in his office was being roped into his party. Akua Afriyie scanned the room. Lloyd sat by James. Next to him was Salamatu, looking as surly as ever. Akua Afriyie didn't know what she'd done to the woman but she was always hostile. Ekow was sitting almost across from Akua Afriyie and kept staring at her, his hands on his glasses. Akua Afriyie shuddered.

"Thank you all for coming out on this Saturday morning, when I know most of you would rather be digging into your morning *kenkey*," John Barnor said. Ekow laughed loudly. "The PPP, good men and women," John Barnor went on, his voice booming and steady, "is a party I've planned for years. The Progressive People's Party. This party will be based on the venerable traditions of Danquah and Busia."

"Do we all have to be involved in this?" Salamatu asked.

"No, no, dear lady. I just thought, since most of my employees, especially those of you in the newspaper office, shared my values and belief that this country is being destroyed by our current head of state," he chuckled, "you'd be the best place to start." He looked around at the room. "Feel free to walk out now, if you don't want to be part of this." Nobody made a move. "The Progressive People's Party," John Barnor went on. "We have a lot of work to do if progress is what we want. We need to do research, comb the streets of Accra for what the people want, and yet always stay true to the traditions of Busia and Danquah."

What if what the people want is different from Busia's tradition? Akua Afriyie wondered.

"What is our motto?" James asked.

"That's why we're here. We're here to brainstorm," John Barnor said. "I want the motto to reflect the fact that the time for change has come, yet I feel very strongly about keeping our forebears in mind."

"How about *sankofa*?" Akua Afriyie suggested. "You're going back to Busia's ways but using them to propel Ghana forward."

"I like it!" Barnor said. "That makes for a recognizable symbol too. Excellent."

"Isn't *sankofa* too quotidian?" Salamatu asked.

"Dear lady, in politics you want simple symbols," John Barnor said. "The elephant of the Republicans and the donkey of the Democrats in America. Very simple, you see." He smiled.

Aren't we going to vote on this? Akua Afriyie wondered.

"Next item is …" John Barnor said.

"Er, John," Akua Afriyie said, "can we vote on that?"

"Yes, yes. The PPP is all about democracy. All right then, all in favor of *sankofa* as the PPP's symbol?"

Most of the hands in the room went up. John Barnor pointed at the hands, counting quietly.

"All opposed," he said.

Salamatu and two others raised their hands.

"Great! With an eight to three majority, *sankofa* is our symbol."

Claps dispersed themselves dryly across the room.

"Right. Next item, groups," Barnor said. "The teams I have in mind are," he said, looking at his paper for the first time, "Research team. You will walk through Accra talking to the everyday man. Find out what he looks for in a leader. Ask him what his needs are.

"The next team is the art and logistics team. You will come up with logos, party paraphernalia etc. The third team will be the meat of the PPP. You will help shape what the party stands for, organize rallies, and if you prove yourselves, you'll be allowed to speak at them.

"Lloyd, I want to you to head the research team. Afriyie, I know you have all this artistic talent in you which has been lying dormant for too long. You're in charge of the art group. Your first assignment is to come up with a logo. Salamatu, I had you in mind for the last group, that is, if you're interested."

"Oh, I am," Salamatu said, smiling for the first time that morning.

John Barnor went on, placing the remaining employees into the three groups. Akua Afriyie was reeling from the lack of democracy he was already showing. Delegating her to a task without asking the others about it. She sighed. Ghana was full of such types trying to be president.

"John," she said, raising her hand.

"Yes, Afriyie?"

"We need to vote on the teams and team leaders."

"Right, let's vote." Most people stuck to Barnor's selections. "OK, team," he said, rubbing his tummy, "we'll convene here next Saturday morning. Team leaders, I'll want progress reports from each of you. After our general meeting, we'll break up into groups. But arrange to meet at least once before next Saturday."

This is the end of any possibility of a life, Akua Afriyie thought. And what am I going to do with Sugri? she wondered. Since the day she'd forgotten to pick up Sugri, she'd decided to become extra-vigilant. She'd just have to keep bringing her to work.

She walked into her office. Sugri's head was buried in her open exercise book.

"Sleepy head! We're done."

"Already?" Sugri asked.

"We spent so much time in there. Let's go home." Sugri closed her book. "Did you get your work done?"

"My homework? I finished it in five minutes and got bored."

"I'm so sorry. You know what?"

"What?"

"For enduring all this, you get to have a burger from Dolly's for lunch."

"Yes! Can I come with you every Saturday?"

"Yes, but don't expect to get treated all the time."

*

Akua Afriyie stood in a white room. The room's shutters, also white, were flung open to the sea, a deep aqua and turquoise. The white curtains fluttered in the wind toward the sea. Dressed in a white summer dress which was blowing in the strong breeze, she looked down at the beach— a pristine white layer of sand. A man in white shorts cut off at the shins and a short-sleeved, unbuttoned shirt looked up and waved at her. She waved back. She couldn't quite see his face.

Then the man was in the room, standing by her. He seemed to be nobody she knew. They stood dangerously close to the window. The wind alternated between disrobing them and wrapping their bodies in their white frocks. The man's dark brown chest was sculptured into ridges. She touched his chest, looked up at his face. He pursed his lips. His face became the pastor's. A dimple appeared and disappeared. He inched closer to her. His lip grazed hers. Then his tongue licked her lower lip, begged to be let into her mouth. He wrapped his arms around her body, bent her over. Everything became black. She was falling into a chasm.

She kept falling and woke up during the rush of the fall, landing in her bed. She switched on the lamp on her bedside table. She was in her orange-hued room. No white curtains, no white clothes, no deep blue sea and definitely no pastor. She put her hand on her head. Why was he in her dreams? She'd met him once. And since he told her he was a pastor, she'd pushed him out of her mind. She picked up the red alarm clock next to the lamp. It was 3:36 a.m. She was wide awake. She slid her hands down and touched herself. She felt wet between her legs.

When her eyes opened again, it was just after nine. She sat up in bed, stretched her arms and rolled out of bed. She pushed Sugri's door open. Sugri was cocooned in a blue and white wrapper. Akua Afriyie stood over her deciding whether to call her or whether to rough her awake. Sugri could sure sleep deeply.

"Sugri," she said in a small whisper. The girl didn't stir. "Sugri!" she said, louder. Sugri's body moved but she didn't make any attempt to wake up. Finally Akua Afriyie shook her shoulder.

"Hmm?" Sugri asked, removing the cloth off her face. She looked up at Akua Afriyie.

"Morning, sweetie. Rise and shine!" Akua Afriyie said. "It's time to go to the office. Bring your homework with you."

"Can't I stay here?" Sugri asked, not ready to end her sleep.

"Nope. Come on, wake up."

"OK," Sugri said.

When they walked into her office, Akua Afriyie strode over to the air-conditioner below a set of louver blades. After turning it on, she pointed at her seat. "It's all yours," she said to Sugri. She was feeling so springy and refreshed.

"Thank you," Sugri said, her voice heavy and groggy, as if she'd just woken up.

Akua Afriyie picked up a folder by the typewriter. "See you later, sweetie," she said, making for the door.

"Bye," Sugri said.

Akua Afriyie opened the newspaper office door and the first person she saw was Edem Adomza. She thought a horrible trick was being played on her. What was he doing there? She was too embarrassed to look his way.

Barnor hadn't arrived yet, but most of the team had. Not sure what to do with herself, she went around the room, shaking people's hands.

"Good morning, Ekow," she said.

"Hello, beautiful," Ekow said. "I've found a man who says he can make T-shirts for us, at a cheap price."

"Great!" she said. "Good job." She shook more hands, slowly, trying to delay each greeting so that John Barnor would walk in before she had to greet Edem. No such thing happened. She shook Edem's hands, stole a glance at his face, smiled and hurried off to Salamatu.

Barnor walked in twenty minutes later, sweating and wiping his forehead with a blue handkerchief. "Apologies, team," he said, mopping his brow. "My wife had me running errands." He moved toward the large table in the middle of the room. He wore black shorts that showed off hairy skinny legs. His blue and white striped polo shirt didn't hide his round stomach. "We have a visitor this morning," he said. "I invited Mr. Edem Adomza to join us, to serve as a fresh voice and a spiritual advisor. Thanks for coming, Edem."

"My pleasure," he said, his dimple playing hide-and-seek with Akua Afriyie's eyes.

"Let's start with administrative details," John Barnor said. "Research team. Afriyie, please take notes." No! she protested internally. Let somebody else take notes! I'm a team leader, this is just too much. She grinned at John Barnor, opened her folder and extracted a piece of paper. She poised her pen over it, ready to be the amanuensis.

Lloyd looked around the group, seeking support from his team members. "We haven't had enough time to comb the streets, so what we did was start in our own neighborhoods. I live in Jamestown. I walked around asking people what they thought of the state of the country. My impressions are that most people in Jamestown—the market woman, the fishmonger, the shoemaker—most people love Rawlings. The market women say he's Ghana's most handsome head of state. Others in my team got the same message. People say he's charismatic and they are going to vote for him."

Someone in the room laughed. It sounded like Salamatu.

"Thanks," Barnor said, his voice without its usual ebullience. "Art team?"

"Ekow's got a contact who can make T-shirts for us," Akua Afriyie said. "Maame is not here, but she's in charge of key holders, pens and other items. She said she found a supplier. I have three samples of logos. As soon as we vote on one, we can start printing it on the T-shirts ..."

"Show them to us," John Barnor said.

Akua Afriyie opened the folder and passed one drawing to her left and the other two to the man sitting to her right. On all three drawings the same long-necked bird picked up an egg on its tail feather with its beak. People oohed and aahed over the designs.

After the pages had been passed around the room, John Barnor said, "They are all fantastic, but we have to pick one. Let's say option one is the red bird surrounded by a vertical blue bar on the left and a green bar on the right. Option two is the multi-colored bird on a white background. Option three is the blue bird in the middle of two horizontal bars, the first green, the second red. Let's vote."

The majority selected the last option.

"Who did these drawings?" Edem asked.

"I did," Akua Afriyie said.

"Good job, Afriyie," John Barnor said. "Edem, why don't you tell us about yourself?"

"Thanks, Mr. Barnor," Edem said, getting up to join John Barnor. "I recently started the Center of Christ Church in Teshie Nungua. It's non-denominational and aims to attract people from all walks of society, especially the youth." He moved his hands around each other with each sentence. "In talking to Mr. Barnor, I suggested that the PPP also target young people. These are the people who are unemployed. These are the people who have been educated but can't find jobs and are genuinely disillusioned with the way the country is being run. Target them and they can influence their market women mummies and daddies to vote for you." Laughter spread across the room. "Keep in mind always that God is the one running the show. He's running Ghana and He'll determine what happens in November next year. He knows what's right for the country. Putting your party in God's hands is the best advice I can give you this morning." Akua Afriyie's eyes glazed over. Why was she getting a sermon this early? And on a Saturday morning! She blocked out his voice and looked at his face, his thick lips. She imagined puckering her lips and planting them on his. "… I'll give Miss Afriyie my information and you can ask her for it." She sat up on hearing her name. "You're all welcome to worship with us. Thanks for your time."

"Salamatu?" John Barnor said.

"My team has drafted a constitution," Salamatu said.

"Go ahead," he said.

After Salamatu gave a long speech on the party's constitution, people filtered out. Akua Afriyie lingered around the room and called for Ekow.

"Hello, Miss," he said, his eyes boring into hers.

"Can we meet during the week instead of today? I'll have copies of the logos made for all of you then. I don't think there's much to discuss now."

"All right, I'll tell the others."

Just as Akua Afriyie stepped out, Edem came up behind her.

"Don't forget my information," he said, handing her the card that was in his hand. "You still haven't come to my church! I really want you to come to our services but I don't want to steal you from your church."

"I actually don't have one," Akua Afriyie said. "God and I have been having some issues."

"I knew it! Something—God—keeps pushing me to invite you. Please come. Our doors are always open."

"Thanks," she said now at the door of her office.

"See you next time."

"Yes," Akua Afriyie said, trying not to look too eager and yet not too distant.

Twenty
Good Soil

Early Saturday morning, Akua Afriyie, Salamatu and Sugri were the only ones in the newspaper office. Akua Afriyie bent over to pick up a T-shirt from a box.

"Forty-four ..." she said. Sugri wrote on a pad.

"... our country has been run to the ground by people who thought they had the best in mind for Ghana. The best meant getting rich and fat on Ghana's money," Salamatu read aloud, pacing by the large table. Her thick hair, piled in big curls, bounced as she marched up and down.

"Fifty," Akua Afriyie said. "You can tape up that box now."

"... The PPP doesn't promise instant change ..."

Sugri pulled taut a strip of packing tape, biting it with her teeth. She clasped the box between her knees, bent over and stuck the tape over it.

"Salamatu," Akua Afriyie said, "are you giving a speech too?"

"No," Salamatu said. "This is Barnor's speech. I wrote it yesterday. I need to read it aloud to see if it flows."

"He hasn't seen it at all?" Salamatu shook her head. If somebody had written a speech for Akua Afriyie, she'd want to at least read through it once. "He doesn't want to go through it before reading it out?" she asked.

Salamatu shrugged, then pointed at Sugri. "Is she coming with us?"

"Sugri? Yes," Akua Afriyie said.

"Children shouldn't be involved in politics."

"She's not. She's just helping me," Akua Afriyie said.

"The way you keep her around here isn't healthy."

257

"I don't think this is any of your business," Akua Afriyie said. Why Salamatu couldn't wait and had to say all that in front of Sugri was what was grating on her nerves.

"I have children too," Salamatu said.

"You do?"

"Yes, three actually. But no one in the office needs to know that. You have to separate your working life from your personal life …"

"Well, some of us can't afford to hire maids and nannies," Akua Afriyie muttered. She turned to Sugri. "Are the boxes heavy?"

Sugri picked up the box she'd just taped. "No," she said, eyeing Salamatu.

"Let's carry them to the car. We're going ahead," Akua Afriyie said to Salamatu and picked up the other box. She walked out behind Sugri. Sugri's shoulders were high and straight and gave off the innocence of the child that she was. Her sleeveless pink and white blouse hung loosely around her thin frame.

Akua Afriyie placed her box on the cement ground and unlocked the trunk of her Fiat.

"Mummy," Sugri said, resting the box on her knee.

"Huh?" Akua Afriyie asked, lifting the trunk open.

"Why was Auntie Salamatu bothering you?"

"Sugri, I don't know," Akua Afriyie said, dropping the box in the dusty trunk. "Give me yours." She put in the other box. "People love to tell you how to raise your own children. They love to tell you how to do everything. Period."

"Don't mind her," Sugri said, sitting in the passenger seat.

"You should wear this, you should go to this school," Akua Afriyie ranted on as she started the car and backed out of the parking lot. "You should go to church. But no, not this one. That one is better. Oh, I'm so sick of it!"

The drive was smooth, mainly because most of the traffic lights weren't working and there weren't many cars on the road.

At the entrance to the Nima Primary School, Akua Afriyie inched her car in slowly, trying not to run over a girl wearing her brown and beige school uniform. She honked.

"Wow, Uncle John managed to get a lot of people to come to the rally," Sugri said.

"I just hope after all this they vote for him," Akua Afriyie said, jockeying into an area filled with women, men and school children. She stepped down and unlocked the trunk. Sugri picked up a box with her long arms and Akua Afriyie took out the other. The dust from the trunk seemed to have already settled on the boxes. They walked to the back of a yellow school building. Up on a cool verandah facing a green football field, John Barnor, Lloyd, Ekow and others from the office were arranging plastic chairs and setting up a microphone. Akua Afriyie and Sugri walked toward them.

"Morning," Akua Afriyie said to the group.

"Morning," they chorused back.

"Afriyie," Barnor shouted, mopping his forehead. "Where's Salamatu? I thought you were coming together."

"I left her in the office, but I'm sure she'll be here soon," she said. He grunted. Wet patches stained his back. "John, I think you should read through the speech before you deliver it," she said, not sure if it was her place to say so.

"Why? What's wrong with Salamatu's speech?"

"Nothing's wrong with it. You should just make sure you agree with everything in it."

"Oh," he said loudly. "I trust her. She's a smart woman." Akua Afriyie clicked her tongue and went back to her boxes. She cut through the tape on them with her car keys. Ekow, dressed in a dingy white shirt, walked over and bent over the boxes, breathing heavily, his right hand clasping his glasses.

"Need some help over here?" he asked.

"Yes," she said. "We should start distributing them. I was going to get Sugri to help me, but I think it's better if *we* do this."

"Yes, yes," Ekow said, grabbing a white T-shirt. "We should wear them." He pulled it over his head and its neck-hole caught the handle of his glasses. "Yes, that's it," he said, the shirt too small on him. "The logo looks very nice."

"Thank you. Let's set the boxes there," Akua Afriyie said, pointing to a ledge by a sunflower garden. They moved them over. She put on a small T-shirt. "Please form a line," she shouted to a group that had gathered around her. Children who looked younger than Sugri scrambled to join the line.

"Can I wear one?" Sugri asked.

"No," Akua Afriyie said.

"Why not?" Sugri asked.

"Because I said so. Go sit over there by Uncle John and co." Sugri bent her head and walked away. Akua Afriyie hadn't meant to be harsh, but she could still hear Salamatu's voice. "Here you go," Akua Afriyie said, handing an old man a T-shirt. "Vote for the PPP!" She smiled.

Two children jostled each other to get their T-shirts. Akua Afriyie looked at Sugri, her legs dangling over the verandah, her eyes wide open, curious, longing. She handed the children T-shirts.

"Finally!" John Barnor's voice boomed over the noise of the crowd gathering around her. Akua Afriyie looked over and saw Salamatu walking toward him.

"Sugri," Akua Afriyie shouted, signaling for her to come over. "Give this to your Uncle John," she said, throwing her a T-shirt.

"Yes, mummy."

Interference from the microphone drew the attention of Akua Afriyie and the people she was serving toward the verandah. John Barnor in his tight party T-shirt stood behind the microphone, clutching sheets of paper. Salamatu, on his left side, seemed to be basking in her being up there. Edem stood to his right. Akua Afriyie hadn't even noticed him come in. Had he been there all along? she wondered.

"Gather round," Salamatu said, craning her neck toward the microphone, her hands slicing the air, beckoning the crowd forward. The throng of mainly old people and young children moved closer to the verandah. "Good morn…" she started, interference drowning out her last word. "Thank you for coming out to the first rally of the Progressive People's Party. We are a party of change, a party for you, a party of progress. I present to you John Barnor, founder of the PPP!" She clapped. Some people in the crowd clapped along. Most looked confused.

Barnor wiped his brow. He smiled broadly and said, "I am so sorry for taking you away from your morning plantain and beans." Akua Afriyie rolled her eyes. His jokes were getting tired. "Really, thank you all for showing up this morning. You are not wasting your time, being here. The time for change *has* come." He raised his sheet and read loudly, "Our dear country Ghana, has suffered. When we achieved independence on March 6, 1957, ours was a success story. We had enough money to loan to the people who had colonized us.

"But somewhere along our path toward true freedom, something went wrong. Our dreams were shattered as we saw our own liberators imprison us. Downhill our country went. Soon, coup after coup ravaged the country and it was always you and I, the common woman and man, who suffered.

"Our country has been run to the ground by people who thought they had the best in mind for Ghana. The best to them meant getting rich and fat on our money. Rawlings used another tactic. He sucked this country dry using violence, fear and corruption. Ladies and gentlemen, the time for change has come. No more thieves, no more murderers." He mopped his brow. "The PPP promises change. True change. Change that the Big Six dreamed of for this country, change started by Kwame Nkrumah, change that Busia believed in …"

Akua Afriyie's gaze moved to Edem. His lips were pursed, his dimples deep. His dark skin was flawless, dry, especially compared to Barnor's face, bathed in sweat. He seemed so comfortable with himself in a simple white shirt and khaki trousers. What was such a beautiful man doing as a pastor? she wondered. How had he found his calling? At thirty she still wasn't sure of what hers was. She wasn't fulfilled at all. Sugri was the only part of her life she could call a success.

"… but change comes slowly. We're not saying that if the PPP gets into power, you'll be rich overnight. The PPP doesn't promise instant change," John Barnor went on. Akua Afriyie looked at him. He didn't seem to believe in what he was reading. And yet that was actually an earnest speech Salamatu had written. She wondered if the people, like Barnor, wanted to hear that message. They wanted change now. She looked at Edem, who nodded as John Barnor read. She wanted to touch him. She wanted to share in his peace. Yet she still hadn't taken up his offer to go to his church. The least she could do was go, she decided. To find out who this man was—this man who'd been invading her dreams.

She'd been having the white dream—as she called it—at least once every week.

"... make sure you pick up a T-shirt," John Barnor said. "Our party headquarters is located in Adabraka, in the same building as the *Morning Guide*. Please come around anytime and spread the word about the PPP."

Yes, she was going to go to Edem's church! She just had to satisfy her curiosity. She didn't realize the speech was over, until people crowded around her, stretching out their arms for T-shirts, pushing each other over. The first box was empty. Ekow had conveniently left her behind to deal with the hungry crowd by herself. Sugri wriggled through the crowd, joining her mother by the bed of sunflowers. Akua Afriyie threw a bunch of T-shirts at her. Together they distributed them, not bothering to look at sizes or who they were going to. Even after both boxes were empty, a thick expectant crowd was still gathered around them.

"We want the T-shirts the man promised," shouted a boy, not more than fifteen. Akua Afriyie didn't have the voice to shout loudly, to explain that they hadn't expected so many people to show up. She looked at the verandah. Edem was looking her way. He walked over. She needed help, but wished it was Ekow coming toward her and not Edem. She couldn't look him in the eye.

"What's the problem?" he asked her.

"We're out of T-shirts," she said, looking at the crowd. "Barnor said to bring only fifty."

"Ladies and gentlemen," Edem said, turning to face the people, "Thank you for coming out to support the PPP. Your presence was inspiring. We didn't realize so many of you would come. Next time," he smiled, "we'll come better prepared. Make sure you tell everyone about the PPP. Thank you." He held Akua Afriyie and Sugri's shoulders and pushed them out of the crowd, toward the verandah.

"Thank you," Akua Afriyie said.

"My pleasure." He paused, looked at her and then at Sugri. "I'm sorry," he said to Sugri. "I just dragged you along."

"Oh! This is my daughter, Sugri," Akua Afriyie said.

"Daughter?" he asked, his brow raised. "Hello, Sugri."

"Hello, sir."

"His name is Pastor Edem Adomza."

"We still haven't seen you at church!" Edem said. "I keep thinking about you. You have to come."

"I'll come." Did he say he thinks about me?

"Can I just tell you how much Sugri looks like you? It's uncanny."

"Really?"

"Yes."

"I'll come to church," Akua Afriyie said. You keep thinking of me? How? Romantically, I hope! she thought. "I'll surprise you."

A woman sucked her teeth loudly. "Me, I'm voting for J.J.!" she shouted. "Even cheap T-shirts they can't make enough. What PPP?" She kissed her teeth again.

*

November 1991

After their usual morning battle—Sugri sleeping deeply, Akua Afriyie struggling to rouse her—they walked downstairs. Sugri was dressed in a blue and white sailor dress, Akua Afriyie in black pants and a grey blouse. She wanted to wear something with more color, but she decided to tone it down for church.

Akua Afriyie was extremely nervous. She kept her eyes glued to the road.

"Mummy, next Saturday, there's a funfair in school," Sugri said. "Can I go?"

"Sweetie, when you're older you'll get to go to all such things."

"It's not fair," Sugri said under her breath.

"Look, an accident," Akua Afriyie said, knowing that Sugri could see the accident, but saying that in an attempt to lessen the tension that had built up in the car. She wasn't being difficult, but she figured Sugri would be less likely to get into trouble if she didn't take part in such activities. A blue *trotro* was turned over on its side, a man in a green T-shirt who looked like he was the driver of the car directed traffic. The passengers stood at the side of the road. No one looked hurt. "Too many accidents in this country."

Because of the congestion caused by the accident, they arrived at the church fifteen minutes late. Akua Afriyie parked on a laterite road, where four cars were parked outside the church. The exterior of the church was grey—the color of the exposed brick.

"We're here," Akua Afriyie said.

"Why can't we go to St. Mary's, like grandma does?" Sugri asked, getting out of the car, stretching. "I haven't been there even once."

"I already bribed you. You accepted it. No complaining. We'll visit grandma after church. That was our deal." They walked by a pile of white sand. Blocks were arranged next to the entrance. A handwritten signboard read, CENTER OF CHRIST CHURCH.

They walked inside. A group of teenagers was singing "A Mighty Fortress is our God." They had actually managed to turn what Akua Afriyie had always thought a drab hymn into a funky song. The room looked dark, even though above three fluorescent lights were on. Wooden school chairs and plastic seats were arranged in rows. Only a third of the room was full. They walked to a row next to the last of three standing fans. As they sat down, a young girl walked to the pulpit.

"Today's reading is taken from Matthew, Chapter fourteen, reading from Verse one to eighteen."

Akua Afriyie listened as the girl read the parable of the sower in a small sweet voice. "Amen," the girl finished and walked off.

"Amen!" people in the congregation responded.

"God is good!" a woman shouted.

"All the time!"

The choir came back on and sang a Twi gospel song. The sparse congregation stood up. Akua Afriyie swayed to the lively tune. As she was getting carried away, Edem came to the pulpit wearing a black robe, a kente stole draped around his neck. He danced as the choir finished off their song.

"Good morning! Let's take a minute to say good morning to each other," he said and walked down from the pulpit.

An old woman turned to Sugri and Akua Afriyie. "Good morning and God bless you," she said, clasping Akua Afriyie's hands in hers.

"Good morning," Akua Afriyie responded. People left their seats, moved to the front row and came over to Akua Afriyie and Sugri. It seemed as if they were greeting everybody in the church. Edem was also working his way down. Akua Afriyie stayed rooted in place.

Edem walked up to her. "You have surprised me!" he said.

"I did? Oh, good," she said, her voice rising an octave.

"Sugri, how are you?"

"I'm fine, thank you."

"Welcome! I hope you enjoy the service."

"Thank you," Akua Afriyie said.

He walked back to the pulpit and waved at a little girl sitting on her mother's lap. "God bless you all," he said, smiling. His skin looked almost blue under the fluorescent lighting. "Matthew thirteen is one of my favorite chapters," he said. "Maybe because I grew up in a farming town." A woman laughed loudly. "It has these great parables about farmers and what they do—sowing seeds, planting. From Verse three, Jesus tells us the story of a farmer in Kpando who went out to sow his maize seeds.

"Some fell on a path, but birds came out and ate them. Some fell on rock. Those seeds grew fast, but had no firm rooting. The sun came out and dried them. Some fell among thorns. They were choked to death. The maize seeds that landed on good soil sprouted, giving the farmer a bountiful harvest.

"In Chapter eighteen, our Lord explains that this is how we enter the kingdom of God. It is through his word. His word is the Kpando farmer's seed. The seed lands in our hearts. Sisters and brothers, let our hearts be like the good soil. Allow the word of God to grow bountifully in your hearts. You won't be snatched away by evil, nor will you have a fleeting romance with God. You won't let the world sway you. With God, you will get that job you've been praying for, that husband, that wife…. Amen?"

"Amen!"

"Sisters and brothers, for me, this parable applies to Ghana as well, although in a different way. We are the seed of our leaders. Our new leaders must lead us toward good soil. For too long, we've been led onto rocky paths, into thorns. But winds of change are blowing our way. We pray that our new leaders take us, firmly root us in rich loam, with Christ as our bedrock, leading us all toward the kingdom of heaven. Let us pray."

Akua Afriyie closed her eyes. He was calm, inside and out. And his sermon seemed tailor-made for her. She had been tossed onto a path with no direction. No roots to keep her grounded, no light to make her sprout. She'd been lost for too long. He was right! She did need to come to church. Lord, she prayed, bring me back to you. Amen.

After the closing prayer, Akua Afriyie and Sugri walked toward the brown pulpit. Akua Afriyie noticed it was made out of cheap wood, nails sticking out of it dangerously. Edem stood by the elderly gentleman who had read the announcements. He had taken off his stole and robe and was wearing a light blue shirt and black trousers. "I hope you enjoyed the service," he said, shaking Akua Afriyie's hand. "Brother Carl over here will give you some pamphlets."

"I enjoyed it," she said. "It's been so long since I came to church, I forgot how a sermon could just speak to your current situation in life. You did that for me. Thank you."

"I hope you'll start coming then."

"Definitely."

Sugri and Akua Afriyie walked out of the church.

"That wasn't so bad," Sugri said.

"You see!" Akua Afriyie said waving the pamphlets in Sugri's face. "The choir can sing."

"Pastor Adomza's sermon was really good too, right?"

"I think you like him."

"What are you talking about?" Akua Afriyie asked, trying to sound surprised. "The pastor?"

"Yes, mummy."

"What do you know about any of this?" she said, sucking her teeth and laughing.

"A lot."

"I'll find out just how much, Miss Smarty Pants."

They drove to Asantewa's house. Akua Afriyie steered her car through the narrow gate into the compound. The ground was a sickly tan color, waterlogged and choked with weeds.

"Poor Auntie," Akua Afriyie said. "Her landlord is useless! He can't even try to find good soil for this place. It's been like this since we lived here." She looked back and reversed out through the narrow entrance.

She parked in front of the electrical supplies store. Babasam sat in front of it. When he saw them, he stood up and waved.

Akua Afriyie waved back. "I have some clothes the office people gave me. I'll have to bring them to him."

"Where does Babasam live?" Sugri asked.

"I have no clue!" Akua Afriyie said as they walked into the compound, which seemed even more crowded than before. As they walked by Gloria's house, Akua Afriyie thought of stopping by to say hello, but decided she didn't want another sermon—not especially when the first one had made her feel good. There was no telling what Gloria's sermon would do to her.

"I miss living here," Sugri said.

"I don't," Akua Afriyie said. "I only miss your grandma."

Asantewa's building looked freshly painted. The smell of grilled chicken lingered outside. They knocked on the front door.

"Who is it?" Asantewa asked.

"Akua Afriyie and Sugri."

Asantewa opened the door. "Surprise, surprise!" She hugged Sugri and then Akua Afriyie. "Come in, come in. Sugri, I'm sure you'll be happy. I've made some nice *jollof* rice and chicken."

"I can't wait," Sugri said. "Church made me hungry."

"Church?" Asantewa asked, her brows raised. "You people didn't go to church once when you lived under this roof."

"Hmmm," Sugri said.

"Auntie, believe it or not, I think I've found a church," Akua Afriyie said, sitting on the cane sofa. "And why didn't you go today? You never cook on church days."

"Lizzie's out of town with Ernest," Asantewa said, turning over a ladle of deep orange-colored rice speckled with tomatoes and carrots. "She's the one who forces me to go every Sunday. Sometimes I need a break."

"I know what you mean," Akua Afriyie said. "She can be intense."

"Have you spoken to her recently?"

Akua Afriyie shook her head. Asantewa smiled sadly and bent over to open the oven door. Akua Afriyie smelt the chicken marinating in ginger, garlic and onions. "Auntie, that smells so good."

"Thank you. So where's this church?"

"In Teshie Nungua. It's a new church. But I like the pastor."

"Grandma, she *likes* the pastor," Sugri said.

"Ei, really?"

"Don't mind that child. She doesn't know what she's talking about," Akua Afriyie said, laughing. "He's very eloquent and is not one of those people who forces messages down your throat."

"I'm so happy you're going to church now. Now all you have to do is call your mother," Asantewa said, pulling a stack of plates from a wooden rack by the stove, "and you'll be all right with God." Akua Afriyie could have killed her aunt. She was always putting her foot in her mouth.

"Mummy," Sugri said, "why did grandma say you should call your mother?"

Akua Afriyie looked at Asantewa. "Because that's what I call her sister. It's something I did when I was younger and it stuck. Can we eat? I'm starving."

Asantewa dished huge helpings of *jollof* rice onto their plates. Akua Afriyie was rattled. Sugri was beginning to ask too many questions.

Twenty-one
Forgiveness

August 1992

Edem was wrapping up his sermon. Since he began, Akua Afriyie hadn't taken her eyes off him. She wiped a tear from her right eye.

"… it's a hot day, you're stuck in a traffic jam, a *trotro* driver cuts in front of you, making you hit the brakes, it's hard to remember Christ's message of love," Edem said. "But I urge you today, to try to live up to love's values. First Corinthians thirteen tells us that love is patient and kind. Love never envies, love is never rude, love is never self-seeking, love is never quick to anger. The heat has a way of making us forget …" he smiled, "… but let's try hard to love our neighbors, the person who wronged us years ago, the taxi driver …"

Akua Afriyie removed a handkerchief from her black purse, wiped her eyes and nodded to everything Edem was saying. Her heart swelled— she wasn't sure if it was with the love Edem was talking about or if it was her lust for him. Lust? No! It couldn't be. She clutched her black Bible. Her orange scarf shook as she soaked in all of Edem's words. Her gaze followed him even as he left the pulpit and made for the door to the left of the altar.

Brother Carl walked up to the pulpit, dressed in a black suit and a crisp white shirt, a red rose sticking out of his breast pocket.

"God is good," he said.

"All the time."

"Center of Christ Church has grown to seventy members. Amen?"

"Amen!"

"Pastor Adomza preached about love today, brothers and sisters. He said God loves us no matter what our past is. No matter what we did or thought of yesterday. He loves us. As Christians, we have to live like our Lord, loving one another. When Christ lives in our hearts, we live in love. If there's anyone here who is ready to accept Christ today, we ask that you come forth. Come to the altar."

From the corner of her right eye, Akua Afriyie saw a woman walk forward. The congregation broke into applause. Tears welled in her eyes again. She put her Bible on her seat, exhaled and followed the woman. Yes, she was ready to fill the void in her life.

Another woman behind her, wailed loudly, yelling, "Yes, Lord! Yes, Lord!" Akua Afriyie walked quietly forward. Edem came back out and joined Brother Carl at the pulpit.

"Praise the Lord," Edem said. "Let's pray." Tears kept flowing out of Akua Afriyie's eyes. "Father," he said quietly, "our sisters Akua Afriyie, Phyllis and Ama, have decided to open their hearts for you to enter. They've chosen the road to your kingdom. We commit them to your care and to your guidance. Their lives will be changed from this moment," he said, his voice crescendoing. "Lord, watch over them. Cloak them in the blood of your son, Jesus. Protect them against the forces of evil. Thank you, Lord, for their lives. Thank you, Father. We pray in the glorious name of your son Jesus. Amen." In a subdued tone, he said, "Please see me in my office after the service."

Akua Afriyie and the other women walked back to their seats. She caught Sugri simpering, but she didn't care, she felt happy, content. She stood in front of her seat, bent her head and prayed, "Lord, I don't know why you pushed me up there, but thank you for giving me the courage. Amen." She opened her eyes and looked at Sugri. The girl was grinning.

After the service, Akua Afriyie walked down to Edem's office. The door to his small room was ajar. The coral-painted walls were bare. An unpolished bookshelf stood next to Edem, who sat behind a small tan table.

"Afriyie!" he said, reaching for a booklet from a bookshelf on which a King James Bible, Good News Bible and New International Version were stacked next to each other. "I wasn't surprised when you walked up today," Edem said, handing her the booklet.

"Why not?"

"I knew there was a reason we met. Today it was explained when you walked up to the altar." Akua Afriyie furrowed her brow. "I've been praying and asking God why He kept you constantly on my mind. Today, I realized he wanted me to bring a lost sheep back home. Welcome back."

"Thank you," Akua Afriyie said, irked that "lost sheep" was as far as Edem was going to take his explanation of why she'd been on his mind.

"Pastor, I'm here," Phyllis said, standing outside the door.

"One second. All right, Afriyie," he turned to Akua Afriyie, "the *Daily Word* is a wonderful devotional. I'll give you a copy for this month."

"Where can I get copies for the coming months?"

"You should subscribe to them."

"OK. Thank you," she said, still a little annoyed.

As she was about to leave his office, Edem said, "Afriyie, from now on, it's a struggle. I'm here as a guide. You can talk to me whenever you want about anything at all."

"Thanks, Edem," she said, walking out. Upstairs she caught Sugri in the middle of a wide yawn.

*

Akua Afriyie arrived at the Village Kitchen at just after twelve. She was sure she'd get there earlier than Eunice, Fati and Dede—yes, even Dede, whose restaurant this was. She walked to the back of the thatched enclosure. Fati was already seated.

"Miracle of miracles," Akua Afriyie said. Fati stood up, enveloping her in a hug. "What happened today?" She pulled out a cane chair, thinking that Fati was putting on too much weight. Or maybe it was the frumpy peach dress she was wearing.

"Nothing happening at work today. It's just election-mania in the Ministries. Everybody keeps asking if Rawlings is going to run for president …"

"Of course he will. Dede isn't here?"

"She is, but she said she can't sit with us today." Akua Afriyie was sure it was because Fati was there. Relations between the two had cooled over the past few years.

"Pity," Akua Afriyie said. "She's done up this place so nicely," she said as she looked around. The restaurant felt earthy with cane chairs and tables painted a deep rust color. She saw Eunice strutting over in a black miniskirt and a cream blazer.

"Hallo, hallo," Eunice said, her heels clicking loudly on the concrete floor.

"Hello," Fati and Akua Afriyie chorused.

"Where's the boss lady?" Eunice asked.

"Extremely busy," Akua Afriyie said.

"*Dommage*," Eunice said, sitting down.

"You look sprightly today," Akua Afriyie said.

"I always get this way when we win cases."

"Ah, defender of the press," Fati said.

"Somebody's got to do it. This was a small case. Some Minister said Fred Tetteh had written things about his family that weren't true."

"And?" Fati asked.

"Of course, they were true. The man sent his wife and children abroad and has a mistress who's half his age in the university. Fred didn't make that up!"

"I love Fred's columns," Akua Afriyie said. "Barnor needs to hire people like him at the *Morning Guide*."

"Speaking of Barnor! How are you, Miss Politician?" Eunice asked, batting her eyelids, dark with eyeliner.

"What politician? All I am is John Barnor's pawn," Akua Afriyie said, laughing.

"I heard your congress went smoothly," Fati said.

"Well, people voted for John Barnor. I was hoping they wouldn't have—just to rattle him a little. But he is the PPP, after all."

"Why are you in that party? Just because you work for Barnor?" Eunice asked, placing her purse on the table. Akua Afriyie could smell its strong, new-leather scent.

"Can we not go there?" she said. "Fati, I know you'll be voting for your chairman," Akua Afriyie wanted the attention taken off her, "which I completely don't understand."

"Yes, your party of choice surprises me," Eunice said. "You used to be so critical of his government and now you work for Rawlings."

"I think he's taken the country out of the rut it was in … in the seventies," Fati said. "Even though it took some drastic measures. And who are you voting for?"

"The NPP of course. *Kukurudu* all the way," Eunice said. "Akua Afriyie, tell Barnor he should just join forces with us, and in eight years, he can run for president. We stand for the same things."

Akua Afriyie had been thinking about telling him that since the NPP had come onto the scene with a much larger following and the same message. But, who was she? Akua Afriyie saw Dede walking over, her hair cropped close to her scalp. "Dede's coming!" she said. Even though years had passed since Dede's aunt was murdered, Akua Afriyie felt uncomfortable talking about Rawlings's politics with Dede around. It was bad enough that Fati worked with Rawlings.

"I was about to complain to you about the service," Eunice said.

"This is Ghana! You know complaining gets you nowhere," Dede said, sucked her teeth and laughed. She hugged Akua Afriyie and Eunice. "I'm so sorry, ladies. I can't join the party." Akua Afriyie caught her glaring at Fati. "Everyone and their grandmother is coming here today. To think I just opened a week ago!"

"You know nobody likes to be left out," Akua Afriyie said.

"All right, tell me what you want to order. This might be the last time you see me this afternoon."

"I want *fufu* and chicken light soup," Fati said.

"I'll have the same," Akua Afriyie said.

"Can I have a salad? But no baked beans or salad cream, please."

"But, that is not a salad," Dede said. "That's leaves and …"

"I'm on a diet! Mawuli says I'm putting on weight."

They laughed.

"Ho," Dede said, looking around her restaurant. "Since when do we do what men tell us to do? I'll put your orders in." She walked toward a bamboo bar.

A young man brought their steaming dishes over fifteen minutes later.

"How are the boys?" Akua Afriyie asked Fati as she washed her hands.

"Fine. Their school is getting more expensive by the minute."

"That's what you get for taking them to GIS," Eunice said. "There are plenty of good private schools that don't cost as much."

"I know," Fati said. "But their father wants them to go to the 'best' school in Ghana."

"How's Sugri?" Eunice asked.

"She's fine. She's writing her B.E.C.E.s next year. She's already started studying. I'm glad she's not like me."

"You were a good student," Eunice said. "Better than I was, at least." And now you're a lawyer and I'm a secretary, Akua Afriyie thought. Now you're married and I'm.... "Is she going to go to Achimota too?"

"That depends on her."

"This *fufu* is amazing," Fati said, slurping soup from her fingers.

Eunice played with her salad and looked over Akua Afriyie's shoulder. "A woman just walked in who looks like your mother," she said.

"Whose mother?" Fati asked.

"Akua Afriyie."

"Oh, no! Are you serious?" Akua Afriyie asked.

"I think it's her."

Akua Afriyie turned around slowly, hoping Eunice was wrong. This would be too awkward. Yes, it was Lizzie. She was dressed in a green and yellow *boubou*, a gold taffeta wrap piled high on her head. Next to her was Mercy. They looked like two plump hens. They walked to a table close to the bar. Akua Afriyie turned round. "I hope she didn't see me," she said.

"Are you two still feuding?" Fati asked. Akua Afriyie ignored her. "Isn't it very un-Christ-like to not forgive your own mother?"

"I'm working on it," Akua Afriyie lied.

"I never understood what happened anyway," Fati said.

"That's enough," Eunice snapped.

"Akua Afriyie, your child doesn't know her own father. She thinks he's dead ..."

"Fati!" Eunice said, a dull green vein in her neck popping out.

"Fati, I'm working on it, OK?"

"Hmmm," Fati said. "Talking of Sugri's father.... Guess who will be working in my Ministry soon?"

"I don't want to hear of it."

"You're not even curious?"

"No."

When they paid for their meals, Akua Afriyie turned to see where Lizzie was. She saw her round shoulders. Her back looked soft and frail. Her mother was aging. "All right, ladies," she said. "I have to get out of here without being seen."

"Do you realize how ridiculous you sound?" Fati said.

"I know. But that's life," Akua Afriyie said. Eunice smiled at her. "Please tell Dede thanks. I'll talk to you later." She blew them kisses and stood up. She kept her eyes on her mother's huge head-wrap, which was bobbing up and down. Mercy might catch her if she didn't move fast enough. She bent her head, placed her orange bag next to her face and ran out of the restaurant, almost knocking over a waiter.

At her car, she fumbled with her keys. Her hand trembled. Tears had built up in her eyes. She felt ashamed. This is ridiculous! she thought. The woman is going to die and I wouldn't have made up with her. She wiped the corners of her eyes. I have to talk to Edem this about this.

*

September 1992

Akua Afriyie picked Sugri up from school. As they drove to Osu, she thought of one thing only. How to tell Sugri about her grandparents. Edem had told her the first step was to come clean to Sugri.

"I want to buy some stuff from Top in Town," she said, coughing. A thick still cloud of dust hung in the air.

"Why is there so much dust?" Sugri asked.

"Rawlings wants people to vote for him, so he's started fixing the roads," Akua Afriyie said. "How was school today?"

"Fine. Actually, Mr. Ayivor is starting classes next week for people who want to write the New School International exams."

"New School is the one in McCarthy Hill, right?"

"Yes. People in my class said it's much better than GIS. Can I take his classes?"

"Has Mr. Ayivor been trained in what the New School people want? Obviously we'll have to pay for these classes. Are you sure his teaching will guarantee you a spot?"

"Well, apparently," Sugri paused, "the New School people have syllabuses, so Mr. Ayivor will know what to teach by going through them."

"Don't get sassy on me," Akua Afriyie said as she drove around Danquah Circle. "OK, let's say that you do apply. That means you'll be in the first batch. Do you want to be a guinea pig? They have no track record to speak of."

"The principal was headmistress of Wesley Girls for over ten years and they did really well. I'll get the brochure for you."

"I'm sure their school fees are just like GIS's—expatriate prices."

"They have scholarships."

Akua Afriyie stopped at a traffic light just before the shops. A boy in a tattered brown T-shirt plastered his window cleaner onto her windscreen. Soapy water drained down the glass.

"Nooo!" she yelled at him.

"Too late," Sugri said.

"This school system that Rawlings created hasn't helped anyone. This boy should be in JSS or is it SSS? He looks quite grown. I guess he should be in SSS …"

"That's why you should let me apply to the New School," Sugri said under her breath.

The boy swiped the windscreen deftly. In under a minute he was done.

"See if I have coins in the glove compartment," Akua Afriyie said. Sugri's fingers combed through the glove compartment. She handed a hundred-cedi coin to her mother.

"Thank you," Akua Afriyie said to the boy. "We'll talk about the New School when we get home. I have something to tell you." She parked in front of the colorful storefront of Top in Town.

"What?" Sugri said, getting out of the car.

"Let's call this a family lesson," Akua Afriyie said and picked up a metal basket just outside the shop. Inside, she pushed through a metal barrier. They walked to the detergent aisle. She swallowed. "Sugri, you know how I call your grandma 'auntie'?"

"Yep. I've always wondered why. I even asked you once."

"Eh, yes. Well, she's your grandaunt."

"I don't understand."

"Asantewa isn't my mother. She's my mother's sister. Your real grandmother lives in Labone." She picked up a box of Omo and placed it against the metal grid of the basket. "This weekend, if you want, you'll meet your real grandparents."

"I'm confused. Why didn't you tell me about them?"

"Sugri, families are strange things. Most times we're strangers thrown together. My mother and I couldn't be more different. I fell out with her. But now, I know the right thing to do is to forgive her." She reached for six bars of Lux and packed them by the Omo.

"Wow," Sugri said. "When was the last time you saw them?"

"I saw my mother last month."

"And you talked?"

"No. I haven't spoken to her in ... twelve years."

"Wow."

"Do you need body cream?" Sugri shook her head. "Seeing her made me think I was being too harsh, too silly."

"What's she like? Are you like her?"

"No, not at all. I already told you."

"Am I like her?"

"You can be," Akua Afriyie said, walking on to the food aisle. "You're both drawn to science, I guess."

"What are you going to say to her?"

"I'm sure God will guide me." Sugri rolled her eyes. "Why did you just roll your eyes at me?" Akua Afriyie asked, holding on to a can of milk she'd just picked up.

"God has been in charge all these twelve years, hasn't he?"

"Now you're being disrespectful." They walked toward a cashier dressed in yellow and red. Akua Afriyie unloaded the contents of the basket onto the checkout table.

"I'm sorry, mummy."

"Four thousand cedis," the cashier said. She looked bored.

"Are you upset that I just sprang this on you?" Akua Afriyie asked as she looked through her bag for her wallet.

"No, I'm not. I can't wait to meet them. You shouldn't have kept this secret from me! I've always thought our family was too small."

Thank you, Lord, Akua Afriyie thought.

*

Sugri stepped out of her room clad in acid-washed jeans and a faded blue T-shirt. Akua Afriyie stopped her.

"I hope you're not wearing that to your grandparents," she said. She herself was dressed in a yellow and green tie-and-dye wrap-dress.

"Why? It's my favorite outfit. I want them to love me for me."

"Please, Sugri, for this, wear something nicer," Akua Afriyie said, pressing a tube of lipstick to her lips. "Thank you!"

Sugri stuck out her lower lip and walked back to her room. "Tadaa!" she said, walking back out in a three-tiered yellow skirt and a blouse with shoulder pads that raised already high shoulders.

"Much better," Akua Afriyie said. "But you could have ironed them a little." Sugri pulled out her lower lip again. "Oh, never mind. Let's go." Akua Afriyie was extremely nervous. She wasn't even sure if Lizzie would be at home. She opened the front door for Sugri to walk out.

As they made their way toward the Fiat, their neighbor came out of the house.

"Good morning, Akua Afriyie, Sugri. How are you?"

"I'm fine, thank you," Sugri said.

"Fine, Ewuresi. Later," Akua Afriyie said, keeping her reserved distance.

"Oh. I wanted to talk to you about something," Ewuresi said.

"Yes?" Akua Afriyie raised her eyebrows.

"My husband is not around a lot these days," Ewuresi said. He never seems to be around, Akua Afriyie thought. "I was thinking we should pool our money together to get a watchman."

"Why? You don't feel safe here? I think we live in a safe area … or?"

"Well, most of the time I'm here alone with the children, and you never know … with Babasam and people like that around…. But you're going somewhere. Please think about it."

"I will," Akua Afriyie said. "Babasam?" she said as they drove out. "That man would not hurt a fly! I mean, it's a good idea, but I can't afford it."

"Why not?" Sugri asked.

"Aren't you starting classes for the New School?"

"Mummy, are you serious? You're letting me?" Sugri shouted. "Yes! Thank you so much," she tried to hug her mother.

"Sugri, I'm driving!" Akua Afriyie said, steering the car along Wireless Road. There was nothing but green grass. On a ledge on the curb of the street, Akua Afriyie saw Babasam seated. He wore a PPP T-shirt and black trousers and stared at the thick clouds gathered above him. "Look at him," Akua Afriyie said. "He's just lost is all." She turned once, twice, drove into a cul-de-sac and stopped in front of a sandy-red gate.

"What a big house!" Sugri said. "I thought everyone in our family was poor."

Akua Afriyie laughed and banged on the gate. Things haven't changed, she thought, their watchman sleeps and sleeps.

Abokyi's head appeared over the gate. He was still there! He looked at Akua Afriyie then at Sugri. He looked at Akua Afriyie again and clasped his hand over his mouth.

"Small madam!" he said, smiling broadly. The skin under his eyes sagged slightly, and he looked rounder than she remembered, but his smile was still as resplendent as ever. "Eish! Small madam! Is this you? A big woman!" He opened the gate for them.

Akua Afriyie laughed. "Abokyi!" she said. "It's me, oh!" He leaned forward and hugged her awkwardly. Akua Afriyie looked at Sugri, who wore an amused smile and was straining her neck to look at him.

"And who is this? Eish, eish, eish," he said, jigging. "Is this small small madam? She looks just like you!"

"Really?"

"Yes. Welcome."

"Thank you. Is Mamaa in?" Akua Afriyie asked.

"Yes, but your father has traveled." That's nothing new, Akua Afriyie thought. She was convinced that her father had another woman abroad or even several. Who knew with men? She still loved him, though. She held Sugri's hand and they walked toward the solid wooden front door. She looked around at the garden. The royal palms loomed larger than when she was last there. She knocked on the door.

The door opened. Lizzie stood in a white polo-neck T-shirt and grey capri pants. She looked at Akua Afriyie and shifted her gaze to

Sugri. Tears coursed their way down her face. She stepped forward to hug Akua Afriyie, who hadn't been expecting this kind of reception. She thought Lizzie would be her usual stoic self.

The air outside cooled. Grey clouds thickened.

"I just understood what my mother felt the day I went back home," Lizzie said.

"Mamaa, this is Sugri," Akua Afriyie said.

Lizzie turned to Sugri. "Look at you! You're beautiful. Welcome, my nana." She hugged Sugri, held her, swayed with her. She leaned back and looked at her. "Thank you, Akua," Lizzie said. "I've really missed you."

"I have too," Akua Afriyie said. She looked at Sugri, who seemed to possess an instant love for her grandmother. She seemed to be lapping up Lizzie's smile and warmth.

"It looks like rain! Come in," Lizzie said.

Akua Afriyie looked around. She felt a chill go down her spine—in a good, bittersweet way. She missed this house. Yet, the memory of the last time she was there kept bubbling up. Her paintings were displayed all around. Ernest and Lizzie had framed the drawing of the coconut trees kissing she'd drawn on the beach.

"We're making *fufu*," Lizzie said. "You haven't eaten lunch, have you?"

"No," Akua Afriyie said.

"I'll tell Senam to make more."

"Senam is still here?"

"Yes."

"You've kept all these people. Abokyi, Senam. That's great."

"They've all become fat!" Lizzie said, laughing loudly. "I've become fat too."

"You're not fat, grandma," Sugri said.

A deafening boom startled them.

"Sounds like a storm," Lizzie said. "And Sugri, it's Mamaa. Call me Mamaa. It makes me feel less old." She cackled.

Akua Afriyie felt the ripples of her mother's laughter all around her. Why didn't I like this woman? she wondered. "Papa's away, I hear," she said.

"Business in Germany," Lizzie said. Just business? Akua Afriyie wondered. She knew better than to bring up her suspicions this time. Lizzie walked into the kitchen and came back out. She wrapped her right arm around Sugri's waist. "Tell me all about you." They sat on the leather sofas. "What are you studying? I hope you'll be going to Achimota, like your mother." She folded her plump left leg under her buttocks.

"Mamaa," Sugri said hesitantly, "I'm thinking of applying to the New School International."

"What's that?"

"A school that's supposed to be better than GIS," Akua Afriyie said.

"Achimota is just fine. Isn't it?" Lizzie asked. "So what are you studying? Tell me, tell me!"

"A bit of everything. My favorite class is general science."

"Oh, good! You inherited the science gene. Hallelujah!" Lizzie said. Akua Afriyie rolled her eyes. That's why we had problems, Mamaa, she thought. "I hope we're going to have a doctor in the family," Lizzie went on. "Sugri looks just like Efua Serwah."

"Who's Efua Serwah?" Sugri asked.

"Your great-grandmother."

"Wow, my great-grandmother is still alive?"

"She's beautiful," Lizzie said. "Tall and dark, just like you. Thank you, Akua. You've made my day. You've made the rest of my life!"

*

The lights in Akua Afriyie's living room were dimmed. Sugri and Akua Afriyie, slouched on the cane sofa, were watching *Indiana Jones and the Temple of Doom*. Indiana Jones was watching the evil Mola Ram dig a man's heart out of his chest.

To be continued….

Akua Afriyie sucked her teeth. "Trust GBC," she said, "to cut off a movie, right in the middle." The image on the screen changed into that of a man with a cloth wrapped around his waist, drumming. "It's already seven?" she asked.

"Yep," Sugri said.

In today's news, five candidates successfully registered to take part in the December general elections. The Chairman attended a workshop in the Central Region ...

Akua Afriyie walked to the front door and pressed down a black switch next to the door, turning on more lights.

"Earlier today," the female announcer read, "five presidential candidates and their running mates successfully filed their nomination papers. They are Flt-Lt. Jerry John Rawlings of the National Democratic Congress ..." Akua Afriyie sucked her teeth.

"You really don't like Rawlings," Sugri said.

"Nope, I don't. And if you weren't so young in the eighties, you wouldn't either. He did some atrocious things."

"... Professor Albert Adu-Boahene of the New Patriotic Party, Dr. Hilla Limann of the People's National Convention, Mr. Kwabena Darko of the National Independence Party and Lt. Gen. E. A. Erskine of the People's Heritage Party. Three candidates failed to show up by the four p.m. deadline. They were the candidates for the Ghana Democratic Party, the Democratic People's Party and the Progressive People's Party."

"What an idiot!" Akua Afriyie screamed. "I can't believe it. What could he have been doing? He better have a good explanation."

"Maybe he was sick," Sugri suggested.

"Sick? He could have sent a proxy. I could have gone for him! Really, Barnor! I don't understand that man. He made us put all this work into the party. Ah well. Good thing he's paid me."

"Are you going to quit?" Sugri asked.

"Quit? Over this? No. Don't you want to go to an expensive school? I can't believe that Barnor!"

Akua Afriyie stared at the screen. In a way she was relieved. She didn't have to feel guilty any more. She would vote for the NPP.

Twenty-two
Higher Learning

May 1993

Plastic chairs had been lined up in rows in a large, freshly painted, grey auditorium. Lizzie, Akua Afriyie and Sugri walked to a row in the middle.

Akua Afriyie looked at Sugri, dressed in faded blue jeans and an 'I-love-NY' T-shirt and then at Lizzie, clad in a flowing purple and white *boubou*. She was glad they got along.

A grey-haired man in a purple political suit waved frantically at them from the front row.

"Mamaa," Akua Afriyie said. "Some man is trying to get your attention. I don't think he wants to talk to Sugri or me."

"Who?" Lizzie asked, opening her bag and extracting a pink case. She pulled out and put on gold-rimmed glasses. "Ah, Otchere! Your father's friend. I wonder what he's doing here. I'll go say hello." She got up and ambled to the front. The man in the suit sprang out of his seat, flung his hands in the air and hugged Lizzie.

"Wow, that man must really love Mamaa," Sugri said.

"I know!"

As Lizzie toddled back to her seat, a woman with grey hair, permed into a bob, made for the podium.

"Welcome, families and friends," said the tall dark-skinned woman, enunciating her every word. Her half-moon glasses rested at the tip of her nose. "My name is Esi Otchere. I am the principal of the New School International."

"That's Otchere's wife," Lizzie whispered to Akua Afriyie.

283

"Oh, right," Akua Afriyie said, wondering what difference that made to her life.

"First of all, congratulations to all of our new students. In our first year of launching, we are honored to have you and your children put your faith in us," Esi Otchere continued. "Twenty students passed our examinations, squeezed through the interview phase and have been accepted as the pioneer group of what we hope will become a fertile training ground for the next crop of African leaders. The New School International will train students to serve Ghana, to serve Africa and to serve humanity. Our four-year program will prepare students for the International General Certificate of Secondary Education and the International Baccalaureate in lieu of the system the government has in place."

Akua Afriyie snickered.

"I'm sure you are all anxious to be taken on a tour of our facilities," Otchere's wife said, whisking her hands in the air, "so I'll be brief with my speech. Our staff is made of teachers who have been trained in reputable institutions in Ghana and abroad. Our arts, languages and science programs are all well developed and fitted with the best equipment. Your children will be able to settle comfortably into programs of their selection. Don't forget to send us your deposits by July 15. Now, I invite you to tour our facilities. Four teachers stand in the four corners of the auditorium. Students with last names beginning from A to F, meet Mr. Kyei at the back and in the left corner. G to L, meet Mrs. Addae in the back, right corner. M to S, Miss Lamptey in the front, left corner. And finally, T to Z, meet Mr. Mahamadu right here, in this corner," she pointed to the corner to the left of the audience. "Feel free to pester the teachers with all the questions you have. Thank you for coming."

In the front stood a petite woman with her hair pulled tightly back, brandishing a sheet in her hand. She was dressed in a knee-length grey skirt and a light blue blouse. Lizzie, Akua Afriyie and Sugri walked over to her.

"Mensah, Morglo, Nahr, Odartey, Puli and Safo," she shouted as she looked at her sheet. "I should have six students' families." The families clustered around her. "Good. Hello, everyone. Lydia Lamptey. I'm a literature teacher here. Let's start with this building. Normally, this is the basketball court, but it will also serve as our assembly hall and auditorium. Please follow me."

"Your teachers will be smartly dressed," Lizzie whispered. "In my day, teachers came to class with patched-up trousers."

They stopped in the middle of a courtyard dotted with ferns, anthuriums and rosebushes. Two cream and maroon story buildings bordered the courtyard. In the middle, a flame tree burst with orange flowers.

"The classrooms, language labs and science labs are housed in these buildings," Lydia said. "Each classroom can seat up to fifteen students and is air-conditioned."

Akua Afriyie looked at an old man in a snug blue suit whose arm was wrapped around the shoulders of a girl Sugri's age. He kept nodding at everything the literature teacher said.

"All right," Lydia said and strutted on the brick-paved ground toward a classroom. "Please come in."

The air inside the classroom was cool and slightly musty. Lydia switched on the lights and a group of fluorescent lights above them flickered and then turned on.

"Very nice," the man in the blue suit said loudly. "In my day, classrooms were out in the open. We had natural air-conditioning." He guffawed and ended up coughing. Lizzie rolled her eyes and smiled at Sugri and Akua Afriyie as if to apologize for the man from her day.

They scaled a flight of terrazzo stairs and Lydia opened a door to a cold room. It was filled with desks with glass casings. Through the glass, Akua Afriyie saw headphones and cassette decks.

"This is our state-of-the-art language lab. Students are all encouraged to take French."

"Is French the only language you teach?" asked a woman with a high-pitched voice. "What about our local languages?"

"Since we're an international school, we focus on languages spoken in more than one country," Lydia said. "As we grow, we'll add more languages. Any more questions?"

"Will my child be guaranteed entry into a university in England after attending this school?" another woman asked, her face lighter than the rest of her body. She had penciled in her eyebrows in a jarring black.

"We'll encourage our students to write the SATs, which are a step toward an education in America, but we won't stop anyone who wants to enter one of the local universities or one in a country of their choice," Lydia said.

The group marched back down the stairs to a rectangular building with netting all along its walls.

"We have top chefs who cook up lunch for students who have to stay for afternoon courses. There's a fee per term, if you opt to eat in our cafeteria."

Next to the cafeteria, bare-chested men, their skins glistening with sweat, weeded a large overgrown patch of grass.

"Our soccer fields," Lydia said and looked embarrassed. "The swimming pool is still under construction," she pointed to an outhouse by the bushy field, "but by the end of the first term, your children will have a modern swimming pool, where they can take lessons …"

"Maybe you can learn how to swim," Akua Afriyie said to Sugri.

"… at a reduced fee, for students," Lydia said. Maybe not, Akua Afriyie thought.

They gathered back at the auditorium.

"We can't wait to see you in August," Lydia said. "Don't forget to send in your deposits."

Lizzie, Akua Afriyie and Sugri made for the car park outside the school's gates.

"It's a nice school," Lizzie said. "I would have loved for you to go to Achimota, but this program seems stronger."

Akua Afriyie thought maybe Sugri should go to Achimota. She didn't think she'd have saved enough money by July 15. She earned a hundred thousand cedis a month. Rent was forty thousand cedis. By the time she paid that, electricity and water bills, she had very little left over for petrol and food.

"I can't wait for August," Sugri said.

Lizzie's driver, Sammy, got up from under an Indian almond tree and walked to Lizzie's black Mercedes Benz. He opened the seat in the back for her.

"I approve! Later," Lizzie said, kissing and hugging them.

"OK, Mamaa," Akua Afriyie said. "Bye."

Sugri and Akua Afriyie boarded her battered Fiat. When Akua Afriyie started the car, the red petrol light flashed on and off. Great, she thought. The red light flashing, her thoughts agitated, she reversed out of the car park and drove down the laterite road. Tossed on it were large red stones, ice-cream wrappers, and empty rusted tins. Turning right onto the tarred Accra-Cape Coast road, she saw the red and yellow Shell logo. She pulled up to the station.

"One gallon," she said to the attendant. "Sweetie," she said softly.

"Yes, mummy?" Sugri's eyes opened her eyes widely and she'd spread the sweetest smile on her lips. Her skin was the same color as hers, her nose, the same aquiline shape. It was her round eyes that Akua Afriyie liked the most, and yet the biggest reminder of who her father was.

How do I put this? she wondered. "I'm glad you got into the New School. I'm so proud of you. It's just that ..."

Sugri's eyes widened.

"Eight thousand," the attendant said.

Akua Afriyie handed him well-worn notes and started the car.

"I can't afford to send you there. I don't think I can rake in enough to pay the deposit. Even if I do, each term I'll have to scrape around for money. And did you notice how they kept reminding us about the deposits? They love money!"

Sugri didn't laugh. She looked away. "This is my dream," she said.

Akua Afriyie felt horrible. She saw, from the corner of her eyes, Sugri raise her hand to her face. She heard her suck in phlegm. She wondered what she should say. I'd be upset too, she thought. It had taken her years to forgive her mother for not giving her the chance to complete her schooling. She knew what it felt like to have dreams snatched away.

"Sugri," she said. "Tell you what? I think you should have a backup. I'll see what I can do about the New School, but don't slack on your BECE exams, just in case things don't work out. You need to have a plan B, like Achimota or Wesley Girls."

"Fine," Sugri said. "You shouldn't have let me apply then."

"Sugri! Don't use that tone on me. I said I'll see what I can do."

*

Akua Afriyie entered the bathroom, just as Sugri plodded out wiping her thin body with a coral-colored towel.

The pink and brown tiles of the floor were wet with puddles. Tiptoeing around them, Akua Afriyie stood in front of the fog-filled mirror in a silk morning gown. She was reaching for a dirty face towel she'd thrown into the wicker laundry basket that morning, when she saw Sugri's panty bunched up on the basket's lid. She picked up the blue and pink bikini-shaped panty, which was streaked with brown lines. This girl needs to be cleaner, really, Akua Afriyie thought. She looked closer at the marks. They were dried bloodstains.

"Sugri! Come here!" she shouted.

Sugri walked back, still wiping her body. Akua Afriyie waved the panty under Sugri's nose.

"I was going to come back and wash it," Sugri said, grabbing it from her mother.

"Look at it," Akua Afriyie said, smiling.

"Eeek!" Sugri said, when she saw the brown streaks. "What's that? My stomach isn't running. And why are you smiling?"

"You're growing, child. It's your period," Akua Afriyie said.

"Really? Finally!" Sugri said. "But why is it so brown? I thought it would look red, not strange like that."

"I didn't know you were waiting so eagerly for your period," Akua Afriyie said, thinking about how she was horrified when she got hers.

"Mummy, you don't understand," Sugri said, opening the faucet of the sink, wetting her panty and rubbing it with a green bar of Rexona. "I'm in JSS 3. Junior secondary three! Girls in my class were sprouting breasts and getting their periods four years ago! Whew! I'm glad this has come before I start senior secondary school."

Akua Afriyie laughed, but was a little bothered. She tied the belt of her gown, opened the brown medicine cabinet above the sink and extracted a packet of Faytex sanitary towels behind the numerous bottles that sat in it. "We have to talk," she said.

"I already know everything," Sugri said, squeezing the water out of her panty.

"Oh you do, huh? Everything about what?"

"About women's bodies. And how now I could get pregnant. Everything. I'm now a woman." Sugri smiled widely.

"I know you're Miss Smarty Pants, but this is part of my job description. Parenting 101. No matter how smart they think their daughters, mothers should not take anything for granted." She thought about Lizzie, and how she'd completely avoided talking about sex. She didn't think that had anything to do with her getting pregnant so early, but she wasn't taking chances. Akua Afriyie dragged a hesitant Sugri into her room. She opened her drawer and took out a black brief with tags dangling from it. Biting off the tags, she said, "Before you sit down and stain my bed, please put this on." She tore apart the plastic packet and pulled out a thick pad. She removed the protective strip and handed the pad to Sugri, who stuck it on and drew up the panties.

"That was easy," Sugri said. "Can I go now?"

"Nope. You said it, that was the easy part." Akua Afriyie didn't even know how to start. She exhaled and said, "All my mother told me was how in the olden days her mother's mother in the north had to sit on a hole anytime she had her period. You, my dear, get a little more information. How do I start this?"

"Mummy, please don't make this painful or I'll have to die."

"OK, so now that you have your period, you have to be extra careful around boys. You already know about sex and how that can get you pregnant and how if you get pregnant at thirteen, well, that will be the end of your dreams of becoming a doctor. I know you're smart, and now that we've started going to church, it makes it easy for you. Just keep sex for after you're married, all right?"

"Fine," Sugri said. "Mummy, I've been adding. You know, doing some math. You had me very young. At seventeen, if I added properly. You weren't married to my dad at seventeen, were you?"

Akua Afriyie hesitated. The girl was too bold. "No, I wasn't."

"Explain ..."

"It's complicated. If he had lived, I don't know if he'd have been responsible and married me. He was years older than me ..." You were an accident, Akua Afriyie kept thinking and was trying to stop herself from saying. I shouldn't be lying about this, she thought, but this is something I can't tell the poor girl, especially not after lying for all these years. Maybe when she's older.

"I'm curious about who my father was. I want to see what he looked like," Sugri went on, her eyes widening. She had sprawled on Akua Afriyie's pink and red sheets. "What kind of music he listened to ..."

"The accident was just before you were born. Sugri, I felt like he'd played some cruel joke on me. We weren't married and I didn't even know his family. I was so devastated I needed to remove every trace of him from my life." Sugri clicked her tongue. It was a deep guttural sound. "I've told you to stop making that noise," Akua Afriyie said, changing the subject. "Hey, I was going to take a shower," she said springing off the bed. "You should keep a diary of your period. Mark when it starts and ends. If you're ambitious enough you can describe what it's like."

"What do you mean, 'what it's like?'" Sugri asked, getting up.

"In your entry for today, for example, you'd write 'brown streaks.' That way you know if your period comes regularly or if there's a problem."

"Thanks, mummy. We should have these talks more often."

"You're being sarcastic, right?"

"No, seriously. I'm glad you tell me these things. Thanks."

"You're welcome." She looked at Sugri. Then she remembered she still hadn't solved the problem of how she was going to pay for her to attend that school. She picked herself off the bed and walked back to the bathroom.

*

July 1993

Akua Afriyie drove with her heart beating so fast, she was sure she was a road hazard. Edem sat in her passenger seat, so close she could touch him.

"I still don't understand why you're taking me," Edem said.

She looked at him. His dimpled cheek was sweating.

"Sorry, I don't have an air-conditioner in this car," she said. "One day, the Lord will provide."

"Amen," Edem said. "Why don't you become a preacher woman?"

"I can be the preacher's wife," Akua Afriyie said and then wished she could take back the words.

"We'll have to find you a husband in that case," Edem said. "You still didn't answer my question."

"I need moral support," Akua Afriyie said, honking when they were outside the sandy-red gates of Lizzie's house. "I won't ask her for the money in front of you, but having you around will soften her."

"That's almost blackmail," Edem said, pulling on his nose.

Abokyi stuck his head over the gate. "Small madam!" he shouted as he pulled the gates apart.

Akua Afriyie drove in. "Abokyi, good evening," she said. "Is my mother in?"

"Yes, yes," he said. He greeted Edem.

Akua Afriyie looked up and saw a flock of white birds flying against an orange sun. Breathtaking, she thought. Now, to siphon some money off my mother.

She knocked hard on the door. Lizzie answered it. She was wearing a green shin-length shirtdress belted at the waist with the same fabric as the dress. On her feet were patent lime green heels with three straps.

"Hello, Mamaa," Akua Afriyie said, kissing her on the cheek. "Where are you off to all dressed up?"

"Auntie Mercy's children are throwing a surprise dinner for her tonight. I have to pretend I'm taking her to some boring state function. It's in an hour and a half. Hello," she said, extending her hand to Edem.

"Edem Adomza," he said, shaking her hand.

"Akua's pastor, right? She's talked a lot about you. Come in," she said and pointed to the black leather sofas. "Make yourself at home. What would you like to drink?"

"Just water, please."

Lizzie, a spring in her steps, strutted to the kitchen, with Akua Afriyie on her tail. Akua Afriyie knew she didn't have any time to waste, especially since the woman was going out.

"Mamaa," she said. "I need help."

"What's wrong? You're not pregnant by your pastor, are you?"

"That was cold," Akua Afriyie said. If she weren't doing this for Sugri, she'd have walked out right then. "I need help with money."

"How much?"

"I've saved fifty thousand cedis for Sugri's deposit. I need another fifty in two weeks. I don't get paid till the end of the month. I'll pay you back."

Lizzie arranged a striped red and white napkin on a metal tray. She placed a glass with pink flower etchings and a bottle of water on it. The bottle sweated and wobbled. She laid it on its side. "Here," she said, thrusting the tray at Akua Afriyie. They moved back into the living room.

"No problem," Lizzie finally said. "I'll write you a check."

Akua Afriyie placed the tray on a black side table by Edem.

"Do you want beer instead?" Lizzie asked him. "Oops! You don't drink, do you? My priest drinks beer like no one's business." She laughed loudly.

"No, I don't," Edem said and smiled. Akua Afriyie wondered why her mother was in such good spirits. She always thought of her mother as a reserved, proper woman, but maybe, she realized, she didn't quite know her mother.

"Come with me," Lizzie said to Akua Afriyie. "We'll be right back." Lizzie led the way, Akua Afriyie trailed behind her. Akua Afriyie turned to Edem, winked and stuck out her thumb. Why did she wink at him?

They climbed up the stairs.

"Where's Papa?"

"In Germany." Lizzie opened the door to her bedroom and out rushed a gust of cold air. The air-conditioner droned loudly. Akua Afriyie threw herself on the bed, the way she had when she was three years old. Lizzie's shoe collection looked like it had grown even more with pumps and sandals in oranges, yellows, turquoises and snakeskin, suede and Italian leather detailing. "I love these!" Akua Afriyie screamed and picked up a pair of flat sandals with teal ribbons that crisscrossed in front.

"You can have them. They're more your style. Tsotsoo sent them from America for me."

"Thanks."

"Here," Lizzie said, handing Akua Afriyie a check. "You don't make enough to pay for that school, Akua."

"I know."

"Why don't you marry that pastor and you two can pay for Sugri's school fees?"

"Mamaa! There's no romantic interest." Akua Afriyie bit her tongue. "*Agyee*," she said.

"So what is he doing downstairs?"

"We have a prayer fellowship tonight. I saw him on the way from work and offered him a lift." Why do I still lie, when I have you in me, Lord? Akua Afriyie wondered.

"Honestly, you need to either quit that Barnor job or ask him for a raise," Lizzie said. "Hmmm, you know what?"

"What, Mamaa?"

"Otchere's wife is the principal of Sugri's school. Your father did so much for the man when he was thrown in jail after Nkrumah was overthrown. I'm sure they can arrange a scholarship for Sugri. I would offer to pay Sugri's fees, but you know your sister's in school in New York and we're paying full American tuition ..."

"No. It's OK," Akua Afriyie said, regretting having come in the first place. She was surprised that Lizzie had no qualms about milking the system. Then again, Barnor could be difficult. Since his failed presidential election bid, he'd cut back on company benefits. Everybody took bribes, once in a while, didn't they? And this was for Sugri. "All right, Mamaa," she said, feeling awful. "Please ask Otchere for an economic difficulty scholarship or something like that. Not for a bribe." She wished her father was there, so she wouldn't have to go through this. "When will Papa stop going away?" she asked, subdued.

"He has a family there," Lizzie said quietly.

"Huh? Another family?" She'd always suspected her father wasn't faithful, but she was hoping it wouldn't be true.

"He had a child there before he met me. He divorced the woman before marrying me. Every time he went to Germany, it was to see his daughter."

"Mamaa, you could have told me this years ago. Then I wouldn't have said the things I did," Akua Afriyie said.

"Akua, parents keep secrets all the time. You adore your father, I didn't feel you needed to know that then."

"You could have told me ..."

"Who is Sugri's father? You haven't told me. I'm sure you haven't told her." Lizzie opened a round, burgundy face powder case and spotted her face with the tawny puff.

"Mamaa, the man was married with two children. I put myself in his wife's shoes and decided not to cause her any stress. I told Sugri her father's dead. Raising her has been the best thing that has happened to me."

"You've done wonderfully," Lizzie said, tapping her on the shoulder. "But lies always catch up with people. Anyway, you've left your lover all alone." She cackled. "I'm done."

"He's not my lover!"

Downstairs, Edem was admiring Akua Afriyie's sketch of two coconut trees kissing.

"Did you do this?" he asked her.

"Years ago," she said. "Shall we leave now?"

"This is really good. You should go back to art and leave John Barnor and his politics!"

"I was just telling her the same thing," Lizzie said.

They strode outside.

Abokyi, sitting on a reclining chair in front of his house, got up and shouted, "Sammy! Sammy! Madam is ready."

"As if I don't have a voice to shout myself," Lizzie muttered under her breath. "Very nice meeting you, Edem," she said, shaking his hand. She hugged Akua Afriyie.

"Thank you, Mamaa."

"You're welcome," Lizzie said. "Give my love to Sugri."

Twenty-three
The Secrets Mothers Keep

June 1995

Akua Afriyie lingered in her kitchen, a spoon dangling from her mouth. She heard the front door whine open. That had to be Sugri. Where did she think she was going? She put the spoon on the white tiles of the kitchen counter and walked out to find out.

Sugri, T-shirt tucked into her jeans, was wearing bright yellow headphones around her head. She seemed determined to make a clean break.

"Sugri," Akua Afriyie said. She could hear the music booming out of the headphones. She walked over and yanked them off.

"*Agyee!*" Sugri screamed, rubbing her left ear. "Why did you do that?"

"Where are you going?"

"To Mamaa's."

"I'll drop you off. I'm going to work."

"I want to walk."

"Have you walked there before?"

"No, but it's not far," Sugri said, her lower lip jutting out, marking the beginnings of a pout.

"With the likes of Babasam around, I don't think you should be walking anywhere by yourself."

"Mummy, I believe you're the same person who once said that Babasam wouldn't hurt a fly."

Akua Afriyie knew she'd chosen the worst possible defense but she didn't want Sugri walking on the streets just like that. She wouldn't forgive herself if something happened to her. "I'm already on my way to the office. Don't you want a free ride?" she asked.

"Oh, OK," Sugri said, plopping herself on the cane sofa and putting her earphones back on.

Akua Afriyie walked into her bedroom, picked up an off-white manila folder and a bright yellow bag. She strode to the bathroom, looked at her face in the mirror and applied a tube of purple plum lipstick to her lips. "I'm ready," she said.

"Finally!" Sugri said.

"I'm giving you a lift. No cheekiness."

"I was going to walk. You forced me to accept your ride."

"Fine, but this is my house. My house, my rules. Daughter doesn't just wander about Accra whenever she wants."

They strode out of the house. Sugri waved at Ewuresi and her two children, sitting around metal basins, washing their clothes. Akua Afriyie thought she never saw the woman's husband. But it wasn't her business…. They never got that watchman.

Akua Afriyie steered her car onto Lizzie's road. She honked at the gate. Abokyi's head appeared, a grin on his lips. He waved at them and opened the gate.

"Ei, small madam. And small, small madam," Abokyi said, once they had descended from the car.

"Abokyi! Is Mamaa in?" Akua Afriyie asked. He pointed at one of the royal palms in the garden, where Lizzie sat on a bronze garden chair reading a newspaper.

They walked to her. A glass of milk-colored liquid sat on a table in front of her. After two seconds, she looked up through her half-moon glasses.

"Hello, hello," she said. "I couldn't take my eyes off this story a student wrote."

"What's it about?" Akua Afriyie asked, kissing her cheeks.

"Let me tell Abokyi to bring chairs."

"Just one," Akua Afriyie said. "I have to go to the office."

"But why? It's a Saturday, and last time I checked you work Monday to Friday, nine to five."

Akua Afriyie rolled her eyes. "It's Barnor. He's not running for president this time, thank God! But the NPP has given him a senior role and he's signed *me* up for all sorts of projects."

"Oh, nonsense!" Lizzie said. "Stay a little."

"OK, but not for long. Sugri, help Abokyi bring the chairs over."

Sugri strode over to Abokyi's little room. Akua Afriyie stared at the newspaper Lizzie was reading.

President Cautions Opposition.

"Isn't this an old paper?" she asked.

"Yes," Lizzie said.

"Rawlings makes too much noise," Akua Afriyie said.

"Hopefully people won't vote for him next year," Lizzie said.

"Mamaa, Ghanaians are unpredictable. Who would have thought they would have voted for him in 1992?"

Lizzie shrugged. "Last week was insane at the hospital. I had to be there almost every day. I'm now catching up on my reading."

Sugri dragged over a garden chair.

"Why didn't you let him bring both?" Lizzie asked.

"Mamaa, it's no problem," Sugri said.

Abokyi came over with another.

"It's fiction … a short story," Lizzie said. "This student wrote about how she met a Minister who got her pregnant. In the end, she manages to unleash a scandal and get the man fired."

"Intriguing," Akua Afriyie said flatly. She didn't understand why her mother had such gaudy taste.

"How's school?" Lizzie asked Sugri, folding the newspaper and placing it on the tabletop.

"It's fine. I'm finishing up the IGCSE exams. Then after that … in August I'll start the International Baccalaureate and then I'll be off to university," Sugri said, playing with her hair. Akua Afriyie reached forward to flick Sugri's fingers out of her hair.

"It's already time for you to go to university?" Lizzie asked.

"Almost."

"I know," Akua Afriyie said. "Time flies, doesn't it?"

"In August I'll have such a busy schedule," Sugri continued. "I'll be taking all these science classes."

"I'm so happy you inherited the science gene," Lizzie said. "It skipped your mother."

"OK, Mamaa, maybe I'll leave you two to bond over your science genes," Akua Afriyie said, getting up from her seat.

"No, no. I'll stop," Lizzie said. "Do you know why I get excited about doctors and medicine?"

"No," Akua Afriyie said.

"You know, my first love wanted to be a doctor."

"Eish! First love," Sugri said. "Tell us about him, Mamaa!"

"Do you want some coconut juice?" Lizzie asked.

"Later, Mamaa," Sugri said. "I want to hear the story!"

"I'll bring you some anyway."

Akua Afriyie looked at Lizzie's disappearing back. The color of her skin was lighter than she remembered. She had aged. Lizzie walked back with two glasses. In her grey leggings and black polo shirt, Akua Afriyie could tell she didn't feel old.

"All right, ladies," Lizzie said. "This is for your ears only. If your grandfather hears this story, he'll be extremely jealous. But it's long. Are you sure you want to hear it?"

"Yes!" Sugri said.

"You're making me miss work. This story had better be good," Akua Afriyie said.

"When I was just about your age …"

"Whose age?" Akua Afriyie asked.

"Sugri's. When I was your age, I had five impossible children and a husband …"

"Oh, excuse me!" Akua Afriyie said, laughing.

"I was fifteen and living in Adukrom No. 2—Sugri, you have to go there one of these days to visit your great-grandparents …"

"I know," Sugri said.

"The story, Mamaa!" Akua Afriyie said.

"All right, all right. It was during the vacation of my last-but-one year of secondary school—Suaadie Girls. I was working on my father's cocoa farm. He was the worst bully, especially when he drank palm wine.

Though age seems to have tamed him…. Anyway, I was helping him harvest his farm. We were plucking the fruits off trees that weren't swollen shoot-infested. Here I was standing on a stool to reach for the fruit. He was much taller than I and had an easy time plucking the pods. I suggested, nicely, that we borrow a ladder from the Aduhene—the chief of Adukrom No. 2, Sugri.

"Oh, that did it. Papa Yaw started yelling at me. Telling me he had thought about that himself and did I think he was foolish? Anytime he gave one of his tirades, I looked over his shoulder, pretending to listen. So, I looked over Papa Yaw's shoulder and I saw these intense white eyes staring at me. I lost my balance and fell to the ground. I was really, quite startled. I looked up and they were gone. Papa Yaw continued his yapping: 'If I needed a ladder, I'd have had bought one for this farm.' He didn't even bother to help me up."

"Oh, Papa Yaw!" Sugri said.

"The eyes haunted me for a while and even gave me nightmares." She took a sip of her coconut juice.

"You didn't tell anybody about them?" Sugri asked.

"No. It was my little secret. I shared a room with three of my sisters. Nothing was private. Experiencing something like that was rare. I kept it to myself. But, I soon forgot about them and went back to school. This happened around the rainy season."

"You have a good memory, Mamaa," Sugri said. Akua Afriyie wasn't convinced. The story was taking too long to get to its point and even though she was happy to delay going to work, she was so sure her mother was embellishing the story.

"You never forget your first love," Lizzie said, her face taking on a pensive air. Akua Afriyie felt a strong urge to throw something at her. "I came back home for the Christmas holiday," she continued. "One evening, my big sister fell to the ground, outside our compound …" She grew quiet, her eyes glazed over. Akua Afriyie became aware of the sound of water hitting leaves. She looked behind her. Abokyi was watering plants. "My sister, Owusua, was epileptic," she said after she'd composed herself. "The day she fell to the ground, I heard Asantewa scream shrilly. I ran out to see why. And there she was. Owusua. On the ground, writhing. You could only see the whites of her eyes. I shrieked.

My mother came out of her hut. She sent me to call Opanyin Nti, the village traditional doctor.

"When I walked into Opanyin Nti's hut, I was shocked to learn that those haunting eyes belonged to his apprentice. With my sister on the floor, I wasn't about to exchange pleasantries. I didn't even greet the man. I asked to talk to Opanyin Nti. I felt the eyes on me as I told Opanyin Nti that Owusua had fallen in a fit and we needed him immediately. We went back ..."

"The eyes too?" Sugri asked.

"Yes, all three of us ran back to my house. My mother had put a spoon in my sister's mouth. Opanyin and the man with the eyes ..."

"What was his name?" Sugri asked.

"Bador Samed," Lizzie said.

"Bador Samed?" Akua Afriyie asked. "Why does that sound familiar?" Bador Samed. *Bador Samed*, Akua Afriyie rolled the words on her tongue. The name rang such a strong bell, but she couldn't make any connections.

"They carried her into my mother's room and Opanyin Nti told us to wait outside. I was so worried, yet I was intrigued by this new fellow. He stood outside, keeping guard, while Opanyin Nti treated Owusua. He kept looking at me and I was flattered. You know what it's like when you're fifteen and getting noticed for the first time. Oh, why am I telling you this, Sugri? You're fifteen and should be concentrating on books, not boys."

Sugri and Akua Afriyie laughed.

"My sister died that evening. Nothing they did could save her." Akua Afriyie heard Abokyi whistling a tune the radio stations played incessantly.

"Sorry, Mamaa," Sugri said.

"Oh, that was years ago!"

"I'm sure it still hurts. I didn't even know my father yet, when I think about his death, I feel so sad."

Lizzie looked at Akua Afriyie. Akua Afriyie glared at her mother. She hoped she had an expression that read, "Back off!"

"He waited for a long while, before talking to me," Lizzie said. "I went back to school and he hadn't said a word to me. Not one word."

"Why not?" Akua Afriyie asked, realizing that she was being roped and woven into the story.

"Maybe he was shy. Maybe he was biding his time. During the rainy season of 1953, I'd finished school and was wasting away at home. One day, he sent one of the aimless children in the village to call me. I wasn't really surprised. At first I wanted to be coy, and send him a message saying I was busy, but I went almost immediately. It was partly because he had piqued my interest a long time ago, but also because I just wanted to get out of the house. People in the house were still not over Owusua's death.

"We always met under the tallest tree in the village, by the Insu River. It was all very romantic."

"How old was he?" Sugri asked.

"Then he was twenty-three, and I was just about sixteen."

"Go on," Sugri said.

"He told me he'd walked all the way from up north, where the grass was tall," Lizzie said. "Up there, they sat on horses and their kings sat on dried animal skins. But his story was actually very sad. His father died when he was very young and his mother was accused of causing his death. She was banished to a witch camp and he grew up with his grandmother. In small villages, you know nothing is sacred. He found out what happened to his mother and was convinced his father had died from a disease, and that his mother was innocent.

"Because of that he left home for Accra to learn the white man's medicine. But first he wanted to make sure he knew our medicine. He knew Opanyin Nti and other traditional doctors had a lot to teach him, but their ways weren't always right. Their ways didn't always work. Their ways didn't save Owusua."

"Wow," Sugri said, sitting at the edge of her seat.

"I'd sit by the river, watching the water bubble on, and he'd be full of all the wisdom in the world. When I was angry with Papa Yaw, for being a bully, or my mother, for being too docile, he had a way of calming me, telling me that families fought because they were made up of people thrown together in a stew and sometimes some ingredients were too overpowering."

"I agree completely," Akua Afriyie said. "What happened to him?"

"One day he disappeared. Just like that. Nobody in the village knew of his whereabouts."

"Why?" Sugri asked.

"Girls," Lizzie said, becoming quiet as if she was on the point of revelation, "to this day, I don't know why." Akua Afriyie was disappointed. This story was going nowhere.

"And you didn't try to find him?" she asked.

"Oh, but I did. The whole reason I left Adukrom No. 2 was to find him. Please don't tell your grandfather this! But I stopped looking when I realized he'd left me without even saying goodbye. He didn't deserve me … though, I always wonder what my life would have been like if he had stayed. Who knows if we'd ever have left Adukrom No. 2? There are all these unanswered questions."

"This is intriguing. You have no idea where he is?" Akua Afriyie asked. She was beginning to think that her mother had cooked up this whole story to get back at Ernest for having a wife and children before he married her.

"It's too sad and embarrassing!" Lizzie said.

"Why?" Sugri and Akua Afriyie chorused.

"He's mad!"

"What?" Akua Afriyie said. She knew the tale was too good to be true. Sugri had a flummoxed expression on her face.

"You both know Babasam?"

"No!" Sugri shouted. "We were just talking about him!" Her face betrayed a look of pure amusement.

"Aha!" Akua Afriyie said. "Bador Samed. Babasam. That's it!" This woman has gone too far, she thought, dragging poor Babasam into this.

"I saw him for the first time since his disappearance a few years after I moved to Accra and he was already deteriorating," Lizzie said, her voice softer. "You were with me then, Akua."

"Really? I don't remember. What did he have to say for himself?"

"I didn't give him a chance to speak. I thought he deserved what happened to him—whatever it was—for leaving me behind."

"And now?" Sugri asked.

"Now, I just get sad when I see him."

"I heard that he's looking for someone," Sugri said.

"I think it's you, Mamaa," Akua Afriyie said. "He keeps getting closer. You should watch yourself." She wanted to laugh. Babasam!

"Oh, I'm very vigilant," Lizzie said, hugging her arms. "I avoid him like the plague. I think his past eventually caught up with him."

"That's so sad," Sugri said.

"This is the first time I've told anyone about him."

"So, grandpa doesn't know about him?" Sugri asked.

"No," Lizzie said. "And he doesn't need to," she said, sniffling. "Before I forget, ladies, July 1st, there's a Republic Day celebration and your grandpa will be out of town. I'd love for you to be my chaperones."

"Of course! Thanks Mamaa! I never get to go anywhere."

"Rawlings and company have managed to turn such things into NDC affairs. Count me out," Akua Afriyie said.

"It's about Ghana celebrating her full independence, not about the NDC," Lizzie said.

"But you know very well it's going to be all about NDC people. You know how they carry on at these functions. In those red, white and green colors."

"Fine, I'll go with only Sugri then."

"It's just that I work for a company that doesn't believe in the same things the NDC people do," Akua Afriyie said. "My ... Barnor's paper criticizes their lavish spending and then you drag us to one of their events...."

"But, you're not going! I'm taking my granddaughter."

"I've always wondered, Mamaa. Did you vote for him?"

"I didn't vote at all," Lizzie said. "Sugri, it's not a big deal. "You don't have to go."

Sugri looked at Akua Afriyie. "Mummy, please," she said in a sweet falsetto.

"Fine," Akua Afriyie said. "Are you picking us up?"

"Yes!" Sugri said, clapping her hands.

"Did you say 'us'?" Lizzie asked.

"Yes, I did. And now, I'm going to the office," Akua Afriyie said, getting up. "Thanks for the coconut juice, Mamaa. Sugri, I'll pick you up later."

*

July 1995

In Lizzie's air-conditioned Mercedes Benz, grandmother, mother and daughter sat in silence. Akua Afriyie was brooding. For her mother, this was normal—she lived for such events. Akua Afriyie figured that having grown up in a village, to become a recognized member of Accra society was an achievement. She was also sure that Sugri was excited. She could smell her keenness. As for her, she was angry with herself for cracking under pressure and going to an event where she didn't want to be seen.

"That cloth looks beautiful on you," Lizzie said to Sugri. "I knew it belonged on you."

"Thanks, Mamaa," Sugri said.

As Lizzie's driver turned into the entrance of Christiansborg Castle, Lizzie said, "All right, ladies, we're almost here. Whenever you get bored, let me know. If I'm not done jamming, Sammy will take you home." Good to know, Akua Afriyie thought, because I know I won't be staying long.

Sammy stopped the car. He got down to open Lizzie's door. Akua Afriyie opened hers. She didn't want Sammy to do that for her. She looked around. The brilliance of the cars in front of them was blinding, even in the dusk.

They walked on red carpeting into a large room. Red, green and gold drapes hung from the wooden ceilings to the floor. Akua Afriyie looked around the room, amused that her prediction had been right. She saw a man dressed in a green, red and black-striped smock. In another corner, she saw a woman in a white *boubou,* with a shawl printed with those same colors draped around her neck.

Lizzie looked at her invitation. "We've been assigned table fifty one," she said, leading them to their table. A man about Lizzie's age sat by a woman who looked Akua Afriyie's age. "Hello," Lizzie said to them, pursing her lips into a polite smile.

"Hello," they responded.

As a waiter in a black waistcoat with a kente sash around his waist brought a tray of champagne glasses over, the younger woman tugged at the sleeve of her husband or sugar daddy. Akua Afriyie decided he was her sugar daddy.

"They're here," she whispered, all too loudly.

"Who?"

"The Minister of Trade. The one who they said was chasing students at the university."

"Oh," her sugar daddy said, seemingly uninterested in her gossip.

Lizzie picked a glass of champagne.

"Can I have a glass of orange juice, please?" Akua Afriyie asked the waiter.

"I don't think that's the wife," the woman was still going on. Akua Afriyie rolled her eyes. That's why Ghana was going nowhere. People were wrapped up in tackiness and idle gossip. Rawlings has a mistress. Rawlings does this. This Minister's children are abroad. That Minister does that. If only people would let them live and call attention to real issues. She was already bored. Maybe her mother would have some interesting story to tell.

"Mamaa," she said.

"Hmmm?"

"You're quiet."

"Oh, am I? I'm just wondering if any of Ernest's friends are around. I want to tell them Ernest sends his greetings." Her mother was no better. She was so caught up in the world of appearances. Same as the woman gossiping about who the Minister had come with.

"When is dinner served?" Akua Afriyie asked. "I'm starving!"

"Me too," Sugri said. Lizzie glared at both of them. Akua Afriyie looked at her mother, who was scanning the room with the eyes of a hawk—no a vulture, more like.

"Ah!" Lizzie said, springing out of her seat. "I'll be back!"

"Sugri," Akua Afriyie said. "Want to do something crazy?"

"Like what?" her eyes popped open widely.

"Let's walk around," Akua Afriyie said.

"Oh. That's not crazy, but sure. I'm bored."

"Me too." They stood up. "We'll be back," Akua Afriyie said to the odd couple. She grabbed Sugri's hand. She was really not a social butterfly fluttering about the place like her mother. Besides, who would she know in this place?

"Mummy," Sugri whispered, "is that Rawlings?" She pointed at a man with caramel-colored skin, his hair peppered white and black, sitting at a table like theirs.

"No! When he comes, if he comes, he'll be sitting up there," Akua Afriyie pointed at a long high table, covered with a white cloth, "not down here. And Rawlings is fatter …"

"Hello," Akua Afriyie heard a familiar voice say. A chill ran down her spine. No! Not here! But, of course! Why hadn't she thought of him? "Afriyie! Surprise, surprise."

She turned to face him. "Rashid!" she said, trying to stay calm.

"Eh, Afriyie, you always abandon me." Akua Afriyie looked at Sugri who was studying Rashid. Their eyes were exactly the same. An onlooker would mistake them for one happy family. "And who's this?"

"My daughter," she said. "Sugri, say hello to Uncle Rashid."

Sugri stretched out her hand, which Rashid shook vigorously, and she curtseyed.

"She's so polite!" Rashid said, running his left hand along his circle beard. His gold and silver ring shimmered. Akua Afriyie was caught in the resemblance between Sugri and her father. They both opened their large round eyes when they were excited, like now. "What are you studying?" Rashid asked her. "Where are you in school? Do you get all As?" He laughed loudly.

"I'm at the New School International."

"Very impressive. One of my daughters wanted to go there but didn't get in. I'm proud of you. Very nice."

"Thank you," Sugri said. "How many children do you have?" Akua Afriyie was scared. Scared that somebody would ask the wrong question, say the wrong thing. Yes, Sugri just asked the wrong question.

"Two," Rashid said, staring at Akua Afriyie right in the eye. "I'll be right back," he said.

"OK, that's enough of a walk," Akua Afriyie said, grabbing Sugri's hand.

"Why? We haven't even started! That man was intense. Let's walk!"

"I just got tired."

"Are you OK, mummy?"

"I'm not feeling too well," Akua Afriyie said. Oh, dear God, here I go again with my lies. "I've had a dull headache all day. It's getting stronger now."

"Do you want to go back home?"

"Let's sit for a bit and we'll see."

Lizzie was back at the table talking to the man and his girlfriend. "… Fine Goods. There you two are!" she said. Akua Afriyie rubbed her temple with her left hand and gulped down her orange juice. "You all right?" Lizzie asked.

"Slight headache."

A brass band started, *God Bless our Homeland Ghana.*

Akua Afriyie felt a palm on her shoulder. The palm squeezed it. She looked at it. The gold-silver blend ring on it glistened.

"Hello," Rashid's voice boomed over the table. "Afriyie, can I have a quick word with you?" he said.

"Sure, why not?" she said, trying to wear a smile. "Be right back, Mamaa and Sugri."

Rashid led her to the buffet table. A waitress lit a candle, placing it under a long metal-lidded pan.

"Afriyie," he said, "that girl is mine. I know it!" His eyes, bulbous, looked like they would pop out of his sockets.

"No," she said, shaking her head.

"Who's her father?"

"He's dead."

"Afriyie, why are you doing this?"

"Rashid, I was responsible for her when my mother threw me out, when you wanted me to end the pregnancy …"

"I suggested …"

"Don't interrupt me. Through those horrible eighties…. I have worked crazy hours to send her to the best schools. I'll decide who and where her father is. He's dead."

"Fine," Rashid said, rubbing the sides of his beard. "Afriyie, you've done a lovely job. I can tell she's well-behaved and smart. *You* cut me out of her life. But no hard feelings. I'd love to help out. With school, anything she needs."

Akua Afriyie was shaking her head. "Rashid, it's too late. The best way to help is to stay out of our lives."

"Afriyie. She's mine too."

"You weren't so enthusiastic about her fifteen years ago. Rashid, I know you have a cushy bank job and whatever it is you do at the Ministry of Finance. I'll spare you the scandal." She said piano-keying her fingers. She knew it was low, on her part, threatening him, but her life was complicated enough as it was. To unweave the lies she'd told, she was going to have to hurt somebody. That somebody was Sugri.

"Oh, Afriyie. She's also my daughter. Be reasonable," Rashid said.

"Rashid, I work for an opposition newspaper. I'm making it easier for you."

"I don't understand why you'd want to put this in any paper. I'm not being negligent. I'm *offering* to help."

"Listen, I told the poor girl her father died. This is not the time to shake up her whole life."

Rashid was quiet. "Don't say I didn't try to help," he said, storming off.

Akua Afriyie wanted to cry, because she was being difficult. Because she was being complicated. Because she'd lied over and over to Sugri. Because Rashid seemed to be genuinely interested in helping. He was no longer the villain. She was. She walked back.

"Mamaa, Sugri," she said. "My head is throbbing now."

"Are you sure you're not making this up to avoid being here?" Lizzie said.

"I came, didn't I?" Akua Afriyie said. "I'll take a taxi home."

"No, no," Lizzie said. "Sammy will drop you off. He'll come back for us."

"Thanks, Mamaa. Sugri can stay with you. I'll pick her up for church tomorrow."

Twenty-four
Farida

April 1997

Akua Afriyie inhaled. Her nostrils drew in the odor of water mixing with earth. It was the cool, spicy smell of the air just before rainfall—her favorite scent. She drew the orange curtains along the window overlooking the flame tree. She looked at Sugri sitting on the magenta rug, envelopes spread between her legs. She looked up, at the raffia lampshade casting shadows on the walls.

"Mummy, I'm so nervous," Sugri said. Akua Afriyie herself felt a tremulous excitement. In a way, this was the moment when she was getting a return on her investment in Sugri. Having spent so much at the New School International, this moment would define her success or failure as a mother. She sat on the cane sofa behind Sugri. A flash of lightning cut through the air outside. The room shook with the rumble of thunder that followed.

"It sounds like it's going to pour," she said, for the first time unsure of what tone to take with Sugri. For the first time at a loss for words that were encouraging, hopeful, motherly. Open the letters, she wanted to say, impatience seeping in. She saw Sugri arrange the letters in her lap. Why were they all small envelopes? Akua Afriyie wondered. So far all the other letters that had arrived in similar envelopes were rejections. Wellesley College, Amherst College, Hamilton College all sent letters with the dreaded, "We regret to inform you …" opening.

Sugri hungrily tore open the Macalester College envelope. Akua Afriyie got off the sofa and plopped herself right in front of Sugri, whose eyes danced across the page. They watered.

"Oh, sweetie," Akua Afriyie said. "This is just the first …"

"Yes," Sugri said, folding the letter and putting it to her left. She opened two more envelopes. The pile to her left was growing.

"I don't understand," Akua Afriyie said, unable to hold her quiet anymore. "You had fourteen hundred on your SATs. Your IGCSE scores were great. Your teachers love you and, I'm sure, wrote great recommendations for you. What's going on?"

"Mummy," Sugri said, her voice thick, as if a huge lump of food were stuck in her throat, "it's because of financial aid."

"Oh. OK," Akua Afriyie said, feeling her inadequacies as a mother rise. She'd been able to send her daughter to one of the best schools in Ghana, but outside of Ghana, she needed to be richer or more something else. What? More aggressive? More interested in money? "I thought schools gave scholarships. That was the impression your college counselor gave me."

"Yes. But, think about this. Everyone in my class applied to the same schools. Half of them paid their way through the New School International easily. Their parents are rich. Some of them don't even have great scores or grades, but their parents can afford to pay more than we can. I mean, we're asking for almost a full scholarship." Large drops of water pummeled the window.

"True," Akua Afriyie said. She felt awful. "Listen, Sugri. God is in control, all right?"

"OK," Sugri said in a muffled voice.

"I'm going to get us some ice cream. Don't open any more envelopes without me."

Akua Afriyie strode to the kitchen. Lord, she prayed, I have worked hard to give this girl everything I couldn't have. She's a good child. She's worked hard. You help those who help themselves. She has. She opened the freezer. Cold mist rushed out, as she pulled forward a drawer. She wrested a tub of FanIce that was wedged between two packets of frozen chicken. Rum raisin. Sugri's favorite flavor. She placed it in the metal sink, ran tap water over its white plastic. She reached for the yellow cabinet above the sink and brought down two clear fish-shaped bowls.

Lord, I'll do anything for you, just make the girl's dreams come true! She dug a tablespoon in the frozen white and wine swirl of ice cream. The spoon skidded on the surface of the ice cream.

"Yes!" she heard Sugri shriek from the living room. Akua Afriyie dropped the spoon. You did it, Lord, she thought, running out.

"What? Who?"

"Columbia! And Williams College!"

"Praise the Lord!" Akua Afriyie said. "Amen! This is wonderful!"

"They'll both be sending their packages soon. I got a full ride with Columbia!"

"Amen," was all Akua Afriyie could say. Tears had gathered in her eyes. Thank you, Lord, she thought. "Why didn't you wait for me?"

"I was too anxious. And when you were sitting there, saying all those things, you weren't really helping."

"I'm sorry," Akua Afriyie said. "Oh, this is a wonderful day! You have to call your grandma! And Asantewa! And all your aunties and uncles! Let me see the Columbia letter."

"What about Williams?"

"Oh, yes. Where are they again?"

"In Massachusetts."

Akua Afriyie couldn't care less for big names and name-dropping, but come on, her daughter got into Columbia! "Did they give you a full scholarship?" she asked.

"No," Sugri said. "We'd have to pay at least two thousand dollars."

"That's it! You're going to Columbia!" Akua Afriyie said, getting up. She threw her right hand in the air, then her left. "God is good! And why am I more excited than you?" she asked, walking back to the kitchen.

"I was just asking myself the same question," Sugri said, trailing in behind her. "I'm excited too, mummy. Just in shock. I'm really leaving home. In a couple of months, I'll be living in a whole new country."

Akua Afriyie picked up the spoon she'd carelessly dropped. It had ended up in the sink. That was true. In all her excitement, the implications of Sugri getting into university hadn't sunk in. Till now. She'd been living for Sugri all these years. She scooped out a dollop of the ice cream. What was she going to do now? Her excitement waned. Her daughter was really going to be independent now. What—who was she going to live for now?

*

311

October 1997

Akua Afriyie sat behind a huge cream computer monitor. She clicked on the Queen of Spades, dragged it onto the King of Hearts. She sighed. She was bored at work. But what was she doing there? There really wasn't much work to be done these days. No big elections. No getting roped into Barnor's politics. No Sugri to go home to. She knew it was unhealthy, not dealing with the fact that her raison d'être was away in university across the world and she was holing herself up in the office. She picked up the *Daily Graphic*. Earlier in the day she'd seen an ad that she'd found interesting. She unfolded the paper and flipped through the black and white pages. There!

> *Farida's Studio*
> *Looking for a space to work?*
> *Looking for artistic instruction?*
> *Want to meet promising artists?*
> *Come visit ...*

She looked at her watch. It was just after five. Everybody had left the office half an hour ago and she was sitting there playing solitaire. She might as well go check out this place. She got out of her seat and shut down her computer. She picked up her bright green purse. This was the first time, since Sugri left, that she was leaving the office before seven.

Farida's studio was not far from John Barnor's office.

Akua Afriyie parked her car along an open gutter. Before she rolled up her window, the smell of kebab wafted into her nostrils. She would have to get some of that on her way home. She locked her door. The kebab man stood behind a grill as high as his waist, his dreadlocks shaking to their own music as he dabbed the meat with oil. She looked around for Farida's and saw a small yellow bungalow two uncompleted houses away from the kebab man. She strode to it. A signboard posted on the maroon door spelled the letters FARIDA'S. Akua Afriyie straightened her skirt, pulled off the thin ribbon holding up her ponytail, smoothed her hair and retied it—not that this was an interview, but she still wanted to make a good impression.

She knocked feebly on the door and didn't hear a response. She tried the door handle. It yielded and led to a semi-dark room, hidden in shadows. As her eyes adjusted, she saw that the room's walls were covered in paintings. She made her way toward a lit second room.

The first person she saw was a voluptuous woman, completely naked. She was seated on folds of white cloth, staring straight ahead. Three women and a short man stood behind easels. The woman closest to Akua Afriyie had sketched the naked woman in red conte crayon. Out of nowhere, a thin woman with skin the color of coffee beans materialized. Her blue turban, patterned with white and aqua triangles, seemed bigger than her whole body. Her dress, straight and sleeveless, matched the blue of her head-wrap. It was stamped with two pockets with the same print as the turban. She noticed Akua Afriyie and put up her right hand. Blue bracelets clanged from her wrist down to her elbows.

"One minute," the woman said. Her voice—gravelly, scratchy, a cross between Nina Simone and Louis Armstrong—shocked Akua Afriyie. She couldn't believe that a sound like that would come out of a woman, and from such a tiny woman. "Miss Quaye, you've thrown a voodoo head-shrinking curse on your sketch," she said to a woman behind a grey easel. "Fix it." She turned to the short man. "Brilliant! Carry on!" she croaked, walking toward Akua Afriyie. "Yes, my dear?" she asked.

Akua Afriyie could tell she had once been beautiful. Now, her skin looked too dry. "I came because of the ad in the *Daily Graphic*," she said.

"Excellent!" the woman rasped, putting her palm on Akua Afriyie's back. "Farida," she said, extending her arm. "Let's sit out here. Come." They walked back to the shaded room. Farida brought over two foldout chairs and switched on a light. "Please, have a seat!" she said, walking toward a desk behind them.

Akua Afriyie looked around. Her eyes darted from painting to painting—a nude man painted in green, fruit still lifes, abstract swirls and arrows, posted on a black wall. She looked up, saw rafters up above, and beyond them, an exposed zinc roof. Three spotlights hung from wooden planks nailed just under the roof from one end of the wall to the other.

Farida walked back and sat across from Akua Afriyie.

"Are you here to make me rich, or to steal my knowledge?" she asked in her gravelly voice.

"Yes," Akua Afriyie said, not sure how to respond. "I'm here to do both. I'd like to take lessons."

"Do you have an artistic bone?" Farida asked, shifting her turban with her right hand. Her bangles slid down to her elbows.

"I guess…. That's what I studied in school. But I haven't drawn in years. I'm so rusty."

"Well, we're very serious here," Farida said, batting her eyes. "You pay me upfront. Per month. I start from basics with each person. It's all about discipline, discipline and discipline. And of course, you have to have talent and passion. *La passion.*" She reached into her pocket and pulled out a packet of Camel cigarettes and a green butane lighter. She stuck the cigarette between her lips, lit the tip of the Camel, took a drag and coughed. "Courses are twice a week," she continued, "for the first three months. Once you've proven yourself worthy of my time, the studio is open to you. So, when do you want to start?"

"As soon as possible. What do I need to bring?"

"Well, money." Her expression remained stoic. She looked Akua Afriyie straight in the eye, then burst into a haughty laugh that ended in a coughing fit. "Here," she said, handing Akua Afriyie brochures. "These are our rates. If you need special instruction, that's more money for me. I've also taken the time to suggest places from which you can buy good art material *et cetera*. I provide you with recycled paper for your drafts but for serious work you need stellar paper and canvases." She coughed. "*Oui*, yes. I think that's it. I'll let you go marinate in, or is it ruminate on your thoughts, but I'm sure I'll be seeing you soon." She smiled. Yes, Akua Afriyie thought, the woman had once been very beautiful.

"Thanks," Akua Afriyie said. She looked back at the studio and walked out. She loved it! And that Farida! Who better than a liberated woman to teach her art? She ambled over to the kebab man's stand, a cloud of fragrant smoke hiding the man from her view. "Evening," she shouted.

"Evening, sister," the dreadlocked man said. "How many?"

"Two sticks, please."

"One thousand cedis," he said, becoming more visible as a breeze blew the smoke up. He took two sizzling pieces of the grill, handing them to Akua Afriyie.

"Thanks!" she said, grabbing a piece of meat with her teeth. The meat melted on her tongue. She was finally going back to her first love.

*

A nude male model lay on his side on a white bed sheet. His left hand lay under his shaved head. His right knee jutted out under his straightened left leg. Farida, a cigarette dangling precariously from her left hand, was touching the knee. If Akua Afriyie wasn't mistaken, she seemed to be massaging it. Today, her turban was teal. Her dress was black, straight, with teal pockets that sat on her hips.

"For some of you, this is your first nude drawing, or nude any-thing," Farida said, flourishing her cigarette hand in the air. "I want you to leave all your prudishness outside the door. Ladies and gentlemen, be bold. If this is your first nude, I will let you get away with some things. What I want you to grasp is how body parts relate to each other. Draw a small circle for the head." She took her hand off his knee and drew a circle in the air near the model's head. "Then come to the torso. That's a bigger circle. He has one bent leg. Show that with a circle. A circle for his penis. Or an oval. Use ovals! Get the general direction. All right, children, go crazy." She bent down to say something to the model.

Akua Afriyie stood behind her easel, an off-white sheet clipped to it. She poised her pencil in front of the paper. She looked at the model. His head was more oblong than oval. On her sheet, she traced the outline of an oblong. His torso was long. She drew an elongated oval. She outlined the positions of his legs using circles, just as Farida had instructed, then she started detailing his shoulders and arms. She stared at his neck bones and tried to reproduce them. She was so engrossed in getting every detail right, she was startled when she felt heavy breathing on her neck.

"Miss Mensah," Farida said, placing her palm on Akua Afriyie's shoulder. "Don't get bogged down in details. That's how you create cari-catures. Get the general sense, the density of things. Details come later. No need to be persnickety here." Right, Akua Afriyie thought, big pic-ture. "Mr. Ansah!" Farida screamed, and walked away from Akua Afriyie.

"From you, I will allow no such mistakes. Step back please. Look at your drawing. Look at the model. What's different?"

Akua Afriyie didn't want to blatantly stare at Mr. Ansah, but she couldn't help it. The man, just as small as Farida, stood back.

"I can't tell," Mr. Ansah responded, barely audible.

"Don't be lazy. Proportions. Where's the model's right hand?"

"By his buttocks." Someone in the room snickered.

"And Mr. Ansah, where is your drawing's hand?"

"By his waist."

"Good, you're not blind. Please rectify at once."

Akua Afriyie struggled over her drawing. She wasn't sure she could finish it without focusing on the small details. She stepped back, looked at her work. The head looked too big. The limbs were thin and longer than they should have been. Farida walked over.

"No, no, no," she said. "Trying to draw yourself, Miss Mensah?" What? Akua Afriyie thought, almost choking. "True, we tend to put ourselves in our work, but please don't. The model is fleshier."

"How do I fill out the details?" Akua Afriyie asked, even afraid to utter the question.

"It's a question of space and density. You have the big circles. Now block out the negative space."

"Negative space?"

"What did they teach you in school?"

"It was a while ago."

"In the space above his head, below his folded arm, what shape do you see?"

"A triangle."

"Good. Shade out a triangle. Shade out blocks of light. It's just like sculpture. The body will start to take form on the paper."

"Thanks," Akua Afriyie said.

When the lesson ended, Farida walked up to the model. "Thanks, Quincy," she said. "You must be exhausted, poor baby. All right, boys and girls. Thank you. Your homework for the day is to learn to express yourselves. Go home, have sex, drink, and come in next time holding nothing back. That is art."

*

Akua Afriyie walked into Farida's studio late. Barnor had made her drive all over Accra looking for cloth that was made to mark Ghana's forty years of independence. The festivities had taken place in March, and why he wanted the cloth now, she had no clue. He needed to hire someone young for these kinds of things. She prepared to have her head bitten off by Farida as she opened the door.

"Don't think you can just stroll in whenever you want just because we fucked," Farida said. Apparently someone else's head was being clawed off. The woman didn't even notice her. Akua Afriyie rushed by and quietly set her bag on the floor. She placed a canvas on her easel and waited with the three other students who were watching the scene with rapt attention.

"This is professional work," Farida went on. "I expect you to show up before all the artists get here. And you come in an hour late, reeking of alcohol. Really!" Her bright orange head-wrap, stamped with brown suns and moons, bopped aggressively up and down.

"I'm sorry," the young man said, his voice dull and slow.

"I'm not sure I want to see your face or your body tonight. In fact, I think I'll have the class work on still lifes. I'm really quite peeved."

"I'm very sorry," the man said.

Farida pointed at the stage, which she'd decorated with plants and flower pots. He walked over to take his place.

"I'm too annoyed to give a speech," Farida said. This was the first time they'd started a session without her pep talk.

After sketching the model, Akua Afriyie splashed green and brown oil paints on the canvas. Farida came round. "Very nice," she said. "The colors are bold, and I love how you've let that fool fill in the space. The battle of man and nature. *Très bien.*" Officially the first compliment Farida had given her.

At ten, Farida closed the studio. She didn't linger to talk to the model or the students she found interesting. Akua Afriyie saw the tiny woman storm off to her blue Golf. She made her way to the kebab stand.

"Kwasi," Akua Afriyie said. "Good evening."

"Hello, sister. Two?"

"Yes, please." She heard Farida's car start. It sputtered and died. Farida tried again. Start, sputter, stop. Start, sputter, stop. After paying for her kebabs Akua Afriyie walked over. "Do you need help?" she asked.

"The forces are against me today," Farida said, turning on the ignition, trying once more. "Oh, forget it! I have a headache and I'm too tired to deal with this. Which way are you going?"

"To the Cantonments area," Akua Afriyie said. "Where are you going?"

"To Airport Residential, but I'll just get off at Sankara Circle and take a taxi home. I haven't sat in one of those in years."

"I can drop you off at home. It's no problem."

"You are a godsend!"

In the car, both women remained quiet. Akua Afriyie tried to think of something to ask Farida to fill in the silent void.

"Apart from the models, I don't get to know my students," Farida said.

"OK," Akua Afriyie responded, not sure why Farida was telling her that. Was that a hint that she wasn't interested in getting to know her?

"It's just a self-protection thing," the woman went on. "I know my students' traits from their work. Like you … you have all this suppressed energy in you. I felt it the first day you walked into my studio."

"Life has a way of suppressing energy, doesn't it?"

"In art, you need to let the suppressed energy erupt. You've started doing that these days. Letting go. You've been producing amazing work."

"Thanks," Akua Afriyie said. Where did I go and sleep last night? she wondered.

"You seem to be reaching into a store of experiences you buried a long time ago that you are allowing to come to the surface. I'm sure your abstract work will be orgasmic. Why did you say life suppresses energy? It shouldn't."

Akua Afriyie was chuckling at 'orgasmic'. "Having children," she said. "That burns inspiration. Do you have any?"

"To ruin this figure? *Non merci.*"

Cigarettes are doing worse, Akua Afriyie thought. "But you're married?" she asked.

"I was. Once."

Akua Afriyie turned down her indicator. "What happened?"

"My husband died," Farida said, her gravelly voice attempting a hit at a high note. It failed. She cleared her throat. "My husband uprooted me to Paris when I was impressionable. Mind if I smoke?"

"No," Akua Afriyie said. "But roll down the window."

"The bastard got tired of me and started sleeping around with whores from all over the world." She lit a cigarette.

"Literally?" Akua Afriyie asked. She wasn't sure if she was allowed to have this conversation, but it was too entertaining.

"I don't know if they were, but I made sure he took care of me."

"How?"

"He paid for my art lessons. I painted in every reputable art studio in that city."

"Wow! How did you meet him?"

Farida took a drag of her cigarette. The smoke assaulted Akua Afriyie's nostrils. "I went to Tamale Secondary School. In my last year of school, I met him when he came to work on a rice-planting project."

"You married him that young?"

"No. I went off to the University of Science and Technology. We wrote to each other often. He came back to Ghana and whisked me off to Paris."

"It sounds like a fairytale," Akua Afriyie said.

"No. Far from one. My parents never forgave me for it. They had a Nigerian Alhaji lined up for me. I simply dashed their hopes. Then that bastard went around chasing every thing in a skirt."

"Was he white?"

"Yes. Yet he only chased black skirts. *Le con!*"

"Have you patched up things with your family?"

"Somewhat. But they know I can't live in Salaga anymore."

"Why not?"

"Accra is as close as I'll get to the comforts of Paris in this bloody country."

"I never married," Akua Afriyie said, not sure if Farida would even be interested in that boring piece of information.

"Well, you haven't missed anything," Farida said. "But you said you had a child! Now you're getting interesting. So you bore a child out of wedlock? _Quel scandale._ Oh, do tell."

"It's a long story," Akua Afriyie said, driving by the Akuffo Circle. "I can't stand my daughter's father." Farida brought out the worst in her.

"Intriguing!"

"Well, she's in university now. I raised her all by myself."

"Good for you, woman. Bravo! Now, we have to find you a new distraction."

"There is someone I'm interested in," Akua Afriyie said, amazed at how Farida squeezed out information from her. In Farida's hands she was a squishy juicy orange.

"Who? Not Ansah in the studio, I hope!"

"Oh, no, no," Akua Afriyie said, laughing. "Where do I go now?"

"Oh, I forgot myself. Turn right. It's the third house on the left."

"He's my pastor."

"I'm liking you more. Have you two done anything?"

"We've known each other for about five years, but no, we haven't done anything," she said pulling along the curb of Farida's house. "I don't even know if the feeling is mutual."

"Have you told him?" Akua Afriyie shook her head. "You're not in high school. You need to ask the man out and I expect a progress report." She was right, Akua Afriyie thought. If even Sugri was now going out with someone, she also had the right to be happy. "_Merci_ for the ride!" Farida said, getting out of the car. "See you next week. And go after that sugar!" Akua Afriyie laughed. How had this woman ended up in her life?

*

December 1997

Akua Afriyie danced along to Anita Baker, as she stood in front of the open oven door. She prodded the golden brown chicken. She pushed the tray back into the oven and shut the door. The mashed yam was already done and in the fridge. She took the lid off a small pan. Her brown gravy looked perfect. She dipped a wooden spoon into the thick smooth sauce, patted it against her palm and licked it. She buzzed around the kitchen, dizzy with excitement. She lowered the fire under the gravy and dashed to the bathroom, hoping Edem would arrive late.

She stepped out of the bathroom, dabbed herself and planned what she'd wear, trying not to give too much thought to how the night would play itself out. She knew what she wanted. Edem. But was that the right thing to want or do? As she was drying the water off her shins, the bell rang.

No! She ran out to her room, pulled out her underwear drawer. She dug through it, trying to find the sexiest pair. Black. Look where your mind is going. This is just an innocent dinner, she chided herself. She opened her wardrobe. He's way too early, she thought, slipping into a black chiffon dress. She buttoned it and fussed with the ruffles at the collar. She picked up a bottle of perfume—*Havoc*—and sprayed it behind her ears and on her collarbones. She fluffed up her hair, hoping it didn't look too messy. The bell rang again.

She ran to the door and unlocked it. He stood there, dressed in a white dress shirt over black trousers.

"I'm so sorry," she said.

"You look nice," he said to her.

"Thanks. You're early!"

"Am I? I try not to arrive late like most people. I guess I've gone to another extreme."

"No, no! Don't worry. Come in."

"Nice flat," he said.

"Thanks. Are you starving?"

"Almost," Edem said. His dimple danced in and out of his cheek.

"Good. We can sit here and talk for a bit," she said, pointing to the cane sofa. "You probably haven't had a good home-cooked meal in a while." She sat on the sofa perpendicular to his.

Edem raised his left brow. "I cook, you know."

"Really? I just assumed, with your being a man and all, that you couldn't cook. I can't imagine my father in a kitchen!"

"I've been living on my own for years now."

What have you done to me? I can't eat. I cannot sleep.

"I'm sorry," Akua Afriyie said, realizing that she'd left Anita Baker playing all this while. "I hope you don't mind that it's not gospel ..."

"I like good clean R&B every so often. I love Aretha Franklin."

"You're full of surprises," Akua Afriyie said. "What else don't I know about you, Edem?"

"I'm sure I've preached about my whole life behind that pulpit."

"I remember you telling us about your mother's death. I liked that sermon. Your father still lives in Sogakope?"

"Yes. I've been trying to get him to move to Accra, but he hates the city."

"You're an only child?" Akua Afriyie asked.

"Yes."

"Really? Your father and mother's only child?"

"Yes."

"That's rare. At least in Ghana."

"You had just Sugri ..."

"I meant in those days. How old are you, anyway, Edem?"

"Thirty three."

"You're a child!" Edem laughed loudly. It was the first time Afriyie had seen him completely let go, let a laugh shake his whole body. Up on the pulpit even in his most heated deliveries, he seemed too composed.

"And how old are you?"

"Old enough to be your mother! I'll be right back," she said, walking to the kitchen to turn off the gravy and chicken. She took out the mashed yam, grabbed the pot of gravy and walked back to the living room with them.

"Need some help?" Edem asked.

"No. Just get ready to eat." She placed the pots on the cane table. He looked so good! She brought out the chicken. In a cabinet across from the dinner table she took out her best, guests-come-to-dinner plates: white plates with green Adinkra symbol trimmings. She set the table and stared at him from the corner of her right eye. "Dinner is served!" she said.

"How come you don't have any of your drawings up on your wall?" he asked as he joined her at the table.

"I'm not confident about them yet," she said, carving the chicken. "Which part do you want?" she asked him.

"Any. I'm not fussy."

"OK, you get the breast. You need to put on some weight!" she said. Edem laughed.

"You don't have any meat on your bones either," he said. They both laughed. A hush fell over the table. He bowed his head, prayed quietly. He cut into his chicken breast. As she took a bite of her chicken, she heard his knife clinking against his plate. The silence was killing her. Maybe he didn't talk when he was eating. "To what do I owe this nice treat?" Edem asked after he'd swallowed the last morsel of chicken on his plate. She was relieved he'd started talking, but his question required her to be honest, and she wasn't sure if she should be.

"Well, you've been such a great spiritual advisor. I thought this was the least I could do for you."

He smiled. "Thank you," he said. "This was delicious."

"I hate to admit it, but my mother is a better cook."

"This was wonderful. Better than anything I'd make."

"What do you want to drink?" she asked. "I have pineapple juice."

"Pineapple's perfect."

She walked back to the kitchen and opened the fridge. How was she going to bring up what she'd really invited him over for? she wondered. Edem, I really like you.... Edem, how do you feel about having a girlfriend? Ugh! She was so rusty in this game. She walked out with two bottles of pineapple juice.

"We can move back to the couches," she said.

"That was really delicious," he said, settling on a couch. She sat perpendicular to him. "Why are you sitting so far away?" he asked. Had she heard right? No, that had to be her imagination making him say the things she wanted to hear.

"Huh?"

"You keep sitting so far off. It's awkward," Edem said. He was right. She was at the extreme end of the sofa. She slid down. They were now sitting almost face-to-face.

"I wanted to talk to you about something," she said.

"I knew there was no such thing as a free dinner!" Edem said.

"Oh, Edem!" Akua Afriyie said, laughing. "No, it's not like that."

"I'm joking," he said.

"Now I don't even want to ask you anymore."

"Come on!" Edem said. They were acting like teenagers.

"How do you handle romantic relationships?" she asked.

"Good question," he said, boring into her eyes. "I don't."

"What does that mean?"

"God does." He was so difficult!

"Do you have a girlfriend?" she asked.

"No, not now."

"Have you ever had one?"

"Of course!" Edem said. "Can we not talk about that, though?" he said, his voice noticeably raspier than before. He stared at Akua Afriyie. She stared back at him. Their eyes locked. This is it, Akua Afriyie thought. Her heart boomed against her ribcage. Was it going to happen? Or was he going to stop her? He leaned forward. His lips grazed hers. Their lips pressed harder against each other. She moved over to his sofa. He held her shoulder, pushed her into the cushions. His tongue probed her mouth urgently. Akua Afriyie felt the release of several years of repressed desires. She sensed his release, even stronger than hers. His tongue shoved, pulled, flicked, curled and licked. His hands searched for her body but he seemed afraid to touch her. She placed his hands on her breasts. He grew bolder orbing them with his palms. He unbuttoned the top of her dress, groping under, searching for her. She, also emboldened, reached for his belt, unclasped the metal. She unzipped his trousers, pulled them down to his ankles. He raised her dress. He seemed in such haste. His tongue touched her triangle, made her toes curl. It had been so long. It felt wonderful—his tongue. It felt … orgasmic. Farida's word. Who would have thought they'd be doing this?

"Do you have protection?" she asked him.

"No, I didn't come here with that on my mind," he said.

"I might have some …"

"Afriyie," he said, sitting up. "I don't think this is a good idea."

"Why not?" she asked, frustrated. "Is it a sin to give in to your feelings? Haven't we already crossed the line?"

"It's not about that," he said.

Disappointment sat on her chest like a meal cooked in too much oil. She'd dreamt of this day so many times, and now the fantasy was crumbling. She looked at his feet, where his trousers sat in a bunch. "What do we do now?" she asked.

"Afriyie," he said. "I'm really attracted to you. I've been since I met you. Why do you think I didn't stop asking you to come to church?"

"But ..." she said. She didn't know whether she should jump for joy, knowing that he at least liked her. But that, apparently, didn't mean anything. "But?" she said, her voice more insistent.

"Yes. But. But, God doesn't have marriage in his plans for me."

"I haven't mentioned marriage," she said. "We like each other. We're both grown up. We can have a grown-up relationship. What's wrong with that? Or would that be fornication?"

"No ... yes," he said, his eyes betraying confusion. "Listen. Supposing we'd slept together today. Eventually you'd expect marriage. Especially since you've never been married.... That's how most of you women are. Marriage is your goal in life."

"That's not true," she said, shaking her head. "You can't just label me as some marriage-hungry person. No." She buttoned her dress. "If I wanted to get married I could have done that years ago. You really don't know me."

"Sorry," he said. "All I'm saying is God has a plan for my life, as he does for yours, and he hasn't spoken to me about marriage, so to start something will just be wasting your time."

"I think you should go," Akua Afriyie said. She felt so ashamed. A seductress who had failed at her task. That was who she was! She wondered why God hadn't spoken to her, warning her. Telling her that seducing a pastor was a horrible idea. Edem stood up, pulling up his trousers.

"If you want to talk some more about this, we can talk on Sunday, after church," he said.

"Please, go," she said, her voice cracked. Her eyes clouded with tears. She cringed when she thought about how eager she'd been to find condoms. Condoms she probably wouldn't even have found! Would she ever live down this embarrassment?

Twenty-five
Brushes

The Center of Christ Church was now International. Akua Afriyie walked toward the newly completed church, impressed. She'd taken a pause for almost a year now, but she'd decided that it was time for her to return to church. She looked at the church building. Its cream walls now stretched beyond the one-story building that it had started with seven years ago. Adinkra symbol engravings ran up the church's front facade. The car park had also been expanded, but wasn't large enough. Cars spilled out on to the narrow Teshie-Nungua streets. And they weren't the battered-up kind, like her Fiat was. They all shone with the kind of newness her mother would appreciate.

Inside, she realized that the construction was still going on, as particles of dust hung in the air, and quite a few irritated chests burst out into whoops of coughing.

She sat in the middle row of the left aisle. She wasn't going to take any chances and sit in the front row. Edem had been calling her, trying to bring his lost sheep back to the flock, but she'd been too embarrassed to answer any of his calls.

She looked at her watch. The service was taking too long to start. It was fifteen minutes late. Is that what came with popularity and expansion? Rudeness?

A woman in a wide, red, suede hat settled in front of her and completely blocked her view of the pulpit. She didn't want Edem to see her, but she hadn't come to church to look at a red suede hat. She slid over to the left.

"So, he's set a date, they say," she heard a woman say. The voice sounded like Agyeiwaa's, the church's most notorious gossip.

"Is that so?" another said. She sounded like the one who always wore bright red lipstick in a shade that was just not right for her.

"It will be hard being a pastor's wife," Agyeiwaa said.

"But, Pastor Adomza will be a great husband," wrong red lipstick said. "The way he gets his messages directly from God, it will be heaven living with him."

Akua Afriyie felt a huge knot form in her stomach. She felt queasy. Edem was getting married? After she'd thought there could be a rapprochement between them, this is what she had to hear from someone else? She didn't want to hear any more of the gossip, but like a mosquito drawn to the warm blood of a man who would probably end up killing it, she stayed, fixed in her seat.

"That woman is so lucky," Agyeiwaa said. "I heard the number of women in this church that tried to seduce that man," she added loudly. "Hmmm. Good thing he's a man of God!"

"Amen. Someone else would have taken advantage."

Akua Afriyie tried her best not to turn around. She was convinced they were having that conversation for her benefit. She couldn't take it anymore. She moved back behind the woman in the red hat.

She stood up when the youth choir broke into praise songs.

My comfort, my shelter, tower of refuge and of strength …

Shout to the Lord was one of her favorite songs. She moved her lips but no voice came out. She couldn't move her hands up to the ceiling. She couldn't shout to the Lord. She didn't listen to the sermon. As Edem's voice floated through the dust-filled congregation, her thoughts jumped to the last time she'd been able to face him. When they'd almost slept together. The time when he'd told her that he was sure all she wanted was marriage. How he'd told her God hadn't planned marriage for him.

"… and sisters, there's a reason God sent us Nkrumah," Edem said. "There's a reason he sent us through years of coups. He sent us President Rawlings for a reason. He has plans for Ghana. Almost forty years after independence, Ghana is one of the most God-fearing countries in Africa!"

"Yes, it is true!" an old woman in front shouted. "Amen!"

Tears kept forming in Akua Afriyie's eyes. His voice was no way helping. She decided the only way to deal with how she was feeling was to find out the truth from him.

She stood up when new converts were called to the altar. She put money in the collection basket when it came around. She stood up when the closing hymn was being sang.

After the service, she made for Edem's office.

"Ei, Sister Akua!" Jennifer said, cutting in front of her. "Long time no see!"

"Yes," Akua Afriyie said. "I was out of town."

"Is that so? Well, the hospital is starting an outreach to build a clinic in the Dedenya village ..."

"I'll be back," Akua Afriyie said, when she saw Edem walking down. She knew she sounded too curt, but she didn't want anybody getting there before she did, or she'd lose her nerve. She rushed down the stairs and caught him trying to open his door. He turned around.

"Amen! Afriyie! Long time no see," he said. "I was beginning to think I'd never see you again." His dimples darted in and out. He unlocked the door to his office and let her in. He left the door open. Akua Afriyie wanted him to close it, but she didn't want him to get the wrong idea either.

"Congratulations. I heard the news," she said.

"Wow, news spreads fast, doesn't it?" he said. "Your first day back and you've already heard. Well, thanks."

Akua Afriyie had expected him to pretend or apologize, but that was asking too much of him.

"So, how are you doing? I hope all is well between you and God."

Akua Afriyie was sure he was trying to change the subject and that was beginning to irritate her. "Why did you tell me God didn't have marriage in his plans for you? Why didn't you just tell me you weren't interested in me? I'm not a child." Her voice rose higher than she wanted it to. She heard footsteps behind her, but didn't turn to see who it was.

He looked at the door, then said quietly, "At that time, God didn't. Afriyie, a lot of time has passed since last year. I'm sorry about what happened between us. I really valued having you as a friend, as a sister in Christ, but *at that time* I really wasn't ready for marriage. I've grown a lot since then, and now God has decided I am ready for a family."

"Don't use God as an excuse," she blurted out. "You took part in an adult act…. You shouldn't have touched me at all." She heard a woman clear her throat. She turned around and was mortified to find out it was Agyeiwaa.

"I'm very sorry about what happened," Edem said, as he rose to close the door. "We mere mortals plan but it's God who disposes. I really didn't plan to get married, but He sent me Faustina. She's wonderful. God is doing wonderful things. The church is expanding. Did you see the cars in the park? We have grown!"

Akua Afriyie sat up. "I shouldn't have barged in here like this." She was angrier with herself than with him. He had been right. If they had slept together, marriage would have been the next expectation. That was exactly why she was reacting the way she was. He'd been the bigger person to stop what they'd started before it went too far.

"Afriyie, seeing you is always a pleasure," he said. "I hope you'll start coming back to fellowships. We miss you."

"I'm sure people are lining up to see you," she said. "Thanks for seeing me." She walked out quickly.

"I'll pray for you," Agyeiwaa shouted.

As Akua Afriyie walked up the stairs, a thought she didn't want to acknowledge rose in her. Finally, she relented and listened to it. Her born-again feeling had been a farce—it was lovesickness for Edem disguised as a strong love for Jesus and all humanity. She saw Jennifer coming toward her with the cane basket. She dashed past the pulpit, through the side door and out of the church.

*

Akua Afriyie drove to the Bassline Jazz Club to meet Farida. As she turned off the Ring Road, she saw Babasam sitting on a short wall. A few flecks of grey peppered his bushy hair, but he seemed to be ageless. He wore a neat shortsleeved shirt and brown trousers. They hung loosely on him. Those were probably John Barnor's clothes, she figured.

She walked into the dimly lit jazz club. She smoothed her white summer dress, which she'd complemented with a yellow scarf around her neck. In a corner of the room she saw a live jazz band performing, complete with saxophonist and backup singers.

Farida wasn't hard to spot. A brown and orange cloth was wrapped high around her head. Instead of her usual long dress, she wore a short brown skirt, showing legs that were remarkably trim. Akua Afriyie hadn't expected her to have such nice-looking legs. Farida was toting a young man on her left arm and held a glass in her right hand.

Akua Afriyie walked over. "Hi, Farida," she said.

"*Salut!*" Farida said, air kissing Akua Afriyie. "After you told me about that false prophet, I knew you'd need this. Have a drink. Scotch? A shot of brandy?"

"Oh, just a glass of juice will be fine."

"Stop giving me that pious act. You need some alcohol, but if you want to be her holiness, Nii," she said to the hot young thing on her arm, "another scotch for me and pineapple juice for my darling here."

The band started playing *Take five*. Farida lit a cigarette.

"You know what?" Akua Afriyie said.

"What?"

"I could do with one of those," she said.

Farida offered her the pack. She didn't seem surprised. She didn't even as much as raise a brow. Akua Afriyie hadn't smoked since secondary school. She pulled out a cigarette, placed it between her lips and lit up. After inhaling, she coughed and tried not to make a fool of herself.

"Some American woman, Karen-something, came by the studio today and was enthralled by your work," Farida said.

"Really?" Akua Afriyie said.

"Yes. You know, a lot of people come in and can't stop raving about your work. I think you've outgrown me. You need to find your own space."

"It sounds like you're kicking me out," Akua Afriyie said, suppressing a cough.

"Yes, I am," Farida said. "I don't handle competition well. When my students start showing more talent than I have, I get extremely jealous. This American woman—one of those plain, odiously overweight types—says she's a curator in a Manhattan gallery. She left her contact information." Farida opened her brown leather bag and brought out a bright yellow business card. "If I were you, I'd be on the phone calling her now. But first have your pineapple juice and find yourself a nice young man for the night."

Akua Afriyie laughed. She stubbed out the unfinished cigarette. Her mouth tasted like an ashtray and now her lungs were irritated.

She had begun a religious series when Farida had let them work on abstract pieces. They were bloody and way too morbid. She loved them, but didn't think they'd appeal to anyone else. Truth was, she didn't think she or her work was good enough.

The next day Akua Afriyie woke up coughing. She vowed never to go near a cigarette again. She lay in her bed and stared at the light coming through her sheer orange curtains. She could lie in bed all day. She thought of Edem and was about to wallow in self-pity when she remembered she hadn't called the American woman.

She got out of bed and walked into the living room. She looked on the sofa where she'd dumped her purse the night before. She rummaged through the black cloth bag and found the lemon card.

As she dialed the woman's number, she stared at a black and white picture of five-year-old Sugri she'd blown up and placed above the TV.

"Hello," a woman's voice answered. It was awake and full of verve.

Wish I had that kind of energy this morning, Akua Afriyie thought. "Yes, hello," she said. "I'd like to speak to Karen Sanders."

"This is she."

"My name is Akua Afriyie. I'm an artist at Farida's. She told me you were interested in some of my paintings."

"Yes, Akwa Afriyie, your work is really amazing. Your pieces had me staring at them over and over again. I love how your work expresses spirituality and motherhood at the same time. I bought one from Farida."

"Oh, thank you," Akua Afriyie said and then coughed.

"I'm going back to the States tomorrow. Tell you what? I'm gonna show your work to the other curators and the gallery owners. Let me take down your information. What's your number?"

"229916."

"Great," Karen said. "Stay posted. I'll be calling you, hopefully with good news. It was great talking to you."

"Thanks, Karen. Safe journey," Akua Afriyie said.

*

November 1998

Akua Afriyie inhaled. She walked toward John Barnor's office, an envelope in hand, unsure of what mood he'd be in. But she had to do this.

"All my co-curators at 171 Gallery loved your work, Akwa Afriyie," Karen Sanders had said to her. She was sending a contract and hoped Akua Afriyie would say yes to their offer. They wanted to showcase twenty new pieces, which she'd have to ship to New York for an exhibition in December next year. Farida told her she'd be stupid to say no.

She stared at the beveling on the polished mahogany door and rubbed her index finger along the envelope. She knocked on the door.

"Come in," John Barnor said. "Afriyie!" His voice boomed. He was too happy. It would have been better if he was in a bad mood. "Kufuor's people just called me. I told them we'll personally handle his publicity and public image. You should have come to the NPP congress. The energy was *butubutu*. I feel like time has definitely come to an end for Rawlings and the NDC. Afriyie, I feel it. I will personally make sure J. A. Kufuor wins the 2000 elections."

Why this now? Afriyie thought to herself.

"You're not saying anything," John Barnor said. "I have this idea I want to run by you. Getting young people ..."

"I'm so sorry to interrupt you," she said, thinking if she let him go on, she'd get pulled in and tied down. "Here's my two weeks notice. I'm resigning, John."

Barnor seemed at a loss for words for a good second and a half. Then he said, "You've sprung this on me. Have you been unhappy here? Do I treat you badly? Good Lord, what am I going to do without you? Can I increase your salary? Why?"

"John," Akua Afriyie said. "These fourteen years have been the most rewarding of my professional life. You've been a wonderful boss. I've just decided to go back to art."

"Art?" He said it flatly. It sounded almost as if art were a repulsive thing. Art. "Oh! You can earn extra money from this project. You can still work here and do your art on the side."

"I want to develop my art professionally."

"You can do art on the side and still be professional. Afriyie, have you thought this through?"

"I can work for another two weeks and help you hire somebody else." That came out a little too coarsely, she thought. She softened her tone and added, "It's just that I'm not getting any younger and for this job, John, you need someone full of life."

"I'm really heartbroken, Afriyie. I didn't see this coming. You could have given me more time." His voice was shaky. "I hire you with no skills, as a favor to your parents, and after everything I've helped you with … you just want to walk out," Barnor said, looking Akua Afriyie in the eye.

Akua Afriyie cringed at the mention of the 'favor.' "Thanks for all that you've taught me. I'll make myself available as and when you need me. Thanks for understanding," she said and walked out of his office. She knew why he was upset. She was his ticket to getting on Kufuor's good side. If he handled the man's publicity he was as good as guaranteed a Minister or MP position if the man came to power. Well, she was through with being a pawn in his game of politics.

*

December 1998

"You need to grow wings and fly," Farida said loudly to Akua Afriyie. "Build your own studio! Besides, it's way too early for you to be here."

"Lots of work to be done, so little time," Akua Afriyie said, as she stood behind a large canvas she'd painted blood red. She rubbed her hand through her hair, which she'd recently cut into an afro. She couldn't see Farida's face. All she heard was the scratchy voice, and the striking of a match against a matchbox. "I already have a studio—my living room," she added, laughing. "But try as much as you want, you can't get rid of me. Especially, not if twenty big pieces have to be produced in a couple of months. Sorry, Farida."

She penciled in wings to the blood red heart in the center of the canvas. She painted them light pink. In the background was the faint image of a mask. Akua Afriyie had conjured up the oval shape of Edem's face and eyes. She was finding him useful, after all. With a thinner brush, she drew a network of veins and arteries in grey and blue around the heart and used the same colors to make the wings come alive.

"You're my muse," Akua Afriyie said.

"I'll be charging you rent," Farida said, coming around the easel, a cigarette dangling from the corner of her mouth. "And fees for ideas."

They both burst out laughing. Akua Afriyie felt a strong connection with Farida. She realized that they were similar kinds of women—they simply had no luck with men. Marriage wasn't written in their destinies and once they accepted that, life was much, much sweeter. For the first time in years, she felt that her own life had direction.

***

PART THREE

Twenty-six
America

Sugri walked down Broadway. Fruit vendors had set up shop on the pavements. Two groups of chess players were focused on their boards. Sugri was surprised that above the avenue's cacophony she could still hear the chess pieces hit the flat wooden surfaces. She loved the vibe of the city and loved being so free.

She walked into her dorm, a red brick and grey concrete building, and entered an ancient elevator.

The door of her room was slightly ajar. She heard her roommate, Rachel, cursing into the phone. She walked in and saw the girl's mop of brown curls bobbing vigorously with every "fuck."

"… isn't the point. No. You know what, fuck you, Chad." She hung up. "My Ghana sister," she said cheerily. "That was Chad," she volunteered. "I like hanging up on him."

"Hi," Sugri said.

They had shared the room for less than a week and she was already grating on Sugri's nerves. Not that she had done anything wrong. It was just that she was always talking about her boyfriend Chad and always sounded absolutely patronizing each time she said, "My Ghana sister." Just because her sister had been to Ghana for two weeks didn't mean they had a connection.

"Are you going to the party tonight?" Sugri asked, trying to get over her irritation.

"It's so cute how you say party: *pahtee*," Rachel said. "Um, what party?" She was looking at the phone, expectantly, her verdant eyes flashing with disappointment when it didn't ring.

"The *parrrdy's* organized by the BSU," Sugri said. "The Black Students' Union."

"Oh, OK. Maybe."

Sugri thought Rachel could be stunning, with those magnetic green eyes. If she got her hair styled and wore less hippie-like clothes, she would really be prettier. And then she realized she herself needed a makeover. She had no idea what to wear to the party. She dialed Ije's extension.

"*The mo' money we come across, the mo' problems we see,*" Ije sang into the phone. "Whassup?"

"I have no clothes."

"Bring yourself here and get ready for an Ije intervention."

As Sugri hung up she saw her roommate pick up her phone.

"Hey," Rachel said. "Why didn't you call me back?"

Sugri smiled as she walked to Ije's building. She was sure people thought she was crazy. She found herself grinning constantly since she'd arrived in America. And that was exactly the opposite of what her Auntie Tsotsoo had told her to do. At the airport, with Lizzie, her mother and all her other aunties and uncles, her aunt had told her it was best to avoid eye contact. People in New York were crazy, she'd said.

Sugri knocked on the door to Ije's room. Notorious Biggie's music oozed out of her walls. Ije opened the door and the walls were papered from ceiling to floor with posters of Tupac, Biggie and pictures of her family in Nigeria. Sugri had bonded with Ije at the international students' orientation a week before. Ije had been the most energetic coordinator, with her hoarse voice shouting across the auditorium.

Sugri walked into the room, her ears ringing from the music. Ije was jigging her shoulders and folding clothes.

"R.I.P. Biggie!" Ije screamed hoarsely.

"Nice outfit!" Sugri said, admiring Ije's denim miniskirt and a spaghetti-strap top that showed off her midriff, while silently praying she wouldn't be dressed similarly. Ije threw a white miniskirt and a flimsy top with straps at her. "Let's make a deal," Sugri said. "I'll wear the skirt but I need a top that shows less. My mother would kill me if she saw me in this." She picked up the blouse by the straps.

Ije ignored her and started putting face powders and lipsticks on Sugri. After she had pinched her cheeks, applied powders and pencils, erased and applied again, Ije let down Sugri's braids and shoved her in front of a full-length mirror behind her door.

Sugri looked at herself. Her thin legs looked longer under the mini-skirt. She looked at the bright pink sleeveless top she was wearing. And her face. Her face! Her lips were pink, her eye shadow was purple and her eyelashes had never been this long. She didn't recognize herself. She looked nice, but like a nice prostitute.

"I hope you like your new look. Come on, let's go," Ije said, leaving Sugri no time to react.

They walked up Amsterdam Avenue along with students trekking in little groups towards the bars lining the avenue. Sugri kept pulling down her miniskirt, while Ije click-clacked away, talking about the tall Jamaican boy who'd transferred into her year, who she was hoping would be there.

Ambulances drove in and out of the Columbia-Presbyterian Hospital entrance, whining dolefully. Sugri found that all the sounds in New York—people endlessly going and coming, music blaring from radios, sirens and honking cars, trains chugging underground—blended together and gave the city a heartbeat.

"… year has been so bad. First Notorious Biggie, then Princess Di and now Mother Theresa," a high-pitched voice said behind her.

"Yeah, you know that Israel Kamakawiwoʻole died too?" a male voice responded.

"Dude, who's that?"

"The 'Somewhere over the rainbow …'"

"Jeez, 1997!"

"Leave your skirt alone," Ije growled.

They arrived at Lerner Hall, where pockets of people had gathered outside on the grass. A group of teenage boys in Yankees and Knicks caps, large T-shirts and jeans falling to the ground had blocked the entrance.

"… we gotta be in the basement?" a heavyset one groused.

"It's the system. They always tryna to keep us down," a boy in glasses responded.

Ije and Sugri squeezed their way into the building and walked down to the basement.

Two lines led into the room the party was being held in.

A woman with a weave-on held up in a crazy chignon patted down Sugri and slowly pressed on her legs, from the top of her thigh all the way down to her ankles. Sugri shuddered and looked back at Ije who didn't seem worried in the least bit.

Another woman was placing hot pink paper bracelets around wrists. Sugri stretched out her arm.

"You got ID?" the woman asked. Sugri looked at Ije.

Ije shook her head. "Nope. We're not drinking. We're not twenty-one!" she said loudly and smiled, as if not being twenty-one was something to celebrate.

Inside, the dimly-lit room was half full. A DJ stood in a corner, behind a table set up with his equipment, surrounded by his large posse. Shouting out lyrics to songs, they seemed to outnumber the people who'd come in for the party.

Ije dragged Sugri toward a group of girls.

"So cute!" one of them was saying.

"He's got such a politician air about him."

"I'd say it's more of a revolutionary vibe."

"Whasssaaap!" Ije yelled and stuck her tongue out. The girls did the same. "This is my girl, Sugri. Sugri, meet Angie, Shawna, Lisa, Dee, Jamie."

Sugri said hello. Before she had a chance to go round the circle to make sure she had the names right, she felt somebody place a moist palm on her shoulder.

"Hello, ladies!" he said. He turned to Sugri immediately, his eyes betraying confusion. "I'm sorry. I just put my palm on you as if we were the best of friends and I don't even know you. You must be new. Ellis." He extended his hand. She shook it.

"Sugri."

"We were just talking about you!" Dee, Shawna or Lisa said.

"Favorably, I hope," he said and turned to Sugri. "Sugri, I'll come back and try to convince you you're BSU material. Ladies, party up!" His dark smooth skin contrasted with his light hazel eyes. He was beautiful. His eyes were small and his hair was adorable—a mop of black curls.

Ije talked to the other girls and Sugri looked around. People kept filing in. At some point a drove of people walked in and the DJ started playing Notorious Biggie's "Juicy." The new arrivals pushed into the middle of the dance floor, cheering and rapping, "It was all a dream …" Sugri watched as people radiated from their corners onto the dance floor.

"R.I.P. Biggie!" Ije rasped and dragged Sugri into the throng of dancers.

Sugri kept a simple one-two step. She loved to dance but only in her room, hence the one-two step. She looked over at Ije who had lowered her body close to the ground. She brought it back up, wriggled her *derriere*, put her hands up in the air, sashayed her hips from side to side and went back down to the ground.

Out of nowhere, a huge man, with cornrows that reached his shoulders, plastered himself onto Ije's wriggling backside. She didn't push him away. Sugri looked on, mortified. Ije and the guy, stuck together, moved up and down, held hands, and ground their pelvises into one. He turned Ije around and all Sugri saw were his ample buttocks thrusting in and out and up and down. Soon, all around them, couples were grinding into each other, though not as intensely as Ije and her guy.

Sugri was about to move away from the dance floor—everyone around her was coupled up and she was feeling foolish, dancing by herself—when she felt a thin body wrap its arms around her. She turned around and looked up but had to lower her gaze. The body belonged to a man a good number of inches shorter than she. His tongue stuck out by the corner of his mouth and he bobbed his head, signaling that she turn around and do like the others. She continued her one-two step, refusing to succumb to this bottom-to-groin dance. Before she knew it, the man had walked off. How rude, she thought as she walked to the drinks table tucked in the corner of the room. Was it by force to dance like that?

"Sugri," Ellis called out.

"Hello, Ellis," Sugri said.

"Where are you from?" Ellis asked. "You have a great accent."

Sugri was skeptical. Two words and he was able to glean a great accent? "Thanks," she shouted. "I'm from Ghana."

"Wow, you're so far from home! Do you want a beer?" he asked, rubbing his hands in his curly hair. A naughty smile traced his lips.

"Huh?" A bean?

"I was joking," he said, a smile raising the right corner of his lips. "That is, unless you really want to drink one."

"Oh, a beer? No thanks. I don't drink," Sugri said.

"Ah, that's what we all said when we first came!" he said. "So how's Ghana? It's the next place I want to visit."

"Really? Why?" Sugri asked. What was special about Ghana? She didn't think there was anything to see. No skyscrapers, no subways….

"Oh wow, you don't sound encouraging," he said. "Ije is all about everybody should visit Naija." His "Naija" sounded funny but she kept a straight face. "I want to go to Ghana and Nigeria and everywhere on the continent because we all come from there. It's our motherland."

"True," Sugri said, beginning to feel stupid. She wanted to say something smart, but found herself speechless. Since she'd arrived in America, she'd been ousted from her Miss Smarty Pants position and she didn't like the feeling.

"On another note," Ellis said, "you should seriously come to our first BSU meeting next week. Then you can tell me about Ghana."

"I'll come," Sugri said. She could feel a million eyes on her and stole a glance around. She saw the girls from earlier on—Dee, Jamie and crew—looking her way. Their faces were hidden in shadows. A part of her was relishing the idea that they were jealous of her, but she was so nervous, she didn't know what to say to him.

Ooh baby, gotta get you home with me tonight.

"Want to dance, Ghana?" he asked with a smile full of mischief.

"Sure," she said, her stomach knotting over because she was afraid she'd be a bad dancer and then he'd lose interest. And more over, she didn't want to dance like *that*.

Come on, come on, Foxy come on.

Ellis stood across from her and didn't make any moves that intimated that he wanted her to assume the bottom-to-groin position. Sugri moved slowly, thinking about every move she was making. She looked at him. He moved smoothly, without effort, as if all his joints had been rubbed with oil.

Quickly, smoothly, before she could protest, he held her waist and turned her around with the lightest touch. Sugri swallowed. Just as she was about to give in, the woman who'd been dishing out the pink bracelets came over and whispered in Ellis's ear.

"So sorry, Sugri," he said. "Duty calls. But don't go far."

Sugri left the dance floor, relieved. If they had danced like that, she was sure she'd have lost all respect for him and for herself.

Ije sauntered over.

"Isn't he the finest?" she asked.

"Who?"

"Don't pretend," Ije said hoarsely. "Ellis! All the women in the BSU are in love with him. There's a long line, you can join it if you want."

"I think I'll pass," Sugri said, trying more to convince herself.

"If that's what you want to do, fine. By the way, that fine Jamaican boy is not here."

"Sorry," Sugri said.

"I'm so bummed out. Usually I stay till the end, but I'm not in the mood. So ready when you are," Ije said.

"If this was your 'I'm not in the mood,' I can't imagine what you'd have done if you were," Sugri said. "I'm ready."

As they walked out Ellis was emphatically talking to a man who looked like he could have fathered him, "I'm sorry, sir. But those are the rules. No ID, no band."

"Ellis, peace out," Ije shouted.

"All right, ladies. Sugri, next Thursday, BSU." He turned to the man. "Sir, either you go in without the band or kindly leave."

Sugri and Ije walked down Broadway. Ije limped in her high heels and hooked Sugri's arm in hers.

"How about you?" Sugri asked.

"How about me, what?"

"Do you like Ellis?"

"I have eyes only for Andre from de Islands," Ije said, with a horrible Jamaican impersonation.

Sugri said nothing. She hoped her sudden infatuation would pass. It was really too soon to be interested in someone. If everybody liked him, it was because he had a nice personality and was nice to look at, so there was no point in joining the long line because she wouldn't even have a chance with pretty Dee and all those other stunning women standing in it. Besides, she was here for school, not fooling around.

An ambulance whizzed by. At the corner to Sugri's dorm, a girl in a tight miniskirt, bent over, hurling all the contents of her stomach onto the sidewalk.

"These people drink too much," Ije said. They turned onto Sugri's street. "Hope you enjoyed that."

"I did. It was eye-opening."

"Ha! You haven't seen anything yet. Peace out, my dear!" Ije said.

"Peace out!"

*

Sugri sat behind her desk, cramming from her Paula Bruice *Organic Chemistry*. The surface of the table was covered in a pink plastic tablecloth. She was trying hard to focus on her reading and not look up to give Rachel a window of opportunity. She looked at the alkene reactions page, and three seconds later her eyes drifted to the framed picture of her mother on her desk. Akua Afriyie was wearing a white shirt and a tie-and-dye skirt, posing by her car. In another plastic frame, her grandparents were standing outside their house. She imagined Lizzie erupting into laughter after they had taken the shot.

"Sugri," Rachel said, her voice thick with mucus. "I'm sure he's found someone else. I know it. We were together for five years! Five years! Why would he want to break up now?"

"I'm sorry," was all Sugri could think to say. The music Rachel was playing wasn't helping her concentrate, nor was Rachel's interrupting every time she noticed she wasn't focusing.

Rachel was tucked under her covers, a box of tissues on the faded floral duvet. "We had the most amazing sex," she said. "I'm sure he's not going to get it that good with anybody else." She blew her nose.

Sugri had never heard anybody, *anybody,* speak about sex so openly. She looked at Rachel. Her hair was plastered to the side of her face. Her face was red, the tip of her nose the most scarlet. On the wall above her, were glued posters of the Backstreet Boys, Britney Spears and Christina Aguilera.

"We promised each other," Rachel went on, "Chad and I, that we'd give each other enough notice, if we wanted a break...." She started crying again.

Sugri had had enough. She opened her pink Hello Kitty planner: *BSU meeting. SIPA 2A.* Good, an escape. She called Ije. Notorious Biggie serenaded her.

"Whassup?"

"Going to the BSU meeting?" Sugri asked.

"Nope."

"Why not? I need you to introduce me to the group."

"Sorry. Got a lab report to work on. *We just sitting here tryin' not to sin,*" Ije rapped.

How rude, Sugri thought. "You're partying in your room. Come for ten minutes. Please," she said.

"I only go to BSU parties," Ije said. "Why are you so eager to go? It's just a meeting. Nothing special."

"I didn't go last week and I want to become a member."

"Are you sure? Is that the only reason?"

"Yup." Now that Ije was insinuating, she wondered if Ellis would be there. Since the party she'd pushed him into the crevices of her mind but now he was resurfacing. Of course he'd be there, he was BSU president.

"I seriously have to work. Go by yourself. It's not scary. Besides, your friend Ellis will be there," Ije chuckled hoarsely.

"OK, I'm going to go now. Peace out," Sugri said.

"Peace."

Sugri got up from her desk and looked over at Rachel, who was sleeping. She tiptoed to her wardrobe and pulled out a light blue jacket. She threw it over her jeans and T-shirt, held up her braids and crept out of the room.

She walked up Amsterdam Avenue. It was eight and the sun was only just setting. She still found the late brightness disconcerting. Her palms started sweating. Was Ellis the reason why she was going to this meeting? she asked herself.

She entered the SIPA building. When she made it up to 2A, a handful of people were seated. Ellis was standing by the board writing the agenda in a numbered list. He turned around.

"Ghana!" he said and signaled for her to sit in front. He was wearing a pair of jeans and a white shirt. He kept adding to his list on the board and making people move to the seats in front as they walked in.

After five minutes, at least twelve people had come in. Ellis stopped writing and sat on the desk in front.

"Thank you all for coming," he said. "We'll start with introductions. Some of you weren't at our first meeting and those who did come must surely have forgotten all our names. We'll go round the room, say our names, class year, where we're from and whatever you want to add."

"Why don't you start?" said a girl who Sugri was convinced was Dee.

"Since Shawna insists I go first.... My name is Ellis Williams. I'm this year's BSU president. Class of 2000 ..."

"Two thousand!" shouted the skinnier of two boys who just walked in. His voice was deep and boomed across the room.

Ellis laughed and went on: "... and I'm from Hot Atlanta! Those are the BSU mascots who just walked in. Why don't you introduce yourselves next?"

"What, what!" the skinnier one said, and pumped at the air with his left hand. "Otis, representing 2000!" he used the deep voice again.

"Marcus," the other said, putting on a high-pitched voice. "2000."

"Clowns," Ellis said. "Let's continue from the back."

"Andre Walker. Class of 2000. I'm from Jamaica."

"Shawna Thomas. 1999. Representing Queens."

"Jennifer Love. Class of 2001. I'm from Trinidad and Tobago," she said in a beautiful singsong of words.

"Great," Ellis said, after everyone had introduced themselves. "I love that we have lots of fresh blood." He smiled with a glint in his eye. He walked them through the dates of upcoming BSU events, community service ideas and the next BSU party. "Internationals!" he said, a little too theatrically. "My dear internationals! We want to celebrate you. Please let us know when your Independence days are. We'll organize campus-wide events to celebrate you. We'll let the ignorant masses know that there are places outside America. Enlightenment and entertainment." People laughed. "Finally," he said, pointing to the last item on the board. "Officers. We'll be voting in three weeks. New students, you're welcome to sign up for positions. We need class representatives, so don't feel shy. Thank y'all for coming. See you next week. Same time."

Shawna and others crowded around Ellis.

Sugri walked out of the classroom. She was glad she came. Should she run for class representative of 2001? That way she'd surely get to see more of Ellis. Silly girl, she said to herself. She saw Jennifer Love walking ahead of her. She had to talk to her, just to hear that melodious accent again.

"Hi, Jennifer!" Sugri said. "Did you come straight from Trinidad?"

"Yes, it's actually Tobago," Jennifer said. She was small and looked thirteen. "I saw you at orientation. Where's your friend? The energetic one."

Sugri laughed. "Ije? She couldn't make it."

"What are you majoring in?" Jennifer asked.

"I'm premed."

"I'm thinking of that or majoring in Sociology. Sorry for springing the question on you. I'm so confused about what to do."

"We don't have to decide yet, though," Sugri said, trying to sound comforting. In Jennifer, she saw a little bit of herself and didn't like what she saw—an overachieving child. She'd rather exude Ije's nonchalant brilliance.

"I know," Jennifer said. "But I'm trying to decide ... do I please myself or please my parents?"

"Tobago is just like Ghana then."

"Girrrl, I'm sure," Jennifer said, rolling her eyes.

"I'm beginning to hate people telling me they love my accent, but I have to tell you, *you* have got a wonderful accent."

"Thanks," Jennifer said.

They were now on Amsterdam Avenue and were headed in opposite directions.

"I'll see you next week then, if not before," Sugri said, wondering how her accent sounded to other people.

"Ghana!" she heard Ellis shout. She turned around. "You left so fast!" he said. "I'm walking down on Amsterdam. What happened to telling me about your country?"

"I didn't want to disturb you," Sugri said, her heart starting a sprint. "You seemed so busy."

"Going to Ghana is more important to me than buying paper and tacks for BSU any day! What street do you live on? I'll walk you there."

"You're too kind," Sugri said. "112th and Broadway."

It was dark, but she could still make out his features. He could pass for a dark-skinned Ethiopian.

"I hope the meeting didn't bore you," Ellis said.

"No. I made a friend and everybody seems really nice," Sugri said.

"You didn't come last week," he said. He'd noticed her absence! Victory was hers! "That whole classroom was full," he went on. "The numbers wane as it gets cold. From then on BSU meetings will just be Ellis and the random loyal member. Hey, you should run for class representative."

"Maybe I will," Sugri said.

"Where's Miss Nwamadi?" he asked. "Playing truant as always?"

"She was listening to Notorious Biggie and doing lab reports," Sugri said.

"Damn, your accent is so sexy," Ellis said under his breath.

"Thanks."

They arrived in front of her building.

"I used to live in this dorm my first year!" Ellis exclaimed. "How fast the year went by! Oh my goodness, memories. The amount of drinking we did freshman year! It was insane!" He paused and put his hands on his waist. "Well, Ghana, we have a lot of talking to do. Would you like to have dinner with me sometime this weekend?"

Sugri was taken aback. "I'd love to!" she said, sure her voice came out squeaky and overeager.

"What day works for you?" he asked.

"Saturday?" Why had she said that? It was two days away.

"It's a date. What's your extension?"

"24139."

"Thanks. *Ciao, bella.*"

"Bye!" Sugri said, dashed in and ran up the stairs.

In the now dark room, Rachel was still asleep. Amen, she thought. She picked up the phone and immediately dialed Ije's extension. As usual, Notorious Biggie's voice floated lazily in the background.

"Guess what?" Sugri whispered.

"What, my dear?" Ije asked.

"Ellis wants to have dinner with me on Saturday!"

"I knew it! You went to the meeting just for him! It's nice that he's interested too. You're going to make a lot of enemies."

"It's not a date, date. Is it?" Sugri asked. "He said we had talking to do. But, he said, 'It's a date.' I'm confused ..."

"Why are you whispering?" Ije shouted, a hint of annoyance in her voice.

"Rachel is sleeping," Sugri said. Ije's mood wasn't going to bring down her high.

"Oh, whatever, Miss Thing. It's a date. And let me guess, you'll need my magic once more. You'll have to start paying for my services."

"Thank you so much, Ije! By the way, Andre was at the meeting."

"Damn! I should have come with you," she said. All traces of annoyance had left her voice. "Damn! Did you talk to him?"

"About what?" Sugri asked. "No, I didn't. Now I have to finish my homework. Later!"

Sugri lit her lamp and bent its neck so the light wouldn't wake up Rachel. She put her textbook on the bed and opened up the page she'd been staring at all afternoon. She still couldn't focus. She was imagining what their date would be like. He'd come for her, dressed in a tuxedo and they'd walk to a nice, cozy restaurant. It'd be perfect.... But why was he interested in her? she suddenly wondered. Maybe this was really just a chance for him to learn about Ghana. That was more probable, she thought. Discouraged, she opened the textbook and painstakingly finished the reactions of alkenes problem sets.

Twenty-seven

Losing Innocence

Sugri walked as fast as she could to *Le Monde* Restaurant on Broadway. In three-inch high heels she could not walk in, she was forty minutes late. Ellis was pacing back and forth in front of the restaurant. He was dressed in a black shirt tucked into his jeans.

"I'm so sorry," she said before she even got to him. "I was going to come earlier. I'm almost an hour late, right?"

"No worries," Ellis said. "Marcus and Otis were entertaining me. They just left."

Sugri couldn't tell if he was being honest. She was always punctual for things, and for this, she especially wanted to be on time. "The girl must always make the boy chase her," Ije had said. "Make him wait. You'll feel good wielding the power." She didn't feel good. All she felt was embarrassed.

"CPT comes from the continent, after all," Ellis said.

"CPT?" She raised her brow.

"Colored People's Time."

"Oh, in Ghana it's GMT," Sugri said, glad Ellis hadn't made a big deal of her lateness. "Ghana Man Time."

"Hilarious," he said, leading her into the restaurant. It was dimly lit and filled with Columbia students and professors. Waitresses clad in all-black bounced from the kitchen to customers, from customers back to the kitchen. The mirrored walls of the restaurant, framed by wooden trefoil arches, made the place look bigger than it was.

Ellis knew everybody in the restaurant, it seemed to Sugri. He'd say hello to this person. Call somebody's name. Shake a professor's hand. A politician, just like they'd said, Sugri thought.

A hostess led them to a seat by the window and a waitress took over.

"Ellis," the waitress said.

"Oh, hi. Sugri, this is Victoria."

"Hi," Sugri said. Victoria seemed to be watching him with hungry eyes. Had they been together before? The tension between then was palpable.

"We took Intro to Sociology last year," Ellis said, as if he'd read her thoughts.

Sugri stared at the menu, pursed her lips and stared at the menu some more. Partly, she was still not over her embarrassment of arriving late. Partly, she was annoyed that Ellis's ex-whatever was their waitress.

"I recommend the *moules frites*," he said.

"Thanks, I'll have that then," Sugri said.

Ellis ordered steak, rare, and a glass of Merlot.

"Will you have some wine?" Victoria asked Sugri.

She shook her head.

"How's Columbia treating you?" Ellis asked after Victoria had walked away. "Do you like your roommate?"

"Well, I've never had a roommate," she started. "I've always had my own room ..."

"Ah, a rich kid," Ellis said.

Sugri laughed and said, "No, not rich. Only child."

"Me too!" he said, his eyes lighting up.

"Really? You don't have the spoiled only child air," Sugri said. Now it was Ellis's turn to laugh.

Victoria brought over a steaming pot of mussels and a white plate with a piece of bloody steak and French fries.

"*Bon appetit*," she said and walked away.

Sugri looked at the pot of mussels and was not sure how to attack them. She picked up a black shell, put it on her plate, and dug in the orange meaty part with her fork. Ellis wasn't staring at her with a look of horror, so she figured she was on the right track.

"Tell me more about your family," he said.

"You don't want to know about my family!" Sugri exclaimed. "I was raised by my mother. My father died in a car accident."

"I'm sorry. Lots of kids grow up in single parent homes here."

"My mother was suffocatingly protective. There was one day when she forgot to pick me up from school. I think that after that moment, she decided to never let me out of her sight."

Ellis cut a piece of his steak. Blood oozed out of the pink meat and floated under the fries. Sugri flinched and hoped he hadn't seen her. Why was he eating raw meat? "That must have sucked," he said.

"Plus she became super born-again and everything was about Jesus-this, Jesus-that. Now you know all about my family. What's yours like?"

"Oh, just po' old black folk in the south who managed to send their only son to a good school," he said. Sugri was sure Ellis's parents were wealthy, but politician-like, swiftly, he turned the conversation back to her. "Do you go to church too?"

"I used to go every Sunday. Since I got here I haven't been."

"I don't believe in God," Ellis said.

"Why?" Sugri hoped he'd at least tell her more this time.

"Maybe I shouldn't say I don't believe," he said. "I'm more agnostic."

"And your parents?"

"Good ol' church goers," he said. "I like that you're innocent." He put on his trademark naughty smile and took a sip of his Merlot.

"So you can corrupt me?" Sugri asked. He almost choked on his wine. "Sorry, but that's what you've been trying to do since the day you met me, offering me alcohol. Remember? And now …"

"Yes, I just wanted to talk to you. You looked so cute and lost."

"I'm not that innocent," Sugri said and pouted.

"Yes, you are."

"How do you know?"

"My innocence radar is going off."

Sugri didn't want him to think of her as a saint who hadn't done anything, but she also wanted him to know that she wouldn't be getting up to any naughtiness with him. But she wanted to steer the conversation back to him. "What's your major?" she asked.

"Sociology and African American studies. Don't tell me yours. I know," he paused and raised his index finger at her slowly, "you want to be a doctor."

She was annoyed that he'd made an assumption about her. She was even more irked that the assumption was true. She saw him smiling slyly and then laughed. "Like all international students, right?" she said. "Yes, I do."

Ellis paid for the meal. "Thanks so much for coming out with me," he said when they stood in front of Sugri's building.

"Thanks for inviting me," she said.

"I'd love to do this again," Ellis said and leaned in so close she could feel his breathing.

"Before we go on," Sugri said, feeling her heart thumping, "I have to let you know something."

"Uh oh," Ellis said.

"I'm keeping myself for marriage," she blurted out and felt like a complete idiot.

"I already knew that," Ellis said. He was being presumptuous again. She opened her eyes widely. "And that is a beautiful thing that I respect and I'm OK with," he added. He pressed his lips against hers. Sugri was woozy. Her first kiss and it did not disappoint. Ellis's lips were soft, slightly moist.

"Goodnight, Ghana."

Her thoughts a royal mess, she stammered back, "Goodnight."

*

October 1997

After a lecture on benzene, the matronly Chemistry professor, Linda Crosby, asked people to pick up their graded midterm exams as they walked out. Before the class was over, the students had already stampeded their way down to Crosby's table and were hunting ravenously for their papers.

Sugri found hers but didn't want to look at it just yet.

"Good job, Sugri!" Professor Crosby shouted, as Sugri made for the door.

Sugri was shocked. She didn't think the woman knew anyone's name in the class—except for the overachievers—but she smiled back.

She looked at the sheet and saw an A written next to a smiley face. She flipped through the booklet. She'd missed one answer. Simply left it blank. It annoyed her that she'd been sloppy. She looked around, hoping people weren't staring at her—they weren't. A girl with bright pink hair smiled smugly as she looked at her exam. A boy with curly dark brown hair didn't seem too pleased. He kept stealing glances at his paper and scowling.

Finding her room empty for the first time since she'd moved in with Rachel, Sugri jumped onto her bed, elated. She stared up at the ceiling and decided to call her mother. She scratched a phone card with a picture of the Statue of Liberty on it. She called home. No one picked up. She tried John Barnor's office.

"Hello," Akua Afriyie said.

"Mummy!" Sugri said too loudly, too happily.

"Hi, dear. Long time no hear. How are you?"

"I just had to tell you. I think I got the highest grade in Orgo."

"Org-what?" Akua Afriyie said.

"Sorry, we contract everything here. Organic Chemistry. My professor actually congratulated me."

"Well done! I have no doubts about you, Miss Smarty Pants. Show them how we do it!"

"And mummy ..."

"Yes, sweetie?"

"I have a boyfriend now."

"Ei, you!" Akua Afriyie said, laughing. "I want the details! I hope you two are being good. What's his name?"

Sugri had expected her mother to overreact. "Ellis. But, Mummy, I called you. You tell me how you are."

"Fine," Akua Afriyie said.

"How's pastor Adomza?"

"He's fine. I'll see him at fellowship tonight."

"What are you still doing at work? It's at least six there." *You have one minute.* "Oh, my card is running out. Love you!"

Beep, beep, beep.

These useless cards! It didn't even last a minute. She hoped her mother was well. She worked too hard. That John Barnor probably had her working on some project.

*

Sugri and Ellis sat in an intimate room in the basement of a Greenwich Village brownstone.

Round tables had been dotted around the room, covered with red table cloths and adorned with candles. Sugri looked at the array of braids, dreadlocks, bone straight hair and colorful weaves people in the room wore. She shifted her gaze from the afro-centric crowd to the framed pictures of Malcolm X, Martin Luther King, Bob Marley, Angela Davis and Michael Jackson. In a corner of the room sat a plastic pink flamingo and a plastic green and yellow palm tree. They seemed out of place.

A woman in a long leopard print dress and thick dreadlocks that swished at her waist, walked onto the small spot-lit stage.

"Hello, beautiful sisters and brothers. I'm Lisa, your host tonight. We have a full program of acts for you. We've got some music, lots of soul and a line up of comedians from all over the country. Give it up for James Turner, y'all."

The crowd clapped loudly.

James Turner walked on stage with a glass of golden brown liquid that looked like dilute coke. He was a portly, thirty-something with a round baby face. He wore a checkered blue and white shirt and jeans.

"Hi, y'all," he said and paused. The audience was quiet.

"A man can't get no respect around here. Aretha done taken all the respect for herself and now a decent man can't get any. I said, hi, y'all."

"Hi," the crowd finally responded, bursts of laughter spreading through the room.

"My name is James Turner, great-grand descendent of Nat Turner. Now, let me see who's in the house." He bent his round body, shaded his eyes and looked around the room. "Ladies and gentlemen, I see some ghosts in the house," he said, straightening his body.

Sugri laughed.

"Some ghosts! Big Punisher, ladies and gentlemen, is alive and kicking and sitting in the back of this room," James Turner said and pointed to a large man wearing a red T-shirt with a green bottle of beer in front of him. He laughed and raised his right hand in the air. "Yo, Big Pun, if you want a second chance to keep crushin' a lot on earth, you need to lay off them *chorizos*," James Turner said. "You need to chill out on the pork, and get some chicken in your life." People erupted in laughter. "Now don't get me started on us black folk and chicken." He paused. "No, I won't go there. On my way here … just outside, some Chinawoman ambushed me," he stopped and held his sides as he laughed. "She said, 'My blotha, I have Chanel, I have Chanel.' Chinawoman's eyes are darting from left to right. I told her, 'Chinawoman, relax. Before po-po shows up, me and the Chanels would have disappeared faster than you can say 'five dollah.'" Turner took a sip of his coke. "You know how every African you meet is a king or prince?"

"Yes!" Sugri heard a deep voice shout.

"Well these kings sold us," James Turner said and held his glass up, "for rum and guns and ladies and gentlemen, they're still at it. On 125th! The other day, I'm walking with my homie Tyrone, and this black Kunta Kinte walks up to me. And Kunta needs to get some serious deodorant on. He says to me, 'My broda, you know James Turner? Dis his latest CD.' Can you believe that shit? Kunta was trying to bootleg me my own shit! 'All for you, for ten dollars,' Kunta said. I told him, brother, I only got fifty cents. Kunta didn't even breathe, he said, 'OK, broda, take it.' Damn!" he said and paused. "Kunta Kinte sold me for fifty cents! They sold us for some shells and cloth, they're still doing it and they'd do it again. For fifty cents! Ladies and gentlemen, James Turner y'all." He walked off the stage. The crowd was in stitches.

Sugri looked around self-consciously. She looked at Ellis who seemed amused. She had never thought of slavery as Africans selling off their people. To her it had always been Europeans who were responsible for pillaging Africa dry. Europeans were the only ones to blame. At least that was what she'd been taught in school. Hearing James Turner say Africans had sold "them" into slavery had shaken her awake. She hardly listened to any of the acts that came on after.

After the show ended they walked out onto West 4 Street.

"Ellis," Sugri said, as she pulled her hands through her jacket sleeves. "Aren't Africans and African-Americans … aren't we the same people? I mean, we all come from Africa, so why is there a big separation?"

"Yes we are …" Ellis started.

"I just find it strange that you have all these people in there calling themselves *afro*-centric, wearing clothes from Africa but sit there agreeing that basically Africans sold them into slavery. Then why not reject Africa altogether?"

"What did you want them to do? Start jeering?" Sugri glared at him. "I'm sorry. There are lots of people who don't call themselves African-American. My parents, for instance, consider themselves Black-American. They said they've never been to Africa, and don't feel a connection with the continent. I see it as really flawed, but I can't quite disagree with a system of thinking that's helping people who've been lost for so long form an identity."

Sugri didn't say anything.

Ellis went on. "And I'm sure half of the people in there didn't take him seriously. He's a comedian …"

"But people like James Turner will give others the wrong perception of Africa," Sugri cut him off.

"It was true, though, Sugri. African middlemen and Europeans worked together to get the slave trade rolling. Europeans couldn't have done that all on their own. But let's not let Turner ruin our two-month anniversary," Ellis said, kissing Sugri's forehead. "Some of them had original jokes, though, right?"

She heard him, but her mind was far away. She was thinking of the role some great-great grandparent of hers could have played—snatching an innocent person and selling them off to get rum and guns.

They walked to the 1-train on Christopher Street. On the stairs that led into the subway station sat a man in brown torn rags holding a sign that read, THE WORLD IS ENDING. BUT FIRST, SPARE SOME CHANGE. Sugri smiled and clasped her fingers in Ellis's.

Turner's words and the faces of the people in the bar resurfaced in Sugri's mind. Somehow the night had shaken her peaceful knowledge of the way things were. She felt weak. This was the first time something someone had said had taken a physical toll on her.

"You OK?" Ellis asked her when they stopped in front of her building.

"Yeah."

"Can I come up?" he asked.

"I'm kind of tired, Ellis. Thanks for taking me out," she said, kissing his cheek.

As she walked up the stairs to her room, she realized that what was upsetting her the most was her lack of education. She hated being ignorant.

*

September 1998

Sugri and Ellis sat in a dim corner of *Le Monde* Restaurant. She thought he looked absolutely dapper in his charcoal-grey shirt, his naughty smile permanently fixed to his face. She reached out for his wine glass filled with a deep burgundy Merlot. She looked at his face and waited for him to stop her. He didn't. She set the glass against her lips and took a sip of the wine. She'd taken quite a few sips.

"To us," she said, lifting the glass a little uncertainly, a little dangerously.

"One year!" he responded. He turned around, waved his hand in the air for the waitress. She came over, curly-haired, in her black uniform. "Can we have the check please?"

"I've got this," Sugri said, taking out bills from her wallet.

"Well, thank you," Ellis said.

They walked out slowly from the restaurant. She staggered. She looked at the street that was Broadway. People, lights, cars and trees were blurring into blobs of color, blobs of luminescence. She liked the nebulous shapes they were forming and the lightness she felt. She didn't drink that much of the wine, did she?

"That waitress was totally checking you out."

"She was?" Ellis asked.

"She was," Sugri said, smiling. "I don't mind, though, because even though she's cute, I know you'll never do anything with her. You'll never do anything like that."

They stopped in front of her dorm.

"Do you want to come back to my place?" Ellis asked hesitantly.

"Of course!" Sugri said. "It's our anniversary."

"Great," Ellis said.

They walked up the stairs into Ellis's room. He unlocked his door.

"Music?" he asked.

"Yes," Sugri said, taking off her sling back sandals. He walked to his stereo, took out a CD and replaced it with another.

When we turn out the lights, the two of us alone together ...

"Good choice!"

Sugri sang along off-key. Dancing sinuously, her hands oscillated in the air. She passed her fingers through her braids and caressed her body. She unzipped her dress from the back and stepped gingerly out of it. She slunk toward Ellis who was leaning against his chair.

"I should give you wine more often," he said.

"Shhh! Let's dance," she said, wriggling in front of him. She turned around. He leaned in to kiss her. She felt hot. Her lips, her breasts, the space between her legs, her everywhere yearned for him. She unbuttoned his shirt.

"Sugri," Ellis said, swallowing, "are you sure about this?"

"Huh?"

"What about 'I want to save myself for marriage'? Are you sure this isn't the wine talking?"

"I'm so tired of being perfect. Of being the teacher's pet, of playing the innocent girl. I'm tired of living up to other people's image of me. I feel horny. All the time, and what do people want me to do? Suck it up while they have fun? Ellis, I want to do this. Now, let's stop talking."

"O—K then. Condoms?"

"Of course!" She turned around and rubbed her *derriere* on him. She felt him pulsing. It seemed to be its own creature—a snake breathing behind her. "Is it growing?" she asked.

Ellis laughed. "You're so cute. Turn around." He held her right hand above her head, pirouetting her. He held on to her as they danced to Joe's crooning. He led her gently to the bed.

"Are you sure you're ready?"

"Ellis! Shut up." He climbed by her and unclasped her brassiere. He suckled her breasts. His teeth pressed harder. His hands worked down her stomach. She felt his fingers slide up between her legs. For the first time since the night started, she felt a little squeamish. Save that for marriage her mother had told her. Had her mother done that herself? She looked out the window and saw drops of water sprinkled on the glass. She closed her eyes. She heard the rustling of plastic, drops of water hitting the window, Joe still singing.

"Guide me," he said. She, unsure of what to do, did nothing. He placed her hand on his sex, rigid, with its own heartbeat. She wanted to take her hand off the foreign object. It felt so strange. Hesitantly, she led him into her. At first she felt as if a fist was being rammed into her body. Her eyes watered as she felt a warm, bitter-sweet pain in her womb. After Ellis pulled out of her, she held him tightly. Somehow she felt if she let go of him, her world would come crashing down.

"You OK?" he asked her. She nodded.

The next day she woke up to Ellis staring at her. "That's creepy," she said, taking her eyes off him and looking around the room. A searing pain ran across her forehead. "Ouch!" she spat out. "My head hurts!"

"You have a hangover."

"I have to go medicate myself," she said, getting up to put on her clothes. Then she felt the burning between her legs. "Later, Williams the Third."

"Bye, Mensah."

On the walk back to her room, everything was muddied. The streets were strewn with newspapers, orange peels, yellow leaves, a plastic doll and a broken phone. She was sure things were going to change now that she'd slept with Ellis. She didn't know how or why, but she sensed it. It was true, sex changed everything. And now it was too late. It absolutely couldn't be undone. She limped up to her room.

Twenty-eight
Goldilocks

Sugri lay on her back, staring at her ceiling. Since Ellis had come back from winter break, something had changed. She didn't know what, but it was there, like an invisible cloud. Her phone rang. Her heart leapt and she hoped it was him.

"Whassup!" Ije's voice rasped through the phone.

"You're back!" Sugri said, trying to erase the disappointment that she was sure came through her voice. "How was Naija?"

"So much fun! You know how home is. Good food, family drama, parties after parties. Anyway, there's a party at NYU tonight. Do you want to come?"

"Let me call you back in a sec," Sugri said.

"Don't forget and call me tomorrow with excuses," Ije said. "I'll be waiting."

Sugri hung up and dialed Ellis's extension. It rang but he didn't answer the phone. She tried again.

"Hello?" Ellis said breathlessly.

"Hi!" Sugri said. "Where were you?"

"I was outside my door, heading out when I heard the phone. What's up?"

"Ije says there's a party downtown tonight. Do you want to go?"

"Sheesh, I can't, Sugri. I have to meet the new black students. I'll probably be too tired after that."

"No problem. I'll tell her we can't come."

"You should go."

"It'd be boring without you. Have fun with the new students."

She called Ije back.

"Sorry, we can't make it."

"We?"

"Oh, I asked Ellis and something's come up," Sugri said. She knew she sounded ridiculous, but it was true—without Ellis there she wouldn't have fun.

"No problem," Ije said. "I'll tell you all about the cute boys I meet. Peace."

*

February 1999

Midterm exam in hand, Sugri sat on the steps of the Low Library. She knew she wasn't looking her best, wearing her red bubble jacket, her hair—what was left of it—held in a scrunchie. A C-minus on the first exam of the semester! Where was Ellis? She looked behind her, at the concrete steps that led to the Low Library with its gigantic colonnades. From Broadway she heard the honks of cars and the cries of protestors. She took out the exam. Her eyes clouded with tears as she studied the pages, blotted with red marks. Someone flicked her ear. Startled, she turned around. Ellis sat down by her.

"Hi," she said, trying to blink out the tears.

"Sorry, I'm late. I had to meet the new kids."

"Still? They're hardly new now."

"Yes, but I'm trying to recruit them for our first BSU meeting next week. They have so much energy. What have you done to your hair?"

That was the problem. Since he'd come back, he never had anything good to say about her. If it wasn't her hair, it was what she was wearing. If it wasn't how she wasn't on the street protesting against Amadou Diallo's shooting, it was that she should be doing more community work. Truth was, she didn't quite feel a part of the community. She could feel him looking at the wisps on her head in disgust.

"Mr. Williams, didn't your mama teach you not to talk about black women's hair?" she asked, hoping she sounded chirpy. "You didn't even ask how I'm doing." She arranged her exam papers on her lap.

"Sugri, I'm sure you have great hair. You can let it grow and be nice and bouncy." He passed his hands through his nice and bouncy curls.

"Ellis, can we please talk about something else? I had a horrible day. How was yours?"

His face softened. "I'm sorry. What ruined your day?"

"I bombed my Chemistry exam. This is the first midterm and if I've started this way, I'm just not going to do well. I have to start well to finish well."

"You got an A-minus?"

"Come on, Ellis, if I got an A-minus and I was acting like this, I'd be the biggest ass."

"You said 'ass.' But you know you do act like an ass sometimes."

"Ellis!" She showed him the exam.

"Ouch! Sorry," he said, his naughty smile tracing his lips. "Listen, this is only the first midterm. You can make it up. Cheer up."

"Thanks. And what's got you so chipper?"

"Those new spring students have mad energy and want to be involved in everything. I love the vibes I get from them. They transferred their good energy my way."

Sugri thought of the new students. There were only three of them. One boy was from Tanzania. He didn't strike her as the most dramatic. The other boy was from D.C. and seemed to only be interested in gangster rap. The third was a girl from California, with skin the color of caramel and big golden locks. Of the lot, surely, she was the only one who'd possess the kind of energy that would make Ellis excited. It had to be her! "Will you come with me to the post office?" she asked.

"Sure," he said. "What are you sending?"

"My application for the hospital internship."

"At Bronx-Lebanon?"

"Yep. You know, Professor Crosby took so long to give me her recommendation."

"She was probably busy."

"She handed it to me with my exam paper. I'm sure she was thinking, 'I need to tell you, Bronx-Lebanon folks, this one is not good enough for your hospital.'"

"No, she wouldn't think that. I'm sure you'll ace your next exam." As they walked out the gates toward Broadway, Sugri saw the throng of protestors wielding wooden pickets, waving cardboards with felt pen inscriptions and marching down the avenue. Blue police barricades had blocked them off the sidewalks.

"Forty-one shots, for what?" an old woman shouted above the cries of the other demonstrators. Sugri saw a tall man in a brown jacket, who looked like Abokyi's doppelganger, repeatedly thrust a wallet toward a policeman. As they passed by, she read the pickets.

NYPD PIGS; FIGHT POLICE BRUTALITY; JUSTICE FOR AMADOU DIALLO

Sugri hooked her arm in Ellis's. His arm felt limp against hers. "Amadou! Amadou!" the crowd chanted. She felt her skin pock. Rage built up in her heart for the first time since she'd heard of the police riddling the young Guinean man's body with forty-one bullets because they thought he was taking out a gun.

"The BSU should raise money to give to Amadou Diallo's family," she said.

"That's a great idea," Ellis said flatly. Maybe he thought she'd said that only for his benefit. She meant it. As they left the crowd of protestors and walked into the quiet post office, she realized she'd never felt so distant from him even though he stood right by her.

*

March 1999

Sugri walked into the classroom where BSU meetings were held.

By the chalkboard, Ellis was looking on as the girl with big golden curls pointed at a pink sheet. He was eating up her every move with his eyes. The girl was annoyingly attractive, Sugri had to admit. Her jeans hugged the curves of her hips. The white blouse she wore squeezed her breasts out. Compared to Goldilocks, she was a pole. Ellis smiled at Goldilocks. Sugri felt a sharp pain in her chest. They were staring at each other. Goldilocks handed him the sheet and walked back to her seat, her skin tinged a shade redder than it had been before. Sugri fought back tears. Stop this! she berated herself. This is not the time to get worked up about something that you might very well be imagining.

After the meeting, she waited outside the classroom. There were always people talking to Ellis. She was always waiting for him. Today, that was the last thing she wanted to do. She felt unattractive. He walked out.

"Hey," he said. "You were quiet today."

"I had nothing to say," she said, hooking her arm in Ellis's. She felt his arm twitch.

"Did you see the flyer Keisha made? I'm definitely going to use it for our party to raise funds for Diallo's family. Did you see it?" Ellis had taken on the Amadou Diallo Family Fundraiser idea and hadn't bothered to ask her to help.

"Yes, Ellis, I saw the flyer. You passed it round. It seems like you really liked her—it."

"Huh?"

"From the way you reacted when she gave you the flyer, I could tell you really liked her work." Sugri pushed the door open and walked out into the cold air.

"What does that mean? 'From the way you reacted?'"

"Well, you must have said something really nice to her, because the girl, what's her name—Keisha?—turned redder than the shirt you're wearing."

"Sugri, what's going on?"

"All I'm saying is you two looked very cozy up by the board. Did you even see me come in?"

"Yo! Yo! Where's my girlfriend? Who are you? Relax, girl. I know. It's your midterm tomorrow, right?"

Sugri smiled. She'd told him about the exam a week ago and he still remembered. That earns you points, buster, she thought. "I'm sorry. I am nervous."

"You'll be fine," he said, kissing her forehead. He retracted his arm from hers. "Girl," he said, "I can't walk you to your room today."

"OK," Sugri said. She didn't want to start a fight. And what was up with this 'girl' he'd chosen to use to address her.

"I have to check out some books from Butler," he said.

"No problem. Good night."

"Good luck with your exam," he said, kissing her lips.

Back in her room, while studying for the Chemistry exam, she kept picturing Keisha bouncing up and down, giving Ellis the flyer and turning scarlet. Somewhere between thinking about Goldilocks and working through radical reactions, she fell asleep.

When she opened her eyes, it was 3:26 a.m. She sat up and groaned loudly. She hadn't finished reading her notes. And she was so tired! In her sleepy stupor, she decided to nap for another hour, wake up and go through the rest of her notes. She climbed back into bed.

On opening her eyes, she realized four hours had gone by. Class would begin in an hour.

"Oh, shit!" she screamed, scrambled out of her bed, rushed to her table and opened her notebook. She flipped through the pages, hoping that their images would magically repeat themselves on the exam paper.

Five minutes before the class started she changed out of her pajamas into jeans and a T-shirt. Please, let my photographic memory save me, she prayed.

*

April 1999

After a tutorial with Professor Crosby, Sugri walked toward Fayerweather Hall. The campus bustled with students and professors.

Spring was seeping back into their lives. Pink, white and orange flowers bloomed along the paved walkways. Where a month earlier, white had covered patches, there was now verdant grass, proudly proclaiming the start of a new season. Students had already staked their positions on the grass, which would probably be wet. She shuddered. She hated wet grass. She hoped Ellis would be done with his Sociology tutoring session. She skipped to the classroom where he held his lessons. Looking at her watch—4:07—she placed her head against the door. She heard absolutely nothing. She knocked. Then she heard chairs scraping.

"One second," she heard Ellis say. Oh, I must be early, she thought. The door opened. Ellis stood behind it. Keisha leaned against the professor's desk. Her skin, ripe, red.

"Hi," he said, in an Aaron Neville falsetto.

"Hello," Sugri said, waving her arms in the air. "You look surprised. Were you expecting the cleaning lady?" She glared at Keisha who was holding back her golden curls with her left hand and picking up her bag with the other.

366

"Thanks, Ellis. I'll go now. See you next week," Keisha said and marched out.

"She couldn't even say hi to me," Sugri said. "Your little girlfriend is rude. I hope I wasn't interrupting anything. Why did Keisha walk out so suddenly? I didn't spoil your little party, did I?" Ellis now stood by the professor's desk, quiet. He packed his books into an brown satchel. It was new. "I wanted to surprise you, so we could go get dinner, but I guess I was the one who was surprised." Ellis walked toward her. She had her suspicions, but it's not like she caught them in *flagrante delicto*. She tried to hug him, but he put up his hands and blocked her. "What's going on?"

"What do you think is going on? You walked in, saw something and jumped to conclusions."

"I didn't see anything," Sugri said. "But it's obvious something just happened here. Where are the other students you were tutoring?" He walked out of the room. She trailed behind him.

"I don't know what's going on with you," he said, when they were outside. "You're so paranoid these days."

The crisp spring air pinched her cheeks.

"It seems I have reason to be. Don't I?" Her voice came out squeaky.

"Calm down, Sugri."

"Why? You're sleeping around with what's-her-name!"

"What are you talking about? I'm not sleeping with anyone."

"I don't know what you're doing with her and frankly, I'm not interested." She descended the first of the Low Library steps.

"Instead of jumping to conclusions, why don't you ask me if something is going on?"

"I already did. OK, Ellis, what's going on with you and Keisha?"

"Oh, now you remember her name."

"Ellis, I'm not playing your game. You know what? I'm having enough trouble with school. I don't need this. I need a break."

"Are you sure that's what you want?"

"Ellis, you're not even trying. Yes, I want a break."

"Fine," he said. Sugri looked at him incredulously.

"Why didn't you just break up with me? This is so typical. You know what, Ellis, you're a pig ..." Her voice broke.

"Wait, wait, wait! You're the one who broke up with me and I'm a pig?" he asked, simpering.

"You made it too easy for me." She ran off, barged into her bedroom and locked the door. The sun's soft rays came in through translucent, green polyester curtains. She threw herself onto her bed and gave in to the sobs she'd been suppressing. She let the emotion tear through her body, swell through her chest, rise to her eyes and flood out in tears. She sobbed loudly. She didn't care if anybody heard her. She physically hurt. Her chest might explode, she thought, with the pain singeing through every one of her cells. Why was she crying over someone who hadn't had the decency to end their relationship before starting a new one?

She stood up and walked to her full-length mirror. Her short hair, standing on the right side, flattened on the left, looked lackluster and dry. Her eyes were the color of Keisha's face when she'd caught them. She looked awful when she cried. She picked up her phone.

Sometimes your words just hypnotize me. And I just love your flashy ways.

"Ije, I broke up with Ellis."

"Oh, my! I'm coming over."

"Thanks!" Sugri said, wiping the mucus yo-yoing out of her nose.

Five minutes later she heard Ije knock on the door. She was about to let her in, when she realized it might be Ellis. "Who's it?" she asked.

"Ije."

"Prove it," she said.

"Open the door, *now*. Ah, ah!" Ije said. She unlocked the door and Ije wrapped her hands around her. "It was because of that Keisha girl, right?"

"How did you know?"

"They were so obvious."

"And I was so stupid! Oh, God!" Sugri shouted. "So everyone knew and I was sticking around like some abandoned puppy." Ije shushed her, leading her back to her bed. "I'm so stupid. How long have people known?"

"They were obvious to me," Ije said. "I'm sorry I didn't tell you. I don't know anything about other people."

"Can you believe when I said I wanted a break, he didn't even beg?"

Ije propped Sugri's pillow behind her. "Listen. Get some sleep. Cry if you want. It's going to hurt a lot. You're going to feel like shit! But you have something bigger to worry about."

"What?"

"The last Orgo midterm, not that fool, OK?"

"Oh, shit!" Sugri said. "Orgo! Next week!"

Later that night, Sugri picked up her notebook. She leafed through the pages, but kept choking up. She opened the first page, where she'd stuck a post-it with a counselor's phone number that Linda Crosby had given her after she failed her second midterm exam. Maybe she should call. She flung the notebook on the floor in a rage.

The next day, she skipped all her morning classes. She called the Health Center.

"Hello," she said. "Yes, I just-just called to make an appoint…"

"Sugri Mensah? You scheduled for later today?"

"Yes. Please cancel it."

"Are you sure?"

"Er … OK, fine, keep it."

"Miss Mensah, I think you should come in. If you can't come on your own, we can send someone for you."

"No, it's fine, I'll come in."

She stood in front of her mirror. Her eyes looked like a bullfrog's. She should call her mother. Nothing the counselor would say to her could beat talking to her mother. She picked up the handset.

The phone rang. Akua Afriyie didn't pick up. She spent so much time in that art studio these days. *I guess this is a sign*, Sugri thought and walked to the Health Center.

It was brimming with students walking in and out. A boy in soccer boots and a football jersey limped in. A girl, makeup running down her face, stormed out. An old woman shuffled around the waiting area.

"Sugri Mensah," a nurse called out. Sugri walked up to the glass enclosure the nurse sat in. "You have an appointment with Rebecca Freedman."

"Yes."

"Room 1F," the nurse pointed toward a corridor.

"Thanks," Sugri said. She knocked on door 1F. A woman, whose hair was crew cut and whose head was level with Sugri's breasts, opened the door.

"Sugri?"

"Yes."

She let Sugri in. Sugri had expected a reclining sofa, flower pots, velveteen curtains, the shrink sitting with her legs crossed, a cigarette dangling from her hand. The office looked like any professor's office, with white walls, thick, hardcover books stacked up in bookcases. Rebecca Freedman pointed at the swivel chair close to the door.

"Please sit." Her voice was small. "Is this your first time at counseling?"

"Yes."

"All righty. Please fill these forms," she said, handing Sugri a stack of yellow sheets. "If you want, sign the confidentiality form and everything you say in here stays with me. Any questions before we start?"

"How often do I need to come?" Sugri asked, signing the forms.

"That all depends on you. We might get to the root of what's bothering you today. It might take four or five sessions. I like to ask openended questions and you can take the conversation where you want."

"OK." Sugri handed her the sheets.

"So, what brings you here?"

"My Chemistry professor suggested this." I want to talk about Ellis, she thought.

"Do you think you need counseling?"

It's just like in movies! Sugri thought. This will go nowhere. It's a good thing insurance is paying for this. "I guess," she said.

"All righty. Let's talk about you for a minute. Tell me about yourself, your family."

"I'm from Ghana. I grew up with my mother. We lived with my grandaunt when I was younger…. Is this what you want from me?" How was this going to help? I want to talk about my boyfriend.

"Yes, you're doing wonderfully," Rebecca said. "Go on."

"I used to call my grandaunt, 'grandma'. When I was twelve, my mother told me she wasn't my grandmother. She told me that I had other grandparents."

"How did that happen? Was your mother adopted by your grandaunt?"

"No. My mother was estranged from them. She told me about my real grandparents when she became born-again."

Rebecca scribbled furiously. "Interesting," she said. "What about your dad? Where was he?"

"He died before I was born."

"I'm sorry. So your mother never remarried?"

"No." Now that the floodgates had been opened, she might as well let the waters rush through. She would expose all her insecurities. "I don't even know what my dad looked like," she said.

"Why is that?"

"My mother said she burned all his pictures. See, they weren't married. His family didn't really know about her. She was so hurt by his death; she didn't want to be reminded of him."

"Do you feel knowing what he looked like would change anything?"

"Maybe. I just feel like a big chunk of me is missing. I don't know his family. Half of me is … a lot of me is incomplete." Wow, I have a lot of issues, Sugri thought. This woman is good!

"How has that affected your relationships with other people?"

"Huh?"

"Do you have lots of friends?"

"A few."

"Do you have a boyfriend or significant other?"

"We broke up yesterday."

Rebecca's eyes lit up. They seemed to say, "Aha! That's why you're here."

"I see," she said. "How long were you together?"

"A year and some. Can we not talk about that?" She wanted to talk about it, but she didn't want to.

"It's fine if you'd rather we didn't discuss him, but he might have a lot to do with your school performance. Can we just talk about your relationship with him, in terms of his role as a male in your life…. Did you see him as some sort of father figure?"

"No, not at all."

"Have you had any older boyfriends?"

"I don't like older men." Almost inaudibly she added, "He was my first boyfriend."

"Sorry?"

"Ellis was my first boyfriend."

Rebecca looked at the plastic watch on her wrist. "I see. Sugri, we have lots to discuss, but I have someone coming in now. Please make another appointment to come back next week. I think we made a lot of headway this afternoon. I'd love to talk to you some more."

"OK," Sugri said. You started making connections, making me reveal everything about myself and then you just cut me off? Thanks for nothing! Sugri thought.

Twenty-nine
A Bite of the Apple

June 1999

A group of interns clustered in front of the main glass doors of the Bronx-Lebanon hospital. A small, blond, forty-something woman in floral nurses' scrubs, came out through the doors, clutching a fat green book. She pointed at each of them.

"Great, we're all here," she said. "Let's move inside." The sound of her voice was drowned out by loud sirens. The doors slid open. Hot morning stillness gave way to cool air inside the hospital. Sugri watched as medics in green uniforms rushed in through a side door, pulling a man on a gurney covered in a white sheet. A large scarlet patch had seeped onto the sheet.

"This way," the nurse said to the interns, pushing open a glass door. "Make yourselves comfortable."

The walls of the room were covered in floral wallpaper. Sugri sat on one of three tan sofas and rested against its arm. She looked at the other interns and realized she was the only black person.

"My name is Dolores Parker. Welcome, to our summer internship program," the nurse said, standing across from the seated interns. She sounded as if she'd lodged a pebble under her tongue. "Your internship lasts two months. You'll be working in pairs with an assigned doctor. This is the internship guide." She waved the fat book in the air with her left hand and flicked her blond hair with the other. Sugri noticed that her uniform matched the wallpaper. "It has information about you guys, emergency numbers, plans of all the floors of the hospital, emergency exits and safety tips for working here at Bronx-Lebanon. For instance, on page twenty, there are a number of color codes I'd advise you to memorize. They correspond to types of potential danger."

"What kind of danger?" asked a girl with big brown curls and large almond-shaped eyes.

"When you see the lights flashing green, you should know it means there's an aggressive person threatening others with a weapon in the hospital. In my ten years of working here, there's never been a code green. Since you asked, why don't you introduce yourself?"

"Cool. I'm Nicole French. I'm a senior at Columbia. Summer '99 is going to be awesome, guys!"

A girl with straight black hair gawked at Nicole and didn't realize it was her turn to speak. After a few uncomfortable minutes, she realized she'd been staring and said, "My name is Solange Cruz. I'm a junior at NYU."

Everyone introduced themselves.

"Great," Dolores said, flicking her hair. "Now, I'll read out the pairs and the sections you're working in. Justin Braves and Marcia Thomas, radiology. Sugri Mensah and Nicole French, emergency room. Zain Ahmed and Lisa Cummins, maternity. Ruben Chou and Jessica Stone, intensive care. Elisa Hunt and Solange Cruz, public health. Okey dokey," she said, softening up for the first time that morning. "Sugri and Nicole. Walk down the stairs on the left, go through the first set of double doors and Dr. Dickson's door is the first on the left. Good luck!" She read out instructions for all the interns and held open the door for the interns to file out.

Sugri could smell the antiseptic following them as she and Nicole walked down the stairs.

"They make their nurses' outfits and wallpaper in the same factory," Nicole said.

Sugri looked at Nicole and burst out laughing. "I was thinking the same thing!" She studied Nicole. Nicole was at least three inches shorter than she. She seemed cool. "I'm so nervous about this internship," she admitted to Nicole. Maybe they could become good friends.

"Oh, hon, don't be," Nicole said, rubbing Sugri's arm. "How come I've never seen you on campus?"

"I haven't seen you either," Sugri said, "and we should have taken similar classes. Then again, I only just finished my sophomore year."

"You're a baby!" Nicole said. "Look, don't be nervous at all. We're going to make these hospital people remember us!"

"Yeah!" Sugri said, sure that came out with such a ring of false-ness.

"Let's see what this Dick—man has to say to us. Do you want to get a drink after this? You should come out!"

"Maybe another time," Sugri said as she pushed the double doors. She needed to be sure that Nicole wasn't crazy before she started hanging out with her. She repeated "Dick—man" in her head. The girl was crazy.

Nicole knocked on Dr. Dickson's door.

A heavyset man with a full grey hair answered the door.

"Well, hello there!" he said. "You must be my interns. Sit, sit." He pointed to two black swivel chairs and put on the half-moon glasses hanging around his neck. He rummaged through the piles of paper covering his table.

"I'm sorry ladies ..." he said, lifting heaps of books and files. "Shit, I can't find it. OK, I'm going to need you two to introduce yourselves. My table eats up things."

"I'm Nicole French. Columbia senior. No! I keep saying that. I actually just graduated, so I'm a Columbia alum, and this is Sugri. She's a baby."

Dr. Dickson and Sugri both laughed.

"I'm also at Columbia and I'll be going into my junior year," Sugri said.

"Nicole and Sug.... Sorry, you're going to have to say your name slowly."

"Sug-ri," she enunciated.

"Sugri. Nice to have you on board. Michael Dickson. Head of the emergency room team. You'll be helping us with mundane paperwork, filing patient cards etc. But don't despair! There'll be exciting stuff. I'm sure you all watch *E.R.* Working here is not as dramatic as on TV, but there are days when you'll see gunshot victims, people being brought in with heart attacks. You'll assist nurses with getting drugs ready for patients. Oh, you'll learn a lot. Questions?" He smiled revealing teeth stained tobacco-brown.

"Do we get to inject patients?" Nicole asked.

Dr. Dickson laughed and said, "When you get to medical school, you'll have lots of chances to do that." He looked at Sugri, who returned a smile. "All right, if you don't have any more questions I'll show you where you'll be working."

Dr. Dickson walked out of his office and led them toward a wooden reception area filled with three large nurses.

"That Cole impregnating both mother and daughter ..." one of them was saying.

"Ladies, you really need to stop watching reruns of *Sunset Beach*," Dr. Dickson said.

The nurses laughed.

"Admit it, Michael, you love *Sunset Beach* too," another one said.

"Not on your life," Dr. Dickson said. "It's a quiet day," he quipped to the girls. "Some days these women work from morning to night. You'll be spending a lot of time in that area."

They moved into a narrow corridor with four doors on the left. He continued: "These rooms are where patients are brought in and where I and the other E.R. doctors go to see them. Come this way." He led them past those doors to a side room lined with metal shelves holding boxes. "One of your most boring but extremely important tasks is to make sure all the patient rooms have suture kits, towels, patient gowns, things like that. This is where you get the stuff from."

"Cool," Nicole said.

"OK, girls, you're free to go home to rest for the last time this summer. See you tomorrow, bright and early," he said.

"Thanks, Dr. Dickson," they chorused.

Sugri and Nicole walked out of the hospital onto the Grand Concourse. Cars whizzed up and down the large highway. Police sirens started, stopped, whined, died out and restarted.

Nicole opened her bag and put on a pair of aviator sunglasses. "Now, about that drink. You're sure you don't want to come?"

"I'm not twenty-one yet," Sugri said. "Plus, I'm not crazy about drinking."

"What's wrong with you? Before I was twenty-one that's all I could think about. Don't you worry. We'll go to this place right by Columbia. They don't card, and I'll buy you a drink. You need to chill. I can tell."

"Next time, I promise."

They walked down the Grand Concourse, the late afternoon sun bearing down on them.

"Juan! *"Si se te olvida la carne una vez más, te voy a matar,"* a woman shouted from a window in an art-deco building. Sugri looked around and saw three boys gathered at the subway entrance where they were headed. Whoever Juan was, he made no sign to show he'd heard the woman.

Across from the woman's building a water hydrant was spraying a full blast of water. Two round girls with curly hair splashed in and out of the deluge.

"Yummy. Chocolate and milk," one of the boys at the subway entrance said. "I like, I like. I gotta have both you sexy ladies with my cookies tonight."

"Fuck off," Nicole said, grabbed Sugri's hand and dragged her downstairs.

"Don't be rude," another shouted. Sugri looked back and saw that the boys had turned around and seemed ready to come after them.

"They're coming!" she shouted.

Sugri and Nicole ran down the stairs laughing. Sugri heard a train arrive just as they put their tokens into the subway slots. They got to the platform as the doors of the train were closing. Sugri stuck her body in the narrowing gap between the doors and the doors opened up. In the almost full car, Sugri looked out and saw the boys standing on the platform sticking their middle fingers up.

After she caught her breath she turned to Nicole. "Lived in New York all your life?"

"Yes ma'am. I don't think I could ever leave. How long have you been here?"

"Two years and don't think I could ever leave either."

Nicole laughed. "So where do you live?"

"Columbia summer housing. It's expensive, but I got a grant that pays most of it. I'm sure, lucky you, you live at home."

"On and off. I have an apartment not too far from Columbia and my parents live downtown."

They got off at 116ᵗʰ Street and Frederick Douglass Boulevard. Just outside the subway, a man bent sideways. He bent so low he almost landed on the ground, but didn't quite get there. His unkempt hair moved listlessly as he straightened himself.

"Crack head," Nicole said and laughed.

"Their dance fascinates me," Sugri said.

They walked through Morningside Park and scaled unending stairs.

"This is me," Sugri said in front of an open gate.

"You're sure you don't want to come?"

"Yes," Sugri said. "See you tomorrow."

*

July 1999

Sugri was sitting behind the reception desk of the emergency room sorting through a plastic box of cards. Nicole sat next to her, behind a cream-colored computer monitor.

"OK. Do this one," Sugri said. "'John Steiker, 54. History: asthmatic, eczema every so often, food allergies. Admitted April 8ᵗʰ. Asthma attack.'"

"John Steiker. Frail, small guy who still lives at home with mama. Loves women with flesh on them. He saw the girl of his dreams. Big mama. Poor guy couldn't find his inhaler before she smothered him in a hug."

"You're crazy," Sugri said. "Now. This will be a challenge. Francesca Bugle. Admitted May 20ᵗʰ. Came in saying her head was on fire and she was seeing stars. No past history of illnesses."

"Easy! Nut case!" Nicole said, laughing. "I hope they sent her right down to psychiatry." Sugri and Nicole snickered. Nicole snorted as an older nurse passed by at the same time. She glared at them.

"I wonder what she had," Sugri said, getting serious. "Seeing stars and head burning …" Interesting, she thought. Since hearing her grandmother's story of Bador Samed, madness had fascinated her.

"Nut case, I said! Forget about her. Hey, there's someone I want you to meet. I think you'll like him. We went to high school together. Let's go dancing. I'll tell him to come. Please say yes."

"No," Sugri said, smiling.

"I'll pick you up."

The emergency room double doors burst open. Two medics irrupted through the doors pushing a creaky gurney on top of which wobbled a huge body covered with a white cloth.

"He's unconscious!" a medic shouted.

Sugri and Nicole got up and led them to the first room in the corridor. They wheeled the gurney inside the room. Sugri grabbed a corner of the cloth under the body. Nicole did likewise.

"One, two, three," a medic shouted.

They started to hoist the body off the gurney onto the narrow bed.

As they began the transfer, the cloth covering the body slipped off. The man was completely naked. His already overweight body looked bloated, especially around his abdomen. His skin was mottled in pinks and greens. On his legs, green veins crisscrossed and formed a network dotted with red and white spots. A putrid stench rose from the body, like rotting flesh and stale beer. They heaved the body onto the bed. Sugri picked up the cover cloth and put it over the unconscious man.

When Dr. Dickson and two nurses came running in, Sugri slipped out. She ran into the nurses' station, shaking. She poured herself a glass of water and sat down to calm her nerves. The man's heavy lifeless body had frightened her. But what was worse was the condition of the body. She gagged. She began to doubt if medicine would work out, if this one body had put her off. That was extreme, Sugri. Breathe, she told herself. She realized she was probably expected to stay to find out what was wrong with the man. She walked out and found Nicole back at the reception.

"What's wrong with him?" she asked Nicole.

"Alcohol poisoning," Nicole said. "Now we really have to go out dancing to cleanse ourselves of that mess."

"After seeing that, Nick, I don't think I want to be anywhere near alcohol."

"I said dancing, didn't I? Not drinking."

"Fine. But if you as much as bring a drop of alcohol near me, I will have to do something really horrible to you."

They took a taxi to 23rd Street, where lines of people and velvet rope had decorated the entire street. Nicole, in jeans and a black T-shirt, didn't look like she had bothered to dress up. Sugri kept thinking of the one-armed blouse she was wearing and felt wrongly dressed. At the back of one line, a girl's skirt was so short it showed the crescents of her buttocks.

"We're not standing in line," Nicole said, pulling Sugri by the wrist. At the entrance to the club, she shouted, "Steve!" and kissed the burly bouncer clad in a black suit.

"You can go in, but it's twenty bucks for your friend," he said, steely-faced.

"Come on, Steve. Twenty bucks?" Nicole said. "Take a good look at this hotness. She's my girl, Steve. We're gonna buy lots of drinks inside."

Steve didn't smile. "Ten," he relented.

"Steve," Nicole whined.

Steve didn't budge. He stamped her palm and said, "You know where the cashier is."

"Asshole," Nicole muttered and walked inside. "I'll get this, hon. I brought you here." She pulled out a flat wallet from her back pocket, took out a ten dollar note and handed it to the cashier, a woman with long fake fingernails, painted pink and white. She stamped Sugri's palm.

"Thanks, Nick," Sugri said.

Inside, the club glowed with orange lighting. Low black stools were arranged in circles, surrounded by dwarf palms.

"Drink?" Nicole asked.

"I'm staying away from alcohol."

"Come on, one or two drinks never killed anyone."

"Just one. I'll have whatever you're having."

Nicole walked to the bar and Sugri sat on one of the low stools. As she looked at Nicole making the order, she began to think that she actually had a life and she was enjoying it. She'd never been freer. She didn't think about Ellis that much and even though she missed her mother, she wasn't itching to go back home, to have her every move monitored. A twenty-something man with close cropped hair walked up to Nicole. She hugged and kissed him. They walked over to Sugri.

"Is this Sugri?" he asked.

"Yes. Sugri, Antoine," Nicole said, winking at Sugri.

He reached out and kissed her cheek, very close to her mouth.

Nicole handed Sugri a glass with a sunset yellow drink.

The club was filling up and the DJ started playing house music. Strobe lights went on and off. Antoine walked to the bar and returned with a glass of golden brown liquid in a tumbler. He took a sip of it and put the glass on a table next to Sugri.

"Let's dance," he said to her.

Sugri downed her cocktail and walked behind Antoine. On the crowded dance floor, all she saw was heads bopping up and down. Antoine pulled her in close.

"How do you know Nicole?" he whispered in her ear.

"We're interns at the Bronx-Lebanon hospital."

"Doctors in the making, huh? Nice."

"What do you do?" she asked.

"I'm a money-maker."

"Modest, aren't we?"

"I'd be modest if the money was mine. I work in an investment bank."

"My sources tell me investment bankers make above average salaries. And bonuses at the end of the year add a few tens of thousands …" Sugri whispered back.

Antoine didn't respond. He kissed her. Softly, briefly at first. He took her by surprise. They barely knew each other. They didn't know each other—at all! Sugri looked at him. He was very attractive. After Ellis, she needed to let go. He pressed his nose against hers. Their lips touched again. They kissed deeply this time. She felt Antoine dig into his pocket. He brought out his hand and showed her three blue pills.

"Want one?" he asked her.

She shook her head. "No, thanks. What are they?"

"Nothing's going to happen to you. Here. I'll take two and you can have one."

I don't think I should do this, Sugri thought. Then again, you live only once. She picked up the pill and held it close to her eye. It was pretty, marked with a butterfly on one side and blue all over.

"Do I chew, suck or swallow?" she asked.

"Wait," Antoine said. He walked over to the low table to pick up his drink. He put the two pills on his tongue and chased it with the drink. Sugri did the same.

They continued dancing. The DJ was still playing trance music. Soon the beats of songs were indistinguishable. They morphed, twisted, mashed up and coursed around in the labyrinth of Sugri's mind. The lights stretched out, brightened for long periods, dimmed slightly, became pink and then red. And Antoine felt really nice. She ran her hand up and down his back. She moved it up to his head and shuddered at the feel of the short bristles on his scalp.

Antoine kissed her again deeply.

"Want to come to mine?" he asked her.

"Huh?"

"Let's go back to my place."

"I'll tell Nicole first," she said.

"OK. Be right back."

Sugri walked toward Nicole who was jumping up and down with a man in a Mohawk and grey T-shirt. Her hair bobbed up, stayed in the air and then came back down slowly.

"Nick," Sugri slurred. She rubbed Nicole's shirt. "Antoine says I should go with him. What do you think?"

"Go where, hon?"

"His," Sugri said.

"I've known him forever. He's a sweetheart. Call you tomorrow," Nicole said and kissed her on her mouth.

Sugri and Antoine walked out of the club. She rubbed his arm as he flagged a cab.

In the taxi, she planted her lips on his while making infinite circles on his scalp. Her heart was pumping so fast. She caught the driver, a man wearing a turban, looking at them through the rearview mirror. He dropped them off in front of Antoine's building.

They made their way up the elevator, feeling each other up. Antoine unlocked his door. The apartment was lit up by the Queensboro Bridge looming large in the distance.

They stumbled into Antoine's room. She was still rubbing his head. He sloughed off her clothes and pulled her down onto his bed. She passed her palm on the silk sheets covering the bed. Completely naked, Antoine climbed on top of her.

She kissed him. His chest was hairy and she repeatedly combed her fingers through the tuft of hair. Before she knew what was happening, she felt a sweet heaviness leave her womb and take over her whole body. He wasn't even in her. Wow, she thought. He entered her and she heard him grunting. The sweet heaviness started again, pulsated and exploded up and down her spine.

The next morning Sugri woke up not sure where she was. Bright rays of light leaked in through glass windows. She looked at the white sheets and saw Antoine's pale body. Oh my God! she thought. How did this happen? She got out of bed and pulled on her panties.

Antoine stirred and turned around. "Hi, sexy," he said.

"Hi," she said, not sure how the night ended like this. She remembered the blue pill! That was her last clear memory.

"We should go for brunch," Antoine said, sitting up in bed now.

"I really should go home," she said. She was confused. She picked up her skimpy top and kept wondering what happened.

"You were amazing last night," he said, clearing some of her confusion.

"I was?" she looked at him. "We slept together?"

"Sugri, you had multiple orgasms last night."

She felt shame seep into her. She didn't even know this guy. She had to leave now. She looked at his bed. The mattress sat on a low, black, wooden bed frame. It was a nice bed.

"Antoine, I'll give you my number." She picked up a pen from a glass table next to the bed and wrote it down. "Thanks for last night."

"Come on, stay! The diner on Third Ave. has the best waffles."

"Maybe next time," she said and dashed out of the apartment. She flagged down a taxi. What the hell just happened to me? she wondered.

*

Sugri sat up in bed. She had to be in the hospital in an hour but she felt exhausted and a strong urge to pee. She hadn't even drunk that much water the night before. She got out of bed and walked to the bathroom downstairs.

She sat on the black-seated toilet bowl. Pain tore through her legs as she tried to pass urine. She stopped. I knew something would happen because of Antoine, she thought. She looked up at the white ceiling. God, you weren't going to let me get out of this one free, were you?

She really needed to pee. She tried again. A tiny trickle made its way out. She felt as if the urine was searing the walls of her urethra. She pressed her eyes closed and forced the urine out. Only half of it came out.

She called Nicole's apartment. No one picked up. She then called Dr. Dickson. He wasn't in yet, so she left a message.

"Hi, Dr. Dickson. It's Sugri. Em, I have a medical emergency so I won't be able to make it today. Sorry for the short notice. Thanks."

She hung up, picked up a pair of jeans and pulled them on. She picked up her keys and walked down to the Health Center.

She prayed for many things as she walked through its doors. She prayed she didn't have some horrible disease. She prayed she wasn't pregnant. She prayed she wouldn't run into Rebecca Freedman, because this would be her victory. "You should have finished therapy," she was sure the woman would say, "then you wouldn't have contracted that STD."

She filled out the forms at the reception room, handed them to a nurse and sat on a blue plastic chair. She stared in front of her. A girl who looked sixteen sat across from her, biting her nails. She looked at the clock. 9:07.

"Sugri Mensah," a tall nurse called for her. "Come this way." She led her around a corridor, opened a door and let her in.

"What can I help you with today?"

Sugri swallowed. This is not the time for squeamishness, she told herself.

"Well, I tried peeing this morning. And I felt this really sharp, burning sensation. I couldn't even finish peeing."

"OK. I know it hurts but I need you to shut your eyes really tight and try to pee into this," she said, handing her a glass beaker. "You can use the bathroom behind the curtain."

Sugri opened the bathroom door. She walked in, pulled down her jeans and panties and squatted over the toilet seat. She pressed her eyelids close.

"Ouch, ouch, ouch," she said silently as she forced herself to get all the urine out of her system in one go. She paused, not able to stand the burning. "OK, one, two, three." She tried again. She filled half the beaker with cloudy ochre urine. That doesn't look good, she thought. She walked out into the room with the beaker in hand. "Here," she said, handing it to the nurse who had a white latex glove on.

"Good. Sugri, please sit. I'm going to ask you some questions."

She sat on the narrow metal-framed bed.

"Have you had a urinary tract infection before?"

"No."

"A yeast infection?"

"No."

"Are you sexually active?"

Sugri paused. "Yes, but not ..."

The nurse went on. "How many partners have you had? If you're not sure of the number you can give a range."

Is this necessary? Sugri wondered. "Two."

"Do you always use protection?"

"Yes." She didn't even know if Antoine had worn a condom.

"OK, Sugri. I think you have a urinary tract infection. We'll test your urine in the next two to three days. Do you want us to check for other sexually transmitted diseases?"

Sugri nodded.

"I'm going to give you Amoxil to take for the next few days. It's an antibiotic. In three days if we find that what you have is not a UTI, or if we find some other STI, we'll call you. If we don't call, all is clear."

The three days that followed were the worst in her life. She didn't go to work at the hospital. On the last day, she woke up at ten and stayed in bed till midday, drifting in and out of sleep. She tried reading, but couldn't concentrate. Around one, her stomach gargled loudly. She got out of bed and opened her cube fridge. She took out a box of chocolate milk and poured it into a blue and white mug with COLUMBIA etched on it. She emptied a box of Frosties that had been sitting on her fridge top for the past month. She put a spoonful of the golden flakes drenched in brown milk in her mouth. Ugh, flat. She left the bowl on her desk and climbed back into bed.

I didn't come to America for my life to end like this, she thought. Goodness knows what I've contracted from that boy. He hasn't even called. Oh my goodness! She screamed, picked up her pillow and put it over her face to muffle the sound. Between crying and trying to read her book, she fell asleep again.

She woke up at four. The sun was still high up. Her stomach began to cry out again. The acids rose up and bubbled over, begging for food to digest. She got up and forced herself to eat the Frosties, which had now absorbed all the milk. After each bite, she tried not to gag. She took the antibiotic tablets.

She climbed back into bed. After five, I should be clear, she said to herself. No, the Health Center stays open all night. After midnight I'll be fine.

The phone rang. Her heart jumped. This was it. The end of her life. She let it ring three more times, then picked it up.

"Hello," she said quietly.

"Miss Sugri!" Ije's hoarse voice cut through. "Whassup?"

"Ije, I'm so happy to hear from you."

"Aren't you supposed to be working at the hospital?"

"I've had something for the past three days, I think it's a flu. Listen, Ije, the clinic might call me any minute to give me medication, so I'll call you later, OK?"

"OK, my dear. Feel better. Call me tomorrow," Ije said.

"Bye," Sugri said, her eyes watering again. I am never having sex again. Not till I get married. That is if I haven't contracted some horrendous disease. Then no one would want to marry me. She looked out her window. She got up and paced through her room. I'm going mad, she thought. Maybe Babasam caught an STD, because surely, she was going to go crazy. She crept back into her bed.

Her eyes opened after seven and she looked at the phone to see if she'd missed any calls. She hadn't. She got up and paced again. Her stomach rumbled. She opened her fridge. An old dried up orange was the only thing left in it. She picked it up and gnawed at it with a blunt, plastic knife. She couldn't cut through it.

She threw the orange at the door and climbed back into bed. Tears coursed down her face. She fell asleep.

She woke up. The bright overhead lights confused her. She looked at the alarm clock. 3:20. She looked at the answering machine of her phone. No blinking red lights.

"Thank you, God," she said, took off her nightclothes, wrapped her towel around her and walked down to the bathroom.

Thirty
Unwinding Tall Tales

August 1999

As taxis sped up and down Amsterdam Avenue, Ije propped open the front door of Sugri's new apartment building with a red fire extinguisher. Sugri reached into an orange mobile recycling cart they'd parked on the sidewalk. She picked up a box, walked into building and scaled the stairs. On the second floor, feeling it slip out of her fingers, she leaned the box against the banister. Why she had to live on the fourth floor in a building with no elevator was anybody's guess. She lifted it and continued her ascent. She dropped the box in front of her room. She dashed back down and met Ije struggling with a box on the second floor.

"You need to get yourself a boyfriend to do these things for you," Ije panted.

"No boys for me," Sugri said. "Boys are the devil." She laughed and went back down. She picked up two black garbage bags, swollen with clothes.

By the time they'd made countless trips up and down the stairs, the entrance to Sugri's room was filled with boxes and garbage bags.

"This is the last one," Ije said, her breath escaping in short bursts. "Damn, I'm tired!"

"Me too," Sugri said. "I'm going to try to stay in this apartment till I graduate." She kicked a box into the empty room.

"You're need furniture," Ije said, poking her head through the door.

"I know. But getting the apartment unfurnished was so much cheaper than paying for a room that comes with a bed and a desk." Not every one has rich Nigerian parents who can send extra money to pay for lavish living quarters, Sugri was thinking.

"You don't need me now, do you?" Ije asked, dragging two garbage bags into the room.

"No, but what's the rush?"

"I have to go the registrar's office to sign this graduation document. Next year it'll be your turn."

"I know. Time is running a marathon to I-don't-know-where," Sugri said.

Ije chuckled. "Peace out."

Sugri looked around the room. The wooden panels of the floor, in dull teak, ran diagonal to the walls. They would look really nice with some good polishing. She walked out and shoved the boxes into the room. Her T-shirt stuck to her back. The air in the room felt muggy. She walked over to the big sash window that overlooked Amsterdam Avenue and slid it up. Guitar strums of bachata music flooded the room, not air. She placed her right palm on her stomach, stuck out her left hand, stepped forward with her right foot and gyrated her waist in a false imitation of bachata or salsa or was it tango? There was something inherently sad about those guitar strums. She made a mental note to find out more about bachata.

She untied her braids and let them fall to her shoulders. She looked around at the boxes, deciding to first unpack the box with her essentials. She grabbed her keys and cut through a taped box. She pulled out a green air mattress, pink sheets, a phone, a white towel and a toothbrush with bristles that looked gnawed on. She plugged in the phone.

She picked up the air mattress and popped the plastic valve open. She stuck her mouth on the valve, puffing air out of her cheeks into the mattress. She puffed her cheek and exhaled. Puffed and exhaled, like a male frog calling for a mate. A mate. She sighed. Since Ellis and the scare from the summer, she'd sworn off boys. It would be nice to have a boyfriend, though. He could come over, and she'd cook dinner, which they'd eat with a bottle of wine. They'd watch a romantic movie. They'd have a steamy make-out session and then he'd go home. She was seriously going to follow her mantra. No more sex. Not till she met her future husband, whatever that meant.

She closed the valve on the inflated mattress, laid it by the window and plopped herself on it. She basked in the glow of her new apartment—her new, unfurnished, box and garbage bag-ridden apartment. With a boyfriend, she'd be making full, grown-up use of the apartment. Her eyelids drooped. Her phone rang, startling her.

"Sugri."

"Mummy?"

"Yes. Sorry the line is not clear."

"Madam, shout into phone …" Sugri heard a deep male voice say to Akua Afriyie.

"OK. Sugri, is it better?"

"Slightly. Where are you calling from?"

"Some communication center. The phone at home isn't working. Some idiots were trimming a tree in the neighborhood and cut the phone line. I've been going to Ghana Telecom for the past week."

"Trust," Sugri said.

"How's your new apartment?"

"I finally moved everything in. I was just about to take a nap, when you called."

"I'll make it quick then. I'm coming to New York!"

"Wow," Sugri said, sitting up on the mattress. "When?"

"In three weeks. The art gallery people are paying for my flight over. It's to discuss my work and so on."

"I'm so happy for you, mummy," Sugri said.

"Thanks, honey. I'll let you sleep now."

"Do you want me to come get you from the airport?"

"They're arranging all that. And a hotel and everything."

"That's nice," Sugri said, disappointment seeping into her bones. She wanted her mother to stay with her, to see that she was taking care of herself. But, she didn't even have furniture! Where would she sleep? It was better this way.

"See you soon!" Akua Afriyie said.

"Two thousand cedis …" Sugri heard the deep voice at the other end of the line say before the connection faded.

*

Sugri checked her outfit in the glass doors of the hotel before pushing the door in. Her mother would appreciate her white lace blouse and black flared skirt with floral borders, instead of her usual jeans and T-shirt. And her not-so-flat shoes! She walked into the hotel reception, a small room covered in olive green carpeting.

"Hello, young lady," the grey-haired, milk-skinned man said to her. "How may I help you?" His teeth were perfect and white.

"I'm looking for Akua Afriyie Mensah," she said. "I can't remember what room she's in."

"No problem," he said. "Spell the name."

"A-K-U-A." He clicked on the keyboard next to a computer monitor.

"Room 18 A."

"Thanks," Sugri said, making for the elevator. She fussed with her skirt. The last time she saw her mother she was a different person. She was a child. Now, she'd been through some core-shaking experiences. She wondered if her mother would be able to tell.

She stepped out of the elevator. Rooms A to F to the left. She quickened her steps, excitement beginning to clutch at her heart. Two years! She knocked on the door.

"Come in," Akua Afriyie said, opening the door at the same time. "Oh my goodness!" she screamed.

"Mummy!" Sugri said, running into her mother's arms.

"You look great."

"Thanks. Like my new look?" Sugri asked, pirouetting herself.

"I approve all the way!"

"You look good too! And I love your afro," Sugri said. Her mother wore a white button-down shirt and blue and green tie-and-dye skirt— one hundred percent Akua Afriyie. "You didn't tell me you cut your hair!"

"I did it when I got the contract. It's liberating. I have some things for you," Akua Afriyie said, bending down to open her suitcase.

"You have such a nice view," Sugri said, looking out the window. She saw motorboats rippling the surface of the East River. "It's not fair!"

"What isn't?" Akua Afriyie asked. Sugri turned around. Her mother held in hand two dresses and an envelope.

"I've lived in New York for two years and not once have I had such a nice view!"

"Ha! When you grow up and become some big shot doctor you can afford such a place. These are from Mamaa," Akua Afriyie said, handing her a short green paisley dress with a turtle neck and an envelope. "She said she wore the dress on her first date with your grandfather. She had her seamstress take it in so it would fit you."

"Cute," Sugri said. Where was she going to wear that to? It smelled of camphor. She tore open the envelope. She pulled out a hundred dollar bill. "Oh, Mamaa! How sweet of her."

"This is from Asantewa."

"Thanks! I've been looking for a *boubou* forever! They're so expensive here."

"Your grandaunt must have communicated with you by telepathy. Do you need a bag for those?"

"Please," Sugri said. "How was the meeting with the gallery people?"

"It went well. They're so nice! Americans are very warm."

"Humph!" Sugri said.

"What was that for?"

"Some are...."

"O—K. These ones were. Although, I'll be extremely hot when I get back to Ghana. I've only done twelve pieces. I have to finish all twenty and have them sent here by the first week of October."

"You'll be fine," Sugri said. "Besides, you don't have me or John Barnor distracting you anymore."

"True! Ei, did I tell you your grandfather got nominated for a Ghanaian Excellence Award?"

"No. What's that?"

"The Oscars of Ghana, they're calling it. And of course, Mamaa is in her element. The awards will be held in December. The weekend before my exhibition here. Can you believe she insists on coming here with me? And she's dragging Papa too."

"Eish, Mamaa!"

"We'll leave the day after the awards show to come here."

"It'd be nice to see her and grandpa," Sugri said.

"I'm ready. Shall we go shopping now?"

"Indeed!"

Mother and daughter walked out into a bright New York summer day.

"Where's everybody?" Akua Afriyie asked. "You made New York seem like a never-ending party."

"They're all shopping. Your hotel is in the dry part! The shopping area is ten blocks from here. Want to walk?"

"Walk ten blocks?" Akua Afriyie shook her head as she slid on her dark glasses.

"It's really not far. I'm wearing heels and I want to walk. That should tell you."

"Since when do you wear heels?" Akua Afriyie asked.

"It's just to impress you. So, are we walking?"

"Sure. Fine."

They walked down Park Avenue. Hot dog vendors pushed their yellow and red metal carts in the same direction. Park Avenue mothers and nannies pushed their babies in prams in the opposite direction. Taxis honked up and down the avenue. On 34th Street, a rabble of mostly teenage girls crowded the sidewalks, in hand bags colored pink, yellow, green and all shades of fluffy.

"Now, this is New York!" Akua Afriyie said. "Overwhelming."

"I avoid this street as much as I can. But it seems like this is what you want. What kind of clothes are you looking for?"

"Just comfortable clothes with a little bit of edge. Now that I'm self-employed, I can wear whatever I want."

"OK," Sugri said. She dragged her mother away from a Payless ShoeSource storefront. "Let's go to Macy's. If you want overwhelming, I'll give you overwhelming." Sugri didn't let go of her mother's wrist, as she shoved, pushed and pulled her way through the throng of shoppers and tourists.

Inside Macy's the story was no different. Women swathed in a thousand aromas, stepped forward with bottles of perfume and testers.

"Amarige?" one of them asked, shoving a red box in Sugri's face.

"No, thanks," Sugri said, walking toward the escalator. She realized she'd become so comfortable in New York, it was like a second home.

In only two years. She was no longer the green, wide-eyed girl, smiling at everyone.

"Why do the escalators look so old? Don't they have money?" Akua Afriyie asked.

Sugri looked at the wooden treads. For some strange reason, she sensed a role reversal after Akua Afriyie asked that. Akua Afriyie had always been the one leading the way, doing the explaining. While it was totally natural for her to be leading the way here—it was after all, Akua Afriyie's first trip to New York—she just couldn't help thinking that she knew a little more about the world than her mother did.

"These were built over a hundred years ago. I'm sure that's how they want them to be," Sugri said.

"Interesting," Akua Afriyie said, clicking her tongue. They walked into the women's section.

"If you're like me," Sugri said, "you go straight for the sales. Oh, I forgot, you're a world famous artist. You can afford things at their full prices."

"Please," Akua Afriyie said. "Sales!" They walked toward racks of clothing. Pink florals flanked black and white stripes. Green and blue spots brushed orange solids. "This *is* overwhelming!"

"Yes. Sale shopping requires skill. Here. You might like this," Sugri handed her a navy blue shirt dress with bright red buttons.

"It's cute, but I don't know about the red buttons."

"I thought you liked color."

"Yes, but as an accent I throw over clothes. I'd rather the buttons were black or blue. That way I could put a red scarf over the dress when I want." Sugri didn't get it. Her face must have registered her confusion. "Oh, OK. I'll try it on."

Sugri picked up a pair of jeans for herself. She was hoping to wangle this out of her mother. With her sale shopping expertise, they piled bright scarves, solid shirts and striped dresses into Akua Afriyie's arms. Akua Afriyie walked into a dressing room and Sugri stole in after her.

"Why did you just dart in here like a frightened rat?" Akua Afriyie asked. Sugri laughed.

"Two people can't be in here at the same time, but to hell with them!"

"Language!"

"That reminds me! How is Pastor Adomza?"

"Can we not talk about that?" Akua Afriyie said.

What could have happened? Sugri wondered. "Too late, I'm already hooked. Tell!"

"I've stopped going to his church." Akua Afriyie unbuttoned her shirt.

"Why? He turned out to be a big time crook who stole church members' money?"

"No. He got married ..." Akua Afriyie stared at the pile of clothes. She picked up the navy blue dress with the red buttons.

"I knew you liked him!" Sugri exclaimed, poking her face into her mother's. "I'm sure someone wonderful and worthy of you will come along."

"Thanks," Akua Afriyie said, pushing the last of the red buttons through the boutonniere. "What do you think?"

"It suits you!"

"Good choice. I guess the red buttons do work."

Sugri wondered what had happened between her mother and that pastor. He was good looking, but she never warmed up to him. He better not have tried any fast moves on her mother.

"Mummy," she said, "why did you really stop going? Just because he married someone else seems a little lame. Did you two have an affair?" She picked up the jeans.

"Sugri, please. Affair?" she scoffed. "He was just a pastor with a great tongue ..."

"A great tongue?"

"He was good with words. But, let's just say I don't believe in what he and his church stand for any more. His wedding was just the icing on the cake."

"O—K," Sugri said, knowing that she'd hit a roadblock. She pulled up the jeans under her skirt. "Ugh," she said.

"What?" Akua Afriyie asked.

"Jeans never fit right. Look at these." She turned her buttocks toward her mother.

"They look fine to me."

"Look at all this extra material at my knees and they make my bum look flat."

"I don't see it. But if you want your jeans really tight, then you should get another pair."

They left Macy's. Sugri dragged her mother up and down 34th Street until, like the girls they saw earlier, their arms toted plastic bags bursting with color and clothes.

"What are we doing tonight?" Akua Afriyie asked.

"You have energy!"

"I have two days left, I better take full advantage."

"OK," Sugri said. "We're going for dinner at a Jamaican restaurant in Chelsea."

"Sounds exciting. I want to clean up first, though. Can we go back to the hotel?"

"Of course," Sugri said.

Sugri and Akua Afriyie stepped out of the hotel two hours later. Sugri looked at her mother in her navy-blue shirt-dress with red buttons. Her afro made her seem much younger.

Sugri stretched out her arm to flag a cab. Taxis passed by them in yellow refusal.

"What's going on?" Akua Afriyie said.

"They see two black women so they don't want to pick us up," Sugri said. "I made reservations for seven. Let's take the subway or we'll never get there."

"Oh. In our nice clothes?"

"Mummy, they're strict about reservations."

"All right," Akua Afriyie said. They walked on Lexington Avenue and entered Grand Central Station through a small entrance after a clothing store with mannequins looking starved. Sugri walked to the ticket booth.

"Two tokens," she said, placing two dollar bills in a slot outside the booth.

The man in the booth slapped the tokens into an opening on his end. Sugri picked them up and handed one to Akua Afriyie.

"Slot it in the hole," she said.

They walked down the stairs. The floor was dotted with saliva and black spots.

"We're going to catch the 7-train, go across town and catch the A-train downtown," Sugri said.

"None of that makes any sense to me," Akua Afriyie said, walking behind Sugri. "If you left me here I wouldn't even know how to get to the hotel!"

They waited at the platform for the-never-arriving-7-train. Sugri's toes were lined with the edge of the platform. She stuck her neck out, willing the train over. Akua Afriyie grabbed Sugri's dress and pulled her back.

"Are you crazy?" Akua Afriyie said. "Why are you standing so close to the edge?"

"*I'm trying not to lose my head …*"

"Huh?" Akua Afriyie said, rubbing lint off Sugri's collar.

"It's a song. Relax, mummy."

"I might not be a New Yorker, but come on, that was dangerously close to the edge." The lights of the train lit up the tunnel.

"Finally!" Sugri said. "*Don't push me. Coz I'm close to the eh-edge. I'm trying not to lose my head. Ah ah ah aah.*"

"Underneath all those new clothes, you haven't changed," Akua Afriyie said. "You're as silly as ever."

They walked through the opened doors and settled across from a fat man sprawled across three of the seats. The doors of the subway slid open at Times Square.

"Are we here?" Akua Afriyie asked.

"One more train." She was thinking of the quickest way to get to the A-train. She absolutely hated Times Square. They walked by a woman fiddling her violin violently, a crowd gathered around her.

"Can we watch?" Akua Afriyie asked.

"Reservations, remember?"

"Sugri!" She heard someone shout.

"Did someone call you?" Akua Afriyie said.

"Sugri!" the voice was insistent, familiar. Sugri turned around. She was surprised to see him. Even though she'd rather have not. He walked over, with his curly hair and naughty smile.

"Hey!" he said, stooping to kiss her cheeks. "I thought it was you. And I wanted to catch you before you turned that corner. Hello," he said to Akua Afriyie, extending an arm. "You must be Sugri's mother."

"Yes," she said, smiling.

"Mummy, this is Ellis," Sugri said.

"Oh, Ellis," Akua Afriyie said. Sugri saw an evil glint flash in her eye. "I used to hear a lot about you."

"Right," he said. "'Used to.' That's a bad sign." He smiled. Sugri really missed him. She hadn't seen him since May. "You look like you're in a hurry," he said.

"We're going for dinner," Sugri volunteered.

"Hey, you look good," Ellis said.

"Thanks," Sugri said, looking down at her shoes. She looked up. "Anyway, gotta go. See you around."

"See you," he said. He went back in the direction he'd come from.

"He's handsome," Akua Afriyie said. "But after that whole cheating thing …"

"Yeah. Don't worry about it, mummy. He's history." She was trying to convince herself more than her mother.

Inside the restaurant, a hostess met Akua Afriyie and Sugri.

"Two?" she asked them, smiling.

"Yes," Sugri said. The hostess led them to a table in the back. The room smelled of sweet plantain and spicy stews. Shaggy's music and lyrics floated around the room, reminding all in the room that they were in Jamaica now. A dreadlocked bartender whisked a silver martini shaker up and down as his head bobbed to the music.

"Your waiter will be with you soon," the hostess said.

"Thanks," Sugri said, sitting down and picking up a menu. "Have you been here before?"

"Yes, once," Sugri said, looking intently at her menu.

"With Ellis, right?" her mother asked.

"Yah," Sugri mumbled back.

"We shouldn't have come here then."

"No, it's no problem. Their food is good. I recommend you go for oxtail or jerk chicken."

"I eat too much chicken," Akua Afriyie said, running her fingers through her hair. "Oxtail it is then."

A man with hair in twists came over. He smiled at both ladies. "Good evening, ladies," he said. "You sisters?"

"No, no," Sugri said, looking at her mother. Akua Afriyie's smile was too broad.

"What are you having today?" he asked, his Caribbean lilt carrying his words.

"Two plates of oxtail and rice and peas. And a side of plantain."

"Very good. And to drink?"

"Cream soda," Sugri said.

"Ginger beer," her mother said. As the waiter disappeared from view, Akua Afriyie said, "Nice accent! And he's cute!"

"Mummy!" Sugri said. She was thinking of Ellis, though. Was this a trick the universe was playing on her? Just as her life was coming back together, was it trying to tempt her into falling into a pit again? Well, she wouldn't fall for it. Not this time. Yet she couldn't ignore the flutter that had danced in her heart when she saw him. Of course she still liked him. A great woman once told her, "You never forget your first love." She didn't think she'd love anyone as intensely after him. She'd give bits of her heart, but never all of it.

"Why so quiet?" Akua Afriyie asked.

"Nothing."

"You're thinking about that boy."

"I guess," Sugri said.

"Did you two … sleep together?"

"Mummy!" Sugri said. There was no way she was going to tell the woman the truth. One, it wasn't her business. Two, she wasn't really proud about having slept with someone who'd cheated on her.

The waiter appeared and arranged square plates before them. He put golden-brown plantains on the table.

Sugri looked at her plate—a ball of brown rice with red beans, oxtail sauce garnished with sprigs of parsley.

"That looks good!" Akua Afriyie said.

"Enjoy," the waiter said.

"Thanks," Akua Afriyie said. "No pressure to tell me. We used to be able to discuss these kinds of things is all ..."

"OK, fine, yes, we did," Sugri said, staring at her plate. She couldn't look her in the eye.

"That's fine. I hope you used protection."

"Yes," Sugri said. Well, I slept with someone else and I'm not sure that we did and I learned my lesson the hard, horrible way.

"I already knew it," Akua Afriyie said. "I just wanted to hear it from your lips."

"How did you know?"

"Mother's intuition. And the way you two acted around each other." Akua Afriyie arranged the napkin on her lap. "What are you waiting for?" she asked, nodding at the plates.

"Aren't you going to pray?" Sugri marveled at how even after two years her mind was programmed for prayer-before-meals when her mother was around.

"For what we're about to receive, we thank you, Lord. Amen," Akua Afriyie said.

Sugri ate quickly. She didn't realize how ravenous she was. She sat back, sipping her cream soda. Now that she'd told her mother that she'd had sex, she might as well let out some other secrets. That's how she worked, if you unlocked her closet to take a peek, the whole pile of unfolded clothes fell out, like a huge waterfall. "Remember how horrible last semester was for me?" she asked her mother, who was leading a piece of oxtail into her mouth.

"Yes, a C in Chemistry. Ellis, cheated.... Uh huh," Akua Afriyie said.

"Well, I saw a therapist," she said and paused.

"You did? Why didn't you just talk to me?"

"Long story. I went for only one session."

"It must have been useless, then," Akua Afriyie said.

"She kept asking me all these questions about our family and the lack of a father figure in my life. Blah blah blah."

"What did she deduce?"

"Nothing. All she did was ask questions."

"What did you say?"

"I told her I felt incomplete," Sugri said, looking Akua Afriyie square in the eye, "that half of me was missing."

Akua Afriyie was quiet. She tried to cut a piece of meat but her knife skidded, clinking loudly against the plate. She looked at Sugri. Her eyes watered. This woman loves crying! Sugri thought.

She lowered her voice, "If I don't do this now I'll keep lying to you."

"Lying to me?" Sugri sat up, fisting her right hand on the table. It landed in a drop of oxtail stew. She wiped her hand on the table cloth.

"Sugri," Akua Afriyie said quietly, "your father isn't dead."

Sugri didn't respond. Her mother was lying. Why was she playing such a horrible trick on her? Why?

"You met him," Akua Afriyie went on. "When we went to the Castle with your grandmother."

The man with big eyes that kept popping open? In primary school they called her frog eyes, but she thought he had extraordinarily large eyes. Bigger than a frog's. So that's who she got her eyes from. Did she feel complete now? No, even more vacuumed out than before. She was a dried up plant cell. The cell wall still stood, but all the cytoplasm had been drained out. She wanted to throw up the food she'd just eaten.

"What's his name?" Sugri asked.

"Rashid. Rashid Adams," her mother said and pursed her lips.

This was bringing back memories of the break-up with Ellis. She felt betrayed. Even the break-up felt better than this. Her own mother had lied to her about such an important part of her life. She took fifty dollars from her bag and placed the notes under the plantain plate. "That's the money for dinner. Mummy, this is fucked up," she said.

"Don't use that language …"

"Listen, I have to go. I need to think," she said, bristling. She rose from her chair. "You can take a taxi to your hotel. You at least know the address. I'll call you later." She didn't look back once and marched resolutely for the door.

"Hope you enjoyed …" the hostess started.

Sugri walked out not even acknowledging her.

New York City, home to all sorts of types, could present you with people looking for trouble when you didn't want any. Today she wanted one of those trouble-seekers to cross her path. She'd give them a run for their money. Tears burned her eyes. She walked west. She retched, amazed at how the brain linked emotions with other systems of the body. Brain to digestive system: Sugri is disgusted. She retched again.

A man in a tight black T-shirt, his biceps and triceps clearly defined, hair slicked back, said, "Honey, drink a little too much? Find a bathroom. Uh huh."

"Fuck you," Sugri said.

"Hey, fuck you too, bitch!"

Sugri rolled her eyes, the fire in her smoldering. She walked toward the looming towers of housing projects. What was she doing there? She'd left her mother all alone. The least she could do was take her back to her hotel. She turned round, composed herself and retraced her steps.

Outside the restaurant, she saw her mother laughing heartily with the waiter who'd served them. A cigarette dangled from his mouth as Akua Afriyie said something to him. Way to be repentant, Sugri thought. Her rage was tempting a comeback but she tempered it, pushed it down.

"Hey," Akua Afriyie said.

"I'll leave you two," the waiter said. "Enjoy de rest of your vacation."

"Thanks, Robert. How are you feeling?" Akua Afriyie asked Sugri.

"I don't feel like talking, but I couldn't leave you here," Sugri said. "I'll take you back to your hotel."

"No need. I'll find it," Akua Afriyie said.

Sugri was sure she was putting on a front. "I'll take you," she said, finally, sticking her thumb out. A yellow taxi pulled up in front of them.

"That was easy this time," Akua Afriyie said. Sugri ignored her.

"Forty-first and Lexington," Sugri said to the driver, complexioned in the same shade of brown as her mother and herself.

"I could have said that. 'Fordy-first and Lexingtin,'" Akua Afriyie mimicked Sugri.

Sugri wanted to laugh, but held strong. She didn't even flinch.

"Truth is, I would have said, 'Lexington Hotel,' which wouldn't have helped much." Akua Afriyie said and clammed up.

"Where you from?" the driver asked, his eyes dancing from mother to daughter in the rearview mirror.

"Ghana," Akua Afriyie said.

"I'm from The Gambia," he said. "Been here long?"

"Me, no. My daughter ..."

Sugri blocked out their inane conversation. She stared at the city through the window. New York was a great city to be sad in. You could cry and nobody would ask why. You could throw a fit and people would walk right by. When you were down, the buildings always stood tall in indifference. They helped you wallow in your misery. Yet at the same time they didn't make you pity yourself.

They stopped in front of Akua Afriyie's hotel.

"Please keep the meter running," Sugri said to the driver. "I'll be right back."

"Don't take too long, now. Nice meeting you, my sister," he shouted to Akua Afriyie.

Mother and daughter walked into the elevator, went up, strode along a lonely hallway not exchanging a word. Sugri picked up her bags and said a terse goodnight to her mother. She didn't want to occupy the same space with her. She dashed back to the taxi.

"That was your mother?" the taxi driver said, as he drove across 42nd Street. He knew she was her mother. Why was he trying to make conversation? Yes she is, but we have nothing in common. I'd never lie to my children about who they are, she thought. "She's very nice," he went on, apparently impervious to the chill Sugri was sending out into the world. She wouldn't speak to her. She didn't want to speak to her till she'd simmered down. Now she was boiling and bubbling over. It had taken almost twenty years for her mother to come clean. She could take twenty years to simmer down.

On Monday, after her African Studies class, Sugri walked into her room. She looked at her inflated airbed—her only furniture. This was home. Her only home. The light on her speakerphone flashed red. She walked to it and pressed the play button.

"Hi, sweetie," Akua Afriyie's voice said. "I know I sprang so much on you this weekend. Trust me, I'd probably have reacted worse. I'm so sorry for keeping things from you. Take your time to think things through. I had so much fun on Saturday. Thank you for taking me shopping and for that lovely dinner. You had some change left over! I forgot to give it to your sulkiness! You better be over your cold war by the time we come for the exhibition, because I will expect you to be there. I'll tell the gallery to send you an invitation. I love you so, so much. I'm checking out of my hotel in half an hour, if you want to call…. I love you."

Beep.

Sugri pressed the delete button. Lies! That's all her mother was good for. And she didn't even leave a tip. The fifty dollars included the tip. The more she thought about the situation, the more the lava in her spat, stirred in itself and threatened to erupt. First, her mother had lied about her grandparents, then about her father. What was she supposed to believe? And the woman said she believed in Jesus. Jesus didn't go around lying to people he loved. She'd never go back to Ghana. New York was her new home.

***

Thirty-one
Calling Lizzie

December 1999

Lizzie looked at her watch. It was thirty minutes past seven. Akua Afriyie kept glancing around furtively. Lizzie couldn't under understand why, but she wouldn't complain. The woman had finally made something of herself. In fact, everyone in her family was doing excellently, and she was extremely pleased.

They stood amidst a large group of people waiting to be let into the event that should have started half an hour ago. A white sign with gold borders posted on the doors of the auditorium read, GHANAIAN EXCEL-LENCE AWARDS.

"Where are your father and Gertrude?" Lizzie asked. "He can't be late for his own award."

"Mamaa, I'm sure they're on their way," Akua Afriyie snapped back. "Besides, we don't know if he's going to win the award."

"What's wrong with you?"

"You know how I get at these events," Akua Afriyie said and waved her fingers in the air.

"Relax."

"Mamaa," Akua Afriyie said. "I don't want you to feel pressured to come on the flight tomorrow. That way you don't have to rush to Aduk-rom No. 2 and you can spend more time with Papa Yaw. After all, the exhibition runs all week."

"No, no," Lizzie said. "I'm coming with you. I'll leave here after Ernie gets his award, go home to rest, leave for Adukrom No. 2 at dawn and be back in Accra hours before the flight. It'll be seamless."

"If you insist," Akua Afriyie said.

Lizzie didn't like the way Akua Afriyie had inherited Ernest's way of giving up too easily. She needed more backbone. She stared at Akua Afriyie's hair. Why she'd chosen to have that bushy hairstyle, she couldn't understand. It looked more presentable when it was straight. And where was Ernest? She'd been feeling a twinge of jealousy, ever since Gertrude had come.

Gertrude had arrived three days ago and because of her Ernest wasn't going on the trip to New York to see his own daughter's exhibition. And Ernest! He was acting so love-struck. It was always Gertie-this, Gertie-that.

"We're here!" Ernest walked in with Gertrude. He wore a black tuxedo and Gertrude, a long red strapless dress, her hair held carelessly back in an amorphous ball.

"Finally," Lizzie said.

"Papa! Gertrude!" Akua Afriyie said as she hugged them. Akua Afriyie's skin was a cool dark mahogany and Gertrude's, the color of a smooth ripe mango. Gertrude had inherited Ernest's bulbous nose and Akua Afriyie's features were finer. They were both skinny as poles and Lizzie felt a strong urge to pass a hot comb through their unruly hair. Both women were beautiful in their own way, she had to admit.

"Why are you standing out here?" Ernest asked.

"They're now setting up, can you imagine?" Lizzie said.

"That's Ghana for you," Ernest said.

"It's the complete opposite of Germany," Gertrude said. Lizzie found her English inflected with a directness, a brusqueness that made her seem cold. Her jealousy abated somewhat. Her children were warmer, she decided and then wondered why she was playing a silly comparison game. Her children were grown, leading their own lives, had all as good as left her, and here she was lining them up in her mind—Lizzie's children on the left, Ernest's child on the right. She was being silly.

"What did you get up to today?" Akua Afriyie asked Gertrude.

"Papa and I went shopping. I bought some cloth," Gertrude said.

"Ernie, where did you take her?" Lizzie asked. "I'm sure to some expensive store!"

"No," Ernest said. "I know how to shop for bargains too."

"Well, make sure you send her to my seamstress," Lizzie said.

People started filing in into the auditorium.

"Let's go in," Lizzie said, huddling her family toward the open double doors.

They handed their invitations to an usher dressed in a pink *kente kaba* and slit.

"Go down the aisle and your seats are in the third row, on the left," the usher said.

They walked down the velveteen stairs of the auditorium. As they took their seats, Lizzie grabbed Ernest's hand. She didn't know why she did, but she need reassuring. He pressed her palm with his fingers.

"Ernie," she whispered. "Papa Yaw is dying. Mama Efua called me this afternoon and said he wants to see me before he dies."

"Goodness," Ernest said. "Is there anything we can do?"

"I think it's just old age," she said. "I'll go tomorrow morning."

"How about your flight? Won't you be cutting it close?" Ernest asked.

"No. I have it all planned. And I can count on Ghana Airways to delay our flight."

"Gertie and I can come with you," he said. Lizzie glared at him. From the corner of her eye, she saw Gertrude, sitting to his right. She was staring at the stage.

"No, I'll be fine," she said. "You two need to bond."

"Well, if that's really what you want," Ernest said and turned to Gertrude.

Lizzie slipped her hand out of Ernest's. She now understood why every year, except for the one when she'd prevented him from doing so, he'd gone to Germany. He'd never been hands-on with her children. He was always a little aloof. Even with his favorite, Akua Afriyie, she'd never seen him so smitten. Maybe it was her fault. She'd been so pushy throughout their marriage and was always running the show, so he'd relaxed and taken a backseat.

After fifteen minutes, the room had filled up but no one had walked to the stage, which was cloaked behind a blue curtain.

"We're so unprofessional," Akua Afriyie said.

"I know. This country has gone downhill, Akua. When I moved to Accra years ago, I'd go to functions and they'd start on time."

"Mamaa," Akua Afriyie said, "our problems started during colonial times. You look back on the old days with such nostalgia but …"

"Yes, but at independence we were much better off than we are now."

A woman walked on stage, swathed in a shiny gold dress. A spotlight shone on her.

"It's about time," Akua Afriyie said.

"*Akwaaba*," the woman said. "Welcome to the first ever Ghanaian Excellence Awards. We're very sorry for the delay. We were experiencing technical difficulties. My name is Nana Ama. I'm your MC this evening. The Ghanaian Excellence Awards are being held to commemorate how far Ghana has come politically, socially and economically. Tonight, we'll be honoring individuals and corporations that have helped propel Ghana forward. But first, a hand of applause for the Asafo Drummers!"

The curtains behind the woman parted and a group of five dreadlocked men pummeled their drums with their palms. As the drum beats pulsed through the auditorium, Lizzie was transported to Adukrom No. 2. She realized she hadn't been taking Papa Yaw seriously. He really could be dying. As much as they had their differences, he was her father. He was the one who'd insisted she go to school when she was six-years-old and that had changed her life. She hoped he'd hold out till she got there the next day. She hoped Ernest's award would come soon. The earlier she set out, the better.

The lights dimmed and the MC walked to a podium in the middle of the stage. "To present the nominees for Best New Business in Food and Drinks," she said, "Mr. Charles Boateng, managing director of the Ghana Water Works."

A skinny man walked on stage. Lizzie almost choked with laughter.

"Mercy's ex-boyfriend from our nursing school days," she whispered to Akua Afriyie and giggled. She hadn't seen him in years.

"The Ghanaian Excellence Awards honor food and drink companies that have been in operation for less than a decade. And the nominees are," he said in a shaky voice and opened an envelope, "Voltic, producers of mineral water; Refresh Ghana, fruit juice manufacturers, and Blue Skies, pineapple producers and exporters. The award goes to Voltic."

The crowd applauded as a man in a grey suit walked up to the stage. Charles handed him a wooden cocoa pod-shaped award.

Lizzie was amused. She hoped Charles had lived a decent life after Mercy unceremoniously left him because of political differences.

An hour passed. Lizzie was growing impatient. They'd announced awards for hospitality, women's development and education, and interspersed those with long pauses where nobody knew what was going on. The MC walked back on stage.

"To present the award for Most Loyal Private Business, Mr. Rashid Adams, managing director of Ghana Commercial Bank and special advisor to the Finance Minister."

Lizzie watched as a tall heavyset man walked to the stage. She held Ernest and Akua Afriyie's hands. Akua Afriyie's was as wet as a sponge. She didn't think she cared much about this award.

"The Ghanaian Excellence Awards honor companies that have served the community for over three decades," he said in a deep steady baritone. "The nominees are Ernest Fine Goods, importers of luxury items; Fan Milk Limited, ice cream and yoghurt manufacturers, and Pioneer Kitchenware Limited, makers of aluminum utensils. The award goes to Fan Milk."

"All right, I'm off!" Lizzie said, springing out of her seat, as the crowd clapped. She'd been so sure Ernest was getting that award, but ice cream sold more than Ernest's goods did. She wasn't upset, was she?

"I'll leave with you," Akua Afriyie said.

"No! Stay till the end," Lizzie said and pressed Akua Afriyie's shoulder firmly. She didn't want Gertrude to be the only one consoling Ernest. She hoped Akua Afriyie got that.

"My love to your folks," Ernest said.

Lizzie walked out of the International Conference Center and looked at the indigo sky. A full moon hung low, painting the sky around it with wisps of white. She walked to her car and unlocked it. When she started the engine, the radio came to life.

"We have to get prepared for the Millennium not just Y2K style," the radio presenter said. "Spiritually, we have to be prepared, politically …"

Lizzie sucked her teeth, turned the radio dial and stopped at a classical music channel.

She drove by a filling station and decided to fill her tank and buy some gifts. That way the next day, she'd drive directly to Adukrom No. 2 and make no stops. She pulled up by a REGULAR pump. A bored attendant walked over.

"Fill the tank," she said to him as she opened the fuel door. She walked into the brightly lit shop.

A woman dressed in a red shirt sat behind a white enamel counter staring at her nails.

Lizzie went to the biscuit aisle. She picked up packets of Digestive biscuits, boxes of Golden Tree chocolate, shrimp crisps and boxes of Refresh pineapple juice.

The shopkeeper stuffed them all into one blue bag.

Lizzie almost asked her if there was a shortage of plastic bags, but decided not to be rude. She paid her and strode back to her car. Another man stood by the attendant. Startled, she almost dropped the bag. She wanted to enter her car as quietly as she could, but hadn't paid for the petrol. She looked at the price display.

"Here," she said, handing the attendant five thousand-cedi notes.

"Thanks, madam," he said.

Bador Samed turned to look at her. "Lizzie," he said quietly. How he still remembered her in his madness, surprised her.

"Not now, Bador," she said and fumbled with her door. Her hand was shaking. A packet of biscuits slipped out of the bag. He could eat them for his dinner—she wasn't picking them up. She sat in the car, slammed the door, started her engine as fast as she could and pressed on the accelerator. She started turning out of the station and almost jumped out of her seat when she saw him standing on the road to her left, waving the red packet of biscuits.

She looked at him, his red skin blackened by the sun and guilt rose in her chest. She'd once loved him. For not trying to find out what happened to him, for not looking for him, she had failed him. Yet, it was a sure thing that her life would have been completely different with him and she'd enjoyed every bit of the life she'd lived.

In the distance, she saw two bright lights approaching. She wanted to scream at him to get off the road. After avoiding him for all these years, the least she could do was save his life. She felt paralyzed. She needed to move herself. In a panic, she pressed on a pedal. The car didn't move. She'd stepped on the brakes. She heard the booming drone of a large truck's horn. It grew louder. She felt a thud and a split second later, her body slammed against the door. As the sound of the truck's horn rang in her ears and blackness invaded her consciousness she smiled. He had always been closer to the spirit world than anyone else she knew. There was no one else she'd go on this journey with.

***

Thirty-two
Art

Sugri lay on her back, her body depressing the airbed. She knew she should get up to inflate it, but she was chewing on paracetamol in her mind and couldn't be bothered about a flaccid airbed. She had to build paracetamol from basic lab chemicals. She really enjoyed organic synthesis. Take a simple organic chemical. On it, perform either reaction A, B or C. The resulting compound depends entirely on what reactions you choose or on what chemicals you add. It was sort of a metaphor for life, she thought. Depending on what or whom you added to your life, you ended up in a different place from where you started. It was all so lovely—chemical reactions. She could start the reaction with phenol. As she thought of what she'd do with it, her phone rang. She stretched over to pick up the handset. Hopefully, that was not Ije telling her she'd found the solution.

"Sugri," Akua Afriyie said. Her voice was soft, sweet, enticing. She's putting that on to win me back, Sugri thought. But no, I won't let her have her way so easily. No.

"Mummy, I'm a little busy."

"Sugri …"

"I have this exam today, and I need …"

"Sugri, listen to me, please," her mother said.

Sugri sat up. She didn't miss that ring of urgency.

"What is it?" she asked.

"Your grandmother passed away."

"No," Sugri said. She felt sick. Brain to digestive system: life is cruel, life does vomit-inducing things to people. "It's not true," she said. "Mamaa is gone?"

"Yes," Akua Afriyie said.

"Oh my God," Sugri said, clutching at the wisps of straight and natural hair fighting for attention on her head. She hadn't thought of loss. Loss happened in chemical reactions too. You could gain or lose electrons, for instance. "How?"

"In a car accident. She was preparing to go to Adukrom No. 2.... Babasam died too. A timber truck ran into them."

"Oh my God!" Sugri didn't know whether to laugh or to cry. Babasam? "Babasam?" she asked.

"Yes. Bizarre, huh?"

"Very. I'm so sorry. Now what?"

"The funeral is in two weeks—just before the new year. This ruins Christmas for all of us this year."

"I have to come home," Sugri said. Then she squeaked, "But I don't have money."

"Don't worry. Your grandpa has already offered to buy your ticket," Akua Afriyie said. "When do you want to come?"

"School is done on the 23rd. So, how about I leave that night?"

"If that's what you want. We'll pay for the ticket and DHL it to you."

"Thanks. What about your exhibition? It starts on Monday," Sugri said, thinking that it was sad that it had taken Lizzie's death to end their war. Life was really cold and calculating.

"I won't be able to come," Akua Afriyie said. "It'll have to go on without me. I was going to fly in tonight with Mamaa.... I have to call the gallery to tell them the bad news."

"I'm so sorry."

"Don't be. I'll call Karen Sanders and tell her what happened. She'll understand."

"I'll go," Sugri said.

"What?"

"I'll go to your exhibition. I'll stand in for you."

"Thank you so much, sweetie," Akua Afriyie said. "That will mean a lot to me."

"How's grandpa doing? How are you doing?" Sugri asked. Her heart felt sore and her head was heavy. She felt like she'd only just met the woman and she'd slipped out of her life. A huge chunk of her just died. Disappeared. Left with years of her life story.

"We're managing."

"I'm so sorry," Sugri said.

"I am too."

"I love you."

"Me too, dear. Good luck with your exam."

"Thanks, mummy," she said, hanging up. She was too shocked for words. She needed some connection with the dead woman. She sprang out of bed and marched to her plastic desk. She searched in an invisible drawer, for her photo album. She'd made a pile of books that would go into a drawer once she had enough money to buy a proper desk. For now, the space under the desk was the drawer, the invisible drawer.

The photo album was once pink. Time had colored it brown. It was her first photo album. She sat down on the floor, spread her legs into a V and started flipping through the album. Her eyes burned. She looked at a black and white picture of Lizzie, taken on the day she'd graduated nursing school, with Ernest by her side. Her smile popped out. She flipped a page. She rubbed her thumb over a picture of her mother, Lizzie and herself. They'd taken it at the Republic Day dinner. Lizzie always looked like a queen.

Sugri heard sirens outside her window. She walked to window and hoisted it up. Frost bit at her cheeks. She looked down at the thin snowfall from the night before. She saw the tops of people's heads as they marched along the sidewalks, leaving long trails of footprints. The sun made everything brighter. Tears danced down her face. As she looked into what she could see of the sky, she said, "Sleep well, Mamaa."

She walked to her bathroom and planted herself in front of the mirror. Her hair was a mess. The straight part stood weakly on end, colored a shade of red or brown or both. She ran her fingers through the mess. The bottom felt rough, like a rough carpet, and the top like cotton wool. Her hair was in really bad shape.

She opened the medicine cabinet above her. She rubbed her palm on the shelf, knocking over small bottles of shampoo. She searched frantically for her nail scissors. The only pair of scissors she owned. It wasn't there. Exasperated, she walked out of the bathroom, searched in a little basket where she kept pens, pencils, badges she'd picked up from bookstores. She found the pair of steel nail scissors buried under the stationery. She picked it up and walked back into the bathroom.

She stood in front of the mirror and looked in her big eyes. Her father's eyes. Her smile was her grandmother's, her nose, her mother's. She tugged on her hair and held it up with her left hand. With her right hand, she sliced through the wisps of cotton wool. She moved to the right side clipping as much of the red-brown hair as she could. She wasn't doing a good job. She snipped the front, cut off all the thin tufts. As she cut, tears formed in her eyes. Her grandmother wasn't even old. She had at least twenty years before her. Why was she so rudely taken away? Sugri couldn't see what she was doing any more. She sucked in a thick glob of mucus and wiped her eyes. Disgusted at what she'd done to her hair, she dropped the nail scissors into the kitchen sink.

Walking to the door, she picked up her red bubble jacket and stuffed her feet into her clunky snow boots. She picked up a blue skullcap and trudged out of her apartment.

Outside, the snow she'd seen from upstairs as a pristine sheet of white, was an unappetizing slushy smoothie. She plodded through the slush, crossing over to the other side of the street. A strong wind gushed up Amsterdam Avenue. She hadn't bothered to take a scarf and now she was paying for it. The cold wind was forcing itself into her jacket. She walked down to 108th Street, where she saw the signboard "Amsterdam Barbers." She didn't know how good they were, but she was sure they'd do a better job than she had.

She pushed the door open and was surrounded by the sad echoes of a bachata song. Everyone in there—all men—turned to look at her. She took off her skullcap hoping that her hair would speak for itself. She noticed no one was actually getting a haircut. Oh, well, good for her. She'd get her hair done faster. Nobody said anything and nobody was coming up to ask what she wanted. Why does this remind me of Ghana? she mused.

"Hi," she said, waving her right hand nervously at no one.

"Hello, mami," a barber in the back responded. He was large, wearing a Yankees baseball cap, a well-defined circle beard around his small pink mouth. "What can we do for you?"

"I want to cut off my hair," she said.

"All?" the barber asked, making the men erupt in laughter.

"Yes, all," Sugri said.

"For real?" he asked, walking over to her. He led her to the chair closest to the entrance. "I can cut off the straight parts if you want."

"No," Sugri said, turning to look at him. "I want to shave it all. I want it to look like your head."

"That's bald, mami!" the barber said, rubbing his ringed finger along his circle-beard. Sugri was reminded of somebody, but she couldn't place her finger on whom.

"Yes, that's what I want," she said, convincing herself.

"Last chance, mami. All?"

"All."

"OK. No turning back."

Sugri closed her eyes and left herself at the barber's mercy. He lowered her chair. As she heard clipping and snipping, she allowed her mind to wander. She thought of Akua Afriyie. She wondered how the news of Lizzie's death had hit her. If her mother died she'd be devastated. Even if she was eighty and Akua Afriyie, ninety-seven. The clipping and snipping stopped. Sugri heard a machine droning. She felt the razor plowing her scalp. She was now afraid of what she'd look like. She wasn't going to open her eyes till all that was done. Her father's image seeped into her mind, like urine leaking into a mattress. That's who the barber had reminded her off with his beard and rings.

"What's your name?" Sugri asked.

"Dave," he said.

"Where are you from?"

"The Dominican Republic. You, mami?"

"From Ghana." She was silent. The music emanating from the four corners of the barbershop wasn't exactly sad, but to her, it rang with echoes of hard times. "Tell me," she said, "about bachata."

"Like the dance? It's easy, you just let the man lead you!" His co-barbers snickered.

"No," Sugri said. "I want to know about the music."

"Oh, OK. Well, you already know it comes from the DR."

"Yes." Yes, idiot, that's why I'm asking you.

"I don't know too much about it," he said. "Except that it developed first in the countryside. It was, like, servant music. Then it moved into ho' houses and now it's all over America."

"Tell me more," Sugri said. She was dreaming of fields and guitars. Hats and melody.

"Bachata, right," he said, "is love music." He stretched out "love." Looove music. "But not the 'I love you, you're my heart' kind of crap. It's about lost love. Like Romeo and Juliet kind of love."

"Dave, you're deep! *Muy profundo!*" a barber shouted. Sugri laughed.

"That's beautiful," she said. Everyone in the barbershop seemed to think so too and kept quiet.

"I'm done!" the barber said, cutting through the hush.

"Already?" She opened her eyes and she was bald. Almost. The barber had been kind enough to leave a thin layer of hair that lay flat against her scalp. She loved it.

"You have a nice head, mami," he said.

"Thanks, Dave. How much do I owe you?"

"Five dollars." She looked at her head. She did have a decently shaped head. The expression, "your grandmother shaped your head well," floated into her mind. It was a sharp-edged expression. It pricked her brain and jagged down to pierce her heart. True, her grandmother hadn't been around to shape her head when she was born, but it still hurt. Sugri paid Dave and walked out.

*

Ije bailed out on Sugri, saying she wasn't feeling well enough to go to the exhibition. Sugri didn't want to go by herself. Ije said she knew someone perfect. Someone who couldn't stop talking about Sugri and who was, in Ije speak, driving her up the flipping high wall.

Sugri looked at her watch. It was four. The exhibition started in three hours. She exhaled and picked up her phone, succumbing to time and friends with excuses.

"Hello," the voice said on the other end of the line. She always loved his phone voice.

"Hi," Sugri said.

"Hey," he said. "What's up, Sugri?"

She was unsure how to ask him. She could spring up the my-grand-mother-died news on him to make him unable to say no. But that would be too cheap. "Are you free tonight? Like in three hours?"

"Yeah, sure," he said. "Why do you ask?"

"I'd like to invite you to my mother's exhibition. She can't be there and I'd love some company," she said. Ugh! Why did I say that?

"I'm game. Do you want us to leave together?"

"No," Sugri said hastily. "I mean, I have to do some other things before the show."

"No worries," he said. "When and where do I meet you?"

"Let's meet at seven at the 171 Gallery on 27th Street between 10th and 11th Aves."

"Great," he said. "See you then."

"Thanks. Especially after the short notice."

"My pleasure."

Sugri hung up. She wanted to take her heart and shove it into a dirty trashcan. It was beating crazily fast. She was sweating in winter. What was all this?

She opened her suitcase and pulled out the green dress Lizzie had given her. She sat on the floor and pulled on black stockings. She stood up, and yanked the dress on over her head. The neckline was rather small, but with her shaved head it wasn't so hard to get it on. She was also glad for once she didn't have to worry about how her hair looked. She walked to the bathroom. As she put on a pair of dangling gold earrings. She took one last look at herself and realized if she didn't leave now, she'd be late. She put on a pair of black, uncomfortable knee-length boots and grabbed her grey woolen coat. She wasn't taking the subway. This was a special occasion; she was cabbing it all the way down.

She arrived at the gallery five minutes after seven. She handed her coat to a woman sitting at the coat-check next to the entrance. She was nervous for two reasons. First, this was her mother's work. She hoped people liked it. Any negative criticisms were slights on her. Second, she had seen Ellis around campus, but this was the first time they were going to spend more than a minute together since …

"Oh my God," he said. "I like your new look!"

"Thanks," she said. "I finally took your advice."

"It suits you. Great outfit!"

"Thanks. I thought I was late."

"I just walked in. I really love your haircut, Sugri."

"Thanks."

There was this hot, awkward air bubble between them. It would pop if someone nicked it. He looked good. Black shirt on denim. She had to remind herself why she was there. To represent her mother. She didn't even know what the Karen Sanders woman looked like. She wanted to introduce herself.

She walked around the room with Ellis by her side. It was a two-roomed gallery, smaller than she'd imagined it would be. In the room she stood in, she saw the name Abhi Shrestha. That wasn't her mother's work.

"I think my mum's work is in the other room," she said to Ellis.

"We should go in there then," he said.

She didn't know if he was just sucking up to her. Whatever the case was, she loved how she had the power. "Can we see this guy's work a little first?"

"Sure," he said.

They walked to a painting. Its caption read, "Nepali sunrise." Sugri looked at the canvas—a pink sky with a round, bright orange sun. Two women were bent in a yellow field. It was pretty. She liked it. She appreciated "realistic art."

"… in Ghana. Her mother died, so she couldn't be here." Sugri turned and saw a portly woman talking to a white-haired man in a grey suit. That must be Karen Sanders, she thought.

"Sugri," Ellis said. "Your grandmother died?" Sugri nodded. "I'm so sorry. Why didn't you tell me?"

"I didn't know how to. It seemed crass to just spill out the words."

"How are you doing?"

"I'm fine. I'm going for the funeral in two weeks."

"I am so sorry, Sugri," he said, putting his palm on the small of her back. The bubble between them heated up.

"I want to talk to the lady," she said. "I'll be right back." Sugri walked after the woman and the white-haired man. She stood awkwardly to the side, hoping she'd catch the woman's attention. It wasn't working. "Excuse me," she said.

"Oh, my, Akwa!" the woman said. "What are you doing here?"

"No," Sugri said, smiling. "I'm her daughter."

"You're the spitting image of her. Oh my word. Karen Sanders," she said, sticking out her hand.

"Sugri."

"My condolences. She told us about her mother."

"Thanks," Sugri said. Suddenly she was at a loss for words. "Well," she said, "I told my mother I'd introduce myself to you, so here I am."

"I'm glad you did. People love her work. We have a reception after this and you're welcome to come."

"Thanks," Sugri said. She walked back to Ellis, who was staring at the face of a child with a palm under her chin.

"The child looks like she's walked the whole earth and seen how hard life is," he said.

"If this depresses you, I don't know what my mother's work will do to you." Sugri hadn't seen any of her mother's new work, except for the one on the invitation. On it, a black hand held a heart that was covered with eyes on a blood red background. She showed it to Ellis.

"Your mother's one morbid woman," Ellis said, shuddering.

"Let's see what else she has in store for us."

The walked into the second room, the hot air bubble at boiling point. Each piece Akua Afriyie had produced was different, but the room screamed of blood. Every canvas had the color red in it. Sugri noticed there were more people in this room than in the other. Apparently people liked abstract, blood red paintings.

She walked to one. It was titled, ABORTION. At one point, she realized, her mother must have considered getting rid of her. She wanted to be mad all over again. But she couldn't be. Not with Lizzie gone. And especially not after everything her mother had done for her. If she had been pregnant at seventeen, she might have considered it too. She looked at the painting:

A black baby was suspended in a sea of red by an umbilical cord. The baby had a beautiful face. The face of a girl with large eyes. The baby was smiling. She couldn't tell if the painting was for or against abortion.

She lingered at that painting for a while then made her way around the room, taking in all the moroseness of her mother's art. The last one was called, MOTHERHOOD. Akua Afriyie had drawn the backs of three women. In the background a faint map of Ghana hovered and had been painted pink. A halo crowned the northern part of Ghana. The image was strangely biblical. And why shouldn't it be, when her mother was born-again. Or was she not anymore? In that case was it a criticism of religion? Sugri didn't know. Art interpretation was not her forte.

She walked to Ellis who seemed to be mulling over a painting of a church congregation in a pink womb. The people's arms radiated toward a priest while a pair of eyes outside the womb watched them.

"Wow," he said to Sugri. "That's exactly how I feel about religion."

"But you don't believe in God," Sugri said. "This painting makes a reference to God watching people worshipping his messengers."

"I'm agnostic, I haven't said …" he said. Here we go again, she thought. She'd really missed him and how he loved to defend himself.

"I know. Hey, there's a reception after this, if you want to go," Sugri said, changing the topic.

"Actually," his naughty smile creased his lips, "I was hoping we could talk."

"O—K …" Sugri said.

"Can we just walk for a bit?"

"I'll tell Karen that we won't be coming," Sugri said. She strode over to Karen who was talking to a woman with curly jet-black hair. Karen saw her this time.

"This is the artist's daughter," Karen volunteered.

"Oh," the woman with jet-black hair said. "Your mother's work is rich. It blends motherhood and spirituality in such a rich way. In her work, the two become almost the same thing. *Mazel tov.*"

"Thanks," Sugri said. "I'll let her know. Karen, so sorry, I can't make it to the reception, but thanks for inviting me."

"No problem. And congratulations. This was a success."

"I should congratulate you," Sugri said.

Ellis was now standing at the coat-check. Sugri picked up her coat. Ellis led the way out. They turned right and walked toward 12th Avenue.

Sugri saw the Hudson River, an ink river, and New Jersey on the other side.

"It's cold, Ellis," Sugri said. "We shouldn't walk for too long."

Ellis was quiet. They crossed the West Side Highway and walked to a wall close to the river.

"Sugri," he said. "I have something to tell you." What? What could it possibly be? she wondered. Did he have an STD? Well, she was clear if that was what he was about to tell her. "I shouldn't have let you break up with me," he said.

"What? Why?"

"Sugri, I didn't sleep with Keisha." Why were people always fucking lying to her? Did she have a stamp on her forehead that read, "Gullible"? She was so sick of this.

"Ellis, I don't want to hear this. I don't need …"

"Please listen. After we slept together, I started believing the stupid, immature thing that people say about virgins."

"What do people say?"

"That they get clingy. And in some ways you were beginning to show those signs. I started to feel claustrophobic around you."

"Why are you telling me this?" Sugri said, her voice cracking.

"Keisha is beautiful, and yes, we kissed. But that was as far as I let it go."

"Why?" She could barely let out the words. Tears had come out of nowhere and with the cold, she felt like they were forming icicles on her face.

"Sugri, I'm still in love with you," he said. "You're so simple. You take me home. You plant me. You're years of history that got severed off. You're goofy. You're beautiful. You're smart as hell."

Sugri looked at him. He seemed to have tears in his eyes. She looked at his beautiful naughty smile.

"Ellis," she said, "my head is freezing."

"Oh, of course! How inconsiderate of me." He held her hand. She didn't retract it. "Want to share a cab up?"

"Yes," she said.

In the taxi, their fingers clasped, she looked up at the buildings. Stand tall, they were saying to her. You won. Your first love. Your long lost child. She smiled. She turned to look at him. He had been staring at her all this time. He leaned in and kissed her. His soft, naughty lips. She'd missed them. She hugged him. Held on to him. Held him tighter than she'd ever held onto anybody. Her chemicals stirred. They wanted to react with his.

"I love you," she said.

"I love you too." One life gone, another returned. Perhaps the universe knew what she was doing, after all.

Thirty-three
Harmattan Rain

Sugri stood at the entrance to Papa Yaw's compound. She leaned against an exposed brick wall, staring at a neem tree which had lost its leaves and had been decorated with black and blue plastic bags. She felt as if by coming to Adukrom No. 2 she'd entered a different world. In a way she felt as if she were standing at the beginning of her story. As she looked up at the neem tree, children darted by her legs, giggling and shouting.

"*Sakora!*" a girl in a dress made out of Lizzie's funeral cloth screamed, running toward hired blue, red, green and white plastic chairs arranged in a circle on a patch of laterite. On the back of each chair, the owner had taken the time to paint in white, the words, DESTINY PARTY RENTALS.

Sugri saw Akua Afriyie talking to Papa Yaw. That morning Akua Afriyie had told her that Papa Yaw had insisted they order a special cloth for Lizzie's funeral instead of the usual black. Lizzie's face was printed in black and white on white fabric with the words, ELIZABETH ACHIAA MENSAH, 1937-1999, arched around her head. Interspersed in the white spaces was the Adinkra symbol, *funtummireku denkyemmireku*—two crocodiles fused at the stomach. Members of the same family or tribe shouldn't fight, her mother had explained to her. Personally, Sugri thought the printers could have done a better job. She looked down at her own *kaba* and slit. Right on her stomach, Lizzie's head crashed into the Siamese crocodiles.

She looked up and kept her gaze on her mother who seemed to be bursting with verve.

Akua Afriyie spoke to Ernest, rubbed his shoulder, hugged him, moved on to Gertrude, hugged her, said a few words, went on to Tsotsoo, hugged her, and moved on to Mercy and Asantewa, whose eyes were blood red. If Lizzie were alive, that would have been her. Lizzie would have been bubbling around, sashaying up and down, greeting the guests. But this was her funeral. Sugri didn't think her mother had it in her to be bubbly, but she was playing the role excellently. Lizzie would be proud.

Sugri turned to look in the opposite direction—at the entrance to Adukrom No. 2. She was sure her grandmother would be pleased at the turn up. The entrance was packed with cars, their brand new bodies glistening in the rays of the afternoon sun. And even more cars were streaming in.

Being back in Ghana was strange. She'd tried to push away her homecoming, but Lizzie had died, cutting short her self-imposed exile. She turned around and saw children running up and down. She should have been doing her assigned task—making sure they didn't invade the food and drinks on the table like ants, but she'd been screaming at them and it wasn't working. The table, covered with a blue plastic sheet, was topped with bottles of beer, coca cola, Fanta, trays of little round donuts, fish balls and tan-colored chips that looked like they'd been soused in a bucket of oil. As had been predicted, she saw fingers crawling all over the table. Children were so funny. She walked toward them.

"No, no, no," she said softly to them. She knew her tone wouldn't work on them but she'd tried shouting and it hadn't worked. Her mother never shouted at her, and she appreciated that. That was one thing she was going to take from her mother. Not the lies she told, though. She walked to her little cousins, whose names she didn't even know—there were just too many of them. "We'll eat soon," she said. "Come on. Be good!"

"*Sakora!*" the children shouted, dispersing in all directions. A little girl fell down in the rush. Her bottom landed on the ground and she was cushioned by her white diapers, but apparently, that didn't help much. She opened her mouth wide, stared at Sugri dead in the eyes and let out a huge wail.

"Awww," Sugri said, walking over to pick up the child. "Shhh! Don't cry." As she tried to calm the caterwauling child, Akua Afriyie walked into the compound.

"Who's this cutie?" her mother asked as the child hiccupped.

"I have no idea. She fell down." Sugri studied the child for the first time, noticing her round cheeks and wide white eyes. The child sucked in mucus and grunted. "I see you're quite the energetic hostess," Sugri said to her mother.

"Ugh. I'm so tired. As eldest daughter I have to go around being nice to everyone. I think your Auntie Tsotsoo would have been more suited to the task. Besides, I'm sure Mamaa would have wanted it that way. Her golden child."

"Mummy, we speak no ill of the dead." Akua Afriyie walked to the table with the food, plunged her fingers into the oily chips and clasped a handful of them.

"Why? I haven't said anything," Akua Afriyie said.

"Since when do you eat so unhealthily?" Sugri asked.

"I'm drained," Akua Afriyie said. "I need energy from wherever I can find it."

Sugri moved closer to her mother.

"*Sakora*," said the little girl on Sugri's left hip.

"These children! That's how she fell in the first place," Sugri said.

"With your haircut, of course they'll call you that," Akua Afriyie said. "It really looks good. I see I had a good influence on you."

"What were your words? 'It's liberating.'"

"Come," Akua Afriyie said. "I have someone I want you to meet," she said, her eyes bloodshot. Akua Afriyie wore misery well, Sugri thought. She looked beautiful when she was sad. She realized that her mother hadn't exactly inherited the happy gene from Lizzie and that was fine. That was who she was. In a way, that explained a lot about Akua Afriyie and why she acted in certain ways. Sugri balanced the little girl on her hip and trailed behind her mother.

They walked out of Papa Yaw's compound, away from the arranged plastic chairs toward the grid of parked cars.

Sugri tried to imagine who her mother would want to introduce to her. Some doctor from whom she could finagle an internship? A new relative? Who?!

They stopped at a Nissan Pajero parked in the last row of cars. Akua Afriyie knocked on the tinted glass window of the driver seat door.

"Yep," a deep male voice said. Rashid opened the door and stepped out. Sugri didn't know how to react. "Hello, Sugri," he said.

"Hi," Sugri said and looked down at the laterite. The black bands of her slippers were covered with the ubiquitous red sand and her feet were dusty.

"He came to offer moral support," Akua Afriyie said.

Sugri was quiet. She stood there with mixed feelings. Her anger was shifting away from her mother onto this man who'd apparently provided the sperm that had produced her. She couldn't bring herself to say he'd fathered her. Fathering involved the kind of job Akua Afriyie did. Akua Afriyie was her father and her mother.

"Thanks for coming," Sugri said. "I guess we can all start from scratch—as grownups." She stretched out her right hand to shake his hand.

Akua Afriyie seemed to have been holding her breath. She let out a huge sigh. "America does things to people! Now she's a grownup!" she said, laughing. She stretched her hands to take the child from Sugri's arms. "I'll leave you two," she said and trudged back to join the people who were filling in the plastic seats.

"Thanks, Afriyie," Rashid shouted at her mother's disappearing back. "I hear you're at Columbia University now," he said to Sugri, rubbing his beard with his hand ringed with his silver-gold blend band. His frog eyes bored intensely into Sugri.

"Yes. I have one year and a semester left."

"Then what next?"

"Medical school. I'm taking the MCATs next summer."

"Wonderful," Rashid said. "I'm very proud of you. If there's anything you need, just let me know…. I'm sorry I wasn't around when you were growing up," he said.

"Don't worry," Sugri said. "I just want to know … what my mother said to bring you here."

"I was with her when we heard of your grandmother's accident. We were at the Ghanaian Excellence Awards. She was telling me she thought it was time I met my daughter properly, when someone called in with the bad news."

"All right," Sugri said, sure it was the other way round—someone called with the bad news and Akua Afriyie decided he needed to be in her life. Sugri didn't know what to say to him. Maybe, she'd been overreacting about the whole feeling of emptiness. Maybe now that Ellis was back in her life, she didn't need a "father-figure" like that shrink had suggested. Oh! She was being too hard on him. He seemed like a decent man.

"I'm really sorry about your grandmother," he said.

"Thank you for coming all the way out here to support us," she said.

"It was the least I could do. We are, after all, family."

Daddy, she wanted to say. To utter the word. To test how it felt. But it was strange, foreign to her tongue. She'd never called anyone that and it seemed too late to be using the word. "I think my great-grandfather is about to give some words," she said, as she saw Papa Yaw hobbling into the center of the ring of hired plastic chairs.

"All right, Sugri," he said. "See you in Accra if I don't get the chance to talk to you again today. You should arrange with your mother to come visit me. We have a lot of catching up to do."

"Definitely," Sugri said. She liked her expanding world. She was one for gain, not loss. She was sure one day she would feel "normal" around him. Isn't that how friendships sometimes started? With unease, uncertainty and mistrust. But they morphed, with time. She walked slowly back to the compound, content. Content that half her story had come back.

Two women clad in black stood next to a white Toyota Corolla, whispering to each other. They didn't realize their voices weren't hushed enough.

"… imagine, him bringing her to his wife's funeral," one of them said.

"Men! Hmmm. After all the woman did for him, he went out and had an affair."

"That's why she died."

Sugri figured they were talking about Ernest and Gertrude. She laughed at how rumors spread. Gertrude was his daughter! And Lizzie died in an accident! Were they suggesting she'd killed herself out of jealousy? Sugri wanted to shout in their faces, but decided not to. They could go around wallowing in their ignorant rumormongering. Lizzie was gone, so they wouldn't be hurting anyone. As she was about to step into Papa Yaw's compound, her mother waylaid her.

"So?" she asked, chewing on a piece of the soggy chips.

"You're still eating those disgusting things?"

"Yes. But tell me, how was it?" She pointed her head in the direction of the parked cars.

"Fine. Listen, people are going around saying grandpa is here with his mistress. How funny is that?"

"I know, I've been hearing all sorts of stories. Papa Yaw is convinced that your grandpa had an affair, and Gertrude is my illegitimate sibling. All morning I've been telling him that he was married before he met Mamaa and that Gertrude is older than I am. He's pretending to be deaf. But, enough about that. How did it go with Rashid?"

"I'll go visit him in Accra," Sugri said. "I almost called him 'daddy.'"

"Really?" Akua Afriyie said, smiling.

"It was strange. It feels too late for him to be my father. I want to know him as a person. But why all the secrecy?"

"I was feeling kind of uneasy about the whole thing. And I didn't know if you'd cause a scene."

"You're referring to my New York outburst, right? Sorry about that."

"I've long forgotten about it," Akua Afriyie said, her bloodshot eyes wetting up. She wiped the tears in her eyes.

"Oh my goodness," Sugri said. "You're not crying because of this?"

"I'm just overwhelmed. With Mamaa gone and now you've reunited with your father …"

"You should work on a painting about that," Sugri said smiling, "Madam Internationally Acclaimed Artist."

"And you're still Miss Smarty Pants, *sakora.*" Akua Afriyie sniffled.

"You follow those children," Sugri said and paused. "Thank you."

"For what?"

"For bringing him here."

"He's your father," Akua Afriyie said. "I should have done that a long time ago. The day Mamaa died, I realized how precious life is. It's sad that it took her death for all this to happen ..."

"I'm sorry too, mummy. Especially for being so pig-headed."

"We all have our moments," Akua Afriyie said. She became quiet and looked at her daughter. "You know, Sugri," she started.

"What?"

"You've become a woman."

"What does that mean?" Sugri asked, laughing. "A few minutes ago, you said, and I quote ..."

"It shows in your shoulders. You seem to have already made some mistakes, but I can tell, you learned from them. You're more confident, you know what you want in life and you're going for it."

"Awww, shucks," Sugri said. "Now how do I respond to that?" Akua Afriyie kept staring at Sugri. "Are you and Rashid going to get back together?"

"Have you seen that pot-belly?" Akua Afriyie asked.

"Hey, that's my father you're talking about!" Sugri said. She heard Papa Yaw clear his throat. "Is he going to give a speech?"

"Yes," Akua Afriyie said. "I've been trying to get him not to do that. The man is so weak. We can't have two deaths in a month!"

The old man stood on laterite, encircled by hired plastic chairs, leaning on a wooden stick. He beckoned for people to settle down in the chairs.

"Thank you all for coming to the sending away of my daughter, Lizzie-Achiaa," he said, his voice weak. "We buried her this morning and she's on her way to our ancestors. I have a few words ..."

Sugri held her mother's hand as they stood outside the circle.

"I want you to remember Lizzie by these words." He paused and looked around. His eyes fell on the neem tree outside his compound. "Like when it rains in harmattan, she left us violently and unexpectedly," Papa Yaw said. "But we know she's at a better place. Her soul can be put to rest, because she lived a full life. She became a person." He paused and coughed. The cough shook his entire rib cage. The whole village was silent. Sugri looked at the faces attached to the bodies sitting in the hired plastic chairs. It seemed like some people were waiting for Papa

Yaw's knees to crumble. Waiting for him to fall over and die. Others were simply waiting for his voice to continue. "My daughter, Lizzie, had a soul that was too big for this village. I tried," his voice broke, "to calm her spirit, but I was doing her a disservice. Lizzie had to leave us to find herself. And she did. She became a wonderful wife, mother, grandmother, stepmother to her husband's illegitimate daughter."

Sugri looked at Akua Afriyie, who looked like she might burst out with laughter. She shifted her gaze to Gertrude, sitting next to Ernest. She looked bemused; she didn't understand a word of what Papa Yaw was saying. Ernest didn't seem bothered at all. If anything, a smirk was registered on his face. He must know his father-in-law well, Sugri mused. She looked back at the bald wrinkled face of her great-grandfather.

"She became a respected nurse in the city. She came back here and built us a clinic. Lizzie," Papa Yaw said, "we know you're on a journey back to *Nananom*. Take with you our blessings, love and peace. Sleep well, Lizzie-Achiaa."

He walked out of the circle toward Akua Afriyie and Sugri. Everyone was silent.

"I need to talk to you, Akua Afriyie," he said. "You can come too," he motioned to Sugri.

They walked by the throngs of people going into the compound looking appropriately solemn and coming out with bottles of beer and smiles on their faces.

Papa Yaw hobbled. He remained quiet, leading Akua Afriyie and Sugri by concrete and mud houses. They arrived at an enclosure filled with long dry grass. "This used to be my farm," he said. "Please sit. This is a long story." Sugri and Akua Afriyie sat on grey bales of grass. Sugri wrapped her legs under her body, wondering what Papa Yaw had to say. Was it about Lizzie's will? Families always had problems with things like that.

"It's hard for me to say this, so I'd appreciate it if you don't interrupt till I'm done," he said.

"Sure, Papa Yaw," Akua Afriyie said.

His yellow eyes focused at a point over their heads. "Back in the early fifties, swollen shoot had spread all over Adukrom No. 2 and all over the Gold Coast. There was a day when I was going to buy seeds to replace the cocoa plants I'd had to cut down. I was about to cross the Insu River when I heard voices. Who did I see when I looked over? My firstborn daughter kissing a man called Bador Samuel."

"Bador Samed," Akua Afriyie corrected. Sugri swallowed. Some how she knew this would explain everything. Her stomach churned.

"You knew him? Yes, him. You have to understand, I had been trying to marry your mother off, and she'd refused so many suitors. I turned around and went straight to the Aduhene's house. It was a hot day," he continued. "The fellow wasn't at home. His beautiful young wife told me he was at the hut of Opanyin Nti—may his soul rest in peace. I walked over and summoned the Aduhene and Opanyin Nti outside. 'Gentlemen,' I said, measuring my words carefully. 'I have a little problem. Opanyin Nti, it involves you.' Opanyin Nti looked at me with those eyes of his. I told him, 'I caught my daughter and your apprentice, that Bador Samuel …'"

"Samed," Sugri now said, beginning to feel sick.

"Please don't interrupt," Papa Yaw said. Sugri clammed up. "I told him I saw my daughter and the apprentice in a compromising situation and I issued them an ultimatum. Bador Samuel had to leave before ruining my daughter, otherwise I wouldn't contribute to the building of any future Adukrom No. 2 projects. The Aduhene saw exactly where I was coming from and sided with me. Of course, Opanyin Nti tried to talk for his apprentice, but we made him realize what a threat that Samuel was.

"Opanyin Nti offered to talk to him, but I knew the likes of that Samuel very well. They don't hear words," he said, sucking in his lower lip. Sugri thought he looked like an aged bald fish. "The Aduhene said the wisest words I've ever heard from him. He said, 'Love is a disease.' He said young people in love are like sick people. They have to be cured. He offered us two of his finest men for us to get rid of that Bador Samuel.

"That night—there was a full moon—I went with the Aduhene and his two henchmen to Opanyin Nti's hut. We each carried machetes. We dressed in black cloth so we wouldn't be seen by the other villagers. What was our luck? We didn't even reach halfway when I saw Samuel walking with such a cocky air back to Opanyin Nti's. We pounced on him. I took out a cloth I had in my pocket and handed it to one of the men.

"One of the other men tied the cloth around his mouth. He thrashed about like a crab that had been caught. He was really strong, with that tall body of his, that Samuel! I lunged at him with a hook as he flapped his arms about like a wild chicken. We managed to drag him to the Insu River. We held him up against a tree, took off his smock and pulled down the skimpy shorts he was wearing. He stood there ashamed. Naked to the whole world."

"No!" Akua Afriyie said. Sugri felt a huge knot form in her stomach.

"We had to. He was too wild, that was the only way we could tame him. I said to him, 'We're poor people, only trying to make a living, and you've come here to shake things up.' I held the cutlass in his face, to make him know I wasn't joking. I told him, 'We don't know who you are. You've lived in this village for two years, but your time is up. You came here with no story, no name we know, and yet we took you in. But corrupting my daughter, you have crossed the line.'

"As I was about to let him go, he said, 'Your daughter loves me. We love each other. In fact, we were going to run away today.' Ho, that did it! I threw the cutlass down. I wanted Samuel to know I wasn't afraid of getting raw. I punched him with a series of uppercuts. The Aduhene's men tried to pull me back, but I was too fast for them. You know, I was quite the fighter. I raised my fist at him, looked him square in his eyes and told him Lizzie was the one who had sent me. And that she had told me everything he'd had done to her and that she was the one who wanted him sent off." Papa Yaw's eyes lit up at the memory of what he'd done.

"Oh, no," Akua Afriyie said.

"He spat in my face and said Lizzie would never do that. He could prove it because he had just made Lizzie his woman. Can you imagine? Spat in my face! Oh, I thrust my knee into his groin! He squealed like a woman. I conked him. He bowled over. I jabbed his head with my knee. I really got him.

"When he was rolling on the floor I said, 'Just keep walking and don't come back here. If I see you anywhere near Adukrom No. 2 or near my daughter,' I grabbed my machete and pressed it against his cheek till it drew a little blood, 'I'll be forced to use this. Know that I have many eyes.' We pushed him out of the village. The fight had gone out of him as he got up, picked his clothes up and walked naked into the forest. I called Lizzie here to confess, but he got to her before I did," he said and bent his head.

Sugri didn't know what to say and she could tell, neither did her mother. They sat there stunned. The trees above them shook in the light dry wind that was blowing. Sugri realized how much the man sitting in front of them had shaped her mother's destiny and hers and how without his intervention they wouldn't be sitting in front of him. As the harmattan blew its dry winds, the clouds above them seemed to thicken.

"It'll be the last rain of the year," Papa Yaw said.

Popenguine, Senegal
October 2007 - July 2008